FLIGHTS AND FALLS

D1444565

B.C. Blues Crime
Cold Girl
Undertow
Creep
Flights and Falls

FLIGHTS AND FALLS

B.C. BLUES CRIME

R.M. GREENAWAY

DUNDURN
TORONTO

Cover image: ©shutterstock.com/rdonar. Select image edits by Chaz Greenaway.
Printer: Webcom, a division of Marquis Book Printing Inc.

Library and Archives Canada Cataloguing in Publication

Greenaway, R. M., author
    Flights and falls / R.M. Greenaway.

(A B.C. blues crime novel)
Issued in print and electronic formats.
ISBN 978-1-4597-4150-8 (softcover).--ISBN 978-1-4597-4151-5
(PDF).--ISBN 978-1-4597-4152-2 (EPUB)

    I. Title. II. Series: Greenaway, R. M. B.c. blues crime novel

PS8613.R4285F55 2019   C813'.6   C2018-903984-1
                                             C2018-903985-X

1 2 3 4 5   23 22 21 20 19

We acknowledge the support of the Canada Council for the Arts, which last year invested $153 million to bring the arts to Canadians throughout the country, and the Ontario Arts Council for our publishing program. We also acknowledge the financial support of the Government of Ontario, through the Ontario Book Publishing Tax Credit and Ontario Creates, and the Government of Canada.

Nous remercions le Conseil des arts du Canada de son soutien. L'an dernier, le Conseil a investi 153 millions de dollars pour mettre de l'art dans la vie des Canadiennes et des Canadiens de tout le pays.

Care has been taken to trace the ownership of copyright material used in this book. The author and the publisher welcome any information enabling them to rectify any references or credits in subsequent editions.

— J. Kirk Howard, President

The publisher is not responsible for websites or their content unless they are owned by the publisher.

Printed and bound in Canada

VISIT US AT

dundurn.com | @dundurnpress | dundurnpress | dundurnpress

Dundurn
3 Church Street, Suite 500
Toronto, Ontario, Canada
M5E 1M2

For Judy

One

TONY

November 26

CONSTABLE KEN POOLE wasn't at his station, and his desk was a mess. File folders in a slithering heap, Post-it memos stuck to other Post-it memos, a half-empty bag of nachos. Pens and bull-clips, and to top it off, a caped action figure of some kind overlooked it all, hands on hips.

Still no sign of Poole. Dion's eyes wandered from the action figure to the file folders, to the label on the topmost folder. It read, "Tony Souza."

Souza was the mystery on everybody's mind these days. Young, handsome, healthy, a new recruit on the North Shore and on the job for less than a month before taking sudden leave, right off the rail of a high bridge. Dion had been shocked by the news, and like everybody else, he wondered why the man had done it.

Jumped.

Back at his own neat desk, he dropped into his chair and tried to work. He couldn't recall ever meeting Souza, and only knew his face from the photographs in the paper. Maybe he had seen the man in passing, a hello in the hall?

Curiosity drove him back to Poole's desk. Using his knuckle, as if a light touch made the act less culpable, he lifted the folder's manila cover, just to see, and clipped to the front leaf was a photocopy of Souza's last words. One short paragraph.

Don't worry about me. I have gone to a better place, it started.

At yesterday's service, snatches of conversation had told Dion more about Souza than the eulogies did. Souza had broken from his family's strict religious tradition, had shrugged off heaven and hell, simply wasn't a church-going guy.

Dion read the rest of the note, and saw it contained anger: *To mom and dad and Sonny, I'm sorry. To everybody else, I'm not.* Sonny was Sonia, Tony's sister. She had spoken at the service, saying her brother was much loved and would be missed. If she had any idea why Tony had ended his life, she hadn't shared that knowledge. Nobody had.

Neither did anybody ask Dion to care — but how could he not? Death by suicide was always tragic. It was the crime that so often went unsolved. It was worrisome, too. What if the person had stepped into oblivion because they had stumbled upon the fundamental, bottom-line truth about the meaning of life, like a message in a bottle, and that truth was too awful to bear?

He shrugged. As pointless as it might be, he would go over the note in his mind for a while, as he lay in bed or ate breakfast or warmed up his car, trying to understand its incongruities. If Souza had found God, as the "better place" suggested, the discovery had not done much for him. The proof was in the fall. Souza blamed everybody but his immediate family for his unbearable pain, but Dion suspected that the *everybody* could be narrowed down to a *somebody*.

Still, Souza was not his brother, not his case, and none of his business, and his death would not haunt him for long. In these moments of pondering, though, he had to wonder if the new recruit blamed the force for his troubles. He wouldn't be surprised.

Two

AMELIA

December 13

DAVE LEITH CAST A TALL shadow as he set coffee cup and newspaper on his desk and said "Morning" to whoever happened to be within earshot. The December sunlight was intense and yellow, the rays low and blinding. It was his favourite time of day, early morning, kind of a mini chance at redemption, a new shot at the old to-do list.

His greeting went to waste. JD Temple, leaning over paperwork at her desk, didn't respond. Neither did Jimmy Torr one desk over, chatting with a stranger. Or rather grilling the stranger, by the sounds of it. The stranger being grilled was no civilian, but a constable in patrol gear, a pale, lanky kid, the only one to return the greeting. And he did so with a peace sign, which struck Leith as disrespectful.

Torr was saying to the kid, "So what the hell were we talking about here, before you sidetracked me?"

"The MVA, I do believe," the constable said. He had a full, loud voice, and a bit of an accent. Irish, Scottish?

Leith dropped into his chair. "And what MVA is this, Jim?"

Torr indicated the Irish or Scottish kid with a thumb. "I'm interviewing him. He saw a single-vehicle up on the Squamish about one a.m."

The Squamish was the informal name for the Sea to Sky Highway, which traced the cliffs toward the winter wonderland of Whistler and beyond. Leith said, "Since when does GIS care about an MVA?"

GIS stood for General Investigations Section and dealt with the more serious crimes. MVAs, motor-vehicle accidents, were only serious crimes if you happened to be involved in one, where even a fender-bender was serious, if it was your fender that got bendered, as Leith well knew. But from the police perspective, an MVA was only serious if there were guns, drugs, or kidnappees in the mix. That, or hit-and-run casualties. The lanky kid stretched his legs and said to Torr, "Lookit, I really don't see why we have to go through it all again, anyway. I already gave a full statement at the scene. It was ghastly and something I'm going to do my best to forget soon as we're done here."

Ghastly was not a word Leith often heard from the mouths of police officers, especially ones who were barely twenty, and somewhere in the back of his mind he decided the kid was out of his league. Or above it. Torr cranked his neck to reply to Leith. "I'm not *on* an MVA. It's a personal favour for Anderson downstairs. He's up to his arsehole with the latest intolerance campaign, and since, lucky us, Craig Gilmartin here is one of ours —"

"Anybody die in the crash?" Leith asked.

"As of eight thirty-five this morning, yes. The driver."

"Amelia Foster, just turned thirty," the kid added, darkly.

Torr waved at him to mind his own business. "Amelia Foster," he told Leith. "Thirty years old. And all I need to know from this punk is one simple thing: did he see the crash? A simple question he can't seem to answer without doing the scenic tour runaround. Seems like someone around here loves the sound of his own voice."

JD muttered something Leith didn't quite catch. He directed his next words at Constable Gilmartin, trying to abridge the bullshit. "Did you see the crash?"

"Like I haven't asked him that ten times!" Torr exploded.

Gilmartin crossed his arms and said loudly that actually Torr had *not* asked that very simple question, not once. "If he had, I would have answered, no, I didn't see the crash. Some guy ahead of me saw it and waved me down. He said this little red car just veered off" — Leith heard *veered* warped to *verred* and thought, *Definitely a Scot* — "just like that, *bam*. We jumped down the ditch right away, and there it was, wrapped around a tree. There was a woman inside. Like I told Sherlock here, we first considered pulling her out —"

"Fresh out of Regina and no respect for his superiors," Torr exclaimed, and pointed a warning finger at Gilmartin. "You smarten up and watch your tongue, hear me?"

JD Temple shouted at Torr that *everybody* could hear him, and to keep his fucking voice down. Torr shouted back at her, quoting some memo on the use of bad language in the squad room, and Leith raised his own voice louder still to ask them both what side of bed they'd each fallen out of this morning.

Torr grunted an apology and turned back to the task at hand, grilling his witness, and Leith turned back to his own task, which right now was getting the lid off his coffee cup without spilling it and burning his thigh, as had happened yesterday.

"You know what?" he heard Gilmartin say, in the same hammered English. "If she'd have veered to her right, she'd have gone into the ocean. I thought she was lucky that she'd gone left instead. But maybe the ocean would have been a far faster and kinder death, I'm thinking now."

Leith turned away from the MVA hubbub to face JD. "How's it going?"

JD had short dark hair, fierce dark eyes, a cleft-lip scar, and an edgy attitude. "It would be a whole lot better if I had some earplugs," she said.

The phone on Jimmy Torr's desk rang, and Torr lifted the receiver. "Yeah? Uh-huh." He grabbed scrap paper and a pen. "Okay, yup. Go on." Phone squished between chin and chest, he scribbled a note. "Uh-huh. No problem." Receiver dropped, he smirked at his notebook. "Yeah, right."

Gilmartin leaned forward with interest. "Something to do with the dead girl, was it?"

"Nope. It's something about a missing guy," Torr told him. "Rory Keefer, forty-five years old. A missing *husband*, actually, which raises flags in my head."

"How so?" Gilmartin asked.

Leith could see one of Torr's tasteless jokes coming.

"When husbands go missing," Torr said, "it's only till they call with a forwarding address. Right, Dave?"

Leith shook his head and fired up his computer. He mentioned to Torr that people were trying to work around here and to keep it down a bit. Torr went back to his questioning of young Gilmartin, and *did* keep it down — a bit.

Three

HIT AND MISS

AFTER A LONG DAY, Leith found himself glancing too often at the little clock he kept on his desk, so he reached over and knocked it face down. He was studying surveillance photographs, trying to pin an identity on a couple of violent offenders caught on a drugstore's CCTV, when a voice called out to him from behind, and the words were alarming: "Sir! I've just been shot at!"

There was a distinct Scottish lilt to the words, but Leith's brain tended to wind down by day's end, and he didn't quite connect the voice to the face until the MVA witness–rookie stood squarely before him. It was young Gilmartin, dressed down in civvies now, ruddy and sweating and out of breath, as if he had run several blocks.

Leith gestured at the visitor's chair across from him and asked for a repeat.

The constable dropped into the chair like a dead weight. "Somebody took a shot at me just now, as I was going down Rogers," he said. "They just missed my skull, sir. Just missed by this much!"

Leith sat back in his chair and looked at Gilmartin's finger and thumb, held about an inch apart. The boy's face was still rounded out with baby fat. He wore a cap, a flat mess of green and red, shoved to one side of his head until he pulled it off to wring in his hands.

"Shot of what?"

"A shot of lead, no doubt," Gilmartin blared. Static created by the swift removal of the cap had sucked his fine brown hair upright. "Sir, I'm dead serious. I was walking down to the Quay to get flowers for Sophie, and a white van drove by, and the bullet whizzed right over my head" — he skimmed his hair with a palm — "and hit the wall beside me. It left a hole this big. Sir? What are we going to do about this?"

Leith looked at the photographs on the desk in front of him: shots of miscreants, faces he should be focusing on. Instead he was thinking about home, and his soon-to-be three-year-old's birthday party, a place he would dearly like to be heading toward in about five minutes. "You should advise your supervisor," he said.

"I already did, sir, and he sent me up here."

"You're sure it was a bullet? There's something called backfire —"

"Backfires don't take chips out of concrete."

Craig Gilmartin had made his point crisply, and Leith was forced to shelve his doubts. Taking potshots at pedestrians was about as serious as it got. What crappy timing, though. Ten minutes later it would have been someone else's crisis. He stuck the photographs into his file cabinet, banged shut the drawer, pocketed the keys. "Okay. Let's go take a look."

* * *

The pockmark was situated at about throat level on a high concrete wall that paralleled the road. The hole, as Leith gauged it, was palm sized, somewhat in the shape of a bowled-over heart, with a deeply cratered centre. Raw-edged, clean, fresh, it could certainly have been caused by a small metal projectile flying at high velocity from the area of the roadway.

The constable stood nearby, back against the wall. Leith placed his thumb beside the bullet hole, which he eyeballed as about 5.5 feet off the ground, and looked at Gilmartin, who was tall — at least Leith's own height, maybe more. "You said it went over your head, so you must have been ducking. Right? You had some kind of warning?"

Gilmartin burst out laughing. He dug in his pocket and presented a shiny silver coin. "This. Would you believe? I was picking it up off the sidewalk. Sophie's lucky penny!" He looked at the coin and tittered. "A lucky penny. Jesus, it's too funny!"

Lying in the kid's palm was not a penny, Leith saw, but a quarter. "Sophie," he said. "Who's that?"

"My girlfriend, who is angry with me, which is why I was going to the Quay," Gilmartin said. "To get flowers."

"And she was with you?"

"What, sir? No."

"You said it was her lucky —"

"I'm saying she's deadly superstitious. It's the Italian in her, I'm thinking. Black cats, birds in the house, misfortune coming in threes, all of it baloney, I tell her. And of course she picks up coins and calls them lucky. I told her it's not lucky; it's unsanitary. I said, how lucky is a nasty virus? But she still does so. And when I saw this coin shining on the sidewalk, I was about ready to step on it, but because she's pissed off at me, and I feel so shitty about it, I picked it up, like on her behalf, sort of thing. Scooped it up, germs and all, and the bullet missed me."

Leith looked at the coin again, still on display, and at Gilmartin's face. "You're kidding me."

"I'm not."

"Keep that coin."

"I will."

Leith went to study the tarmac. From inside his car he made a brief call, then returned to Gilmartin to get more details for his notebook, and when all was said, they stood looking at the pockmark.

"Some kind of month," Gilmartin said. "First Tony —"

"You were friends with Tony Souza?"

"Went through Depot together."

Leith nodded and shook his head, in the way of saying yes, the suicide was awful news.

"Then that girl dying before my eyes," Gilmartin said. "And now this. I've never seen anybody dying before. It was horrible. And my phone was dead. It's the cold that does it, you know, sucks the life right out of it. And then that guy, the one who waved me down, he didn't even *have* a phone, would you believe? Come to think of it, neither did the girl. I'd totally forgotten about her. What are the chances of three people converging at the scene of an accident, where time is of the essence, and nobody having a working phone?"

Gilmartin went rattling on, the release from tension turning him into a chatterbox, and the words began to flow in Leith's one ear and out the other. He nodded sympathetically as he half-listened, keeping an eye down the block as he tried to hide his impatience. Waiting for Ident, listening to Gilmartin, thinking about home.

Ident showed up eventually and parked their vehicles up and down the block, impeding traffic from Esplanade to the Quay. This near Christmas, even at this hour, the city was a flurry of activity. Detour signs went up. The section of wall in question was photographed in macro. A deformed slug was found in the gutter, and the blacktop was scrutinized from one end of the block to the other. Leith organized a team to canvass businesses in the area for witnesses. But it would go nowhere, he realized, standing to one side and watching the pros at work. Random shots never did.

* * *

Leith found his superior, Sergeant Mike Bosko, still in his office, and stepped in to let him know what had happened. He was invited to sit, and from his chair paraphrased his notes. "So the van approached from behind. Gilmartin didn't get a good look at it, didn't see the occupants, didn't note the licence number or any identifying markings. It's a two-way street. He was walking southbound on the west sidewalk, so the shot would have come from the van's passenger side. Just one shot. There's only a right-hand turn at the bottom of Rogers, but the vehicle took a left toward Lonsdale. Gilmartin says there were other vehicles in the area, and someone could have taken down the van's plates because of the illegal turn, but he doubts it. Frankly, so do I. I've been to the scene myself, called in Forensics, notified Ballistics. I observed a fresh pockmark on the retaining wall measuring 1.72 metres off the ground, about five foot eight, sir. A slug was recovered from the gutter 9.5 metres northeast of the bullet hole itself …"

"Excuse me a moment," Bosko said. "How's he doing, Craig Gilmartin? Is he all right?"

Bosko was a good man, a fantastic leader. Smart, kind, patient, and caring. Leith didn't like him much, and had his reasons. Not good reasons, but reasons all the same. "Sorry," he said. "I should have mentioned, Craig seems fine. He has no idea why anyone would shoot at him. He wasn't in uniform. No indication it's targeted or anything to do with his job. He's only been with us for a couple of months, hasn't made any enemies, gets along with everyone, he says. No shell found, but the slug's just a twenty-two, they're saying. Hardly hit man material, so I'd say it's another of those random things we've been getting lately. They shoot to scare, just for the thrill of making people jump."

He paused to re-examine his own doubts. This shooter had seemed to be aiming at the level of a man's head, which didn't strike him as scare tactics. But that was for the next shift to worry about. "I've got the word out, and B watch is on full alert. I told Gilmartin to watch his back. I told him to get a uniformed member to drive him home, to be safe."

"Sounds like you have things under control, Dave. Appreciate it." Bosko stood and tucked his shirttails a bit snugger under his belt. He was young for his rank, younger and taller and heavier than Leith, and best described as bear-shaped. He was also smart and unflappable. "Going to meet the boys for a beer," he said. "Would be great if you joined us."

Jimmy Torr will be there, Leith thought, picturing the crew sitting around the long table at Rainey's, where they often met up to talk shop not so reverently, like briefings from the dark side. JD Temple, Doug Paley, Sean Urbanski — the usual crowd making the usual noise. "Wish I could," he said, "but I have a wife and baby waiting for me with birthday cake."

Though frankly, his three-year-old, Isabelle, would be fast asleep by the time he got there. It would just be him and Alison sitting there with Scotch and what was left of the cake.

"Oh, excellent! Whose birthday?"

"Isabelle's." Leith plastered on a smile. He wasn't a great smiler. He didn't like his stained and imperfect teeth, or the shape of his face when it stretched sideways into a grin. But he knew the value of cheeriness and never gave up trying. "She's just turning three."

"Three, what a milestone! Go home, then, and have fun. One day we'll cut out early, what d'you say? Have a chat."

"Definitely, we'll do that," Leith said, still smiling, though the word *chat* gave him the chills. He and Bosko had history of sorts, issues dormant but not dead: an off-the-record investigation of one of Leith's colleagues, Cal Dion, that wasn't going so well. He shrugged off the anxiety he inevitably felt in Bosko's presence, and they walked together to the exit, gathering their coats and gloves on the way. They remarked on the lull in the North Shore crime scene these past few weeks. Leith hoped aloud that the potshot wasn't the end of a pleasant trend, and Bosko added a heartfelt "amen" — all of which, like a jinx, probably should have been left unsaid.

Four

NIGHTFALL

RAINEY'S WAS THE LOCAL PUB where the gang all met. Tonight it had ramped up the old Christmas spirit, flickering an overload of LEDs and blasting rock and roll carols. JD was a regular, though she rarely stayed long. She sat in her usual place, the bench seat with its good view of the entrance. From here she could monitor the comings and goings of patrons, and also warn her off-duty workmates, should a senior officer show up, to tone down the colourful rhetoric, their views on law and order that didn't always mesh with the force's mission statement.

She spotted one now: Mike Bosko. He darkened the doorway and stood chatting with the hostess. He was removing his gloves, too, which meant he planned on staying awhile. JD spun her index finger once and jabbed it into her cheek, a discreet signal to the others to shut up and be nice.

They all looked around as one, but if Bosko got the hint that a warning had gone out, he didn't let on. He smiled a greeting as he took a chair. *Not as dumb as he looks*, JD thought. She admired Bosko, in a way. He was friendly, quite a talker, yet she had the feeling he could play the executioner, if he had to. And then coolly get on with his day.

There was also something fishy about him, she believed. But maybe only because her favourite detective in the bunch, Dave Leith — who was absent again tonight — didn't seem to care for him. Or maybe distrusted him. There was no overt sign that she could pin down in her mind, but her senses said something was definitely afoot, and usually her senses proved right.

Someday she would put it to Leith directly. For now she contented herself by keeping an eye and an ear out for clues. She watched Bosko now. As usual, it wasn't long before he had taken charge of the conversation. He spoke of an investigation now underway into a random potshot down near the Quay. The target happened to be a new recruit, who fortunately had dodged the bullet.

The potshot discussion took the crew's conversation all over the map, as JD listened and occasionally put in her two cents. They talked about new recruits in general, which got them talking about the suicide of Tony Souza, which got them talking about Christmas, in the way conversations reroute themselves along the path of least resistance.

Again, JD wondered why Leith didn't like this Bosko guy. He was droll. He made her laugh. On the topic of Christmas, he was telling them a story about home decor and ladders. Not his own home, but that of Arlo, a good friend from his Vancouver white-collar crime days, who really liked to over-deck the halls.

"And not just for himself and Sylvia to enjoy, mind you," Bosko said. "The whole neighbourhood gets to enjoy the glow when he's got all the lights up. They're probably visible from outer space. And of course every year I get roped into helping out. I don't know how many hours I've spent untangling extension cords and replacing bulbs. I swear, he wasn't like this before retirement."

Droll, but he does go on, JD thought. She was glad when he finished his beer and said he had to be going. The rude shoptalk picked up where it had left off, but not for long. It was late, and the party soon disbanded.

Back at her apartment, JD was changing into her super-soft indoor clothes when her work phone rang. A bad sign. Moments later, she was shoving her feet into her boots once more and heading out into the night.

* * *

Leith got the call as he was brushing his teeth, feeling logy and primed for bed, and the curt message kicked him awake. The neighbourhood in question was so close he could hear the wailing of sirens as he climbed into his car. They seemed to be converging on the given address from all directions. He arrived moments before the paramedics, and took in the scene. The first cars to respond were parked out front, and one vehicle was lit from within. He crossed the street toward it and found JD behind the wheel. In the passenger seat next to her, a small, pale-faced young woman was staring straight ahead with a stunned expression.

JD rolled down the window to talk. "Witness," she explained. "She called it in. Want me to wait?"

Leith took another look at the girl. "She's okay, not hurt?"

"Not hurt. We'll hang on till you've checked it out."

Leith jogged up the steps to the porch on the heels of the paramedics. Behind him the street was becoming clogged with emergency vehicles, and more were on their way. Constable Alain Lavalle stepped out onto the porch as Leith topped the stairs. "Shot in the chest," he said. "Poole and Sattar responded, and house is cleared. They're inside to your left, sir."

Leith passed Lavalle and entered the house. It was a squat Cape Cod style structure, the kind with small bedrooms and hardwood floors, high ceilings, mullioned windows. To his right was the kitchen, to his left the living room, and straight ahead a generous corridor that would lead to the back of the house. The victim lay at the hallway entrance, attended to by two uniformed constables. Or attended by one, at least. Kenny Poole was in his fifties, the senior of the two — in fact, he was the supervisor — yet he stood back, looking dazed, while his trainee, young Rajesh Sattar, knelt over the motionless man on the floor, hunched forward in the awkward space, the heels of his bloodied hands pressing wads of gauze against the victim's upper-left torso, the heart zone. Only when the paramedics raised their voices, insisted they were here to take over, did Sattar get to his feet and stand back.

The victim was Constable Craig Gilmartin, the kid who had been shot at just hours earlier, the one Leith himself had sent home with a flippant warning to be careful. And no, it wasn't a random thing after all, and he should never for a moment have supposed it was. The boy lay on his left side, propped against a cushion. His face was pale, hair damp with sweat. Blood around his nose had left dark clotted tracks. He'd been injured for a while, then, maybe hours. Coatless, but fully dressed, boots still on, as if he'd just arrived home. His T-shirt, once white, was now a gory carnation as the paramedics removed the mess of gauze left by Sattar.

Mike Bosko arrived, one of the few to be allowed over the threshold. Leith threw him a glance and said, "Dammit."

Blood told at least a part of the story. It streaked across the floor leading to Gilmartin's resting spot, as though he had been dragged several feet. Or crawled. Outside another siren sighed to silence, and yet another rounded a corner. Sattar was saying to the medics, "He's got faint signs. Hardly breathing. What took you so bloody long?"

Bosko asked anyone, "Who reported this?"

"Girlfriend, sir," Poole answered. Don't know her name. She's in the cruiser with JD."

Bosko asked for details, whatever was known, and Sattar told him that he and Poole, responding to the call, had found Gilmartin like this, comatose and covered in blood, with a slow oozing wound. No sign of a weapon. Sattar had propped up the victim to slow the bleeding, and while he tried to staunch the flow Poole had given the house a cursory all-clear. Other members arriving moments later had supplied a first aid kit and completed the search. No sign of the attacker indoors or out.

Poole added to Sattar's report. The blood was barely seeping when he arrived, and he had thought Gilmartin wasn't breathing. He had told Sattar not to move him, as there could be spinal damage. Sattar had ignored him, he said, and shifted Gilmartin to his side and propped him up with a sofa cushion, which shouldn't be done.

"It definitely should be," Sattar said, but for Leith's ears only.

Leith looked around. Aside from the body on the floor, nothing in the room immediately stood out. No damage, no signs of a struggle. The paramedics were moving fast, loading their patient onto the stretcher. In the hallway Bosko was talking to someone on the phone, doling out tasks, and Leith noted the change in the rhythm of his speech. Usually leisurely and — at least in Leith's mind — somewhat circuitous, it was now sharp, fast, to the point. Sattar would attend ER with the victim, and Poole would be on crowd control, keeping traffic in and out to a minimum, till Forensics could get to their scene work.

Leith asked Ken Poole for his Maglite. With the beam flared wide, he walked down the hall toward the back of the house, watching the floor in front of him. A darkened bedroom to one side, and another room that Gilmartin had used for an office, maybe, with desk, computer, bookshelves, and easel, too, with a canvas up and a painting in progress.

The back door he found locked and undamaged, and the sunporch leading off from it was cluttered with summertime junk. Below, the fenced lot was no doubt brighter than it had been before the neighbours were roused by all the police activity, lights blazing on all sides, spilling an orange glow across path and lawn.

He returned to find that Gilmartin had been removed. He passed on to Bosko what little he knew, then left the house to see about JD and her witness.

Bystanders were gathering on the sidewalk, and he scanned faces for one that might shine a beacon of guilty knowledge. It sometimes happened, but not this time. Headlights turned a corner at the end of the street. He blocked the blaze with his arm and leaned down to talk to JD. She gestured to her passenger and said, "Sophie Dewitt, Craig's girlfriend. She called it in."

Dewitt was in her late teens or early twenties. Harry Potter spectacles slid down her nose, in danger of toppling off. She looked waxy, almost catatonic.

Leith bent low to peer past JD at the girl, who could be the shooter, for all he knew. "Hang tight, Sophie," he told her. "JD will take you to the hospital, and I'll get there soon as I'm done here, and we'll have a talk, okay?"

The girl nodded and whispered something he had to cup his ear to hear.

"He's dead, isn't he?"

"No," he said. "I've just seen him. They're getting him ready to transport right now. He's got vital signs. He's young and fit, and there's a very good chance he'll get through this." He turned to the owner of the blazing headlights as the lights doused and the doors banged shut. Jim Torr was striding toward him, Sean Urbanski close on his heels. He looked at Sophie again, and saw that his words of reassurance hadn't moved her an iota.

She had seen Gilmartin herself, he realized. Seen all the blood, knew how bad it really was.

"She doesn't seem injured," JD said, as Leith straightened. "I asked her a few questions, and she says she doesn't know who did it. I'll get her to the hospital now, get her checked over."

He nodded. "See what you can get from her. Give me an hour. Make sure she doesn't wash or change her clothes, and no food, no cigarettes, no sedatives. Just water for now. Right?"

JD knew all this, and the narrowing of her eyes told him so. She began to roll up the window, but he gave it a rap for one last question. "Who drove Gilmartin home today, d'you know?"

"Ken Poole, I think."

JD drove off with their prime witness, tailing the ambulance. The winter night was chilly, but Leith's sense of guilt was making him sweat. It was a guilt sure to set in heavily as he ran out of tasks to keep him busy. He turned to Torr and Urbanski and told them the news.

"It's Craig Gilmartin, and it's not good."

"Gilmartin?" Torr said. "The guy I was grilling this morning? You're kidding me!"

Leith told them about the drive-by he had shrugged off as a random event. Torr and Urbanski said they'd heard about it. Leith gestured at the house, the open door at the top of the stairs. "Ken Poole escorted Craig home late this afternoon, and for all we know, the kid's been lying there bleeding ever since. As long as three hours."

"Gilmartin," Torr repeated. He blinked at the house, a beehive of activity now.

Exhaust billowed about their legs in the chilled air. Bosko came down the steps and joined them at the curb, telling Leith to get a team together from all shifts. A mobile unit was on its way, as was Ident. The drive-by slug was a .22, while this one was a larger calibre, by the looks of it, and the only connection so far was one target named Gilmartin.

Two attempts, two guns, Leith thought. *What's this kid been up to?* "Talk to Kenny," he told Urbanski. "Get down everything that happened today when he drove Craig home. Everything."

* * *

Past midnight, and the hospital corridors were not deserted, but quiet. Together, Leith and JD spoke with Gilmartin's parents. They were in their late sixties, so their son had been a latecomer. They both had thick Scottish accents and an apparent ability to keep their horror masked. But they were devastated, kneecapped, and the questioning went nowhere, really. They didn't know and couldn't guess who had shot their son.

In the end the Gilmartins were left to their vigil, and Leith and JD escorted Sophie Dewitt back to the station to get her version of events.

Five

TOUCH AND GO

December 14

SOPHIE DEWITT WAS NOT quite five feet tall and not quite twenty-two years old. She was also not quite present when Leith sat down across from her in the interview room at 2:15 in the morning. She spoke in dull tones, telling him and JD that it was her fault, what had happened to Craig, because of getting mad at him the way she did after their big fight.

Aha, Leith thought. *Here we go. A slam-dunk crime of passion.*

"When did you have this big fight?" JD asked. She spoke in a kindly way, but she was a bit of a chameleon, Leith knew, and gentleness was only a part of her toolbox.

Sophie didn't fall for it. "We didn't fight today," she said sharply. "I went over there to apologize, actually. It was *last week* that I wanted to kill him. And even then, it was just words."

"Oh, okay," JD said. "What was the fight about?"

"Nothing. We'd gone out for drinks, and he spent a whole hour talking to some girls he didn't even know, while I sat alone feeling like an idiot. Which I am. He's just way more social than me. It's something I have to get used to. And maybe it wasn't a whole hour, actually, but at least twenty minutes, and we still ended up in this big fight, and I broke it off."

"And you believe that has something to do with him being shot?"

Sophie nodded, then shook her head. "I don't know. I called him last night around midnight, but he didn't answer, so I figured he was already out enjoying his newfound freedom."

No, he was at the scene of a car crash, Leith thought.

"I told myself I didn't care if he was out having fun without me," she went on. "I was maybe disappointed, but I knew I'd get over it. I'm not a child."

Her face began to crinkle and redden. She gave in and cried like a child, taking one tissue after another. Then she calmed herself and said to JD with dignity, "And now he's dead, so none of it matters. I just wish I'd been able to apologize for being so petty. That's all."

"I can see why you're upset," JD said. "That's tough. How long have you known Craig?"

"We met this spring. It was serious, too. Until I screwed it all up."

Half a year wasn't long, relationship-wise, Leith knew. But he had been in love at her age, and had experienced the highs and lows, and the misery that followed breakup. With all this emotion flying around, he had to wonder if maybe Gilmartin had shot himself, and this girl Sophie had arrived and disposed of the gun for some reason. Or she was lying, and she had in fact arrived with the gun, after a week of stewing, and shot him.

He looked at her round face, tilted down now and sniffling, her funny round eyeglasses. Like Gilmartin, she seemed like a bit of a black sheep, but level-headed. Smart. He didn't think she had shot her ex, and for now he would stick with his original belief that everything was just as she stated: she had arrived to apologize, had found Gilmartin down and bleeding, had called 911.

"Did you see any vehicles that you didn't recognize, that stood out to you in any way, parked in front of his place?" JD asked.

"Parking is bad around there. It's always jam-packed with cars, so I wouldn't know."

"Do you have any idea at all who might have done this?"

"No, I have no idea," Sophie said. "He's literally the nicest guy on the planet. Why would anyone want to kill him?"

She seemed to realize what she had lost all over again, and began to sob. Leith would have given her a fresh box of Kleenex and a fifteen-minute break, but JD was signalling to him that they should shut this down for the night.

When their witness was gone and Leith and JD were back at their desks, he said, "We could have pressed on, JD. Time is ticking."

"I think she's told us all she knows," JD said. "She's dead tired. She needs sleep."

Leith slumped and pitched paper clips into his empty pen jar, missing the goal on most shots. Hand and eye coordination were starting to go, and so was his mind. He, too, needed sleep. Messages buzzed on his phone, lighting up the screen. He monitored them distractedly.

JD was tapping at her keyboard and thinking aloud as she worked. "The drive-by. It would take two, right? One to drive, one to shoot. Unless the driver's some kind of James Bond, Navy SEAL, DIY sharpshooter type. Not likely. Who could afford that kind of assassin? And what kind of assassin would use a popgun? Must be amateurs."

Leith only half followed, a part of his mind stuck on repeat, contemplating his own carelessness, his dismissal of the drive-by as a random shot, a lark. "Sure," he said.

JD looked up from her keyboard long enough to give him the eye, which meant she was coming up with some kind of zinger. Leith gave up his paper clip basketball and paid attention.

"You're not thinking Sophie hired a hit man to kill Craig, are you?" she asked. He had said no such thing, but he had considered it, and she must have read his mind. "Because you can forget it. Might as well drop her from the list. But if Craig's a real playboy, he could have trod on somebody's territory, after breaking up with Sophie."

She was typing again. Leith got to work as well, answering his messages, reading through Gilmartin's personnel file, making notes, responding to calls from the field. From the hospital updates he learned that the patient's life remained touch and go. Any moment now he would get the bad news. He was a pessimist, and pessimists knew best.

His land line jangled, making him jump. But it was only Sean Urbanski saying he had spoken to Ken Poole. Ken had nothing interesting to relate about this afternoon, when he'd driven Gilmartin home. Conversation en route had been desultory at best, Urbanski said.

"Been what?" Leith said.

"*Desultory.*" Urbanski was a big guy, with tousled blond hair and a beard, who liked his phone apps, his favourite lately being Word of the Day. "Aimless, just small talk. Didn't discuss the drive-by in any detail. Ken says he pulled up at Craig's place, said *ciao*, and Craig walked into the house alone. Lights were off, nobody hanging around that Ken could see. He watched till the door closed, then drove off."

Followed soon thereafter by a deadly blast.

"Right," Leith said. "Get the whole conversation down as best as Ken can remember it, however desultory it was."

A scapegoat would be nice, he thought, as he disconnected. But he couldn't blame Ken Poole for not escorting the kid inside, making sure everything was safe in there. Poole should have been briefed, instructed that the house be properly cleared, and who should have instructed him to do so, if not Leith?

No, for this particular murder-in-the-making, he could shoulder the blame alone.

Six

LOVE LOST

WHEN DION HEARD ABOUT last night's shooting of an RCMP officer — new on the force, critical condition, no names released — he quit buttering his toast to stare at the clock radio on the counter, and his eyes filled with hot, stinging tears.

Angry tears, because he hadn't been called. He should have been there, for a first-hand look at the scene. Should have been given the chance to form his own theories, advance them for consideration, help hammer the facts into an effective line of inquiry.

Instead, he had been allowed to sleep through it all.

It was his own fault, of course. The force had reached out to him, said he could come back to GIS, and instead of jumping on board, he had insisted on staying in the general duties pit. Why? Because the GIS was the Serious Crime Unit, and Serious Crime was dangerous waters for him, since he was a serious criminal. A year and a half ago, out in Surrey with his friend and colleague Looch

Ferraro, he had killed a man. Illegally. It was the deep dark secret that would never let him get back to normal.

These days he had a bad feeling that his deep, dark secret was about to come to light. David Leith's changing attitude toward him was one warning sign. Usually standoffish, Leith was being nicer to him lately, which could be a sign of pity, and pity could be a sign of disaster approaching.

At the living room window Dion looked out through the slats, down on the street, like the desperado he had become. He watched pedestrians and counted up his fears. Leith's pity, Bosko's interest in him — and worst of all, the witness.

She had been up above, on the weed-choked gravel hills that had been built up by excavators over the years and then abandoned. She had been looking down as he stood in the pit below, shovelling earth and grit over the body. She had seen him, and he had seen her. Yet all he knew about her, to this day, was that she was on a dirt bike, she had pink hair, and she had fled.

He had dropped his makeshift spade and jumped into his car, Looch beside him. They had torn out with no grand plan in mind except to cut the witness off on the highway, and instead had got T-boned on the passenger side by a punk in a speeding sports car.

The punk and Looch were both dead now, and Dion would spend the rest of his days trusting nobody with pink hair.

Which was stupid, because the dye would have grown out by now. She could have switched to blue. Or purple. Or gone natural, for all he knew.

But time had gone by, and no witness had stepped forward, and no body in a shallow grave had come stinking to the surface either. The latter was the most baffling of all. The burial was botched by the interruption, and Dion hadn't gone back to make it properly disappear, as per the plan. He couldn't, because he had been in a coma.

The passage of time told him Pink could be crossed off his list of fears, for now. If she was going to come forward, she would have done so long ago. But as one worry faded, another one had risen, hinged on a memory he had retrieved only recently. Hardly a vignette, maybe nothing but/a misinterpretation, but had he turned around as he worked at being a gravedigger, and had he seen Looch standing near the car, his face underlit?

Underlit. In retrospect he was sure he was right, and an underlit face meant Looch was either checking his mail or making a call.

And there was no way he'd be checking his mail.

Looch was a burly man and a big talker, but he could be a real chickenshit in a crisis, and who would he be calling to cry about his predicament to? His common-law partner, Brooke, that's who. Looch thought the world of Brooke. She had the answer to everything. She would tell him what to do.

Dion was still looking out the window, still searching the streets for danger. Had Looch made contact? Had he told Brooke what he'd done, what Dion had done? But if he had, and if Brooke was in the know, she seemed to be keeping that knowledge to herself. *So far.*

He worried anyway, because one thing was for sure: crime had a way of unravelling, and on the day of reckoning his only excuse for killing that man would be laughed out of court, after which he'd be sent to the slammer at whiplash speed.

So keep lying low, then, and pray. Except he wasn't good at lying low. In fact, all this lying low and watching his back was giving him ulcers — not literally, yet, but he was sure to wind up with a doctor's visit and a bunch of Zantac pills, if he wasn't careful.

Eating breakfast instead of staring at it would be a good idea. He chomped on the toast and swallowed, chomped and swallowed.

His shrink had talked about the power of gratitude, and he tried it now, counting off on his fingers what he had going for him instead of against.

Counselling itself was a big positive, in fact. He hadn't gone willingly, but was starting to appreciate the sessions, because Samantha Kerr's psychological soul-digging was inadvertently teaching him how to read between the lines of how others saw him. He was sussing out how to avoid detection. He was perfecting the fine art of being normal.

Gratitude point number two was his improving health. Getting ill would be the last straw, so he had thrown out his cigarettes, cut down on Scotch and beer, and ate meals rich in vitamins, minerals, and fibre. He had bulked out, almost back to normal, bought a road bike and a rack for his car, and went for spins in his time off. On his last checkup his doctor said he was doing great.

So even though his spirit was dragging its knuckles, his cardiovascular system was hopping.

There was probably some third thing to be grateful for, but he had run out of time. He stood at the sink counter, half dressed, his short black hair still damp from the shower, the slice of whole grain, partly buttered toast in his hand blurred through tears. He took another bite and chewed viciously. He wouldn't rush to work, and wouldn't ask questions when he got there. Any details worth picking up he would gather through osmosis as he carried on with his day. If the downed officer died, he would attend the funeral — but nothing further.

He scraped the remains of the toast into the garbage and placed the plate in the sink, irritated by curiosity. Who had been shot? A rookie. First Tony Souza, and now this. Could the two be related? Was last night's victim someone he knew? Probably not.

The tightness in his chest was from the caffeine, no doubt. He poured the rest of the cup down the drain. He put on his street clothes, buffed his boots, would change into his uniform at work. He seemed A-okay, judging by his reflection in the full-length foyer mirror. Nobody could tell from looking at him that he was churned dirt inside. He palmed the shadows from under his eyes, then grabbed his coat off its hook and left the apartment, out to discover who the fuck had gotten shot.

Seven

STEEL

LEITH LISTENED AS Jim Torr opened the debrief with his background report on the victim. "Craig is twenty-two. Grew up in Dundee, which is in Scotland, came to Canada at eighteen, and after some film school classes, he dropped out and applied to join the force. Went through the hoops, got accepted. First day on duty was October 12. No major disciplinary snags, though he's been told to pipe down and pay attention during briefings. That's not on his record, but from collateral sources. His family's got money. Dad's some kind of top-dog executive ..."

A privileged background, then, Leith thought. Fairly unusual for the police force. Torr went on with his review, and nothing stood out as a flag except for wealth. The dad was a big shot with a multinational based in Scotland that Torr was describing at length, and money always attracted an element of danger to any family. A kidnap attempt gone wrong was something to consider.

Sean Urbanski reported on the chronology of the single-vehicle crash Gilmartin had chanced upon — maybe irrelevant, maybe not — as assembled from Gilmartin's statements to the first responders. The only written statements were one badly jotted police report, followed by the more in-depth interview by Torr. "Craig was travelling west on the Sea to Sky, heading home from a house party in Whistler, when he was flagged down to the scene of a crash. See map on wall. This was about one a.m., he says, give or take an hour."

"Give or take an *hour*?" Leith said. "That's as close as Craig could get it?" *What kind of cop rounds his time to the hour?*

"He hasn't been on with us long enough to know how all-important minutes are, I guess," Urbanski said.

"Fractions of minutes, better yet," JD put in.

Urbanski nodded and tucked scraggly hair behind an ear. For months he had not only been improving his vocabulary, but working on the look that would get him into biker bars without raising eyebrows. His dream was to move to Surrey and go undercover with Special O. "Other evidence suggests the crash happened in the area of midnight, going by the 911 calls. Speaking of which, we got three of them. Two came from cellphones, drivers who pulled over at the scene, and one anonymous call from a phone booth in Horseshoe Bay — that's maybe fifteen minutes' drive west from the accident scene, if you're doing the limit — at twelve sixteen a.m."

Torr cupped an ear. "The call came in from a — what did you say? Phone booth? What the fuck is that?"

"In the old days," Urbanski said, "long before you and I were born, Jim, cellphones used to be tied to wires, and if you ripped them off the wall, they no longer worked."

JD interrupted impatiently. "You're saying neither Craig nor the guy who flagged him down had a working cellphone to call 911? How likely is that?"

"Unlikely," Urbanski said. "Maybe even chimerical."

Leith had been tapping his list of questions with his pen, puzzled by something, but the something was eluding him. He thumped the pen louder, for attention. "Any clue as to who this individual was who flagged Craig down?"

"No clue," Urbanski said. "No names were exchanged. Craig pulled over and Mystery Man told him he'd seen the red car lose control and swerve into the trees. That's all we've got, second-hand hearsay. Craig gave just a rudimentary physical description of the guy in his statement to the on-scene officers. Dark hair, medium build. Didn't even know what make of car he drove. Just that it was a mid-sized four-door, *steel*, the officer's got written down for colour. Which I guess means grey. Craig wasn't pressed for details, but of course, who knew it would end up being important?"

"Okay. Carry on."

"So Mystery Man and Craig climb down into a ravine where they find an older red Mazda pretzelled around a fir tree. Get the door open but see the victim's in too bad a shape to move. Mystery Man goes to flag down a car to call for help while Gilmartin stays at the scene. Gilmartin explained to Jim here that Mystery Man hadn't flagged down anyone in the end, but had taken off, so Gilmartin went and did it himself. He says there were some other people who showed up and left again, either three individuals or three parties — no descriptions or details, age, gender, nothing. In retrospect it would have been nice if somebody had asked him for those basics, hey, Jim?"

"I'd like to see you do better with Constable Runaround Sue," Torr snapped back.

Leith remembered what was bothering him, what Gilmartin had said down by the Quay as they waited for Ident to show up, in what had been to Leith little more than aimless chit-chat at the time. "There was a third person at the scene, a female, who also didn't have a working phone, right?"

Torr checked his notes and Urbanski scanned his report. Neither found mention of a third passerby without a phone. *She must have been one of the "other people" who had shown up after*, Leith thought, and told Urbanski to carry on.

"Two cruisers, fire, and ambulance show up," Urbanski said. "Gilmartin gives his statement to the first responders, which is where I got the bulk of this info from. It's here in the file for your perusal."

Leith nodded. "I'm still mind-boggled that neither man had a working phone. Especially Craig, a police officer. His phone is his lifeline, and he should know that."

"That's what I told him," Torr said. "His excuse was a drained battery. He'd spent time outside while in Whistler, and cold must have drained the battery, and he couldn't find his charging cable. As for the other guy, who knows? Maybe he's a luddite."

"Hey, dumbasses," JD said, "Mystery Man took off instead of flagging down cars, Craig says, so I'd bet he's the one who made the 911 call without leaving his name. So even if he had a cell on him, he had some reason for not using it. Didn't want to be tracked down, did he?"

"Good bet," Leith agreed. He invited discussion about the big question right now: were the car crash, Mystery Man, and either shooting related at all, or were they discrete occurrences? Was the afternoon drive-by shooting a first attempt, with a more successful follow-up, or another coincidence, just one supremely rotten day in the young constable's life?

The discussion was as fruitless as he expected. Winding down, he handed out tasks. Paley and Torr would try to track down the man in the steel-grey car, who may or may not have made the 911 call from the pay phone in Horseshoe Bay at 12:16 a.m.

Leith gave Urbanski the task of checking for stolen white vans and re-canvassing the neighbourhood for witnesses. JD would interview everyone at the Whistler party Gilmartin had left that night, see if there had been any interesting interactions, disagreements, rivalries.

"Questioning party animals," JD said. "Just about my favourite thing in the world to do."

With the team dispersed, Leith was left with a difficult task. He went to see Mike Bosko and told him of his own bad handling of the situation. Gilmartin had been shot at as he ambled down to the Quay, and rather than take any of the many precautions he should have, Leith had blithely packed the boy off home with only the briefest word to Ken Poole about the drive-by shooting.

"You know what they say," Bosko said, cleaning his glasses with a small cloth. Without glasses he looked bare, younger than his forty-two years. Even vulnerable.

"Yes, I know," Leith said. "Hindsight. It's no excuse in this case. It wasn't a high shot. It was meant to hit the target in the head or chest. If Craig hadn't ducked —"

"Now, look ..." Bosko said. Eyeglasses back on, he was in control of the world again, a hand flat on the desk as if to keep something from flying away. "I could tell you a few stories about my own lack of foresight. We'll talk about it sometime. Right now it's just getting in the way of moving forward. Right?"

Leith agreed that moving forward was more important than regret. "I'm heading back to Gilmartin's house with Raj and Kenny. Get them to run through their actions, see if they moved anything, forgot anything. Also I need to get Sophie into the house, have her do a walk-through. If something's missing or out of place, hopefully she'll spot it."

Bosko nodded. "Good. I'll look forward to your report."

Leith got on with it. He picked up JD and returned to the Cape Cod house on Osborne, with its bloodstains and crime-scene tape. As JD remarked en route, the upside was that a professional would have left a corpse behind, and whoever had done this had not — quite. "Which means they're new at this, which means they'll have left a trail, which means we'll get 'em," she said with fierce certainty. "No sweat."

Eight

SHOT IN THE DARK

RAJ SATTAR AND KEN POOLE arrived to look over the scene with Leith and JD. Neither man believed he had shifted the furniture or impacted the scene in any way, aside from administering first aid to the victim. Sattar was adamant. Poole seemed less so, but he agreed: nothing touched, nothing moved.

They were now gone, and Sophie was on her way over to go through the same exercise, with the additional task of touring the house to see if she could detect anything missing, added, rearranged, or simply odd.

While they waited for Sophie to arrive, Leith and JD stood in the living room, looking down the broad hallway where Gilmartin had fallen. They looked at the bloodstains and evidence markers and tried to imagine what had taken place that night. It seemed clear enough that Gilmartin had been ambushed. The forensic report was still pending, the one that would give bullet trajectory and, hopefully, point of firing. Until then it was a lot of guesswork. Possibly the attacker had come to the door with a ruse, rang the bell. Maybe he was let in or maybe he had barged in, and Gilmartin, defenceless, saw the gun and turned to run.

If so, he didn't make it far.

Leith looked at the bulky sweater Gilmartin had been wearing last evening, when they had gone together to look at the pockmark on the concrete wall down by the Quay. The garment seemed to have been tossed haphazardly at a standing coat rack in the foyer, and now hung crooked and forlorn. He looked at the foyer's ceiling fixture. "The bulb's missing. Maybe the shooter got here ahead of Gilmartin and removed the light to create a diversion?"

JD looked doubtful. "Why would he remove it? He could just twist it, break the connection."

"Because he's thorough. Wanted to be dead sure it wouldn't reconnect."

"Then where is it? I don't see a bulb lying around. So he took it with him? Seems kind of unlikely, carrying around a light bulb. Why not just toss it aside? Fear of leaving fingerprints behind, you're thinking? Get real. Even a newbie assassin would be wearing gloves."

"You know, I resent your habit of second-guessing me."

Worse was her habit of second-guessing him correctly. All the same, he followed up with the light bulb theory, and imagined the man with the gun sitting in the dark. Somewhere in that nook, possibly. He imagined a flashlight beam flicking on, aimed at the victim, disorienting him, putting the target clearly in the shooter's sights. Aim, and *pow*. "Wasn't much of a hit man, though," he said, echoing JD's earlier remark. "To leave him alive."

JD looked at the doorway and at the place where Gilmartin had been found sprawled. "If you're right, and the ambusher was waiting inside, then Ken Poole would be dead, too, if he had followed Gilmartin in. Then we'd have two bodies to bury instead of one."

Leith reminded her that Craig Gilmartin wasn't a body yet, though even as he said it, he knew it was just a matter of time. The last report from the hospital had been grim.

JD, who outranked Leith when it came to pessimism, said nothing.

"At least Bosko seems to think there's a chance he'll pull through," Leith told her.

"You don't sound like you believe him."

"Bosko's probably the smartest guy I know, but ..." He lowered his voice, as if the walls had ears. "Have you noticed how all his guesses end up wrong?"

JD gave him one of her rare, slight grins.

Leith looked glumly toward the front door. "As for Kenny Poole and whether he'd have been killed, too, that depends. He had his Kevlar on, but if the shooter had a semi-auto, no guarantees. But at least he'd have returned fire. I should have laid it out for Ken, JD. I should have sent him in. It would have been a different story."

"You really want to blame yourself for all this, don't you?" JD exclaimed. "Hey, I know what to get you for Christmas. A hair shirt. You're a size forty-six, I'm guessing."

Leith wondered if Kenny Poole, a normally chummy uniformed cop in his fifties who had shepherded dozens of rookies through their baby steps, including Craig

Gilmartin, felt as guilty as he did. Kenny could have taken the initiative, after all. Could have decided to check out the house as a precaution.

Make that two hair shirts.

He continued to cast his eyes about, searching for something to get a grip on. Markers on the floor showed where Gilmartin had landed and where he had moved or been moved to. The bloodstain pattern analyst had been and gone. Her analysis would soon paint a fuller story, but for now, the drag marks were whispering their tale, Gilmartin's attempt to crawl down the corridor toward the rear of the house.

JD was studying the empty ceiling-light socket in the foyer. "If he was shot in the dark, the killer must have known the place pretty good, right? Must have known Gilmartin enough to recognize him in the dark, too."

Leith gave her his flashlight theory.

"Or that," she agreed. "Creepy."

Where did the assassin wait? Leith wondered. On that boot-removal bench next to the door, cradling his .45, the calibre the bullet had turned out to be? Lights out, the killer just sitting there, waiting. It did smack of a hit man, in a way, except for the, well, frankly, *poor* shot, and moreover the lack of a finishing-off bullet. So who stood to gain? The parents, who had some insurance policies on the kid? Bosko had interviewed them and didn't think they had a place up on the board. Their love for their son and barely contained grief knocked them right off the suspect list, was how Bosko put it.

Having met them himself, Leith agreed — the parents were not behind this. Craig seemed like a grounded young man, and grounded young men usually come from loving homes. Maybe Sophie had done it after all. Shot him, departed, got rid of the gun, came back and made the call, crying onion tears.

Except no way were those onion tears he'd seen spurting from her eyes. And that hyperventilation was real. Regret was another possibility, of course. Or madness.

As he considered and reconsidered Sophie, the girl herself arrived with an escort, Constable Lil Hart. Sophie didn't disintegrate at having to revisit the scene, as Leith had feared she would. Her eyes were red and puffy, but she had pulled herself together, was even smiling. "They say there's a chance he'll live," she reported.

She had placed a brighter inflection on the word *chance* than Leith had.

Seemed she described what she saw when she had come in that night. It was dark, and she had made her way toward the living room carefully, calling out Craig's name. Didn't see him till she was midway across the room, saw him lying at the entrance to the hallway. Screamed.

"Why didn't you turn on the hall light when you stepped inside?" Leith asked, testing her.

She gazed at him, transitioning from her godawful memories to his trite question. "Oh, there is no hall light," she said sadly. "He meant to put one in, but he's incredibly lazy."

There. Either a mystery solved or an amazingly cool liar.

She went with Leith and JD around the house, looking for discrepancies. In the master bedroom an Ident officer stood with graph paper and an electronic measuring device, setting the dimensions of the room to paper. The room was a riot of clothes and magazines, books and dirty dishes. The Ident man glanced at Leith. "It's not been tossed, if that's what you're thinking. Just a real fuckin' mess." Too late, he saw Sophie, and his grimace mirrored Leith's. "Sorry."

"That's okay," Sophie said, staring around at the mess. "I've said the same thing myself."

Leith looked at the large abstract painting that covered one wall — scribbles of dark blue and crimson with speckles of gold.

"Craig did that," Sophie said. "He's quite talented."

Leith nodded. "I've seen his studio." And the easel with the work-in-progress that might never be completed. "He's good."

The rest of the house showcased Gilmartin's creative spirit in haphazard fashion. By the end of their walk-through, Sophie had found nothing missing and nothing amiss, and Leith was no wiser about what had happened.

Sophie left with her escort, and Leith and JD stood on the porch, watching her go.

"She's definitely off my list," Leith said.

"Hmm," JD said.

He frowned at her. "What d'you mean, hmm?"

"I'm just not so sure now."

"Seriously?"

She sighed. "No, not seriously. I just don't like empty lists."

Leith got it. An empty list was a super bad start to their first forty-eight.

Nine

THE MAN WITH FLIES

THE DAY'S ASSIGNMENT took Dion out in the field and onto a boat with Corporal Chris Wallace, investigating a spousal assault in Deep Cove. The inlet air glancing off the yacht's deck was sharp and cold, but every so often the sun would find a hole in the cloud cover and come beating down, warming Dion's head and shoulders. He listed injuries and loss of property as relayed to him by Wallace, who was crouched down beside the victim, a man in his late eighties who whispered his complaints as he lay on his deck recliner. The worst injury seemed to be an abrasion on the forehead, and the biggest loss was a lobster — from Safeway, not cheap — that had bounced off the victim's head and fallen into the waves.

Wallace was nearly as old as the interviewee. Decrepit. *He'll probably need help uncrouching*, Dion thought. He yawned. His iPhone buzzed. He excused himself from the interview and walked along the deck toward the boat's stern, to talk out of the wind. A minute later he returned to tell Wallace of the latest North Shore crisis. "Sir, we've got a girl in a tree."

"A cat?" Wallace said. He had managed to straighten up on his own, gripping the railing and glaring at Dion. Not really a glare, but his default expression.

"A girl."

"In a tree?"

"She won't come down."

"They should call the fire brigade."

"The firefighters can't get to her. She's in the forest. At Maplewood. They're carrying ladders in, but they want a police presence."

"It's not a police matter, is it?"

"It might be."

"Surely there's a patrol close by who can take it."

Wallace was in one of his moods, brittle, shell-shocked, unyielding. Dion wasn't eager to attend the girl-in-the-tree emergency, but he did look forward to leaving the yacht behind. "Everyone's pretty much occupied with the shooting," he said. "We're done here, just about, so we might swing by. It's on our way. Couldn't hurt."

The man Wallace was interviewing had fallen asleep in his deck chair while they argued. He wore a winterized jogging outfit and a lap blanket. His wounds were neatly bandaged, his wife had been taken away for questioning, and the only thing endangering his life right now was age.

Wallace woke the victim to advise him of their departure and they returned to the car. Dion drove out of the marina and southbound on the Dollarton, to the parking lot of the Maplewood Conservation Area, past the gates and onto the service road. An ambulance sat with two paramedics on standby, and a fire truck, now empty, had squeezed in the small turnabout at the end of the road. Dion pulled his unmarked sedan in behind it. Two children were trying to climb the sides of the fire truck. Wallace shouted at them to get off while Dion radioed for directions to the girl-in-the-tree's location. He was told to head over the footbridge and take the upper trail toward the bigger of the two ponds. Did he know the way? He did. It wasn't a huge forest reserve, but getting there would take a few minutes. Orange pylons set out by the crew would tell him where to go from that point.

He passed the news on to an unexcited Wallace, and added, "I can go alone, if you want. You can wait in the car. It's not far, but your shoes —"

"No. Let's get this over with."

They walked down the entrance pathway, strait waters glittering at its end. A footbridge took them onto the pleasant, earthy trail leading through the woods, still green in December, and already Wallace was complaining. "Though why they need *us* ... we can't climb trees any better than them. Firefighters climb. Why can't they get her?"

"I don't know, but they're not sure why she climbed the tree. It struck them as odd. They thought we might be needed."

Maplewood was a micro refuge from the city, locally famous for its wildness. The park sat ocean side, fringed with narrow beaches and thronged with birds in summer. Even in the chill, Dion could see birds flitting about. The path began to incline, and he spotted water through the trees, the flash and flicker of the Burrard Inlet, which made him think of his ex-girlfriend, Kate, and the time they had come here to explore and ended up bushwhacking down to canoodle on a patch of sand amongst the rocks.

Seemed like a lifetime ago. He stopped and watched Wallace catching up, the man looking older than his age as he climbed the path, looking sucked dry, like a strong gust might send him airborne.

"I can see a pylon," Dion told him.

They carried on, and the hint of orange ahead became the marker he was looking for. He and Wallace left the trail and made their way to a small gathering: three firefighters in insulated pants and jackets, the fire chief, and finally a middle-aged civilian couple with worried faces. A ladder stood propped against a rangy tree, a deciduous of some kind bristling with thin branches — not an easy climb, by the looks of it.

Dion peered up into the shadows of the tree, but could see no girl through the foliage. Wallace peered too, shading his eyes and saying something about his damned neck.

"Where is she?" Dion asked. "I don't see her up there."

A firefighter pointed. "She just went higher. Soon as we put the ladder up, she started climbing."

Dion saw her now. He looked around. The fire people were telling Wallace that the civilians here were the girl's parents, Mr. and Mrs. Trask. Mrs. Trask looked wind-whipped and frightened. She edged closer to the group and said, "She's special needs, you know. Fifteen, but mental development of a four-year-old. We're her foster parents. I don't know what's gotten into her. She's never done this before."

"We were out for a walk," Mr. Trask said. "She wandered off. We went looking for her, spotted her in the tree. Ula nearly fainted."

"That's me," Mrs. Trask explained. "I told Leo to get down, but she just started climbing up instead. Leona, that is. We call her Leo."

Dion asked if Leona was hurt, but nobody could say.

"Four," he relayed to Wallace, wincing at the implications.

"Four what?"

"Mental development of a four-year-old," Dion said.

Wallace looked puzzled, and maybe offended, but Dion's focus was on the tree again. He looked up high and fixed on the blue fabric of the girl's jeans.

"That ladder extend any further?" Wallace asked the fire crew.

The chief answered. "Sure, but we wouldn't want to startle her again. Every time we attempt to raise the thing she starts yelling and climbing. I'm afraid she'll fall. We'll have to get out the block and tackle, but same problem — the fuss will scare her. But we got no choice, really. We're fetching the netting, should be here shortly."

"Oh no, she's climbing again," a firefighter said.

With a cry of alarm, Mrs. Trask headed toward the ladder, as if she meant to take matters into her own hands. Mr. Trask held her back.

"I'll go up far as I can get," Dion offered. "Maybe I can talk her down."

The firefighters seemed doubtful, as did Wallace, but when nobody voiced a strong objection or insisted he wait for the netting to arrive, Dion shrugged out of his police parka and asked Mrs. Trask what Leona's favourite TV show was. *Sesame Street*, she told him. Favourite character: Grover.

Dion knew of *Sesame Street*, and in his mind's eye he could see Grover, a furry green puppet thing with a garbage can lid on its head, if he wasn't mistaken. He could see himself saving the day and being commended before an admiring audience. Years ago he had been on a scene like this, had watched as the rescuer coaxed a child out of hiding by getting down on her level, talking about cartoon characters that she could relate to. Easy. He gave his jacket to Wallace for safekeeping, rolled up his shirt sleeves, and set his foot on the ladder's first rung.

* * *

Up in the tree, the conversation wasn't going well. Leona sat six feet above Dion, looking down. He had propped himself on the sturdiest bough he could find and was looking up. Leaving the ladder behind, he had climbed several branches to get closer, but dared go no farther. The thinnish branch she sat on looked strained, and if she got spooked and went any higher, her support structure might start snapping.

From what Dion could see of her, Leona was small for her age. She had fine brown hair in two ponytails.

She didn't seem traumatized, or even unhappy with where she found herself. All she had told him so far was that she had lost her glasses and hurt her knee. He told her that they should both climb down, very slowly, and put a Band-Aid on that knee.

Leona said she didn't want to go back down because of the man in the bushes. She liked climbing trees, anyway.

"What man in the bushes?" Dion asked.

"Dirty man," she said. "Flies."

The image that flashed into Dion's mind was a grubby flasher with his pants open. But Leona was batting her hands around her face in what looked like annoyance.

"Flies? You mean buzzing flies?"

She nodded, looking down. "Yucky."

"That doesn't sound good. Where is this man?"

She pointed unhelpfully to the forest floor below.

"Where? Will you come down and show me?"

No, she wouldn't climb down, wouldn't show him. She wanted to stay where she was.

"I won't let him hurt you," he said. "Your parents will be there, too. We'll hold your hand."

She shook her head.

"Did he scare you?"

"Uh-huh."

"Did he say something to you?"

"He looked at me."

"Did he come close to you?"

She shook her head again. "He was sitting."

Dion thought about the buzzing flies. It wasn't the right season for buzzing flies. West Coast flies didn't buzz much in December, unless there was a free feast to attend. Not the right season for sitting in the woods, either.

His position in the tree was becoming uncomfortable. He called up to Leona, "I'm going down now, get some hot chocolate. And a sandwich. What kind of sandwich do you like? Peanut butter? Aren't you cold? Hungry?"

She wasn't hungry, wasn't cold, was allergic to peanuts.

He told her that her foster parents were worried. "They're really afraid you're going to fall and hurt yourself."

"No, I can fly," she told him, looking dreamily up at the clouds.

"No!" Dion thrust out a hand to stop the thought in its tracks. Only when she made no show of flapping her arms or launching did he breathe again. "No," he told her again firmly. "You can't fly. But you sure can climb. Climb on down here, okay? We'll sit together for a while."

She shifted about as if to climb higher, and in desperation Dion resorted to the last trick up his sleeve. A cheap trick, maybe, but all he had left. He shouted up cheerily, "Hey, Leona, you know who's down there? He heard you're in trouble and came right over. Grover. He's sitting there in his garbage can, and he's really worried you might fall."

Leona stared down at him, and beyond him to the earth below. From Dion's perspective, she appeared to tip forward, and he shouted at her again to be still. "You can't see him from where you're sitting," he bellowed. "Just climb down here, slowly. I — I can see him. He's waving."

"No, he's not," she said.

"Yes, he is."

"In a *garbage* can? Why is he in a garbage can?"

And suddenly she was climbing nimbly down. She bypassed him like a monkey and kept going, all the way to the ground. He followed more carefully, and found the girl angry and confused that there was no Grover to greet her. But everyone else was pleased, and there was a spattering of applause as he retrieved his patrol jacket from Wallace.

Leona was pacified, given a carton of apple juice, and her scraped knee was attended to. She then accepted Dion's apology for his lie, and educated him on the difference between Grover and Oscar the Grouch. Finally she took her foster mom's hand and led Dion and Wallace into the woods. She stopped and pointed, and Dion stepped in front of her and squinted. Now he caught a glimpse of what had scared her up into the tree. It scared him, too. He turned the family away, telling them to go back to the parking lot and wait there. Wallace radioed the fire chief and gave the same advice: take the men back to the vehicles with the family and stick around till further notice.

Now the three of them were alone, two living and one dead. "Some hobo gave up the ghost," Wallace guessed. But the woods clearly unsettled him, and he looked more alert than usual. Dion was eying the shadows. Listening, hearing nothing but the rustling of dry leaves and grasses, the shushing of the tides to the west. Then there was the buzzing.

He moved in closer to look at the body.

The dead man sat rump-down in the bushes, staring forward, his lower face damaged and slack, the flies zigzagging about his nostrils, clothes littered with twigs and leaves. Just sitting with his back against a tree, far off the beaten trail, like a man on a picnic gone drastically wrong.

On closer view Dion could see the dead man wasn't a hobo, he hadn't given up the ghost in any natural way, and it hadn't happened too long ago. His hands were zap-strapped at the wrists, his ankles bound with twine. A rope around his neck kept him fixed to the tree and seated upright. Dried blood drizzled off the top of his head like a black, lacy cap.

Dion retraced his steps, away from the smell of death. He summarized for Wallace what he had seen, then jotted notes: time and coordinates, and all those present, and what brought them to the scene, and the weather (cold and overcast, five above zero, max), and finally a brief description of the dead man. Caucasian, brown-haired, middle-aged, average height and weight. Looked like his skull and jaw had been impacted hard. He wore dark slacks and an expensive-looking brown-leather bomber jacket over a black T-shirt. There seemed to be jagged tears in the T-shirt.

"Could be the Blueridge man," he said, pocketing pen and notebook. A forty-five-year-old named Rory Keefer had recently been reported missing, and the description was a good fit.

Wallace didn't reply. He stood rigid, hands in coat pockets, looking solemnly across at the dead man as if trying to communicate with him telepathically. Unlikely, though. Probably he was thinking about Scotch.

There came a faint noise, like a body shifting or something large inhaling deeply — but it was only the wind tugging at the treetops. Dion looked up. A mess of branches blotted out the sky. Nothing around him but tree trunks and shadows. An odd stretch of silence. Then a crow cawed, and somewhere far away, children yelled and whooped.

* * *

Leith and JD were across the waters in Kitsilano talking to Craig Gilmartin's parents once more. This time they were trying to elicit from them the name, or names, of anyone who could have wanted to harm their son. Rivalry within Gilmartin Senior's business world, perhaps? Some kind of vendetta?

It was slow going. The parents were exhausted, had just come from the hospital and would soon be going back. Loreen Gilmartin kept losing track of the question and needed frequent time outs. And just as she promised she would be all right now to carry on, a phone call came in from Craig's brother in Edinburgh, causing further delay.

Leith was waiting for Loreen to finish her long-distance call when JD turned to answer her own phone. She spoke briefly, and once done, motioned Leith aside to fill him in. A dead man in the woods. "Chris Wallace was first on scene," she said, "and Sean and Doug are on their way out there."

Wallace from general duties being first on any scene was puzzling. "Some kind of accident?" Leith asked. A foolish hope, as Sean and Doug would not attend an accident, no matter how serious, unless their own loved ones were involved.

"Tied to a tree and shot in the head," JD said. "I'd say no, not an accident."

Ten

GUNRUNNER

JD CALLED THE AREA Maplewood Flats. She said Malcolm Lowry had squatted here in the sixties and at that time wrote *Under the Volcano* — and not much else, she added. Leith didn't know the man or the book, and in fact had been unaware that this patch of preserved woods and shoreline existed. He looked around with interest as JD drove in. "Nice place," she said. "Kind of a secret, just minutes from the head-fucking city. And now this."

They left the car in a small parking area jammed with emergency vehicles and two unmarked sedans, and walked down a trail toward the waterline. JD went on griping. "Just don't tell all your friends about it. It's low traffic, and I want to keep it that way."

"I can count my friends on one hand," Leith told her. He held up a hand, thumb and two fingers extended. "And you're one of them."

She put on a burst of speed, and Leith supposed it

was to avoid having to deal with the compliment. He jogged to catch up.

At the end of the path was a small, wild beach strewn with flotsam. The grey-green waves coursed in a climbing tide. Across the strait waters were the impenetrable woods that lined the shores, with Burnaby rising beyond. "This park attracts birders," JD added, turning toward a picturesque footbridge. "I like birders. They're quiet, they mind their own business, and they tend to disappear."

"Are you a birder?"

"Me? Gimme a break."

She may not be a birder, but he knew that JD had her eyes on the sky in a big way; she wanted to quit the job, move up north, become a bush pilot. Shift cargo and tourists for a living — preferably cargo. Her desire to withdraw from humanity disturbed him. Sometimes, when he was feeling magnanimous, he wanted to reach out to her, keep her grounded, but she never made it easy. The closer they became, the harder she backpedalled.

A short hike brought them to the murder scene, where an unidentified male had been found. No wallet, no ID, no visible tattoos. So far he was just an unfortunate John Doe, executed and left to rot. Leith and JD looked at the body where it sat being photographed. An update had come in to them en route: the man had not been shot, as first thought, but impaled and beaten. Leith understood the error: the body looked bullet-riddled.

He spoke to those on-site and got the full gruesome details. The man's torso had suffered multiple penetrating wounds, and his head and face had been impacted at least twice, hard enough to break the jaw and knock out a few teeth. As far as the impact trauma, the likely weapon had been found in the bushes: a jagged rock, small enough to heft with two hands, but large enough to do serious damage. The rock was polluted with blood and hair.

Leith also learned that it was Dion, not Wallace, who had found the body. Of course it was. Who else would stumble upon a corpse hidden in this little woodland glen? Nobody but Cal Dion.

He took brief statements from both men, and by the time he was done the body had been removed and only the forest remained to be combed. Wallace left the area, allowed to return to the beach, where he probably rested on a park bench now, rubbing his knobby knees. Dion remained nearby. He was close enough to be called over, if needed, but had turned away from the gory tree. He was eating a sandwich, which Leith found odd.

JD approached Leith, saying she had Jo-Lee Keefer on the line, and what should they do, meet her at the morgue or what? Leith checked his watch, gauging travel time, and suggested forty minutes.

Jo-Lee Keefer was the woman who had reported her husband missing yesterday. Leith recalled Jimmy Torr taking the call and laughing it off as just another husband who didn't want to be found. Seemed Torr was wrong. There was a good chance this was their missing man, Rory Keefer, and whatever had happened to him, it was most definitely against his will.

Leith walked over to Dion, saying, "Where'd you get that? I don't see any food trucks around."

"Ula Trask had extras," Dion said, mouth full.

Leith didn't know who or what Ula Trask was. Neither could he imagine having an appetite at a crime scene like this. The reek of death had snaked into his nostrils, and it would take several hot showers and a lot of scented soap to get rid of it. "Looks like we have an ID on this guy," he said. "He was reported missing yesterday. Going to talk with his wife now, see if we can firm it up."

"Okay."

"You and Wallace can leave any time now. We've got this place covered."

"Right, thanks."

Clearly, Dion was no longer a ladder climber. Well, literally speaking he was, in this case, but in no other sense. Leith collected JD, and together they went to meet the missing man's wife.

The woman stood waiting in the hospital's foyer, looking miniaturized in front of an oversized Christmas tree, the soothing notes of seasonal melodies tinkling around her. Jo-Lee Keefer was in her midforties and of Asian descent, with nothing notable about her except a kind of flare when it came to jewellery and cosmetics. She jangled and glistened as she turned to Leith and JD and said, "This better be some kind of horrible mistake."

They sat in a lounge-like room down the hall from the morgue. JD described the victim and his clothing, and Jo-Lee said that sounded like her Rory. JD asked if Jo-Lee wouldn't mind looking at the jacket itself, and perhaps a scarf.

Jo-Lee inspected the dead man's leather bomber jacket, which had been removed from the body and bagged as an exhibit, the bloodied portions of it concealed by strategic folding. She looked at the scarf. She said yes, that was Rory's jacket, that was his scarf. Now she knew what was coming, the bad news that lurked in that other room, the sort of room she must have seen in movies often enough. She reached to touch the jacket in its plastic shroud. "Chrissake, what are you hiding? Is there blood on it? What's happened? Let me see the body."

"That's not at all necessary," JD assured her. "If you want, I could show you a photograph —"

"I want to see him. I want to know."

Inside the crypt Jo-Lee identified the body without hesitation. The damaged portion of his face, like the bloody jacket, was concealed. "Oh god, that's him!" she cried. "What'd they do to him? Why? What'd he ever do to them?"

The specificity of her wails pinged Leith's attention. "You think you know who did this, Mrs. Keefer?" he asked.

"Sure do. He was getting guns in through Stewart, eh?" She looked at Leith, at JD. "Drive up north, pick up a load, bring 'em down here, sell 'em at a huge markup."

"Guns?"

She fluttered her hands, as if all this talk exasperated her. "I think so, yeah. Don't ask me. I had nothing to do with it. I hate guns." She looked at the closed eyes of her dead husband and said, "Oh, you dumb bastard, what have you gotten yourself into?"

She was escorted back to the sitting room, where she told Leith and JD about her husband and his precarious lifestyle. "He used to drive up to Stewart about once a month. He was really tight-lipped about it, but when I kept asking and asking, he finally said it's guns. I never thought to doubt him. It's the kind of thing he'd do, eh? Sell guns to schoolchildren, if it made him a quick buck."

Her face was wet, but already she was recovering from the shock. Leith thought about her fast turn-around from grief. Maybe it would seep back in when she returned home and saw the gap her man had left behind. Or maybe not. Some relationships were fairly cool, take it or leave it. He knew Alison wouldn't bounce back quickly if she had to identify his body laid out on a stainless steel table. He was quite sure she would mourn for at least a year. He hoped it wouldn't be much shorter than that, but not a lot longer, either. He made a mental note to remind her that he would want her to get on with her life, if that were to happen, not wait too long to be happy again.

But fifteen minutes? He addressed Jo-Lee. "Did you ever see these guns?"

She shook her head, pulling a face. "God, no. Didn't want to. Once he told me, I never asked again. Plugged my ears."

"Do you know who he was selling to?"

"No idea. Believe me, his friends and mine don't mingle."

JD asked, "Did Rory own a gun of any kind? Small arms or rifles?"

Leith knew Rory Keefer didn't possess a firearms licence, so any guns he owned would be illegal. "I'm sure he did," Jo-Lee said. "I'm sure he ran every calibre available on the planet, and had a collection of his own. Was he shot with one of his own guns, is that what you're saying?"

JD didn't tell her that it wasn't a gun that killed Keefer. The evidence wasn't in yet, she said. But Jo-Lee seemed to reach her own conclusion. "He's been like a scalded cat these last few months," she said with a grim nod. "Very jumpy. Says there's someone named Giorgio after him, a rival gunrunner, he says. The name keeps him up nights. It's Giorgio this, Giorgio that, Giorgio's going to get me, Giorgio's going to slit my throat. He was going to take out this life insurance policy, but in the end he was too cheap. My Alero," she said, her eyes on Leith now, a startling switch of pace. "You guys ever find it? It's technically *my* car, not his. Only got it last fall, brand new off the used car lot."

Her earlier report of a missing husband had come hand-in-hand with a report of her missing vehicle, and up till now Leith had thought the vehicle was collateral damage. Now he raised his eyebrows.

"Not yet, Jo-Lee," JD said. "We're still looking."

And we'll be looking very damn hard, now, Leith thought. "Anything about this car that stands out?" he asked. "Custom paint job, body damage, stickers?"

"No, it's just a boring, clean, well-maintained Alero. Green."

JD had her notebook out. "Okay, so we're going to have to take a look around your property," she said. "And the sooner the better. See if we can find anything to help figure out who did this, all right? Is that okay with you?"

"Yes, of course," the woman said.

"We'll have you escorted home, and the rest of us will be there within the hour. I've got your address right?"

Jo-Lee checked and confirmed the address in JD's notes. "There's an old garage out back I never go near. No clue where the key is, but go ahead and break the lock. That's where you'll probably find them, the Uzis or whatever the hell."

She looked back toward the swing doors as she was led away, and Leith caught a glimpse of what looked like sorrow in her profile. For Rory Keefer's sake, he was glad.

* * *

They found no Uzis stashed in the garage once they had broken the lock. There were no rifles, shotguns, revolvers, or pistols. No BB guns, ray guns, stun guns or glue guns. Nothing but an old plastic dollar-store spud gun lying on a dusty shelf. Neither did a villain named Giorgio pop out of the woodwork. Not yet, though it was a line being followed up in the dead man's computer, phone records, and correspondence. The name had been Googled and algorithmed and put to the RCMP's best informants, with a G, with a J, in various language variants. No Giorgio showed up.

Jo-Lee was their only suspect. She worked for the city. She was not in the databases as any kind of troublemaker, or even a witness to trouble. After a second interview, Leith felt that for a suspect, she was far from exciting.

In the early evening, he and JD and the others who had pitched in to search the Keefer property returned to the office empty-handed. Leith was depressed. The workload was ballooning before his eyes, and many of the best detectives were either on holiday, training programs, or sick leave, all of which amounted to a lot of overtime in the forecast for him. His noble plans of tackling the walls of his new fixer-upper bungalow — first line of attack PolyFilla and spatula — would have to go on hold. Again.

Even the quiet pleasure — well, not exactly *quiet*, with a three-year-old on board — of sitting at the family table for dinner tonight was not to be.

Leith stepped into Mike Bosko's office — Bosko was also working late — to update him on Rory Keefer, the non-guns, the non-Giorgio, the non-Alero, and in the other frustrating case, the lack of progress on the Craig Gilmartin shooting.

"Yes, well, keep at it," Bosko said. "I've been talking to the super, and we're going to bring some guys up from general duties, fill the gaps. Speaking of general duties, I'm still not sure how Dion got from a yacht at Deep Cove to a homicide at Maplewood."

Leith leaned in the doorway. Another big unsolved mystery cluttering up his thoughts like a dull worry, like overdue taxes, was Cal Dion — something to be dealt with, but better tomorrow than today. "It's a long story. If you want, I can recap for you, but —"

Bosko shook his head. "You know what, Dave, I don't need to know right now. But since we're here and talking about him, I'll answer some of those questions you had last month, if you have an extra moment."

This was the grain of sand in Leith's relationship with Bosko: Dion, and what he may or may not have done. Leith took a chair, resisting the urge to cross his arms, and listened.

Eleven

TROUBLE

THE EXPLANATION STARTED with a question so broadly cast that it took Leith a minute to pin it down. "How's it been going?" Bosko asked.

To an outsider, the correct answer would have been something like "not bad." But Leith, an insider who knew exactly what was behind the question, answered frankly. "It's not."

The "it" Bosko was asking about was Leith's investigation into a crime neither of them could even begin to prove, Leith suspected. What he knew about it was virtually nothing. He knew Dion had maybe broken the law, that it had occurred the summer before last, and that Mike Bosko was the lead investigator — if not the *only* investigator. And Bosko's sole confidant and deputy was Leith.

Last summer he had taken on the responsibility to be Bosko's eyes and ears. They were a two-man team on what Leith had thought was a case without foundation.

And yet his prying had made some headway. He had latched a tracker onto Dion's car, and the data had led him to a defunct gravel pit in the Cloverdale area of Surrey. A gravel pit with expanses of crumbly dirt that would make a great spot for disposal of a body, and Leith had thought he was on the verge of discovery.

But it was a short-lived victory. It seemed Dion had an audacious guardian angel, for when Leith had returned, only days later, foolishly equipped with a long-handled shovel, he had found the gravel pit back in business, and dumped over the possible crime scene were, yes, a few kilotons of crushed rock.

The destruction of the possible crime scene had ended his inquiries — a memory he would prefer to forget — and he had spent months pondering whether to share his intel with Bosko or not. For now, at least, it was a resounding *not*.

His hopes that the investigation would fuck off and die were dashed last month when Bosko had explained why his interest was alive and well and going places: apparently there was a witness to Dion's crime.

But the conversation had ended there, in no small part because Leith had decided he was done spying on brother officers. Leave that to Bosko and the internal investigations team, if it came to that. But that was then, and this was now, and apparently Leith wasn't done. Not yet.

"Do you want to hear this?" Bosko asked.

Of course Leith didn't want to. But he had to. He had to end the suspense. It wasn't a fun kind of suspense. It was like getting a free ticket to the execution of a friend. He nodded.

"Remember our first debrief in New Hazelton, just about a year ago?" Bosko asked. "It was in the backroom of a restaurant. Introductions were made, and one young constable in attendance was Dion. The name caught my attention, since a constable named Dion had been involved in a serious crash in Surrey some months before. I didn't know if this was the same Dion, but it didn't take much checking to confirm it."

Leith had first met Dion then, too, and had not been impressed. He'd been the opposite of impressed. He had thought Dion was a rookie, and an inept one at that. He had since learned the man wasn't a rookie and wasn't inept, but just plain difficult.

Bosko continued. "It wasn't until I learned his first name that I began to wonder, though. Because phonetically, *Cal Dion* rang a bell in my mind. It's a strange story, Dave, so listen carefully. In August last year, the non-emergency number of this detachment received an anonymous message. The caller, a female, reported a crime in Surrey. As you know, our front desk is not manned 24-7, and after hours, incoming non-emergency calls go to an answering service. The message she left was muffled. She used a pay phone, and you know how hard it is to find pay phones these days. That told me she probably didn't want to be traced."

An echo of the 911 caller in Horseshoe Bay, Leith thought.

"Probably she was trying to disguise her voice as well," Bosko said. "The pay phone she used turned out to be in a Coquitlam mall. The mall's surveillance video didn't give us a face. So we were left with, basically, a muffled mystery call that went nowhere, filed away and forgotten. I was new to North Vancouver then, and I had a lot to think about, but I didn't quite forget about it. I had to wonder why a caller from Coquitlam would call a North Van detachment to report a Surrey crime. Right?"

Right, Leith thought. A month after Cal Dion, a North Van constable, had crashed his car in Surrey.

Bosko said, "The situation would have been a lot different if the caller had spoken clearly. She says, 'I know' — something indiscernible — '*killed on* killed a man in Surrey.' And it went on from there. Even after enhancing the audio, we thought it was just a stutter, and the name was lost in the indiscernible bit. Follow?"

Barely. Leith nodded.

"So back in the Hazeltons, when I was confirming Dion's identity just out of curiosity, I saw 'Calvin Dion' in his paperwork. It still didn't click. But when I mentioned him to Inspector Stein a few days later, and she called him Cal, I began to wonder. When I got back home, I listened to the message again, and I was about thirty percent convinced that 'killed on' was actually 'Cal Dion.'"

The puzzle piece snapped into place. "What was the rest of the message?"

Bosko had it memorized, it seemed. "'I know' — indiscernible — 'killed on killed a man in Surrey. When you arrest' — indiscernible — 'testify against him. Make the arrest, and I'll call again.' That's all I had at that point. I didn't have a body in Surrey that fit with the crash in any way whatsoever. Just one muffled call-in. Anonymous, with no follow-up. You can see why I didn't open up a file."

"But you pulled strings to get him back here, so you could keep an eye on him. Keeping an eye on him from your position wouldn't be easy, so you got me to do it. Right?"

"Partly that. Partly it was curiosity. Is he brilliant, or just lucky, the way he gets things done? Case in point, the dead man at Maplewood. Either way, as I told you, he would be one incredible asset to the team, if he'd only take the offer."

"An asset, or a suspect in a Surrey murder without a body," Leith said, and realized his arms had crossed themselves. His undisclosed knowledge about a possible gravesite lying under mountains of rock haunted him. When this all came out, he would have to decide whether to confess to his iffy tracking fiasco, or just shut up about it.

Probably the latter.

He uncrossed his arms and linked his hands in his lap, watched Bosko, tried to look nonchalant. The kicker, he felt, was coming.

"A month ago, around Halloween," Bosko said, "I got the second call I'd been waiting for. It came through the main line again, and this time was patched through to me. Same voice, less muffled."

God, Leith thought.

"In fact, clear as a bell," Bosko continued. "With no intro, she said, 'Why haven't you arrested Dion? Haven't you found the body?' So there it was. I was right, and I was stunned. Even with my concerns brewing away, it was a shock to hear his name."

"You recorded the call?"

"The call to the main desk is recorded. Once patched through, it's not. I asked her why Dion should have been arrested. She said because he killed a man. Now, that could mean killed a man in the line of duty, but there's no record of Dion ever having done so."

"Maybe she was referring to the MVA. Dion was the driver, and his passenger, Luciano Ferraro, was killed. Maybe it was somebody who knew Ferraro, who wanted Dion to pay. Maybe the caller was Ferraro's wife."

"Well, except she asked if we found the body."

"Right, of course. No mystery about where Ferraro's body is."

"So that doesn't fit. This caller was talking about an actual murder with intent. We didn't get into the nitty-gritty, as I wanted to nail down her identity and the specifics quick as possible. I asked who the victim was. She didn't answer. I feared she was getting discouraged and might disconnect, so I tried to keep her chatting. I told her that her previous call was too muffled to discern and suggested it would be best to meet in person. She said if I didn't have a body, there wasn't much point in talking further, then implied that I was incompetent. I told her we could maybe find the body if she came forward and helped fill in the blanks. I gave her my personal number, told her to call any time. She said she would think about it. Then she hung up. So what have I got? Confirmation that she is accusing Dion. An informant who is weighing whether to come forward with more details. That's where I stand."

"Chances are you don't hear from her again. Then what?"

"Back burner once more. There's not enough to push it forward. For all I know, it's somebody with a grudge just trying to make trouble for him. I have a feeling, though, I'll be hearing from her again before long. Clearly this knowledge bothers her. She wants resolution."

Bosko's phone was doing its usual blitz of buzzing and flashing for attention, and as always he seemed to know instinctively what to ignore and what to pay attention to. He picked it up now, and the light from the screen lit his face as he read a message. Then, "Anyway, the long and the short of it is" — *Christ, here it comes*, Leith thought — "let's just keep it open for now. If this woman gets in touch, I'll let you know."

"What if I want to distance myself from it all?"

Bosko tilted his head and considered Leith. "I wouldn't blame you. But you won't be doing him any favours. Don't you think?" He didn't wait for an answer, but gave a rueful smile that doubled as a *see you later*, and turned to other matters.

Twelve

BLUE

MONITORING THE PROCESSING of evidence was about as easy as things could get, Dion decided. It was a step down from his tasks in general duties, where at least he was out and about, doing things. He preferred the out and about. He watched the car being processed and worked at adjusting to the slower pace.

Only minutes earlier the vehicle had been unchained from the carrier and dropped into its examination bay. High-watt spotlights glared down, giving the scene an underworld showroom quality. The lock-up was chilly and stank of gasoline. In the after-hours lull every clink and clank echoed. Two members from the Forensics Identification Unit were at work, crawling in and around the car. Dion had taken up an observation post at the sidelines, seated on a plastic stacking chair against the wall next to Raj Sattar, his partner of the hour. Both men were in uniform, with jackets on and collars up.

Sattar was an optional partner, really. Free to leave, should he be called away on other errands that might arise. With no errands to run now, he was studying his smartphone screen, or playing a game on it, and complaining. Dion held a clipboard loosely on his lap, doing as told, observing the car and ready to take notes, though there were none to take at the moment. He was not listening to Sattar much. A mad energy surged through his body, but he felt too heavy to move. He looked at his clipboard and saw that the notes he had made were blocky and childish. The writing style had become habitual, a way of taming his spastic loops. To kill time, he decided to try writing in a more mature hand. He clicked his pen and focused on the facts.

The facts were basic. The car was a shiny newish Alero, trunk and doors sealed off with exhibit stickers. It was confirmed to be Rory Keefer's vehicle, and had been located on Keith Road an hour ago, about 5:30 p.m., at the rear of the Superstore, only a couple minutes' drive from the Maplewood Flats, where the man had died. Like its owner, parked and cold. No keys in the ignition. Dion filled out the form again, trying this time for fluency. Make, model, colour ...

Sattar continued to complain. He seemed disgusted. He was meant for bigger things than watching a car being worked over. "But no," he said. "We need eyes on this. Four eyes, I guess. What about the murder of Craig Gilmartin? I should be on that one. It should be mine. I was first on scene, me and Kenny Poole, but Kenny's useless. Stands there going *what the fuck* like he never seen a shooting victim before, while I jump in like Superman and administer first aid."

Dion nodded. Nodding like a bobble-head to whatever Sattar was talking about seemed to satisfy him. Listening seemed optional.

"Saved Craig's life, didn't I?" Sattar was saying. "And so far nobody says thank you. Propped him up, wound higher than heart level to slow the bleeding. Applied pressure, 'cause if he lost another ounce, man, forget what Kenny says, telling me not to touch him — if I hadn't so-called touched him, you think he'd still be alive?"

"Yeah, no," Dion said.

"Seems he's some kind of *artist*," Sattar said suddenly. "Kenny and me cleared the place, and in one room — you know how you notice things even if it's in the back of your mind, when you're totally focused on something else? Well, there's this big picture up on an easel thing, and there's paintbrushes and shit around, and in the back of my mind I'm thinking, whoa, is that some kind of mishap with a paint can? If that's what he done on purpose, man, he's a bad, bad artist. Really bad. I mean, I could do better drunk with my eyes closed. I mean, nice enough, okay, with little bits of gold and all that. But honestly? Anyway, I shoulda known. He's such a fruitcake, man. Can't stand the guy ..." Sattar fell silent, looking depressed. Fruitcake or not, Gilmartin was his friend, and his friend was dying.

"What colour would you say it is?" Dion said, indicating the car.

Sattar looked at him. "What?"

"I'm making notes. Everybody's calling it green. Isn't it more like blue?"

"It's green," Sattar said. He kept looking at Dion. "You found the dead guy out in the woods, yeah? Guy who owns this car? How'd you know where to find him?"

It took a moment for Dion to recall Leo gazing out to sea from on high. "I didn't," he said. "There was a girl stuck in a tree we had to go check out. She said there was a man in the bushes, and she ended up leading us to the body. I wouldn't call this green."

"A girl in a tree? Like, doing what?"

"Long story."

"Was she pretty?"

"What?"

"So what d'you think all this is?" Sattar said. "Drug deal gone wrong? One of those things you go, yeah okay, he's dead, so what?"

Sattar was somewhere around twenty-five. He had a pushy way of talking, and quickly lost interest in his own train of thought, which made him hard to follow. His voice filled the cold echo chamber as the Ident team worked. They had broken the seals and were inside with lights and vacs, magnifiers and tweezers, employing their magic in the gathering of trace evidence. Sattar bounced his knees awhile, gloomily looking anywhere but at the car. "They say he's hanging in there — Craig. But he's gonna die for sure. I know, 'cause I seen him. Ever met him? An okay guy, I guess. Hilarious accent. Shitty artist, like I say. But totally badass air hockey champ, man. Killed me five in a row. Was hoping to turn that around, reclaim some dignity, but so much for that, eh."

It didn't seem as though the team was finding anything interesting in or around the car. Hard to tell with

Ident people, though. They never smiled. Never shouted *Hallelujah!* Dion's report was bland, so far, and his new, improved longhand looked like squashed spiders. Next to the time of commencement, he wrote in plate number and VIN, transferring the data from his notebook, probably unnecessarily. The data was already spelled out elsewhere.

Next in his notes came a basic description. He had written down *2004 GM Alero, green.* Now he crossed out *green* and wrote *blue.* Then he thought about Kate, who taught at the art school over on Granville Island, who knew the name of every colour under the sun. He had seen her name in the paper last night, an announcement that she was taking part in a group show with two other artists in a Vancouver gallery. Seeing her name in print was both shocking and maddening. He had been doing so well, putting her into cold storage.

When they had been together — again, it felt like forever ago — Kate had been working on giant photographic montages that Dion never *got.* She was now with another guy, a guy who ran an organic food outlet, a guy who *got* it — in both senses. Dion thought about the guy, and for whatever reason, the thought led to Tony Souza jumping off a bridge.

"Did you know Souza?" he asked Sattar, realizing too late he was interrupting some new complaint midstream.

Sattar looked hurt. "Know who? The guy who killed himself? No, not really."

With that there was nothing left to say. Sattar was staring at Dion in silence.

Dion stared back. "What?"

"He looked a lot like you, didn't he?"

"Did he?"

It wasn't the first time Dion had been told he looked like Souza. In the general duty pit some weeks ago, Corporal Doug Paley had called him over, tapping a photograph in a newspaper — a headshot of the young man who had recently jumped off a bridge. "Looks like you in your rookie days, if you squint," he said.

"No, he doesn't," Dion had answered, looking at the photo of Souza, a handsome Mediterranean-looking individual smiling for the camera. Dion was not Mediterranean.

"That's 'cause you're not squinting," Paley had snapped as he walked away.

Now Sattar was making the same comparison, so maybe Paley was right. Dion stretched his back. He looked at the car. He thought of a note he had seen on the whiteboard in the Craig Gilmartin case room just an hour ago. It was a brainstorming list somebody had scrawled in dry-erase marker, points taken from Gilmartin's statement following the crash on the Sea to Sky Highway, as the team looked for anything Gilmartin might have done or said in the days before he was shot, hoping something might link up and produce a lead. Apparently nothing had.

What was the particular note he was trying to remember, and why did it matter?

He looked at the Alero. Two distinct cases, Craig Gilmartin and Rory Keefer, nothing to link them but gender, rough timeline, and the fact that there were vehicles involved. A crash on the highway on one hand, a green car that might be part of a murder scene on the other. It was enough of a link that he had gone through what he knew of the files again and again, searching for commonality. Nothing. He looked at his boots, trying to pull the word he had seen on the whiteboard so recently. What was it?

He stared harder at the Alero. Something about the colour ...

"What's up?" Sattar asked.

"Steel," Dion said, slapping his knee. That was the word. "Maybe he meant blue. Would you call this steel blue, maybe?"

"Definitely fucking not," Sattar said, also looking at the Alero. "Why?"

"They wrote *steel/grey* on Gilmartin's board, but what does that mean, steel grey? Dark grey, or silver, or what? I read his statement, Gilmartin's, the one he gave to first responders on scene, and he said the guy who took off, his car was 'steel.' He didn't say grey, or at least it didn't get written down, so that's just what the team guessed he meant. But if all he said was 'steel,' maybe he meant blue. Steel blue. That's a colour, right?"

Sattar's stare at the Alero became analytical, but not for long. "You're thinking *that* car is *this* car, and that by the way, Craig Gilmartin is colour-blind? Well, yeah, I guess he must be, from what he calls art. But this is not steel anything, man. Especially not blue. This is the shittiest factory green on the planet. It's a bad colour for a car. The worst."

Dion doodled a sunburst around the word *blue* on his clipboard. Then he shrugged, crossed out *blue*, and wrote *green* in its place.

Thirteen

HIGH

December 15

FINALLY, AFTER SOME discussion with the team that went nowhere, and then a private discussion with Dion that seemed a little ridiculous, Leith decided he had better go see Rory Keefer's car for himself. Last night Ident had searched the Alero inside and out, and no signs of violence had been discovered. No scuffs or bloodshed, no slashed upholstery. Seats were not oddly positioned and the rear-view mirror seemed normally aligned. The popped trunk didn't disclose a load of guns or any other contraband. The only quasi-illegal substance was a damp, dirty roach in the ashtray.

Now, with the forensics report in hand, Leith stood with Dion in the vehicle bay and looked at the ordinary four-door sedan. The car was well-lit by sunlight, with an extra blast from the electric lamps. The colour of the car was a dark, unpleasant green, in Leith's eyes.

Not a bright green. Not grass, emerald, sage, or forest, and definitely not blue either, as Dion had suggested at Leith's desk this morning in that baffling conversation, drawing lines between this car and Craig Gilmartin's statement.

"No, well, it's definitely green," Leith confirmed. He tapped the file folder he held to prove it. "The registration papers say green. Keefer's wife called it green. This isn't a blue car, Cal."

There was a lull as he and Dion both studied the car. "It's like a blue-green, maybe," Dion said. "Gilmartin described the other guy's car as 'steel.' Maybe at night, on the highway, he saw it as steel blue. Because what kind of colour is that, steel?"

"Silver," Leith guessed. "Or grey. Probably what he meant was lead grey, like every other car on the road is these days."

"Except he paints. Aren't painters totally specific about their colours?"

"You really want there to be a connection, don't you?"

Dion answered tightly. "It's not what I want. It's what I believe. Two violent events within days of each other, two cars to be on the lookout for — how often does that happen?"

"I could pull up half a dozen more files of cars to be on the lookout for right now, if you want," Leith said. "Maybe you want to link them all in?"

"No."

"No, of course not. Anyway, there's nothing to indicate Amelia Foster's accident was a criminal act. It was a single-vehicle crash. Tragic, of course, and yes, we'd like to find the man at the scene that night who called 911 and was apparently driving a steel-coloured car, because he may be able to shed some light on the shooting of Craig Gilmartin. But I doubt very much he has anything to do with the Maplewood stabbing or this very green car I'm looking at." To bolster his case, Leith turned to beckon over a civilian mechanic who serviced the bays. "Hey, Pat. Settle this question for us, would you?"

The mechanic joined them and followed their stares to the car. "What's up?"

"Is it blue or is it green?" Leith asked him.

There was no hesitation from the mechanic. "It's kind of blue-green," he said. "Believe they call it teal."

Leith hurried back upstairs, followed closely by Dion, and together they studied the statement Gilmartin had given roadside on the night of Amelia Foster's crash, skipping down to the part where he described the vehicle of the man who had flagged him down and then driven off to anonymously call for help.

What was this guy driving? was the officer's question.

Gilmartin's answer, as taken down that night, was, *Standard four-door, didn't catch the make. Not too old. Colour I'd say was steel.*

Or maybe the officer misheard and — as Dion hardly needed suggest now — Gilmartin had actually said, *was teal*.

Still, even if the word was *teal*, not *steel*, it was not much more than a tease, an unsubstantiated link. Yet Leith eyed Dion with a deep-seated suspicion — or maybe superstition — that because that faint connection was Dion's lead, the connection would prove valid.

Hell no, not just valid — *pivotal*. "You might be onto something here," he admitted.

"I know," Dion said with a grimace. "Just not what I *thought* I was onto."

Leith's impulse to clap him on the shoulder and say something jolly, like *good work*, died on the vine. "I'm going to take a look at where they found the Alero," he said instead. "You'd better come along."

* * *

The Superstore wasn't far from the detachment. Along the western flank of the mega-building with its football field–sized parking lot ran Keith Road, leading to the freight bays around back, then petering out to an unpaved turnaround. It was along Keith that Rory Keefer's Alero had been pulled over and left, locked and unblemished.

Leith and Dion got out of Leith's car to inspect the spot marked on the file diagram. It was a quiet, secluded area, almost a lover's lane, with a tangle of blackberry bushes and a patchy view of Vancouver across the water. The bushes and grasses had been combed for evidence, any potentially interesting debris picked up and bagged, but so far nothing popped out as relevant.

Leith walked to the end of the turnaround and thought about stats. There weren't many violent deaths on the North Shore, and few of those deaths were mysterious. He phoned JD and told her to bring in Jo-Lee Keefer, get her to listen to the 911 call from the Horseshoe Bay Mini-Mart, see if by any chance it sounded like her dead husband making the anonymous MVA report.

"You think there's a connection?" JD asked. "Between Craig and Rory Keefer?"

Leith hesitated. "I have reason to wonder if Keefer wasn't the man who flagged down Craig at the Amelia Foster crash. Anyway, it would be helpful to find out Keefer's whereabouts at the time of the crash. "

"Yeah, okay," JD said tiredly. "I'm still trying to find some dirt on Keefer. Seems to be fairly clean, but everybody I talk to has a different angle on the guy. I've been up to my neck in Jo-Lee's bullshit allegations all day."

Leith holstered his phone and walked back to where Dion seemed to be on sky duty, observing the cloud formations amassing like an army overhead. "Couple more things I want to check out. The Sea to Sky accident site, and the phone booth where the 911 call was made from."

Dion got into the passenger seat again. He didn't look happy. "Why take me along? Orders from Bosko?"

"No orders from anybody. Why would Bosko order me to bring you along?"

"That's what I want to know."

Leith could understand Dion's arm's-length attitude. He seemed to think he was under suspicion for something. Which he was. And, naturally enough, he didn't trust those around him, including Leith. Which he shouldn't.

"You pointed out the colour of the car," Leith explained. "And somehow or other that sprang a new lead, and maybe even joined these two files. That tells me you're engaged, and all I want to do —"

"So what? You'd link the two anyway, with or without the car. It's nothing. By the time you end up investigating whether it's the same car, it'll all be solved."

Leith pushed his vehicle into the traffic funnelling off the Second Narrows Bridge. "Anyway, you can't fool me," he said. He idled with the lineup, stop and go. "You want on the case. You want to put your two cents in. Might as well quit playing dead right now."

They were moving again before Dion spoke up. "You're in the wrong lane."

"I know it," Leith lied, and signalled to butt into traffic.

* * *

Dion regretted his uncalled-for interference, drawing to Leith's attention the steel-blue question, which turned out to be — maybe — a transcribing error. By different paths, he had arrived at the same destination, merging two vehicles of interest into one, effectively merging two major crime files into one. Smart, observant, dedicated — but a sheer fluke.

He didn't care that his engagedness impressed Leith. Impressing Leith had not been his objective. Pinning down the doubt was all that mattered. It had nothing to do with work ethic or the goodness of his heart. And as he had told Leith, the team would have arrived at this destination pretty fast on its own.

He noticed that Leith was a good driver, but tense when in new territory, which he was heading into now as they approached the ferry settlement of Horseshoe Bay that jutted into the narrows. He didn't seem to know this route so well, out here beyond his jurisdiction on the so-called Sea to Sky, a road Dion knew colloquially as the Highway of Death, or sometimes the Killer Highway.

"Don't like terminals," Leith admitted. "Too many signs. Go this way, don't go that way, departures here, arrivals there."

"Just stay left."

Leith stayed left, and once in the village he relied fully on Dion for directions to the pay phone. Dion knew Horseshoe Bay well. Over the course of his life, he had taken the ferry across to the Island countless times. He had missed sailings and spent plenty of downtime in this place, had picked up cigarettes from the convenience store while biding his time, and had once used the pay phone affixed to its brick wall off to one side. "That way," he said.

Leith turned the unmarked Crown Victoria as directed and reversed into a parking stall facing the wall. The phone was mounted on the wall with nothing but a Plexiglas windbreak for those who used it. *And who besides a desperado would use it these days?* Dion wondered. The phone looked derelict and sad, as if it knew it would soon be jimmied off and chucked into the junk pile with all its mates — another pay phone hits the dust.

The store's surveillance footage had been gone through, of course. But the outdoor camera was aimed at the entrance, not the side of the building or the shadier parts of the parking area.

Still seated in the car, Dion considered the phone as it related to the front of the store. Through the curve of windshield the sky was grey, end to end. A bit of rain lashed the glass, litter clung to chain-link, and far away he could hear the first rumblings of thunder.

"Middle of the night," Leith said, "The store's open twenty-four seven, but at twelve sixteen a.m. the place would have been pretty empty. Caller probably parked next to the phone, and employees might not have seen him. We'll step in, see if anybody's remembered anything new."

Two employees were in charge of the brightly lit store. Even at midday there were few shoppers in the aisles. Faint music played, and the workers moved slowly through their tasks, maintaining the delicate balance between doing nothing and looking busy. The young woman who came out from behind the till to talk to Leith told him that, yes, she was on shift that night, just herself because her workmate was a no-show, and it took a while to get a replacement. She was the store manager. She had been manning the till around the time the call was made, and as she told the other cop earlier, she hadn't seen anybody driving by, pulling up, using the phone — nothing.

"Sometimes memories fill in over time," Leith explained, handing over his card.

"I'll put it with the other card with the number I'm supposed to call if I remember anything," she said, and laid it on the counter.

"Was there much traffic that night?"

"The usual, probably. Not much."

He showed her a photograph of Rory Keefer. "This guy ring any bells?"

"Doesn't ring *my* bell, that's for sure," she said, and glanced at Dion and grinned.

It wasn't the first time Dion had heard the ring-my-bell joke. Not the first time Leith had, either, judging from the shortness of his smile. "So you've never seen him before? He didn't walk by that window, step into the store?"

"Nope."

"How slow a night was it? One car an hour? Two?"

"Something like that. One or two. Wait," she said, and held up a finger. Leith and Dion waited. "No, maybe that was another night," she finished.

"What was another night?"

"When you said two, it *did* ring a bell. Two pairs of headlights, no customers," she said. "Both vehicles went to the side there."

Dion put pen to paper, making note of her words.

"Along here?" Leith asked. "By the phone?"

"Kind of in that area. You always worry, is this the night I'm going to get robbed? But no customers came in, so for all I know they did their drug deal or whatever and left. Happens. I forgot about that till now."

"Two vehicles together, one following the other? Or some space between them?"

"Kind of together, but not like bumper to bumper."

"How long did they stay there?"

"Well, as I said, I forgot about them, didn't notice them leaving."

"Or whether they left together or separately?"

"Don't know."

"And you don't know what night that was?"

"Let me think about it." She thought about it, gazing at Dion. "That was the night that whole family got shot dead down in Oregon," she told him. "Murder-suicide, you remember that, the contractor who went bankrupt and decided his own life wasn't worth living, so neither were his wife and kids'? I'm sure they were grateful for his sense of togetherness."

Dion wasn't aware of the tragedy.

"It was in the headlines," she said. "I was reading about it on my iPad soon after I wasn't held up and robbed. So that's why I know it was that night. It's all a stream of consciousness, you know? Connecting the dots."

"So Oregon was breaking news when these cars pulled in?" Leith said.

"Yes, for sure."

Leith did a headline search on his phone. He showed the result to Dion, then looked at the clerk. "Got it. If that's the same night somebody made a call from that pay phone, we're getting there. Let's try to narrow it down to a time."

Her best guess was anywhere between 12:00 a.m., about an hour or so after her shift began, and 2:15, when her co-worker arrived. Leith asked her if she had any idea what either of the two vehicles were — cars, pickups, vans, any clue?

"No clue," she said. "They were just headlights."

"High, low, close-set, wide?"

"Wow, don't ask for much, do you? I think the first was low, like a normal car. Second was maybe higher, like maybe a pickup truck."

"The high headlights — how far apart? Wide like a full-sized pickup, or more like a small Jeep-type vehicle?"

"This is where my recall hits a brick wall. Sorry."

"Anything else of interest happen that night?"

"Not that I know of."

"Well, thanks," Leith said.

"Thanks," added Dion, tucking away his notebook.

"Have a nice day," she told them.

* * *

Leith had bought a takeout coffee before leaving, and with it safely lodged in the console, he drove north approximately fifteen minutes, to the accident scene that he had flagged on his GPS, the spot where Amelia Foster had left the road in her red Mazda 323. With no good place to park, he drove past the spot, pulled a U-turn at the earliest opportunity and parked on the ocean side, southbound, with hazards flashing. Probably right about where Gilmartin had parked that night, behind the steel or teal vehicle of the mystery man who might or might not be Rory Keefer.

"Not a great road in winter," Dion remarked from the passenger seat. The engine was shut off and they were both staring across the road at a shallow ravine, the stand of conifers backed by a natural rock wall.

From this distance there was no way of knowing which was the killing tree, but Leith could guess. "Yeah," he said. "I know what they used to call it."

"There've been worse roads in Canada," Dion said. "But not by far. Till the upgrades. That's reduced the fatalities along here quite a bit."

"Some things change for the better," Leith said, and stepped from the warm serenity of the car into a battering cold wind. He stood by the bumper of the Crown Vic and took in his surroundings. The traffic here was not heavy, but steady. Skiers heading to Whistler, no doubt, and Whistlerites heading into town for some Christmas shopping. Cars zipped by doing probably ninety clicks. Limited by geography, this section of road narrowed from four lanes to one lane in each direction: two narrow opposing lanes, twisting in tight curves along the belly of the cliffs, no centre divider.

"Used to be like this all the way to Whistler," Dion said by the passenger door.

Leith stared up. The rock wall rose steeply, then slanted into the dull glare of the sky. To his back was an aluminum guardrail, the only barrier against a deadly plummet into the Pacific.

They waited for a break in the traffic and crossed the highway on foot, and from there climbed down the grassy dip and through some low scrub to where the Mazda had come to rest. The wreck had been removed, but the evidence of destruction remained: the wounded fir tree, the heaved and gouged ground, the crushed bracken.

Leith looked at the ground where the MVA victim would have lain. "It raises some questions," he said. "If the unknown driver arrived before Craig, maybe he was responsible for the accident. Might even have run her off the road deliberately. Or, if he didn't cause the accident, maybe he saw who did."

"If he ran her off the road on purpose," Dion said, after a moment's consideration, "he definitely wouldn't have told Craig. If he'd run her off by mistake, he might have said so. If he'd seen someone else run her off the road, he definitely would have told him. He didn't say anything, so either he ran her off the road, or he didn't see who did, or nobody ran her off the road and it was just an accident. She lost control, like he told Gilmartin."

"Sure. I get what you're saying." Leith tried to imagine the night, from what he knew. He took in the scene, added blackness, seriously reduced the volume of traffic, then threw in some variables. "Maybe Teal had a passenger. Gilmartin might not have noticed a third party."

He knew from the on-scene investigator's report that other passersby had stopped after Gilmartin, but the investigator had not considered them important, as those passersby hadn't seen anything and would have nothing to add. So away those witnesses had gone, unfortunately, without handing over their contact information.

Maybe they would respond to the ads that had gone out asking the public for information, but Leith doubted it. Their testimony, for what it was worth, was gone like the morning mist.

"If the driver of the teal car is Rory Keefer," he said, "and if Keefer witnessed something he shouldn't, that could mean someone tracked him to the pay phone in Horseshoe Bay. Maybe that's the second vehicle the clerk saw pull in. The supposed pickup."

"Kidnapped him after the call," Dion agreed. "If so, there must be more than one person involved. Someone would have to drive Keefer's car away, dump it out of sight behind the Superstore."

Leith nodded, thinking again about Keefer's possible involvement. Keefer owned a cellphone, of course he did, but he hadn't used it that night. Because he didn't want the trouble of being a witness, or some shadier reason? Had he driven Foster off the road deliberately? Was he killed for what he'd done? And was Gilmartin targeted because he had talked to Keefer?

Red paint from the Mazda was smeared, blood-like, across the killing tree's pale bark. Otherwise the ravine was giving nothing away. The two men climbed the bank and studied the asphalt underfoot, the black burnt-rubber streaks of Amelia Foster's wheels heading at them like the twin ghosts of her horror. Again, it told them nothing but the obvious. For rate of speed and all the other fine details, the accident reconstructionist would have to translate for them — another report in progress.

Dion looked to the north. "There's a pullout there, illuminated. Foster would have driven through it just before she crashed."

Leith followed his line of vision. Down the road, ocean side, a scenic viewpoint bellied out over the sea, with the usual info signs and oversized garbage bins. Three taller-than-average lamp standards would have lit that section of highway even in the darkest hours. "I doubt the light would reach this far."

Traffic had increased since they had pulled over to the shoulder. Cars torpedoed past, shredding the air. They waited for their chance to cross and made the dash. Dion went around the front of their car to look over the brink. Leith joined him, and what lay below looked to his watering eyes like a vast brawl: whitecaps rushing in at the rocks, sucking back, rushing in harder, crashing down and breaking into froth.

No wonder Amelia Foster had steered left.

Fourteen

STONE WALLS

December 16

THE BLOCKY OLD HOSPITAL sat across the street from the detachment. At the reception desk, as he showed his identification, Leith was advised of the strict ICU house rules. He was warned again by another nurse outside Gilmartin's door, then left alone.

Inside the room were three empty beds and one shrouded by curtains. Behind the curtain he found a chrome-railed bed flanked by active machinery. Craig Gilmartin lay on his back, an inert, long-limbed cocoon sheathed in blankets and tubes. His eyelids were faintly blue-veined, like a baby's, and the lashes were gummy. His intubated mouth and nose were enclosed in a plastic snout strapped to his head, and the mask, Leith realized, was doing Gilmartin's breathing for him.

The young constable had caught the bullet close to his heart, rupturing the subclavian artery, shattering his scapula and throwing him into hypovolemic shock, if Leith had the lingo right. The bottom line was that he might not pull through. Yesterday, Raj Sattar had managed to weasel past the nurses to visit Gilmartin, to say a prayer over him. Visibly shaken, he had then reported back to the detachment, saying Craig was deader than anyone was willing to admit.

With the doctors' long and grim reports in mind, along with Sattar's pithy one, Leith had come expecting the worst. Instead, to his surprise, what he saw in Gilmartin's form lying before him was not a fading, but a life force slowly surfacing. Strange. Leith was far from imaginative, yet it was happening before his eyes, the frenetic process of demolition and repair, a cellular knitting and relayering. Gilmartin was going to survive.

Only when the machinery broke its pattern of blipping did he wake with a start.

Pessimism firmly back in place, he ran to fetch a nurse. The nurse studied the screen briefly and adjusted something. She thanked him for bringing it to her attention as though she really would have preferred that he hadn't, and whisked off again.

Probably best not to hang around, Leith realized. "Keep up the good work," he told Gilmartin, and left him to his stealthy repairs.

* * *

The meeting Leith called was held in Bosko's office. Rather than taking seats, Leith, JD and Jimmy Torr stood around Bosko where he sat at his desk to share what they had. Torr opened the meeting by holding up a manila envelope and promising that the pictures weren't pretty. "Ready for a little light entertainment?"

Bosko didn't say whether he was ready or not, but accepted the photos as they were handed to him, removed his glasses, and studied each in detail. Leith stood behind him and looked over his shoulder, refreshing his own memory. The first shot was an 8 x 10 glossy of a dead man sitting against a tree, what was left of his face swollen and discoloured, blood tracking down his cheeks from the crown.

"This loose scarf around the throat —"

"Not a garrotte," Leith said. "It was used to gag him. Knotted at the back. Blood on it, and some vomit. Probably slipped off when his jaw broke. His wife identified the scarf as his." He took the photos from Torr, pulled the autopsy set, and showed the first to Bosko. "Note the bruises."

"Ankles, wrists, knees, elbows, all over," JD said. "Like he was banged around in some hard place. Or struggling. Duct-tape gunk all over him. Mouth, too. Riot of fibres caught in the gunk. Chafing. Probably tied at the wrists and ankles and held in close confinement for some hours."

"Like a car trunk," Leith suggested. "Except the fibres aren't off any kind of car-grade carpet. Maybe he was placed on a tarp."

Bosko was looking at the first photograph again, of Rory Keefer tied to the tree. He glanced up at Leith.

"He was stabbed in the abdomen first," Leith said, and the unimaginable suffering of Rory Keefer struck him again. "Stabbed twice. Then left sitting for some time before being finished off with a rock to the face and top of the head. He was stabbed again post-mortem, fourteen times: deep, fast thrusts into the thighs, lower belly, and a couple more to the stomach. There was also a more deliberate stab between the ribs around the heart. Missed the heart, but it wasn't for lack of trying. Strange, since he was already dead."

"Looks like amateur hour to me," Torr said.

Leith nodded. "The rock-to-face blow dislocated his jaw, as you can see. Must have been a heavy swing going right to left. Then a swing downward with the same rock fractured the skull, left a depression about seven centimetres round, and is the likely cause of death. There's blood and hair on the rock and the surrounding area, but not much blood spray. Still, the killer, or killers, would have walked out of there quite a mess."

"You say he was left sitting for some time before being finished off," Bosko said. "How long?"

"We can't say, except it wasn't quick," replied Torr. "At least ten minutes, we're thinking."

"Maybe they were trying to get information out of him," Leith said.

"Or it was just for the thrill," added Torr.

"Revenge," Bosko suggested.

JD had another idea. "The killer never did anything like this before. He was unsure of himself. He stabbed the guy, twice, thinking it would be like in the movies, instant death. When that didn't happen, he started freaking out, trying to decide what to do. Maybe seeing the man in pain got to him, and he used a rock to finish him off fast. Show him some mercy."

"Why do you assume it's a *he*?" said Torr, nose in the air. "Seems kind of sexist."

"I'd hardly call a rock to the head merciful," Leith put in, pre-empting JD's probably regrettable response. "A cut throat would be kinder. It probably wasn't extracting information, either. You'd see more superficial cuts. I'm with Jim — it's a first-timer's thrill kill, plain and simple."

"Whatever the case," Torr said, "even ten minutes is a hell of a long time to hang around the scene."

"'It's cold, wet, and miserable," JD agreed. "Not to mention creepy as hell."

"No, I'm saying it's risky," Torr said. "Even in December, even at night, you get your weirdo nature buffs exploring the park. The guy's got to be wired."

"Why do you assume it's a *he*?" JD said smoothly.

Leith agreed with Torr that the killer or killers — he was quite sure more than one were involved — were on something.

"If only adrenaline," Bosko murmured. He had looked through the horrific photographs with equilibrium, as if they were landscape shots and not stark depictions of torture. He stacked them, handed them back to Leith, and changed the subject. "Bit of promising news for you guys. We have a response to the public request for witnesses to the Sea to Sky crash, a driver who came on the scene and stepped out to help."

"Right on," Torr said.

"I didn't talk to the tipster myself, but she'll be coming in later today to give a statement. Also Amelia Foster's partner, Tiffany Tan — maybe it's time to have another talk with her."

"Yikes, the dykes," Torr said. "Well, what?" he retorted at Leith's glare. "That's what she is. She and Foster were a couple, okay? Let's not be coy here."

"Since we're not being coy here," JD told Torr, "You're an asshole."

Leith's views on many things were old-fashioned and would no doubt fail the PC test, but unlike Torr, he was smart enough to keep his prejudices to himself — and to see them as something he needed to change. He turned his glare on JD, who shouldn't be swearing at the top of her lungs in the presence of Bosko, but she was too busy thrusting her chin at Torr to catch the reprimand. Which didn't matter, as Bosko had ignored the entire exchange. He swivelled his chair around to face Torr and said, "I know you and Doug talked to Tan once already, and I think you mentioned it was like pulling teeth. She was in shock, though, and hopefully she's recovered a bit. It'd be good to get any exchanges she had with Foster that day. It could be nothing, or it could be important, but whatever it is, gently does it. Right?"

"I tell you what it'll be," said Torr, "more of the same: *dunno, dunno, dunno.*"

"Right, so let's switch things up a bit," Bosko replied. "Take Dave this time, and let him do the talking. Okay?"

It was a mild but icy slap, and even thick-skulled Torr seemed to feel it.

Done, Bosko wished them all a good day, leaving Leith and Torr, two straight white guys, to pay a visit to one gay Asian woman. Leith could only hope she was more open-minded than they were.

* * *

Tiffany Tan was thirty-three, with a bleach-blonde asymmetrical haircut and a row of studs in one ear. Her mouth was clamped in a thin line, her eyes red rimmed and bruised looking. She stood reeking of dope in the doorway of the low-income housing unit where she lived with Amelia Foster, and it appeared Torr was right — she was going to stonewall them once again.

No, they couldn't come in, was her first response. They could talk to her from the corridor.

Torr stood back with arms crossed while Leith questioned her. He opened with an apology for intruding at a time like this. He told her some progress was being made on Amelia's MVA case. She looked unimpressed. As far as she understood, he realized, there was no case. A momentary loss of control had cost her girlfriend's life. She didn't need cops coming around to tell her so.

He told her that there could be more to it than a simple MVA, and that he would appreciate it if she could tell him about any conversations she had with Amelia that day. Or that night at the hospital, before Amelia passed. Anything could be helpful. Had Amelia mentioned where she was going before she left? Or managed to say anything as she lay injured?

Tan's answer was a grunt that could have been yes, no, or maybe.

"Sorry?"

She repeated herself more clearly. "Yeah."

"What'd she say?"

"Dunno."

"Well, can you repeat anything she said, Tiffany?"

"Dunno. Couldn't figger."

"She was talking, but you couldn't figure out what she was saying?"

"'S'bout it," she said.

That's about it, Leith translated. "Did she say what happened at all, what caused the crash?"

Tan shook her head, combining it with a shrug, which probably meant *sorry, I'm not sure*.

"Did she recognize you?"

Silence.

He repeated the question.

Silence.

"Do you know the answer to that?"

Silence.

"Did you understand my question? Did Amelia give any indication she recognized you? 'Cause that would tell us —"

"Why don't you leave me the fuck alone," she said, and started to shut the door.

Leith spoke louder. "Sure, we'll do that now. We might talk again, though, okay? And I'd appreciate if you'd give me a call —"

Slam.

On the way downstairs, Torr hooted with glee and punched Leith on the shoulder. "Didn't I tell you? *Dunno, dunno, dunno.*"

Fifteen

INTO THE MIX

NEXT UP ON LEITH'S agenda was talking to the individual who Bosko had mentioned would be coming in, the woman who had stopped at the Amelia Foster crash scene on the Sea to Sky and responded to the media release asking for witnesses.

Judging by her quaint handle, Desiree Novak, Leith expected either an Amazon in Lycra or a little old lady in a pillbox hat, but she turned out to be a tallish girl of seventeen, her tow blonde hair cut short except for a swish of long bangs.

She was at the age where he wasn't sure whether to refer to her as a girl or a woman. There should be a word for those in between, he thought. But she was more of a girl, in his mind. Maybe it was her open expression and her lack of cosmetics. She was also looking around with what seemed like anxiety, so he told her not to worry, and asked again, as he had downstairs, whether she was okay talking without a parent present.

"Oh, I'm not worried," she said. "I've always wanted to have a look around in here, so it's actually kind of exciting. I'm actually planning to join up soon as I'm nineteen."

"Are you really? Good for you."

She nodded. "I also want to say right off the bat that I'm really sorry I didn't come forward sooner, but it's because I didn't even see the crash, and I only stopped for a few minutes to see if I could help. Then I was at McDonald's the day before yesterday, and I saw on TV about how you wanted anybody who even just stopped at the crash scene to come forward."

"And I really appreciate that you did," Leith said. "So tell me about the night of the crash, Desiree. When did you arrive and what did you see?"

"You can actually call me Dezi," she said. "I get totally thrown off when people say Desiree."

"I'll do that."

"Well, I just got my N," she said, referring to her novice licence, "which means I can *finally* drive by myself, so I cruised out to Squamish and back. I kind of didn't tell my mom the absolute truth about that, because I knew she would *not* be pleased if she found out I was on the Sea to Sky all alone — she calls it the Killer Highway. Well, I got home really late and she found out anyway, and she almost took away my licence, but I managed to talk her out of it."

She smiled and her grey-blue eyes lit up. Leith felt that if he was a lot younger and much less married, he might be falling in love right now. "Was it your own car you were driving?"

"Not really. But my mom has two vehicles, and she lets me drive the old Sidekick. So anyway, I was heading home from Squamish, and I saw two cars stopped at the side of the highway with their emergencies flashing, and I figured somebody might be in trouble, so I pulled in behind them. Then I saw some other lights shining across the highway, from the ditch. I went over and saw that a red car had hit a tree and was on its side, and there were two guys down there. I went down and they asked if I had a phone. I said I didn't, which is a long story ..."

Aha, Leith thought, the nagging memory of Gilmartin's half-absorbed statement coming back to him. So this was the girl without a phone.

"And they both kind of swore, and then one guy, the younger one — he said he was a cop, so maybe he even works here?"

"I think you're probably right," Leith said. "Can you tell me what the older guy looked like?"

"I didn't see him much. Mostly I was looking at the girl in the car."

"Sure. What about the vehicle the older guy was driving?"

She shook her head. "It was just lights flashing in the night to me."

"Did the two men have any conversation that you heard?"

"No, other than talking about phones, and how one of them should go flag down a car, and somewhere along the line the young one said he was a cop. Which, if you know who he is, you should totally give him some kind of commendation, because it was really impressive how caring and concerned he was."

"I'll certainly pass that on," Leith said.

"Anyway, he told the other guy to go flag down a car, because 'everybody else on the planet except us three has a phone,' is what he said. So the other guy took off to do that, and the cop said he'd stay with the girl, and he kind of sat down right in the mud and held her hand, like, talking to her."

"Was she talking to him, too?"

Dezi shook her head. "I don't think so. She was in pain, mostly kind of whimpering. It was horrible." She ran a hand over her face as if to wipe away the memory, then straightened in her chair. "But I guess you get a lot of that kind of thing in this job. You have to be strong."

"That's for sure. And what happened next?"

"Well, then a few minutes went by, and a bunch of cars zipped by above, and the cop said, 'Why isn't he flagging them down?' Then we went to check, and there was no sign of the guy. So he started trying to flag one down himself, and I said I really had to go home or my mom would worry, and he said, 'That's okay, you should go,' so I left."

"And you went home, did you?"

"I did. And Mom got mad, and so on and so forth. I didn't even realize I should give a statement till I saw it on TV, like I said. I'm sorry."

"That's all right. When you found out we were looking for witnesses, you came forward, and that's more than a lot of people would do."

"It's not very helpful, though, is it. I wish I'd saved the day."

"Well, if you carry through and join up, maybe you will be saving the day not long from now," Leith said, knowing he was going overboard with the niceness thing. He busied himself jotting down the end time of the interview.

"People tell me joining up is really hard," Dezi said. "Like, a whole bunch of hurdles before you can get in. Is that true? Like, what are my chances?"

"You've got to be physically able, and of good character. If you've got that under your belt, you're off to a running start."

"Do you have to be a genius at math? Because I'm not."

Leith grinned. "Honesty is more important than math. You should see my idea of long division. And I'll tell you what, if you're serious about a future here, I'll see if I can get you a grand tour of the station right now."

"Really? That would be awesome. If it's not too much trouble."

Leith thanked her again for attending, then called Doug Paley and asked if there was somebody around with twenty minutes to spare to give a future recruit a detachment tour.

* * *

"Fuck," JD muttered. Just because she happened to be taking a short break and staring out the window, thinking about a different life, Doug Paley was shackling her with a task fit for a first-year trainee. "Where is she?" she asked him with a sigh.

The young woman she collected from the reception desk looked a little embarrassed, but polite and enthusiastic. JD swore again — but only silently. "Hi, there," she said. "I'm JD. So, I hear you want to sign up."

Fifteen minutes would be plenty, she decided, as she started to show the teen the workings of the building. Dezi showed keen interest and asked a lot of questions. Damn good questions, too, JD thought, pleasantly surprised. Half an hour later they stopped on the main floor, where JD found a souvenir RCMP T-shirt for the girl, because as teens went, this one actually wasn't so bad. The tour was no frivolity to Dezi, either. She was not only enthusiastic about signing up, but determined that it would happen. She told JD what had first inspired her. Several years ago she had watched a policewoman chase down, tackle, and overpower a guy on Lonsdale.

"Made me kind of proud," Dezi said, and JD thought she could detect sadness within her smile.

The tour ended in the underground parkade. They sat in a marked cruiser and talked about onboard computers and changes in policing over the years. They talked about the risks, too. They even talked about sexual harassment, discrimination, the headway women were finally making, and possibilities for the future. Dezi sat in the driver's seat, gripping the steering wheel and gunning ahead down a road of adventure rather than a parkade wall.

What the poor kid didn't seem to be seeing was the mountain of paperwork behind that parkade wall, though JD had given her fair warning.

Dezi had shrugged it off. "I can handle paperwork."

"I'll ask you again in five years."

They left the cruiser and returned to the lobby, where Dezi mentioned the news she'd heard, about the shooting of a local RCMP officer in his own home. "They aren't saying much about it, except he's in critical condition," she said. "I hope he'll be okay."

If she was fishing for the inside story, she wasn't going to get it. "He'll be all right," JD said. She held the door open, and Dezi fairly danced down the steps, smiling up at the light rain as if touched by infatuation. She turned to wave. "I'm already loving this job, JD!"

JD watched the future cadet bounce away and thought, *Let's just hope the job loves you back.*

Sixteen

UNIDENTIFIED FLYING OBJECTS

December 17

ON FRIDAY MORNING Leith arrived at the office to find a fair-sized gathering knotted about the main-floor coffee machine. Bosko was there, beaming, along with Urbanski, Torr, JD. General duty members milled about as well — Kenny Poole, Raj Sattar, Cal Dion. Everyone looked pleased.

"What's up?" Leith asked.

"He opened his eyes," JD told him.

"Beat the odds," added Urbanski.

So Craig Gilmartin had passed Go. Leith beamed, but only fleetingly. He had to get a statement from the patient, and hopfully now he could do just that.

* * *

The constable was awake, but barely. He had been moved to a different room on the hospital's second floor, into a less terminal-looking bed, and stripped of the bulk of his life-support machinery. The door had a guard on duty. The room within was dim and quiet, and Gilmartin lay flat on his back, a tube strung under his nose, his bare arms loose at his sides. He looked up at his two visitors with faint interest, focusing more on Raj Sattar, probably because Sattar was leaning close.

Leith had invited Sattar along, as the young man professed to be Gilmartin's work buddy, and his presence might help put Gilmartin at ease.

"Hey, bro, you're awake! And about time, too," Sattar was telling his friend in a loud whisper.

Gilmartin raised the first and second fingers of his right hand in what looked to Leith like a failed Christ-like gesture, then let them drop again.

"So you've been out for a hundred years, you slack-ass." Sattar's aggressive whispering was more annoying than a bellow, to Leith. Still, he was glad the kid was here, doing all the chummy breaking of the ice, which he would have failed at, badly. "How ya feeling?"

"Shitty," Gilmartin whispered back.

Sattar turned to Leith. His teeth flashed in a grin as he hissed with delight, "He feels *shitty*!"

As pleased as Leith felt, he could see they wouldn't get much out of this visit. He congratulated the survivor for, well, surviving, then tried the one question that couldn't wait. "Do you know who shot you, Craig? Can you give us a name or description?"

Gilmartin shook his head. Not a faint no, but a definite *uh-uh, nope, no chance.*

It was another piece in the puzzle, albeit not a great one. Leith told him to get some sleep, that he would be back later. He walked with Sattar down the monochrome halls — all the gloomier for the twinkle of Christmas decorations — past patients out for slow strolls, past staff and visitors.

"Guess we can skip the mourning lilies," Sattar declared, and jabbed the elevator's down button.

"Bunch of daisies will do," Leith agreed. Daisies reminded him of Dezi Novak — there was another question he would have to put to Gilmartin when he was up to talking. Why did he leave her out of his statement?

They left the hospital, stepping out into the blustery cold now embellished by an icy, fine drizzle, and stood on the curb watching the cars swish by. Leith glanced at the winter sky. In every place he had lived up till now, winter had brought snow. Snow was rare in the Lower Mainland, but rain was anything but. Normally the rain depressed him, yet today it seemed kind of nice. Sattar seemed to think so, too, cheerfully snugging down his patrol cap. The traffic broke and they jaywalked across 15th to the detachment to share the news of Gilmartin's first words.

* * *

Late in the afternoon, Dion was upstairs, working in a semi-seconded mode in the General Investigation Section. His latest efforts to snub the GIS weren't working so well; maybe his attitude was only making him stand out more. Maybe it was time to go with the flow.

He had a desk and a slate of assignments, none too challenging, and for the most part was left to his own devices. The attempted murder of Craig Gilmartin was at the top of everybody's to-do list, as it was on his. Nobody had come up with any good theories so far, but one had taken shape in his mind overnight, further developing this morning. But it was a weird idea, highly unlikely, and one he tried to banish.

Banishing wasn't working so well, and all he could do was face it squarely and work on its logistics. He drummed his fingers on the desktop and thought it through, start to finish.

No. Impossible.

He watched a uniformed member escort a heavy-set girl with short, spiky hair and facial piercings into the section's foyer. She wore jeans and black leather. She fixed her sights on Jimmy Torr at his desk and called out, "Hey."

Torr had a habit of pulling in his gut when approaching women. He did so now. "Ms. Tan, hey. What can I do for you?"

It was Tiffany Tan, then, Amelia Foster's partner. Dion had heard Torr and some others talking about her, putting her down, like jerk-off schoolboys passing notes. Dion had been one of those schoolboys, once. Amazing what being ass-deep in trouble could do to a person's humility.

"Where's the other guy?" Tan asked Torr.

"What other guy?" Torr said. "Dave Leith, you mean?" She shrugged.

Torr looked around, searching for Leith.

"I think he's talking to Bosko," Dion said.

Torr was forgetting about his gut, gesturing like a traffic cop, relieved. "Good. Take her down there, would you?"

Dion led Tan down the hall to Bosko's office and knocked on the jamb. Inside, Leith sat across from Bosko, listening, ankle over knee and file folder in hand. Their conversation paused when Dion apologized for interrupting. "Tiffany Tan's here to see you."

Leith stood. He asked Tan if she wanted to talk in private. She didn't, so he offered her his chair. She refused the chair, too. "I thought 'bout it," she said, coldly. "Why she wiped out, eh. If you wanna know."

"That's exactly what I want to know," Leith said. He remained on his feet, and Dion guessed he would have preferred ushering her off to an interview room, but didn't want to break the connection. He could see why. Tan's commitment to this conversation looked tenuous, at best.

"You've remembered something Amelia said?" Leith asked her.

"Right."

"This was in the hospital?"

"Uh-huh."

"I'm all ears," Leith said. He caught Dion's eye, and his glance said *notebook out, please.*

Dion got out notebook and pen. Tan adjusted her stance slightly, noticed him with his pen, and dictated to him directly. "What she said is, she said it was a bird. She's a birder, right? Obsessed. So she's prob'ly just flipped out on morphine, or Dem, or whatever the fuck they had her on. She was talking weird."

"A bird?" Leith said.

"A dead bird, all lit up and screamin'." Tan's entire body rose an inch or so in a shrug, then settled back with a squeal of leather.

"Huh," Leith said. "Were those her words?"

She shrugged again. "Said, 'Big dead bird come at me, Tiff, all lit up.'"

"And screaming?"

"And screamin'."

"And she spoke your name, hey?"

"Yeah, she did."

"So she did recognize you?"

"Yeah, she did."

"And the bird, she said it was dead? That was the word she used?"

"Yeah. Dead, and lit up, and screamin'."

"Did she say anything else?"

"Not much of nothin'."

"Did you say anything to her?"

"Yeah."

"What did you say to her?"

"Said, 'I love you Amelia' a million times, is all." She sneered at him.

Bosko stopped Tan with a question as she turned to leave. "Tiffany, how long did you know Amelia? When did you first meet?"

She took her time, staring at him, and finally said, "Medinmay. Park."

"What?" Leith said.

She turned her glare on him, said, "Fuck's sake, ears open this time?" and repeated it more slowly. "Medin*may*. The park. I'm outta here."

Leith stepped out into the hall and called at her receding back that they weren't finished, but apparently they were. Dion stood finishing his notes, wondering what park she was talking about, and thinking it probably didn't matter.

"I should have arrested her," Leith said, back in his chair. He looked rattled. He and Bosko debated the woman's response, wondering if Medinmay was a walk-in clinic, maybe.

"They met in May," Dion interrupted. "In the park."

Leith said, "Oh."

Bosko said, "Ah." He smiled at Dion, then at Leith. "Something thrown, maybe. A rock? Foster was driving along, saw it a split second before it hit, and the first thing that came into her mind as she was losing control was a dead bird falling. Have you ever been hit in the windshield by a flying object?"

"Eggs, once," Leith said. "At a riot."

"I mean when you're travelling down the highway, for instance."

Dion recalled being hit by a bird. It was about eight years ago. His car of the day had been a cheap second-hand Corolla, rust-pocked blue, loaded with friends, their destination a house party way out in Hope. On the stereo the Heartless Bastards played, and none of it was relevant to Bosko's question except for the impact.

He wouldn't share the memory, because his pre-crash memory was supposed to be patchy. The patchy memory thing had been a hasty plan thrown together as he lay recovering in rehab, knowing there would be interrogations ahead. Easier to say "I don't remember" than lie, he had assumed.

But he had messed up. Should have limited the scope of his amnesia to the day of the accident, because maintaining chronic forgetfulness was hard work. Now he had to think twice about everything he said, which was turning him into a man with nothing to say. He sometimes wondered if it was worth it. Maybe hiding out was worse than the jail cell he would be escorted to if he confessed.

Distracted by images of a dungeon, he forgot about keeping his mouth shut and said, "I hit a bird on the Lougheed. It obscured my view and I had to pull over fast."

Bosko was interested. "Any idea what kind of bird it was you hit?"

"No clue."

"Because it happened so fast, right?"

Like a meteor. Shock followed by laughter. Stopped along the Nicomen Slough, cars hurtling by. Everybody piling out, checking for damage, trying to clear up the mess. Looch picked up a wing bit between thumb and finger and threatened to throw it at Brooke. *Why was I busting a gut? What was so funny?*

"Nothing left but feathers." Dion could read upside down the words Bosko had scribbled on a notepad: *Lit up. Dead bird.* The Ident report made no mention of bird guts or feathers plastered to Amelia Foster's wrecked car. "Do birds ever die in mid-air?"

"Sure, if they're full of birdshot," Leith said.

It was an unlikely scenario, the chain reaction of a bird dying mid-air and falling on the car, scaring Foster into the ditch. And again, there would be evidence. "Maybe a gull flew at her," Dion suggested. "It was lit up in her headlights before veering off, and it startled her. The bird flew away, but she lost control."

Leith looked doubtful.

"Screaming," Bosko said.

"Could have been herself screaming," Leith said. "In her confusion ..."

Bosko offered Dion the second visitor's chair, waited till he was seated, and said, "I was driving along Bridgeport a few years ago, heading for the airport. Suddenly my windshield shattered with this terrific bang. At first I thought I'd been shot at, but then realized I must have been hit by a large bird. I didn't see it coming, and I don't know where it came from. Just *wunk*. This was broad daylight. It happened" — he snapped his fingers — "like that. So whatever Amelia Foster was describing, I doubt it was a lit-up bird. Unless it was all in her imagination, the lit-up bird she saw would have had to be moving slow enough for her to register as it came toward her."

"Tan did say Foster was flipped out on something," Leith pointed out.

"Could be delirium," Bosko agreed. "Maybe a "dead lit-up bird" is her drugged metaphor for some kind of vehicle. A motorcycle, maybe?"

"Jay Comstock says there was no other vehicle involved," Dion said, referring to the traffic accident reconstructionist who had eyeballed the scene and provided his magic computations. "Single-vehicle accident. An avoidance manoeuvre commenced fifty-some metres before she left the shoulder. She stepped on the gas instead of the brakes, accelerated and swerved, Comstock says."

The quality and quantity of his own words pleased him, a flood of savvy. Bosko and Leith seemed impressed, too. He felt inspired, felt he could beat this brain-damage fiasco he'd invented, start pulling memories back into focus. Not fast enough to reopen the inquiry, but enough that he could stop hiding out. Start being smart again.

"Isn't that bad luck?" Bosko said. Dion blinked at him. "Birds flying into houses," Bosko explained. "At least that's how it started out. I believe the superstition's since migrated to birds flying into windshields."

Dion felt the colour drain from his face. Looch had said that same thing, the day by the Nicomen Slough, once they had cleaned the glass and were pulling back into traffic. Birds in houses, dead birds, birds sitting on the back of your chair — basically anything bird-related was a bad omen, Looch had said, according to his superstitious family. "Better not tell Mama about this," he had joked. "She'll never let me out of her sight again."

Bosko was winding up the meeting, saying this was all good stuff to put on the board for team feedback. "Craig Gilmartin," he added to Leith. "He's had a day to recuperate. Go and see if he's up to talking. And take a recorder. Let's get every syllable."

Leith nodded and stood. Dion knew Leith was partnered with Torr lately, and would be taking him to get Gilmartin's waking statement. He wished he could go instead of Torr, as it could help with his own unspoken, unspeakable theory. Gilmartin had clearly indicated that he didn't know who shot him, according to Leith. But could he be lying? *Why would he lie?* Dion wondered. Fear? If he could be there in person to observe the constable's responses first-hand, he could better judge what was going on. He could decide whether to move forward with his suspicions or trash them.

But no matter. Collating the info after the fact would have to do. He finished up a note on Tiffany Tan's statement, such as it was, and stood to see that Leith hadn't left, but was leaning in the doorway, waiting for him.

"Well," Leith said. And there it was again, an uncalled-for kindness that struck Dion as forewarning. "Coming?"

Seventeen

BIRDS

GILMARTIN WAS VISIBLY BETTER, Leith saw. He sat propped up in bed, still attached to an IV, surrounded by the loot of sympathy. Better, but still not great, more a wraith than a man, with creased skin and raccoon eyes, hair standing on end, and a look of dazed fear stamped on his face.

"Yes," Gilmartin said, when he caught Leith's stare. "I scared the hell out of myself, too, when somebody made the mistake of showing me a mirror."

So the patient was fully lucid, and already on his way to being a chatterbox again. Leith smiled his congratulations, but Gilmartin was peering past him at Dion, as if he might be a hit man lurking in the background instead of a cop. "I'm a little jumpy. Who's he?"

Leith reintroduced himself, then Dion. "I came by this morning with Raj Sattar, but you were pretty out of it."

"Yes, I recall. The brain comes and goes. I'm on massive painkillers. They're wearing off, by the way, so better make it quick."

"Your parents have been to see you, have they?"

"To put it mildly, yes,"

"What about Sophie?"

To Leith's surprise, Gilmartin shuffled himself upright with a show of anger. "No, sir, because she's not allowed. You're not accusing her of shooting me, are you? Because she sure as hell did not."

Leith assured him that Sophie wasn't being accused of anything and that visitor restrictions were only temporary. From his inner breast pocket he brought out his small digital recorder, and he saw Gilmartin tense at the sight of it.

"Ah," the kid said, as he recognized the machine, and his laughter had a hysterical ring to it. "Thought for a moment you were going to taser me."

"Take it easy. We'll get this over with quick as possible, then let you get some rest." Leith stood at the foot of the bed and turned on the recorder. "How about you just tell me what happened that day, in detail, after you were dropped off at home."

It took some moments for Gilmartin to put the ordeal into words, but when he did, it came out in a torrent. "I got home," he said. "Somebody came up the steps, I turned around, and the son of a bitch shot me."

An angry torrent, but brief. "A tad more detail, if you would, please," Leith said.

Gilmartin tried again. "Kenny drove me home. He let me off at the curb. Nothing out of the ordinary there that I can tell you about. I walked inside. I took off my sweater. Hung it up. I walked down the hall to flick on the table lamp, because the overhead doesn't work, and heard somebody coming up the front steps. I figured it was Kenny coming back, maybe he forgot to tell me something, so I went to open the door, but as I turned the handle I saw something wasn't quite right. The door's got that rippled glass panel in it, and I saw through the ripples there was something wrong with the picture."

He paused again. "It wasn't Kenny, not quite, and I felt, like, this cold wash of fear, and before I knew it, this bastard was shoving the door open as I was trying to shove it shut. I turned and ran for the hallway. I had a brilliant plan of escaping out the back way. Then he shot me. To tell the truth, I'm surprised I'm here telling you about it."

Leith was thinking much the same thing. *On a wing and a prayer*. "And you didn't see his face?"

"No."

"You were shot in the upper chest. You were lying on your back. You must have turned around at some point, faced him. Maybe if you thought about it …"

Gilmartin could not remember turning around. He could not remember seeing the man's face. He couldn't remember anything again until he woke in a hospital bed, as he described it, staring up at Raj Sattar's grin.

"How about in general," Leith said. "Anything, even if it's just an impression. Size, age, nationality?"

Gilmartin was losing steam, and clearly wanted Leith gone. "Bulky, Caucasian male. Not as tall as me. Pale, roundish face, dark clothes, and that's all."

Leith turned to check that Dion was getting this all down. Dion's pen was idle and his stare was fixed on Gilmartin's face. Leith sighed and turned back to the patient. "Does the name Desiree Novak mean anything to you? Or Dezi?"

"No. Why?"

"A witness came forward — young woman with short blonde hair — said she stopped at the crash scene, was down there with you."

"Oh, her. Is that her name? I wasn't thinking straight. She came down the ditch. She didn't have a phone either, would you believe? Did I not mention her in my statement?"

"You mentioned her to me, but it wasn't in the statement."

"I'm sorry. She didn't seem important. She must have slipped my mind."

Leith wasn't surprised. "Well, let's get to the nitty-gritty. Can you think of anybody who would want to hurt you?"

Gilmartin blinked as he considered the question. "I can't think of anybody," he said. "Except maybe Ken."

"Ken?"

"I'm joking. My supervisor, Kenny Poole."

"Kenny Poole's got an alibi," Leith said.

"I don't know, then. I'd like to think I have no enemies."

Leith opened his folder and placed a document before Gilmartin. "Recognize this man?"

In the photograph, a jaunty-looking Rory Keefer beamed at the camera. Gilmartin frowned at the image. "Might be the fellow who flagged me down on the highway, at the scene of the accident. Looks like him. A bit, anyway."

"Do you recall the colour of his car?"

Gilmartin was still frowning, but now was directing the scowl at Leith and starting to look cranky. "I gave all that already. How many times —"

"Just once more."

"Teal, I said. *Teal.* It's like a darkish turquoise."

Leith glanced at Dion, who was biting his lip. Gilmartin was staring at each of them in turn. "Did I say something special?"

"I'll tell you, Craig," Leith said, taking the photo back. "We're thinking your attack might be linked to that accident you witnessed. Thinking back on it, can you make any kind of connection?"

But all this talk, combined with meds running their course, was bringing on pain. Gilmartin crossed his arms as if to ward it off, squeezed his eyes shut, pursed his mouth.

Leith sped up his questioning. "Maybe something Amelia Foster said or did, or something you saw at the accident scene, or something you took away with you, even, that made someone come after you? You said in your statement the injured girl was mumbling and incoherent. Can you remember anything she said, even if it made no sense?"

"I'm afraid the whole thing is just a great fat blur in my head."

"All right, then."

"Oh," Gilmartin said. His eyes popped open again. "My engine! It was making a funny noise, like a whine or a whir. I was actually going to pull over just as I got flagged down. Then I forgot all about it. Afterwards, it seemed to be okay, so it must have been a fan belt or something adjusting itself. It happens."

Leith waited for Dion to jot down the info before moving on. "Did you maybe see any other vehicles around the scene at the time you drove up? Maybe parked farther down the highway?"

"Possibly," Gilmartin said. "Possibly not. I don't think so."

"There's a little turnout just before the crash site. Was it empty, occupied?"

"Like I said, possibly, and possibly not."

Which was incredibly unhelpful.

"All I can remember," Gilmartin said, "Is the guy who flagged me down. Besides that, nothing. I checked my mirror before pulling over, and there was nobody close behind me. If there were headlights, which I don't remember, they would have been far back."

"Did you have any conversation with that man at the scene?"

"Mostly about phones. Mine was dead, and he said he didn't have one. Then that girl came along —"

"Dezi?"

"Sure. She said she didn't have a phone. No, she said she used to have a phone, but not anymore. So no phones amongst the three of us. What are the chances? So the guy went up to flag a car, because surely somebody in the world had a functioning phone on them, and the girl went with him. Or no, she didn't, because I recall her talking to me a bit. I saw cars flying by, nobody stopping, and I thought what the heck? So I went up on the highway, and the guy and his car were gone."

The pain seemed to be coming in waves now. "I'm going to die," he said.

"You're not going to die. You want me to fetch the nurse?"

"No. I'm fine. So then the girl said she had to go, and I saw headlights coming, and I jumped up and down till the driver stopped, and thank god, he had a phone and called 911, and the rest you know."

Leith left his station at the foot of the bed and stood by the window, looking out. He had run out of questions, except for the last bit, Tiffany Tan's rather fabulous lead. He heard the hesitation in his own voice as he turned to ask, "Did you see any animals in the area? Around the scene of the accident?"

"Animals?"

"Airborne, maybe?"

Gilmartin seemed to search the air for some kind of logic that was eluding him. "Airborne animals, sir?"

Dion spoke for the first time. "Like birds," he suggested. Leith returned from the window, and he and Dion both watched Gilmartin as they waited for the answer.

"Did I see ... I don't know what you're ... *birds*?"

Again he squeezed his eyes shut, and now Leith was alarmed enough to close down the interview. "Don't worry about it," he said, which was exactly what Gilmartin was apparently doing. He had sunk into his pillows, his temples beaded with sweat. Dion dashed off to get the nurse, and with that, the interview ended.

* * *

Not until they were in the detachment, about to part ways to their respective desks, did Dion gather the nerve to ask Leith the question. "So are you investigating Kenny Poole?"

Leith drew up short and looked at him. "What?"

"Did you really check his alibi, or were you joking?"

Leith's gaze intensified. "What're you talking about?"

Dion pushed his fists into the pockets of his patrol jacket. "When Gilmartin said that Kenny wanted to kill him, he was joking. Then you said that Kenny has an alibi. I just wasn't sure —"

"We were both joking, Cal. It's called dry humour."

Laugh, Dion instructed himself. But he couldn't. "I thought so," he said.

Leith left him, then, but not without a final, piercing stare.

Eighteen

A BEAM OF LIGHT

December 18

AT THE START OF DION'S weekend, the weather gods had banged together warm fronts and cold, draping low-lying fog all over the North Shore. In the late afternoon he walked through the heavy mists on the Spirit Trail seawall, doing his best not to search passing faces. Searching faces and patterns in traffic, reading signals in the air, it had all become habitual over the years. Like the retired carpenter he'd once met, who had complained that he'd go to his grave mentally tape-measuring every board he laid eyes on, would Dion die searching faces?

God, he hoped not. He tried to focus on the West Coast scenery, to relax and "be recreational," as Sam Kerr had put it. Be present. Be real.

He sat on a park bench, insulated in his leather car coat, and watched the ocean heave. He could hear the wet hiss of traffic up the hill and the voices of passersby muted by the cold.

The world is not so full of criminals as you think, Kerr had told him. Kerr the shrink, who may or may not see through his act. *The bad guys are a minority, believe it or not. Let down your guard*, she told him. *Step out of your comfort zone. Believe in life and love.*

Eyes closed, he inhaled deeply, pulling in life and love and a lungful of briny winter air. A shadow passed by, doubled back, sat down on the other end of the bench. Dion opened his eyes and studied him a moment before looking again to sea. His seatmate, a youth in a dark hoodie, remarked it was kind of a crappy day, wasn't it. "Looks to me like you got a bad case of the winter doldrums," he added, and Dion realized this was going to be a sales pitch.

He assured the kid he was just fine, thanks.

"Could've fooled me," the kid said. "But that's okay, 'cause I got for you the guaranteed picker-upper. Or looking to mellow out some sweet lady on your Christmas list? This here is the perfect stocking stuffer."

"I've got a line on all that, thanks," Dion said.

"Sure thing. But a deal like this, man. An eighth — thirty-five bucks, if you can believe it. Or if you want, a single, two singles, however many singles, pre-rolled, extra potent, just fucking bursting with THC. *And* at liquidation prices!"

Dion considered the boy's face, considered the offer. "Who're you muling for?"

"No, man, just unloading something for a buddy. Personal supply but overstocked, strictly a one-time offer."

"Ray Boland?"

"Ray who? No, never heard of him," the kid said, which made sense, since Ray Boland didn't exist.

"Then who? I only trust Ray's stuff."

The kid shrugged. "So I guess you gotta wait for Ray."

"Fuck off, then," Dion said, and hoped the kid would do just that.

"Your loss," the kid said, but instead of fucking off, he shifted a few inches closer. "If Ray's stuff is so good, why you look like shit? Here, give this sampler a try. If you like, four bucks apiece, you can't beat that. And they're fully loaded, with a little something special on top."

A mini joint lay on the park bench between them. The kid should be in retail. Dion crumbled a bit off the end, peered, and sniffed, unsure how pot aficionados tested their product. He asked the kid what exactly the "something special" was. The kid said, seal the deal and he'd reveal, and if this went down well — and he was confident it would — they might exchange numbers.

The mysterious *something special* had sold Dion. He dusted his hands and gave a nod. "Give me the eighth."

He handed over two twenties, and the kid handed him change, along with a baggie of weed. Dion brought out his ID and placed the kid under arrest. Not easy, because the kid had springs in his legs and tried to flee, so it became a short chase up the grassy slope, a tumbling haul back downhill through the squishy wet grass, a bit of a skirmish on the pathway, and in the pat-down process, Dion was nearly taken down himself by two passersby who mistook him for a mugger.

The men unhanded him only after he shouted loud enough about who he was and what he was doing. He'd won no respect from them, though, and from a distance they threw insults, letting him know what they thought about the pot laws in this country and what he should do to himself. "Get lost," he told them.

With the boy subdued in his grip and the hecklers gone, Dion called for backup, then sat himself and his prisoner on the bench, regretting his grass-stained clothes. Without handcuffs available, he had to make do with a firm grip on the detainee's arm.

"I should have known," the kid said. "The haircut. But I figured if you were a narc, you'd do yourself up like a drug addict needing a fix. Reverse psychology, right?"

"Don't talk till you've been read your rights."

With time to kill, they ended up talking anyway — about self-driving cars, drone technologies, solar-powered highways. A man and a woman appeared on the pathway, heading this way, and Dion did a double take. Even at a distance he recognized the woman with the streaming blonde hair: his ex, Kate. She was snugged up against the man, who he guessed was Patrick, the lover he had heard of but never laid eyes on.

He tried to go invisible. But Kate saw him, and it was her turn to do a double take. *Crap*, he thought. How would it look, him holding on to this guy's arm like a possessive lover. Misleading, that's what.

She stopped as if to call out hello, boyfriend paused at her side, but before she could speak, two uniformed members arrived to take custody of the dealer, and Dion stood to conduct the prisoner exchange.

When he was done, he turned to see that Kate hadn't moved on, was waiting patiently for him to come say hello. He didn't return her smile as he approached. No way would he smile with that guy on her arm. There was still hope for himself and Kate, he thought, and smiling at her in a situation like this would send the wrong signals of acceptance and closure. He wasn't even close to closing anything when it came to Kate.

She made introductions, and Dion and Patrick nodded at each other. Patrick wasn't the barefoot Hercules that Dion had pictured when Kate had talked about him in the summer, but still, not bad looking. There was a touch of flint in his greeting smile, Dion noted, and it pleased him. It meant the foundations of that relationship could be pushed with a foot, tested. He returned the flint, but no smile, to say the fight was on.

If Kate noticed the war manoeuvres, she ignored them. "How've you been? Last time we talked you were looking for a new place to live. Any success?"

"Apartment on 14th," he told her. "It's pretty good."

"And you're working undercover now?"

She was referring to the kid on the bench. "That was a mistake," he said. "I'm not undercover, and it wasn't a sting, and I probably should have laid off." Maybe it wasn't so much a mistake as a screw-up, he was thinking. He had thought twice before making the arrest, but three times would have been better. For all he knew, some fine-tuned operation was underway, and he'd just stepped in it. On the other hand, fentanyl was everywhere, killing people like the plague, and the kid had suggested there was something special in the mix. That meant he had to be stopped cold, and the operation, if there was one, would just have to be rewritten. "He tried to sell me some weed. Wasn't much I could do about it. He seemed to be asking for handcuffs."

She tilted her head, caught his eye. "But you two seemed so friendly."

"We were passing time."

"That's good."

He didn't think there was anything good about what had happened here this afternoon. His nerves were still revved from the experience, the dirty trick he'd pulled, the scuffle, being shouted at by the good Samaritans, and now worry about being reprimanded by the drug squad. Nothing good at all. "What do you mean, good?"

"I'd never have caught you chatting with a prisoner before. You'd be grinding his ear with your boot, if anything." She caught his warning glance and changed the subject. "Anyway, you're looking fine."

"You look great," he replied, because she really did.

Patrick interjected. "We're going to miss the show, Kate."

She told her boyfriend to give her one second, and extended another peace offering to Dion. "We'll have coffee one of these days. This time it'll go better, right?"

As they walked away, Patrick turned to say, "Nice to meet you, Cal."

Kate didn't look back, but fluttered her hand goodbye over her shoulder. Which was nice in a way. Un-final.

* * *

The crew had failed JD. She was sitting at Rainey's alone, just her and her beer, which was kind of a twist, since she was the least sociable of the bunch, usually the last to arrive and the first to leave. She wished Leith would show up, because she didn't mind him as a workmate.

No, that was unfair. She liked him. He was a bit of a mother hen, but what was wrong with mother hens?

She also liked Dion, who was on her mind a lot, lately. She had known him well for years before he had crashed his car, back when he had been a lot of fun. He was no longer fun, but he was a lot more interesting. She was fairly sure that he was hiding something, and his claims of head trauma and recovery and all the rest of it were just the armour he had put on to avoid detection.

As if she was so blind.

Maybe, she dared to speculate, whatever he was hiding had something to do with the thing going on between Leith and Bosko, that peculiar telepathy she couldn't help but notice, strung so tight it practically twanged.

Or maybe she should get a life and mind her own business.

Mike Bosko materialized beside her, asking where everybody was, and she stared at him in surprise. Speak of the devil, or at least one of them. How had he snuck in when she had been watching the door? Either her surveillance skills were rusting or he was a leprechaun.

"I don't know, but good thing you're here," she said. "I was starting to feel snubbed. Sit down and have at least one drink."

"With pleasure," he said.

He took the chair across from her. His beer showed up a moment later. JD clinked her glass against his and said, "Well, have you got your buddy's house all lit with Christmas cheer?"

"Stage one is a wrap," Bosko said. "Most of the lights are up. But he's saving the new *pièce de résistance* for next week. Did I mention he's retired?"

"You did."

"Retired and regressing, I think. Last year it was just the reindeer prancing along the roofline. This year he's adding Santa Claus. Stuck in the chimney."

"I've seen those. Really tacky."

"Super tacky," Bosko agreed. "But his Santa is state of the art, homemade, life size. People are going to crash their cars when they get a load of that up there."

"That's not good."

"There's nothing good about Arlo's mania. Thankfully it will be short-lived, just till Boxing Day, when it all comes down again."

"What brought on this mania, besides retirement?" JD asked.

"A batch of grandkids, all under the age of six. He wants to be the best granddad ever."

"That's sweet. But don't break your neck helping him out. Roofs aren't good places to be, especially when you're full of Yuletide cheer."

"I'll be staying on solid ground," Bosko said. "And I'm paid well for holding the ladder, by the way. His wife Sylvia is the best cook I know. Hey, speaking of Arlo ..."

Bosko had a way of segueing through topics with metronomic precision, JD noticed. It was kind of awesome, sitting back and watching it happen.

"I had a dream last night," he went on, "after reading Dave's report of his talk with Craig Gilmartin. My dreams are about as dry as dust, for the most part, but this one was a little fancier than usual. For some reason I was in Arlo's basement, looking for something. It's something I've actually seen there, amongst all his junk. But my dream version of this item was quite different. It was yellow, where the real one I think was blue. And it was up on a plinth, with a beam of light shooting down on it from above, as if to make sure I got its significance. Strange things, dreams."

"Wow," JD said, trying not to sound puzzled. Even stranger than dreams, she thought, was Mike Bosko. "What was it, on the plinth?"

"Oh, a plane," he said, and spread his hands about three feet apart, demonstrating wingspan, JD supposed.

"Interesting dream," she said. "Symbolic. Of something ... I'm sure."

"Well, no," Bosko said. "Not a symbol. Just a theory."

Nineteen

LOOK UP

December 20

THE FOG CONTINUED overnight and into the morning. Dion was late to work, his temples throbbing from a drug-induced sleeping binge. He dropped into his desk chair, swivelled about in such a way that nobody could look at him directly, and prepared to attack the day's tasks. Today would be another stretch of hours under the fluorescents in GIS, in plainclothes suit and tie. He had once preferred the suit and tie — he'd been a sharp dresser — but now he preferred the uniform. It was easier. He hoped he would be sent back downstairs soon, back out on patrol. Upstairs was no longer his goal.

He pulled documents from his in tray and had to blink hard to bring the words into focus. At only twenty-nine, his eyes were starting to go. He slumped like an old man, too. Seeing Kate and her boyfriend had put buckshot in his morale. The small lift of optimism she had left him with had fizzled away overnight. Life was over. He just didn't care.

Doug Paley walked up to his desk with something to say. "Would be a good idea if you started showing up on time."

Dion didn't look up, but could sense Paley there, the shape of him, could see him in his mind's eye, squarish and big-bellied, thick neck, small ass, belt too tight around his waist like it was to blame for the distortion. "I know that."

"Would be a good idea if you looked a smidge sorry for being late, too," Paley added. "Maybe even throw in an apology, eh?"

Dion straightened to glare at him. "I'm sorry for being late. It won't happen again."

"Good. Now go tell it to the boss. He wants to see you."

Dion remained sitting upright, watching Paley. A part of his mind was wondering, what if Paley transformed emotionally for some reason, say a death in the family — would his physical presence also mutate, enough that Dion, who knew him so well, could perceive the change without actually seeing him? Through a pane of rippled glass, say? The question filled him with self-pity, as it related to his private line of inquiry into the near-fatal shooting of Craig Gilmartin. If he proved himself right, whatever his intentions, he would end up in the mud, because no way would Ken Poole go down without a fight. He'd pull his accuser down with him.

"What, is it about that collar yesterday?" he said. "Did I mess up something?"

Paley grinned. "Probably, but all's well that ends well. I hear the mule's spilling drugs like a birthday piñata. And he's talking, too. Maybe he'll crack the network."

"So what does Bosko want from me?"

"I don't know. Maybe he wants to pin a medal on you. Maybe he wants to ship you back to Tuktoyaktuk. Whatever it is, just make it snappy, before he freezes his nuts off out there."

Dion paused on his way to the door that would lead to the hall that would lead to Bosko's office, and Paley explained his last mysterious comment. "He's not in his office. He's down at Waterfront."

"Why?"

Paley walked away without an answer. Dion pulled on his coat and left the building. He drove an unmarked cruiser downhill to the seaside park, not far from where he had nabbed the dope dealer and met Kate yesterday. He parked by the marine school, next to a black police SUV, and walked around to Waterfront Park. The field was nearly empty, he saw. The paths were quiet. No Bosko in sight.

Never had Dion been called to meet a superior outside the walls of the detachment.

It had to be really bad news.

Maybe this was the edge, the drop-off, where he would be told, *the game's up*. The girl with pink hair had finally broken her silence, the body had been dug up, and he would now be reborn into the penal colony, where he belonged.

There was Bosko, not sitting on a park bench twirling handcuffs as he waited, but standing on the grassy verge, his bear-like shape silhouetted against a backdrop of morning mist. He seemed to be frowning at something in his hands, a device with an antenna, and for a moment Dion thought it was a detonator. But coming closer he saw the radio-controlled toy airplane parked at Bosko's feet — blue and white, three-foot wingspan — nosed into the open stretch of lawn, but not going anywhere.

The sergeant turned to greet him. "There you are, Cal. I take it you know how to work these things better than I do. I can't seem to get it going."

Dion looked down at the plane. In his younger years he had been quite a hotshot flyer, but how could Bosko know that? Doug Paley must have told him. "It's a bad place to run a plane, if you don't know what you're doing," he said. "Too many people around, not enough runway. And what if it went in the water?"

They both looked at the nearby waves. "That one didn't even occur to me," Bosko admitted.

"Give it here. Let's see." Dion took possession of the box and fiddled with switches and toggles, and still nothing happened. He crouched to check the plane itself. Some people walking by stopped to watch. On one spectator's advice, he snapped open the panel on the underside of the control unit. Sure enough, one of the batteries was in wrong. A hotshot he was no longer.

He sat on a nearby bench to fix the problem. Now a red light on the control box flicked on. He repositioned the plane on the grass and tried once more.

"It's pretty old," Bosko told him. "A friend loaned it to me. Arlo. He bought it at a garage sale way back when, and he's never flown it, but he assured me it's in running order. Of course, he could be wrong."

But Arlo was right, and the plane began to whir. Above Dion gulls wheeled and screeched, and on the footpath the chatter of the audience was friendly. The sun tried to break through the grey, and the wind was sharp and cold. He thumbed the throttle again, and the plane rolled toward him, gathering speed. He steered it away, ran it in a wide arc, into the wind. It would need a good thirty feet for liftoff. With a nudge of the controls, the plane nosed up. It lifted! He watched open-mouthed and ducked as it buzzed noisily overhead. He turned on his heels to follow its path.

They were airborne, and he was the pilot. He whooped in triumph. The audience clapped and cheered.

Above them all, a small silhouette against the blurry heavens curved in lazy circles. Once he got a feel for the thing, he tried a drunken loop de loop. He was considering a second loop-the-loop body-spin combo when Bosko appeared beside him. "Good job! Now for the hard part. Think you can land it in one piece? Not sure how Arlo would feel if I brought it back in a garbage bag."

"No problem. I think."

Gritting his teeth, he gave the plane another long, curving approach, throttled down and brought the craft thumping to the turf. It bounced, tilted, and landed on a wheel and a wing. He raced to check for damage, found none, and turned to give the thumbs-up. Bosko smiled, and the spectators clapped again and went on their way.

Bosko didn't take over the controls, as Dion thought he would, but instead picked up the plane and led the way back to the vehicles. "Arlo calls it a cheap knock-off," he said. "With a more expensive model and some practice, a person could really fine-tune his manoeuvres, do you think?"

"It would take a lot of practice, but a pro could land on a dime."

"Did you ever land on a dime?"

"Not even nearly," Dion said, still elated, forgetting that his past was supposed to be a blur.

"It's fairly noisy," Bosko said. "A lot louder than a drone, say. Probably audible for quite some distance."

"That's why flying clubs get stuck in out-of-the-way places," Dion said. "It's a noisy sport." Now that the fun was over, he was eying Bosko with wonder. "What's this all about?"

"Oh," Bosko said. "Sorry, I thought the word had spread already. I'm thinking in terms of Amelia Foster's screaming, lit-up bird. What d'you think?"

* * *

A radio-controlled plane as a murder weapon was a long shot, but Bosko wanted it checked out for feasibility, and a day trip was planned. Leith would head up the expedition, along with JD Temple, Dion being included for his plane-flying expertise, he supposed.

JD pulled into the viewpoint close to the Amelia Foster accident site, and the three of them left the car to study the geography. They looked along the highway and up the cliffside, scanning for a spot where the theoretical plane operator could post himself, or herself, to dive-bomb passing cars.

"There," Leith said, pointing. "It's the only place it could work. What d'you say, Cal?"

Up within the young forest was a scrubby crag, mostly hidden from passing vehicles by bushes and small conifers. "I guess with a small plane you could air launch from up there," Dion said. "Then land in this pullout. But it would take a lot of skill. And even then there's a big luck factor. The wind's got to be just right, and you'd better hope no vehicles are filling up the pullout when it's time to land. So if somebody did it with a plane, it couldn't have been premeditated. Had to be some kind of accident."

"If Foster's crash was an accident caused by an RC plane mishap," JD said, "then who chased down Rory Keefer and Craig Gilmartin?"

"A drone wouldn't need a runway, would it?" Leith asked.

"A drone doesn't scream," Dion pointed out. "Foster said the dead bird was screaming."

"But Craig said he heard a buzz or a whir."

"Drones make noise, too," JD said. "They … drone. Some are quite annoying. I've got a niece, and I can attest to how annoying drones can be."

Dion looked up at the outcrop. "A drone's more likely."

"Actually, my niece prefers her micro RC jet that screams bloody loud," JD said. "It's very fast, and agile, too, and I've seen her land it hard and fast in the grass at my feet. No long runway necessary. Not very big, but I guess if that came screaming at your windshield you might crank the wheel hard."

So the options were there.

"Go check it out, would you?" Leith said.

Dion and JD waded through dewy weeds and began the climb. At the top — about the height of a two-storey building — they balanced on the slippery, mossy rock face and surveyed the area below. Good view on the approaching highway, partial on the crash zone itself. Through the brush, Dion could see their black Crown Vic parked across the road, flashers blinking.

"That would have been nighttime, though," JD said. "Can you fly these things at night?"

Dion pointed at the pullout some distance down the highway, with its oversized lamp standards. "At least that section would have been illuminated pretty good."

A car appeared in the distance and drew close, giving a rough idea of timing, no more than twenty seconds from first viewing to when the vehicle blazed past. "The jet's probably already circling," JD said. Though they don't have great battery life. At least my niece's doesn't."

On their return to the base of the rock, Leith crossed the road to join them. "I couldn't see you up there."

"We could see the road and parts of the crash site," JD told him. "It would be tight, but like Cal says, with a lot of skill and a little luck, I guess it's possible. I'm actually starting to like this dipshit idea of Mike's."

Leith didn't look convinced. Dion wasn't going to say how unconvinced he was, or that this was nothing but a field trip for him. Almost as fun as flying planes by the sea.

But JD was rolling with the idea. "So let's say it's a micro jet. I stand up there, wait for the red Mazda to come into view in that patch of lamplight, then deploy. It swoops down. Mazda swerves and goes shooting into the woods. Meanwhile another car's approaching, also from the right, also southbound, and I just have time to bring the plane in. I drop down out of sight and watch a man get out of the teal-coloured car. That's Rory Keefer. A few seconds later another car approaches from the right — that happens to be an off-duty cop named Craig Gilmartin. Keefer flags down Gilmartin. I can't hear what's happening, because it's way down there in the trees, but I see both men go down to the crash site."

In Dion's opinion, the idea was already collapsing. In Leith's, too, by the look on his face. "And then what?" he asked.

JD frowned at the roadway as Leith advanced her scenario through to its conclusion. "Supposedly you're going to now follow Keefer to the Mini-Mart in Horseshoe Bay and kidnap him. Where's your car?"

"Crap," JD said. "Where's my car?"

There was nowhere close by that another car could have hidden, not that Dion could see. Gilmartin had said there were no other vehicles sitting on the road within view besides his own and Keefer's.

Leith went on killing the idea. "You just go crashing out of the bushes, do you, and jump on his tailgate as he pulls out?"

"I've got an accomplice," JD said. "We're in radio contact."

Leith shook his head. "No. The boss has blown this one. It's getting way too high-tech and unlikely."

"And anyway, what's the point?" JD agreed. "What's wrong with a good old-fashioned high-powered rifle? Or what's wrong with following the Foster girl, say, like he did with Keefer? Wait till she stops somewhere, throw her into the trunk, deal with her later. Who needs this fancy shot-in-the-dark RC business?"

Listening to the argument, Dion believed that both of them were missing the point. Not that he was getting it himself, but it was in there somewhere.

"And besides," Leith was saying, as they recrossed the highway back to the car, "even leaving aside the follow-up of chasing down Keefer, say you're out here in the bushes with your gizmo, and you successfully crash the Mazda. Then what? How do you get away? The crash happens, and pretty soon people are swarming all over the place, onlookers and ambulance attendants and police. Someone might have seen your gizmo gunning for the car, and you'd have them out beating the bushes looking for you. And look around." The three of them stood on the ocean side of the highway and looked around. "There's nowhere to run, is there? There's rock face there, ocean there, road there. You're cold and uncomfortable, you're terrified of being discovered, and the place is a beehive of activity."

"How about this, then," JD said. "Some A-hole on a bicycle was riding along here with his plane strapped to his rack. Stopped, decided to give it a run, did the deed by accident, then laid low, trembling in his boots, till the place cleared out, and made his getaway, followed by us jumping to wrong conclusions all over the place. The Rory Keefer killing is unrelated, a business deal gone wrong, something along those lines, and Gilmartin stepped on somebody's toes. Possible, right?"

They got in the car, Leith saying an A-hole on a bicycle toting an RC airplane along the Killer Highway in mid-December was such a remote possibility that he wouldn't bother putting it on the board.

"Fine," JD said. "I tried." She fired up the car. From the passenger seat, as they pulled away, Leith looked back at Dion, maybe as an invitation to pitch in. Dion had nothing to pitch, but he was still looking for that point he was missing. He leaned and tilted to look sideways and up — way up — at the rock face sloping over the band of trees, an almost sheer tower of stone blotting out the sky and casting this segment of highway in cold, almost perpetual shadow.

Twenty

FELLRIDGE

AT DEBRIEF, LEITH SAT through Jimmy Torr's report of nothingness. Little had surfaced about Rory Keefer. Though unemployed, he'd had a healthy bank account, but his wealth was explained by an old inheritance and wise investments. The mysterious Giorgio that Keefer's wife, Jo-Lee, had suggested as a lead was no lead at all. Inquiries in Stewart had gone nowhere, too. A friend of a friend of Keefer's thought he had mentioned getting a hold of some guns underground, but that too died as a single puff of hearsay.

Sean Urbanski reported that he had nothing much on Amelia Foster, either. She had worked for the last two years as a housekeeper in an assisted living facility in Lions Bay, but had recently been laid off and was job hunting. She had a minor criminal record — shoplifting — was openly gay, and eked out a shared existence with Tiffany Tan in a one-bedroom apartment on 1st Avenue. Tan had no criminal record, scraped by working in a produce store on Commercial Drive earning twelve hundred a month gross, and that was it. There was nothing more he could wring from her.

At the end of the Keefer/Foster debrief, Leith told the team about Bosko's scrapped theory involving an RC airplane or drone. The theory generated laughter and not much else.

* * *

Late that night Leith got a call from Craig Gilmartin.

"I've thought of something," the constable said. "I don't know if it's anything, but I was teaching Raj how to play chess when he said something that struck me."

Hoping it would be some breakthrough revelation, Leith grabbed pen and paper from his bedside table. "Yes?"

He heard only silence.

"Damn," Gilmartin said. "I've forgotten."

Leith flipped the pen in the air. Next to him, Alison laid down the novel she was reading and looked at him over her glasses.

"Sorry," Gilmartin said. "I was quite doped at the time. It seemed important."

"Retrace your steps," Leith told him.

Gilmartin tried. "I was playing chess by myself, and Raj came along. I was glad to see him. I'm going crazy in here — nothing to do but watch TV. He said he could only stay a minute. I told him to sit down and at least play a game of chess with me. I told him he could be white. He said he didn't want to be white, and he doesn't play kids' games." Gilmartin stopped to laugh, a raspy sound that didn't improve Leith's mood.

"It was so funny," the kid said, still tittering to himself. "I set up the board anyway, and was showing him how each piece moves, right? I'm going, this is a rook, he can only go straight, and this is a knight, he hops along like this, one, two, three, and so on, then Raj grabs the white king and it kicks my black king right off the board, and he says, 'This guy knows kung fu! Checkmate.'" When Gilmartin was done laughing, he said, "Where was I?"

"The white king knows kung fu."

"Right. Then Raj threw a packet of gummy bears at me and left."

"And that's it?"

"That's it."

"And somewhere in there is something important you wanted to tell me. Something to do with Amelia Foster. Something she said at the scene?"

"Man, I'm so sorry," Gilmartin said. "It's just gone."

"No worries," Leith said. "If it comes to you, call me right away. Good night." He banged the phone down, maybe a bit harder than called for, and rolled over to get a few hours' sleep.

* * *

In the morning, though he hadn't heard from Gilmartin with any update on his non-revelation, Leith went across to the hospital with Dion. The patient looked almost chipper, seated like an oversized child in pajamas on the edge of his bed, waggling his toes. He invited the men to unbury a couple of chairs and make themselves comfortable. "I touched these today," he said, pointing at his feet. "Well, not without the help of my rehab specialist. She made me do it."

"Good for you." Leith cleared a chair of magazines, a fruit basket, a dancing beer can, saying as he worked, "I'm not sure if you were talking in your sleep last night, Craig, but you called me with something important you'd remembered, but then you forgot. I'm hoping it's come back to you since." He sat down and waited.

"Oh, for sure it did," Gilmartin said, to Leith's surprise. "I'm sorry, sir. I should have called you, but it's nothing. It seemed like something at the time, but it wasn't. The problem is that I remember the conversation *surrounding* what it was, but not the *it* itself. It just didn't stick firmly in my mind, the name of it. Didn't stick at all, to be honest, which is the whole problem, I guess."

"Hold it," Dion said. "Back up and start over. I'm losing your *it*s."

"Like I said, it was nothing. When the fellow and I went down to see if the girl, Amelia, had survived, she was lying there trying to say something. I just can't remember what it was. All I remember is our response, which is what I was trying to remember last night." Gilmartin glanced at Leith, then addressed Dion again, as he was the one taking notes. "She said something — I think she told us to run away, or something — then said something else, and this guy and I said, or maybe I just thought it in my head, *What's she doing talking about kids' games?* Something like that. But I can't remember what the kids' game was."

Dion summarized aloud from his notes. "Amelia Foster said something. You talked about what it was she had said, or thought about it, and believed it was a kids' game she was speaking of. Have I got that right?"

"Yes. It was so depressing," Gilmartin said. "This girl bleeding to death in front of me and talking about kids' games, like maybe she was flashing back to childhood. Did you find the guy? You could ask him. Maybe he'd remember."

Leith didn't tell Gilmartin about Rory Keefer and his new home in the ether. He was trying to think of a game to suggest, to see if he could jog a memory, but Dion beat him to it. "Tag?"

"What, sir?" Gilmartin said.

"The kids' game, was it tag?"

"No. It wasn't tag."

"Hopscotch?" Leith said.

"Definitely not hopscotch."

"Cops and robbers?"

"It definitely was not cops and robbers, either."

Dion seemed to have run out of possibilities after tag, so Leith searched his early years for more suggestions. "Jacks?" he asked. "Snakes and ladders? Pin the tail on the donkey?"

"Nope, nope, nope."

"Hide-and-seek?"

He saw Gilmartin's eyes light up like two green Christmas baubles.

"That's what it was!" the constable cried. "Hide-and-go-seek! 'Hide,' she said. Not run away. 'Hide, hide.' And when I got closer, she said, 'Hide-and-go-seek.'"

* * *

Reflecting on Gilmartin's revelation, Dion believed it was a game of some kind, the whole thing, the dead birds and smashed cars, sheer cliffs, toy planes, hide-and-go-seek, the corpse in the woods tied to a tree — not just stabbed, but beaten with a rock. Some kind of twisted, sadistic, giddy, out-of-control game.

How the killing of Rory Keefer linked with the shooting of Gilmartin was too obscure to consider for now. One thing at a time. Crack one case, and the other will fall open, too.

When lunch hour arrived, he left the detachment for some off-the-record investigating. He drove to the Maplewood Conservation Area, thinking like a killer. He timed a hike through the woods — not a brisk walk, but hauling his imaginary victim through the dark, prodding him along, helping him up when he stumbled, all the way to the execution tree. From here he stood and took in the setting. Scary. His exhalations hung pale in the cold air. Remnants of crime-scene tape remained snagged in the bushes behind the tree. He walked forward and touched the bark. He turned his back to the tree, squatted down, and looked outward at the woods from the murder victim's eyes.

He was doing too good a job of being there, channelling Keefer, getting a hint of the man's horror. He was down on his rump, tied to the tree, the killer moving toward him. To be here, alone, facing the faceless … fill in the face, name the assassin, win the game.

"Local," he said, watching the killer approach with

knife in hand. He rose to his feet as the fear became too visceral and stepped away from the tree.

The killer was a local, and young, still a boy.

He thought of the red Mazda, and Bosko's scrapped theory, and the cliff that rose up opposite the dizzying drop to the ocean, and the answer came to him so abruptly that he said it aloud. "Fellridge!"

Fellridge was nothing but a gravel parking plateau, an offshoot of Cypress Bowl, a minimally controlled hump of mountainside veined with trails that people hiked or biked in summer and cross-country skied in winter. Some of its trails led to lookouts over the Sea to Sky Highway and the inlet waters where the ferries came and went. Maybe one of those lookouts was close enough to the highway that it could be used as a launch pad for a killing toy.

He could remember the area as though he and Looch were there yesterday. Now all he had to do was find it again, and then explain to David Leith how he'd remembered, with crystal clarity, something he should have forgotten in his supposedly murky past.

Twenty-One

HIGHER

December 21

AFTER REHEARSING HIS request a few times, Dion approached Leith to ask for permission to follow up a lead. *Keep it vague*, he told himself. Knowing Leith would ask the reason, he had rehearsed that part as well. "Just an alternative idea I want to rule out, up at the Mazda crash site," he said. "It's to do with Bosko's plane idea. I'll just look around, report back if it pans out at all."

"What alternative idea is that?"

"A possible vantage point the pilot could have taken."

Leith frowned. "You and JD scouted it out thoroughly."

"Not a hundred percent thoroughly."

"Don't go alone."

"No, it's nothing. I can handle it."

Leith called after him, "Remember, you have a counselling session at four."

Dion's second-to-last mandatory chat with Samantha Kerr. He had mentioned it to Leith earlier and then forgotten it completely. "Of course," he called back.

Down in the parkade he signed out a Suburban four-wheel-drive. He left the city northwest toward Horseshoe Bay, cruised through the hundred kilometre-an-hour speed zone, but instead of zipping out past the ferry terminal to the crash site, as Leith would be expecting, he took the exit ramp to Cypress Bowl and began the climb from gloom and rain into clear skies and snow-dusted roads. Close to the top he exited again, off the main road and onto a rough offshoot toward what he knew as Fellridge, a swatch of hiking and cross-country trails with views on the giant inlet waters of Howe Sound.

Fifteen minutes of slow and bumpy driving brought him to a good-sized parking plateau, where half a dozen winter-worthy vehicles sat, but without a soul in sight. He parked his Suburban and stepped out into a crisp stillness that promised more snow on its way. The last time he had set foot here, maybe seven years ago, the plateau had seemed smaller and the woods wilder. He walked along the main trail, looking for a certain path that would veer off in the direction of the ocean. *Great lookout down there*, Looch said from somewhere at his side.

He and Looch had been on mountain bikes. It was day's end, and others in the group had returned to the cars, but Dion cycled after his friend along an earthy trail.

"It won't be the same this time of year," Dion now said to Looch then. "The snow changes everything."

Hikers' tracks went before him in the whiteness. He walked for five minutes, then five more, and stopped in surprise when he recognized the small path that Looch said would lead to the amazing view. Just like it was those years back. He couldn't see any boot prints heading down that way. He was alone with Looch's ghost.

He started to walk, visualizing the viewpoint. It looked out westward on a span of ocean, but also, if he recalled, onto the highway not far north of Lions Bay, where Amelia Foster had crashed her car. Walking was a lot slower than cycling, and he adjusted his estimate accordingly. Surprised again, he found it exactly where he recalled it being. *Right here.* In his mind's eye, Looch dropped his bike, and he did the same, and they started single file down an even smaller trail, not much more than a dusty mule track weaving through boulders and scrub.

The path was now snow-frosted instead of dusty. It dipped away through the evergreen treetops and vanished. Dion gripped the jags of a stone wall as he found his footing, and Looch gave an encouraging shout over his shoulder. *Just about there! It's worth it, man. Top of the world.*

Another patch of woods, a thinning of the trees, a sudden falling away of terrain, and finally he stood on the brink, the prize Looch had promised. Back then he had looked out and whooped his delight at the view. He looked outward now at the same curve of ocean with the same sense of exhilaration, minus the whoop. He held his breath and looked down, and disappointment rushed in. He let out his breath with an obscenity. Not even a glimpse of the Sea to Sky. He'd been wrong. This wasn't the answer.

Anger welled within. At himself for believing, and at Looch for bringing him here and then abandoning him without so much as a *sorry, pal*. All that buildup for one mediocre view that wouldn't advance the case an iota.

He sniffed back his rage and tried to reason away the cascading sense of failure. The ocean continued to shine, blinding even under clouds. He was on top of the world, and so what that he'd killed his friend and was a fugitive from his own matrix? He hadn't been nabbed yet, and that was something to celebrate. He ground his heel in the dirt and told himself how grateful he was.

In grinding his heel, he noticed a path leading downward from where he stood. He followed it with his eyes. He wasn't dressed for mountain climbing, but it appeared fairly traversable. Maybe that was the answer. He hesitated, afraid to go on, and the fear had to do with serious falls and questionable motives. Then there was the sense of time running out. He looked at his watch.

He imagined the glory of success if only he could nail this down, the kudos he would get from the team. "Just make it quick," he told himself, and started down the slope.

* * *

A pretty girl sitting on the steps outside the detachment gave a friendly nod as JD started down past her. JD stopped in surprise. "Dezi."

The girl stood. Today she wore a bright blue parka, and underneath, the navy T-shirt with the RCMP coat of arms on it JD had given her.

"I'm just working up the nerve to talk to the lady at the front desk," Dezi explained. "I have a question about the application process, but she was really busy."

"Well," JD said, "I'm stepping out for coffee. C'mon, we'll see if I can help."

"Thank you! That would be great. I'm supposed to be at work soon, so I appreciate it. They're just really lame questions, and it's not like it can't wait, but I want to get as much lined up in advance as possible …"

They were walking now. "Where do you work, Dezi?"

"The pet supply store on 19th, plus I walk dogs on the side."

"So you're serious about taking this big step, are you?"

The young woman didn't leap to answer, but nodded reflectively. Which was good, JD thought. Life decisions like this should be approached with care, unlike her own flip of the coin. "I think I'll be good at it," Dezi said.

"I think you will, too."

"I just wish I was nineteen, like, now."

"Hey, don't ever wish you were older," JD warned her. "Time is a one-way street. And it gets faster as you go."

"I know that. My mom says so all the time."

"What does your mom think about you signing up?"

A cloud seemed to darken Dezi's eyes, but it rolled by and she was smiling again, pulling a face. "Mom thinks I'm absolutely insane to want to join the police. She thinks I should become an RN, like her. But she'll support me all the way, when it comes to it."

"Yeah? You get along with your mom?" JD asked. She wasn't a detective for nothing.

"Yeah, we're good."

But not great. "And your dad?"

"I don't actually have a dad."

"I'm sorry."

Dezi shrugged. She looked as if she was about to say something, but changed her mind.

Over coffee, Dezi asked not one question, but half a dozen, most of which JD was able to help her with. For the rest she offered resources that could be followed up on.

Only after they were back on the street did Dezi broach a topic that seemed to be worrying her. "Is family background very important for applicants? I've never been to church, and my mom and I yell at each other a lot, actually. Constable Leith says honesty is more important than anything, so I'm going to have to tell the recruiting officer. I'm working really hard to get along with my mom better, but still. Is that going to hurt my chances?"

"No, Dezi. Most families have their yelling matches." JD studied the girl's profile, again catching a glimpse of sadness. "As long as you're not getting physical with each other."

To her relief, Dezi burst out laughing. "No knives, no baseball bats, no flame-throwers. Not so far!"

As they walked along, JD realized she didn't want this to be goodbye. She liked Dezi's enthusiasm, and was enjoying her new role as mentor. *Who'd have thought?* "Hey, d'you feel like checking out the shooting range?" she asked. "I'm heading out in a couple days. I don't know how you feel about guns, but it's something you have to learn about sooner or later."

Dezi's eyes went round. "I can go with you? Is that

even allowed? Oh my god, yes! Yes, thank you, JD! That would be so awesome."

She smiled as she accepted JD's card with her number on it, along with one last piece of advice. "If things ever get rough, you tell somebody, all right?" Those shadows that sometimes darkened Dezi's eyes, like dips into sorrow, continued to worry her. She pointed at the card Dezi was still examining with wonder. "You tell *me*."

Dezi looked at her, not smiling, face so grave that JD expected her to divulge, confess, admit to something, plead for help. Instead, the girl grinned suddenly, waved, and turned to dash off to work.

* * *

The path had become nasty. Dion made his descent mostly sideways, sometimes feeling carefully for footholds, other times forced by gravity into a jolting jog. He was on one of those jogs when the world dropped away before him, and he skidded to a stop, the soles of his shoes starting a small avalanche of grit and pebbles. A quick back step and a low crouch, and he was safe. On all sides were small scrappy bushes and a few stunted pines, all enclosing a plateau large enough for a man to lie spread-eagle, but not much more.

The drop offered a promising view, though. On his feet again, he edged forward. Gripping the knot of his necktie, he stared down and gulped as he realized how close he had come to a free fall. Another inch or two farther and he'd be dead.

But now he was smiling broadly, because Looch hadn't failed him after all. Down there was the highway, a narrow strip snaking along the contours of the mountain. On the highway in both directions crawled cars and trucks, toy sized from here. Beyond the road, the ocean stretched across the horizon, speckled with small boats and big ferries negotiating the narrows.

He tried but couldn't pinpoint where he was in relation to the Mazda wipeout. Judging by the trajectory of the ferry he could see heading inland, Horseshoe Bay must be somewhere off to his left. But how far and at what angle he couldn't tell, due to the lay of the land. Would someone be able to attack cars with an RC plane or drone from here? Leith would have to talk to an expert, bring in a chopper, get some aerial shots.

Looking at the ground he stood upon, Dion saw what might be a path continuing downward into the brush below. Not a man-made trail, but some kind of jagged fault line, likely headed toward Lions Bay. It would need to be followed to its end, but not by him and not now. Other than that, the ground was made up of hard, wet rubble that would leave little in the way of footprints. Something black caught his eye, half-hidden in the dry grasses. He crouched for a closer look.

It was a small, round piece of black plastic, crushed and embedded in the grit, as if it had been stepped on, hard, and left to bake in place over the summer. Not a recent bit of debris, unfortunately, but interesting all the same. He snapped a picture with his phone, then used his car key to pry the object loose and marked the spot for follow-up with a triangle of rocks.

With the artifact pocketed, he retraced his steps back to his car, moving fast now with the wooded solitude beginning to weigh on him. Once on the level trail he began to jog. Twigs cracked in pursuit and he could see flashes of movement through the blackness of the trees. Reaching his vehicle, he jumped into the driver's seat, slammed the door against the dangers of the wilderness, and hammered the steering wheel in relief and triumph. The clock on the dashboard when he fired the engine reminded him of his missed four o'clock appointment, but he knew how to deal with it.

He switched the engine off again and phoned his shrink. He apologized, told her he had honestly forgotten, gave his excuse. It was a good one, unbeatable, one that would put her in her place: "It's just that I'm in the middle of investigating a double homicide here."

"S'okay." She sounded muffled, like she was eating. "I'll break protocol and slot you in after hours. Five o'clock. I'll see you then, hmm?"

"Why don't we just write today off," he suggested.

"Why don't you just come down at five," she suggested back.

He ended the call and drove downhill to the highway.

Five. That left him just enough time to return to the office, where he would let Leith know about the bit of plastic, once it was sealed, labelled and delivered to lock-up. If he had time — which was starting to look doubtful — he would describe Fellridge and the view, and suggest that aerial shots could best confirm or rule out the lookout as a possible extension of the crime scene, a place from which someone might possibly operate a radio-controlled plane to scare motorists off the road. He thought about how impressed Leith would be once he learned of this possible breakthrough. *Awed* might be too strong a word, but *admiring* was appropriate. He smirked to himself as he drove along, imagining himself on a pedestal. On the car radio the Heartless Bastards played, like a déjà vu of the road trip to Hope. This new song was slower, though. More introspective, even melancholy. Melencholy enough, as it played to its end, to nearly move him to tears.

* * *

At 5:15 p.m., in the company of Jim Torr, JD Temple, and the exhibit custodian, Leith stood at the counter of the exhibit room and looked at the bit of black plastic submitted minutes ago by Dion, who hadn't hung around to explain, but rushed off to his counselling appointment.

"Now, what could that be?" Leith asked his colleagues.

"I know what it is," Torr said, and asked JD, "Know what that is?"

"Sure, I know what that is," she said.

"Anybody can see what that is," put in the exhibit custodian. "At a glance."

Leith still didn't know what it was, and said so.

"Off the small end, by the looks of it," the exhibit custodian said to Torr and JD.

"Definitely off the small end," JD agreed. She looked at Leith and dropped him a clue he couldn't possibly miss. "The end you look through, Copernicus."

"Ah," Leith said. A binocular lens cap, of course.

Twenty-Two

RUSH

December 22

FOLLOWING THE MORNING briefing, Leith went over the Fellridge discovery with Dion once more. Using Google Earth and topographical maps, it had been determined that the lookout did indeed line up fairly well with the Mazda crash site. Still, Leith wasn't quite as pumped about the find as Dion apparently was. Maybe it was the wariness of his extra years of experience, but he suspected the new lead was likely nothing but an expensive tangent that had to be ruled out.

There was also the question of the new lead's mystifying source. Looking again at the Google Earth printout, with the crash site and the lookout both marked, he asked Dion how he had zoned in on that tiny bit of cliff. As far as he could see, it was all one unruly mass of wilderness. "So you've been there before, you say?"

Dion's story from last evening was sketchy. He repeated it now with almost word-for-word sketchiness: he had been hiking out there six or seven years ago, with friends, and discovered the lookout. On the printout he pointed at a small clearing higher up, with vehicles parked. "The trail comes off from right about here. You can't see it because of the trees."

His words had the ring of a false alibi, in Leith's ears. "Sure," he said. "Even as you tell it, though, the viewpoint you guys found is somewhere in here, Cal. But the place you've marked, where you found the lens cap, is down here."

"I went to the viewpoint, couldn't see the highway, so I proceeded downward till I found the ledge. You would have done the same."

Leith would have done no such thing. "So you got there through trial and error?"

"Memory." Dion was getting snarly. "An educated guess, trial and error, luck. In my opinion, the ledge is a possible launch pad, possibly approachable from below, as the path continues down. Might even lead to parking along the highway, maybe via Lions Bay. That'll have to be checked out. The point is, I'm getting things done, right? I'm doing my job. Am I on trial here?"

The heel-kicking didn't deter Leith. On the contrary. "How many times did you and Ferraro go up here, to this lookout?"

"Looch was up there before, I don't know how many times. That was my first time, when he showed me."

"Your first and last time there before yesterday?"

"That lookout, yes. And that particular trail, too, if that's what you're going to ask next."

As usual, Leith and Dion were doing a great job at failing to get along. Whatever divided them seemed built in and unfixable. It was chemistry, probably. But the iceberg tip of a murder investigation didn't help. "Right," Leith said coolly. "The North Shore is riddled with great hiking trails, so you guys had plenty of new places to explore. Every weekend a new trail to check out. Right?"

A pause while Dion considered the question. "We didn't go hiking every weekend."

"And you've only been there once before yesterday. Years ago. Your memory's pretty good, sometimes."

An even longer pause. "Sometimes it is," Dion said.

After a short wait, in case this was confession time — it wasn't — Leith let him off the hook and started to pack it in, thinking of the long, difficult day ahead. The exercise he was preparing for might have been a nice break from routine, if not for the many motorists he was sure to piss off. "Let's see if the crew is ready. I want to get this over with, fast."

* * *

Within the hour Dion was standing on the pullout on the highway, where the marked and unmarked police vehicles had congregated. There was also a civilian car, a white hatchback wearing reindeer antlers. To his right lay the strait waters, ferries and recreational boats that seemed to float in the chill. With some wait ahead of him, he studied the watercraft moodily. Bullshit was going to be his downfall, he realized. That same haze he had invented, that he so desperately needed, was going to envelop him. A year and a half ago he thought he'd been smart, covering everything off to investigators with *I don't remember*.

In fact he did remember, perfectly.

The mistake was not mapping out his memories. On paper. He hadn't studied up hard enough in those rehab days, as his memory came back like a defragging hard drive. It had come back fast and clear, with things he would rather forget. He had taken to sitting in the library at the hospital, his face still lumpy, head still patchily shaved from surgery, looking through psych manuals, the DSM and other textbooks, trying to figure out how best to fake it.

The memories were there, but not the intelligence, clearly. He hadn't realized how lost he would get without a spreadsheet to guide him. No, instead, in his endless discussions with cops and neuropsychologists in the days that followed, he had blurred up his past with reckless abandon. And now he couldn't get it back, not without raising flags and launching a re-investigation into the crash itself. *So, Cal, the fog is clearing — let's talk about Cloverdale, about the death of Luciano Ferraro, about what the hell you guys were up to out there at that time of night.*

Probably, the past was clearer to him than it was for most people. Pre-crash, at least. It was the days following that were murky. Swimmy. Vague. He had flipped the truth, and now keeping track of what he was supposed to have forgotten was impossible. How could he remember what he'd "forgotten" with his post-crash memory deteriorating? It was bad, and getting worse, not at all *excellent*, as he assured anyone who asked. Just another lie he had to keep under his hat at all costs, if he wanted to keep the job.

The dream of keeping the job was the source of his depression, he decided. *Depression is the gap between what you're wanting and what you're getting*. One day soon all his hopes and dreams would hit the wall in a messy explosion that would see him packed off, wearing the wrong kind of stripes. And then what? No choice but to follow in Constable Souza's footsteps and find some great height to jump off of. Even if it meant an in-cell hanging using prison PJs for rope.

He winced through flickering cold sunlight at the team milling about roadside, working out the day's strategy. Leith was doing most of the talking, his words gusting out in officious white clouds, inaudible from where Dion stood.

The civilian RC buff, president of the local flying club, was the owner of the reindeer-gag station wagon. He was being briefed separately by Corporal Paley. The antlers told Dion the buff must be some kind of ham. Dion's task was to take the ham and his plane up to the cliff ledge, and once there, keep him from falling. At the last minute Leith had assigned JD to accompany them, to make doubly sure the ham-president-buff did not fall, Dion supposed. As he watched Leith and speculated on his real motive for assigning JD, Leith turned and beckoned. They were all set to go.

* * *

The president's name was Tom Frey, and he wasn't hammy at all. Middle-aged and serious, in fact. Fairly quiet, too, until he got on the subject of RC planes and drones — then he couldn't seem to put a lid on it, talking possible and actual speeds, cost range, manoeuvrability, transmitters, receivers, rules and regulations, the whole nine yards. Dion wasn't interested, but JD seemed enthralled. It wasn't RCs she wanted to pilot through the air, though; it was herself. Her dream job was flying cargo planes up north, so she said. Dion had never believed she meant it; he had thought it was just her way of griping about the job. But now, as he listened to her chatting with Frey, he realized her interest was real, and it went beyond the need to escape. She actually wanted to fly.

Bad idea. Life was dangerous enough without leaving the ground, and he made a mental note to tell her so, talk her out of it, keep her close.

They were in the SUV making their way up the long, winding Cypress Bowl Road. JD drove, their expert in the passenger seat beside her, Dion in the back. Along with her general inquiries about flight, she made good use of the time, grilling Frey about other members of the flying community, any odd characters he might know. He knew a lot of the hobbyists, he admitted, and yes, there were some young men in the club he considered troubled. If it came down to it, he would name names to aid in the investigation, but only in a pinch. They were all friends, in a way. Family, almost, and he didn't want to tarnish anyone's name unnecessarily. JD said that was fair, and fell silent.

They arrived at the high-altitude parking lot and unloaded themselves and the plane Frey had selected as the most likely weapon, a small wedge-shaped fighter jet, light as a feather, in a custom-made sling bag.

"Doesn't look like much, and I'm not the best flyer in the world," he said. "But super dextrous, and it doesn't need a runway, if you know how to drop it. Which I do."

"And it screams?" JD sked.

"Does it ever."

The man continued talking about the technical aspects of flying to JD as she double-checked her supplies — water bottle, rope, radios — and Dion marvelled at how wholeheartedly people threw themselves into their hobbies. He wondered if he should try throwing himself into a pastime or sport. Yet there wasn't anything he could see himself becoming passionate about, beyond flying under the radar and staying out of jail.

He realized he had been staring at JD, and it now occurred to him why. Seeing her in avid conversation with somebody outside of her work realm really was the event of the century. He lifted his iPhone and snapped a photo of her in profile, evergreens in the background. He looked at the photo. It wasn't a good shot, but he liked it.

Maybe he should take up photography. If only to please Sam Kerr.

He stuffed his phone in his pocket and got to work looping sturdy cord around his shoulder. JD got on her radio to advise the ground crew where they were at. Silent now, the three of them struck off down the path, through the hushed and dripping December woods.

As they neared the shrubby upper lookout, Frey stopped in his tracks. "Look," he said, demonstrating how his boot heel slithered on the frosty path. "It's an ice rink. That looks like quite a drop-off we're heading for, and I don't see any railings. I thought we were going somewhere civilized."

"That's not actually the one we're aiming for," Dion told him. "It's down a ways."

"Has it got a railing? The guy in charge, what's his name, Leith? He said it was some kind of ledge, but he said it was safe."

"It *is* safe," JD said. She turned to Dion for confirmation, "It's safe, right, Cal?"

Dion could not, in good conscience, swear that the ledge was safe, and maybe Frey read the conflict in his eyes, because he said, "God, you people," and turned to head back up the trail. JD went after him, taking his arm and holding him in place.

Coward, thought Dion with a smile.

"We'll go slow," JD was promising their expert. "Holy cow, I've never met a pilot who's afraid of heights before. Where does that come from?"

"I'm not afraid of heights. I just don't overly care for them."

Slowly the three of them made their way down the treacherous path of crumbling rock and scrubby weeds. By the time they reached the ledge, the one that had almost pitched Dion to his death yesterday, Frey was breathing hard. JD asked him if he was okay.

"I'll be okay." Frey set down his bag. "I'm not as fit as I once was."

They stood as a group and stared down at the road. Frey made a brisk beckoning motion to Dion to open the bag and give him the plane. Dion did as told, then went about tying one end of the rope to a solid outcrop, the other to the steel rings of Frey's harness.

"I hope he knows his knots," Frey said.

"Like a Boy Scout," JD assured him.

JD was on her radio, communicating with Leith below. Dion watched the toy-sized traffic rolling to a stop, held up by city flaggers on either side of the stretch in question. A lone black car rolled slowly along the cleared section of road like a plane taxiing for takeoff.

"Now, look," JD told Frey, and pointed. "The guy driving the black car is a real dink, so don't hold back. You get a medal if you send him over the cliff. Okay?"

She smiled at Dion, sharing the joke, because the driver of the target car below was Jimmy Torr. Dion told her it wasn't funny. Even if Torr was a dink, a mishap wasn't out of the question, and nobody wanted to see Torr in a casket.

JD ignored him. "Look at 'em all," she laughed. The people below were mostly members, both uniform and plainclothes. More hands had made themselves available for this outing than needed. "Some kind of trip to the zoo, or what?"

JD didn't laugh often, but when she did, she pulled out the stops, and Dion couldn't help but join her. He was laughing at her laughter when Leith's voice came over the radio and sobered him with a sharp reminder to Frey that the objective here wasn't to hit the car, just take a swoop at it, please and thank you.

"Killjoy," JD said.

Frey was ready, and she radioed Leith to let him know. Dion watched through field glasses as Torr fired his engine and drove north a kilometre or so until he disappeared from view. A moment later the car reappeared, facing this way. He would be going at an average speed of ninety kilometres an hour, cruising westbound past the pullout with its light standards, along the strip of road where Amelia Foster had lost her life. Unlike Foster, Torr would be braced for attack.

Frey launched the plane like he was throwing a rock. Instead of falling, the jet screamed off into the blue, trimmed about like a hawk on the hunt, and dipped with breathtaking speed to the earth below. Even as it flew out of sight Dion could hear its fading shriek. He tried following with his glasses, but lost the darting speck, and focused instead on the target vehicle.

The first run failed, and there was a tense moment as Frey nearly lost the small plane, bringing it down in the limited space of the lookout. He apologized, explaining again he wasn't really top of the class with this particular model. "And I'm pretty good," he said. "Whoever did this thing, he had to be a master."

The crew below took a break. Traffic was allowed through before being cordoned off again. On the second run Frey did better. On the third he brought the plane swooping at Torr's windshield with speed and what looked like pinpoint accuracy. Dion tracked the black car with his binoculars, watched it swerve to an angled stop. A tiny Torr stepped out of the car swiftly and looked up with anger.

Even without binoculars JD had seen Torr's raised fist, and she slapped her thighs in childish delight. Dion didn't join her this time, because in the moment of the car's swerve, he had recognized within himself something unexpected and troubling. A spike of glee, almost a narcotic hit, almost a sexual rush. Could this be the thrill a killer experienced as he snuffed out a life? And had he felt the same thing back in Surrey, swinging his fist even when it no longer mattered?

Was he just plain bad? He looked up with a flinch. The clouds were full of ammunition. A gull coasted, eying the antics below. Frey's voice sounded both sharp and muffled in his ears. "Well? Was that okay?"

"He stayed on the road," was JD's answer. "Otherwise, perfect."

* * *

Down below, Leith, Sean Urbanski, and Jimmy Torr discussed the test results as the pissed-off drivers that had been held up for the last twenty minutes started streaming past. "Okay, so it's not impossible," Torr said. "Could be a random attack, some club of psycho weirdos with a new hobby?"

Leith nodded. "Tom says it would take a lot of air time to get this good. A drone is more likely and would take less practice, he says, but there's the noise factor. And the micro jet has more thrust. We'll have to keep an open mind. Remember, it's likely just a sport to them, and maybe they've done it before. Maybe the only thing that sets it apart this time is somebody died. And there were witnesses."

"So we're saying after the hit they had to eliminate those witnesses, make sure nobody was alive to say it was an RC that did it?" Torr asked. "These guys are total wack jobs, you're saying?"

"To put it nicely, yes."

Urbanski came up with a variation. "Maybe hunting down the witnesses was the object of the game."

Leith looked at him, marvelling both at the idea and Urbanski's ease in putting it forward. He frowned, trying to imagine this being a game to a person or persons unknown. If so, how long had it been going on? Was Amelia Foster the first, or just the first to stand out as a possible crime? He made a note to have the guys check the road reports, with an eye out for MVAs with any shadow of similarity.

Twenty-Three

RIPPLES

LISTS OF NAMES WERE stuck up on the case room wall: model-airplane club memberships from here to Chilliwack, and mail-order lists from all the local hobby shops. Leith had a battery of constables working on the lists. The shops were approached for canvassing, and all names on all lists were entered into the computer to see who pinged in PRIME-BC, the police information database. JD had sat down with the president of the flying club, Tom Frey, and as promised, he had given her some names of possibly troubled teens to look into. Frey also helped Leith understand the bewilderingly varied world of RC and drone flying.

By the end of the week Leith was at least passably familiar with the aerospace rules, the types of craft available, the parks and fields favoured by local hobbyists. He had flipped through the magazines. He had watched YouTube clips of planes doing backflips among stratus clouds, and drones speeding through obstacle courses. He'd gotten sidetracked watching trained eagles take down drones that posed a threat around airports. He knew some lingo, and more to the point, he had formed a fairly good impression of the breadth of the North Shore flying clubs' membership.

This was not the season for flying planes in the park, he knew. The clubs were more or less hibernating or flying indoors. "It's really summertime fun," Frey had explained. The age range of most enthusiasts was either early to midtwenties, or else post-retirement.

Done with flying objects for a while, identified or otherwise, Leith decided it was time to talk to Craig Gilmartin again, see if he had anything to add to his hide-and-go-seek statement.

* * *

Gilmartin was downstairs in the hospital's rehab centre, trying to straight-arm an insignificant-looking barbell to shoulder height as a therapist offered guidance. The therapist noticed Leith and Dion waiting in the wings and left them alone to talk.

Gilmartin lowered himself onto a bench and puffed out a breath. Leith sat next to him. "Looking good, Craig. I'm wondering if you've thought of anything new since we talked last. I hate to say it, but though your hide-and-seek is an interesting clue, it hasn't opened any doors so far."

"Nothing new to tell you, sorry."

"Maybe we can nail down the sequence of events that night a bit better, then. You were a little vague on it before." Leith brought out Gilmartin's statement from the night of the crash, put on reading glasses, and read from it aloud. "You said here, 'The guy went to call 911 and then I did too. I was waiting for the ambulance and some people came along and went away again.' See that?"

"I see that. Should be a couple commas in there."

"This is a police statement. We don't like commas."

"I don't talk like that. I put in commas. Sometimes I throw in a semicolon."

Leith carried on with the quote. "You're asked, 'How many people stopped after you?' and you said, 'Three.'" He looked at Gilmartin again. "If you remember it was three, you must remember a bit about each of them, right?"

"That girl without a phone would be one. Or maybe I didn't count her in there. I don't recall."

"Dezi arrived when you and Keefer were down in the ditch, right? And she left when you were up on the highway flagging down vehicles. "

"Keefer, is that his name?"

"Rory Keefer, we're almost certain."

Gilmartin eyed him suspiciously. "What happened to Rory Keefer? I have a feeling it's not good."

"It's not good," Leith admitted. "But let's not worry about that right now."

Gilmartin sighed. "I can't get it straight in my head, who came and went. We were up on the highway. The guy without a phone was gone, and the girl without a phone took off. Then a whale of a guy stopped, and wouldn't you know it, he had a phone! I told him to call 911, and he did, and I told him to stick around, but he didn't." He scowled.

"Right, we've managed to talk to him," said Leith. "What about after that?"

"Some foreigners stopped, a couple. They asked if they could do anything. I said no, and they left."

Leith asked for more particulars. Age, nationality?

Gilmartin was massaging his left bicep, the one that had been trying to raise the kilo weight. "They were fifty or so. I think they were Bavarian."

Dion had been more or less pacing as he listened, and now he stopped to ask, "The accent, you mean?"

"No, 'cause I don't remember them actually talking," Gilmartin said. "I just got this funny feeling."

"You got a funny feeling they were Bavarian?" Dion blared. "What, they were wearing lederhosen? What do you mean you got this funny feeling?"

"So maybe not Bavarian then, all right? Sue me. Anyway, that's all I remember. That's four, I guess, including the girl without a phone."

"Good," Leith said. "So to recap, you and Keefer are down at the wreck. While you're down there, Amelia Foster says something about hide-and-seek, or something that sounds like that. Right so far?"

"It's hide-and-*go*-seek," Gilmartin said. "You keep forgetting the *go*. But otherwise, right so far."

"Neither of you guys have working phones on you, and then Dezi arrives, and she doesn't either."

"Right. And like I say, I'm utterly mind-boggled by our mutual phonelessness."

"You and Keefer agree that Keefer should go flag down a car. He climbs up out of the ditch, leaving you and Dezi —"

"No," Gilmartin said. "Dezi left, too."

"I thought she left with you later, when you went up to the highway to flag down a car yourself, after you realized Keefer had taken off."

"Bastard," Gilmartin said.

"Keefer actually called 911 from Horseshoe Bay," Leith told him. "Maybe he couldn't get anyone to stop and decided the phone booth would be faster. But what about Dezi? This is the second time you've been unsure about when she left the scene."

"No, she was with me after Keefer left," Gilmartin said. "I remember her talking to me as we watched the cars whiz by. Other than that, I don't know. I was focused on Amelia."

"Of course. What did you and Dezi talk about? Did you tell her anything about yourself?"

"I might have told her I was a cop."

"Anything else?"

"No. It wasn't exactly a tea party down there."

"I know."

"I was a wreck."

"Sure." Leith gave the patient a careful, low-impact pat on the back and told him to keep getting better, and to call right away if he thought of anything else.

As they were re-entering the detachment halls, Leith said to Dion in a fit of temper, "For a while there I thought we were getting somewhere, but I'm lost. Amelia Foster, Rory Keefer, and Craig Gilmartin aren't connected. It's crazy. Amelia Foster startled into a deadly crash by an RC plane? Just because it's possible doesn't mean it's what happened. At this point we might as well add the whale and the Bavarians to the board, stir it up a little. Why not?"

Hearing silence, he turned and saw that he had been talking to himself. Not only had Dion not been listening, he was heading toward the stairs.

"What's up?" Leith called.

"Going this way," Dion said, and did so.

* * *

When the coast was clear, Dion headed back to the hospital. It was time to test out his theory, put it to Gilmartin directly, see if it jarred out the truth. If not, what then? Just let it lie?

No, he couldn't do that. It would be like noticing a ticking package in the basement and saying nothing. Unconscionable. He would have to push it all the way to its conclusion, and that meant first talking to Gilmartin. Depending on what happened there, he would then confront Poole in person.

He crossed St. Georges, and back in the hospital was told Gilmartin had returned to his room. He found the constable getting comfortable in bed with a book and a mug of some hot beverage. He didn't look pleased to see Dion. "You're back," he said. "More questions?"

Dion stood by the bed in a no-nonsense way. The visit was off the record and against the rules, and he didn't want Gilmartin to know it. "Not about Foster," he said. "About Tony Souza. We didn't want to put it to you downstairs, in a public space, this line of inquiry. Okay?"

"Okay."

Notebook out for a prop, Dion began his questioning. "You knew him, right? You went through training together. You both got posted to North Van at more or less the same time?"

"I knew Tony quite well," Gilmartin agreed. "But if you're going to ask me why he killed himself, I'm just as mystified as anyone. I can't help you out here. I wish I could." But he was a lousy liar, like a living mood ring, changing colour with his emotions. Now he was pink.

"Tony's private life, after hours," Dion said. "Beyond the roster. How did it seem to you? He ever talk about his problems? You seem like a perceptive guy. Ever read anything between the lines, Craig?"

Gilmartin was listening intently, his eyes never leaving Dion's face.

"What is it?" Dion pressed. "Whatever it is you know, you need to tell me."

"I have nothing to tell you, honestly."

Dion shifted gears. "You get along with Kenny Poole okay?"

The mood ring now lost colour, went pale. "I get along with Kenny fine. As did — as did T-Tony, far as I know. Why? What's Kenny got to do with anything?"

With the paling and stuttering, Dion's suspicions grew wings. Because he knew Kenny Poole, probably better than anyone. He knew what Poole was capable of. "Just between us, then," he said, and put away his notebook to prove it. "You've been to Kenny's place, right? His apartment just off Chesterfield?"

"Me? No."

"What about Tony? Did he go over there? To Kenny's?"

A long pause. "Might have."

"Might have, or did?"

"Him and some others went over there for a few drinks one night, I'm pretty sure. After shift. It was Ken's birthday, I think."

November 13, Dion knew, because he had celebrated a few of Poole's birthdays himself, over the years. November the thirteenth fell just days before Souza jumped.

"What others?"

"I really don't know."

"But later on, Tony told you about it?"

The questions were hitting nerves, no doubt about it. Gilmartin's eyes had widened, his body had become still as stone. "Told me what, sir?"

Dion let the silence stretch, still considering how much to say, how much to hold back. Leading the witness wouldn't be good, but it was time to give him a nudge. He switched gears again. "The night Kenny drove you home, after you got shot at down by the Quay, did he drive straight to your place from the detachment?"

"No, actually, now that you mention it," Gilmartin said. "He had to pick up something. From his apartment. It was on the way."

Bingo. "Yeah? What did he have to pick up?"

"A camera, I think. He'd promised to lend it to somebody, and he thought he might as well grab it now, since we were passing his place."

"Did he invite you up?"

"No. He was gone for all of two minutes."

Dion knew exactly what Poole had grabbed from his apartment. It was throwaway, and it was loaded. He said,

"You have a good idea what this is all about, and maybe you're not ready to face it, but I'm telling you, it's time to do just that: face the truth."

Gilmartin did not look convinced.

"If you're thinking about the repercussions," Dion said, "you don't have to worry about that. You can trust me. I'm one of the good guys."

"Well ..."

"So talk to me. I'm not writing this down, and whatever you tell me will stay lowest possible profile from here straight through to the end of the process, whatever that process is." He gave Gilmartin an official smile of confidentiality to seal the deal. "What we're doing right now is combining data, putting together a theory, that's all. You're not sure, and neither am I, and of course we don't want to get anyone in trouble unnecessarily. But that's not going to happen. What we need right now is something to work with. If we're wrong, the whole thing is flushed. We'll bury the sources. And we'll keep Tony's memory pure, whatever the outcome. Know what I mean?"

Gilmartin didn't seem to.

"You're not in any kind of trouble, either," Dion assured him. "But if you know something, or even suspect it, and you're keeping it to yourself for whatever reason, it's not going to help anybody. Not you, not Tony, and for sure not all the other recruits coming down the line."

He thought he saw Gilmartin roll his eyes, but couldn't be sure. "So far it's a cast of three, and you're one of them, and without your evidence there's no way justice can be served. Like I said, super-tight line of inquiry, mute button's on. But that makes it even more incumbent on you to talk, on your own. You know I can't lead you. I lead you, and anything you say is garbage. And we want to avoid warrants coming into this. You understand all that?"

Gilmartin sighed and sipped his coffee or tea. "Man ..." he said.

Dion leaned closer and forced eye contact. "If you put your mind to it, you can figure it out. If you think it's not possible, think again. You described the shooter to us. Even distorted by the glass, you can put a name to him. You think he won't try again? Who are you going to trust? Him or me?"

Gilmartin had frozen in place, now paler than his own bleached-blue pajamas. He whispered drily, "I sincerely don't know what you're driving at here. Sir."

"Do the math, then," Dion said. He backed off, dropping his business card on the bed. "Call me 24-7, when it clicks." And he walked out.

Twenty-Four

THE GHOST AND MRS. VLUG

December 23

DION WAITED IN THE DOORWAY to Bosko's office for Sean Urbanski to finish whatever he was telling the sergeant. "Money," Urbanski said. "There was more of it kicking around than Tan told us about."

Bosko looked up from what he was doing. To Dion, Bosko was a data machine who could shift seamlessly between cases, as if a gas station holdup in Deep Cove was on the same continuum as a suspicious drowning in the Seymour River and a counterfeit report from the Holiday Inn. But he didn't seem to be shifting along the continuum now; he'd had his full attention on whatever he'd been reading, and now he looked thrown by Urbanski's words. Disoriented. Not a machine after all.

"Amelia Foster and Tiffany Tan," Urbanski reminded him. "They put fifty percent down on a used camper van.

A Westfalia. They made two monthly installments on the van before Foster died, and now Tan can't keep up the payments, so the deal's been rescinded. So I'd say the funds were coming from Foster. Tan gets a return of most of the money and the dealer gets the Westfalia back." He handed over documents. "Bill of sale. Loan agreement."

"Quite a bargain for a Westfalia," Bosko said, reading.

"It needed work," Urbanski said. "Still, it's big bucks for these girls. I asked Tan where the money came from and she said it was a gift from her dad. I asked her dad. He says the most money he ever gave her was fifty bucks on her sixteenth birthday."

"You'd better talk to her again."

"Dave's sending somebody to pick her up."

"Good, thanks." Bosko went back to his report and Urbanski turned to leave, then turned back again for a last word. "Boss, I hope you haven't made New Year's plans yet. Come on over to our place for the countdown. Come early and join us for dinner. Ky has a whole stack of T-bones, and I do believe one of 'em has your name on it."

Bosko gave a thumbs-up but went about declining the invitation. "I'd love to, Sean. Except New Year's Day is also dim sum day. Long story, but kind of a tradition I've held with a friend from my last posting. I can't possibly break it."

"Some other time, then."

"Some other time."

"You, too," Urbanski told Dion as he brushed past, more an order than an offer. "New Year's, my place, be there."

He was gone, and Dion stepped into the office. "Everyone's busy," he said, "so I've been sent over with the update you were asking for."

"Great. Fire away."

"JD's been going through traffic reports for the Sea to Sky, and here's what she's got." Dion delivered the news in batches, challenging himself to avoid looking at his notebook for as long as possible between refreshers. It wasn't the most exciting memory game, but it had become habitual.

"On January fourteenth of this year," he began, "three people in a van went off the road in the same area where Amelia Foster crashed. Lost control, hit the barriers, and flipped into the sea. They were all in their early twenties, no survivors. The accident was put down to icy roads and inexperience, as the driver had only had his full licence for three months. We've faxed the particulars to the traffic analyst, Jay Comstock, and told him to revisit the file."

He checked his notebook. "On June twenty-first, also this year, a lady named Patricia Vlug reported that a creature flew at her windshield and nearly drove her off the road, in that same spot. Squamish detachment took the report and closed the file. They figured it was a bird. Nothing came of it."

"And she survived to tell?" Bosko asked. "Fabulous. Does she still live in the area?"

Dion nodded. "Leith and I are heading out to see her pretty soon."

"Thanks, Cal. Let me know how it goes."

Bosko returned to his original file. From where Dion stood, he could see the photograph of an infant on an autopsy table, battered beyond repair.

* * *

Patricia Vlug was a frail woman who looked about a hundred years old. She lived on her own in a small ground-floor apartment in Deep Cove with a lot of houseplants, canaries in cages, and a free-roaming purple budgie that flapped by Dion's face and startled him.

He and Leith were ushered into her living room — or conservatory, it felt like — and they sat side by side on a hard brocade couch overcrowded with throw cushions. Leith tried to open the discussion with his first question, but Mrs. Vlug interrupted with a statement: they must have tea. So off she went to put on the kettle.

Some minutes later they each had a cup of fragrant tea in one hand — Darjeeling, she said — and a biscuit in the other, and Leith was able to get to the point of their visit. "It's about a report you made to the police this summer, Mrs. Vlug. An incident on the Sea to Sky Highway?"

She nodded. "I remember it well. The police were quite pleasant, but they didn't believe me." She directed her next comment at Dion. "I didn't insist, you know. If you start insisting, they call you mentally unstable." She gave a lively finger snap. "Lock you up." And to Leith again, "Do you want to hear what really happened?"

Leith gave her a sporting grin. "Why not?"

"Has it been back?"

"It's possible."

She nodded as if this confirmed her worst fears. "It was a dead man," she said. "That's what I told them. Not a bird. A little dead man in a flowing white gown, with a skull and skeleton hands out like this, and long white hair. He appeared at the passenger-side window of my Mini Cooper and followed along, howling at me."

"Howling, like how?"

"I'm afraid I couldn't repeat it for you."

"A long, steady howl, or high-pitched, or intermittent, or —"

"He was speaking in devil's tongues."

Something muttered a question close to Dion's left ear, and he turned to stare into the beady black eyes of the purple budgie, perched on the sofa back behind him.

"Percival," Ms. Vlug snapped, "don't bother the boy. Shoo!" She clapped her hands. "Bad bird! Budgie soup!"

Dion covered his teacup with a hand as the bird flew away. Beside him Leith asked, "And what happened next, ma'am?"

"It was a foggy night," she said. "My sister Margaret had just had a fall where she lives at Skyview Manor — that's assisted living — in Lions Bay, and I needed to drive out there to see she was all right. Even with all the upgrades I'm not comfortable on that road, not at night, not in the fog."

"Who is?" Dion said.

She nodded at him and went on. "Well, I missed the turnoff and had to drive some distance to get turned around. Then as I was nearing Lions Bay again, the little dead man just came down from nowhere, flew at me and startled the living daylights out of me, then flew away again before I could say Jack Robinson. I started to slow down, but I didn't quite stop, and then he came at me again, alongside the driver-side window this time, following me as I drove, his head going back and forth, back and forth. And then he disappeared upward, then came right at my windshield, grinning like a banshee and speaking in tongues." She made a noise in her throat, what sounded to Dion like a fairly good imitation of an angry swarm of bees. "I was sure I was going to hit him."

"What did you do?" Leith asked. He was seated forward now, staring at the tiny woman in wonder. Dion found himself staring, too, picturing the scene: a lone woman in her Mini under attack on a lonely, dark road overhanging the crashing sea.

"Well, I pressed on the gas and kept going straight," she said. "I don't know why I pressed the gas. I suppose I should have stopped, instead, but I was sure he would come at me if I did, and perhaps even get inside the car, somehow. Mercy, but I was frightened."

"I can imagine."

"More tea, Mr. Leith?"

"No thanks, ma'am."

"And you, child?"

Dion raised his brows. "No, ma'am, thank you."

"I would have preferred to smash him to bits," Mrs. Vlug went on, refilling her own cup a little unsteadily.

Dion sat up straighter and crossed his arms. "But?"

She nudged her eyeglasses. "At the last minute he flew upward and disappeared again. And I kept going. After a minute or two I was more angry than frightened, and let me tell you, I had half a mind to turn around and go back and just confront the little brute again, and this time I wouldn't stop until I'd knocked him to the ground and driven him flat. That's how angry I was. But I went to town instead and reported it. I still regret that. They told me it was a bird. A bird! As if I don't know birds from ghosts."

Twenty-Five

WINGS AND THINGS

ON THE DRIVE BACK TO North Vancouver from Deep Cove, Leith's phone rang. Dion listened to this side of the call, most of it monosyllables. On disconnecting, Leith said, "JD's out in East Van trying to bring in Tiffany Tan."

"What for? The money?"

"Yeah. Tan and Foster could hardly pay the rent, yet all of a sudden they were buying a van. We want to know where they got the steady flow of cash. Tan's at work, though, and refusing to leave. She says she'll come in at 5:30, but I'm thinking I'll make things easier for everybody and go see her myself. Want to come along? Child?"

"That lady was two hundred years old. We're all children to her."

"She didn't call me child."

"You're more of a lad."

They were both grinning, until Dion remembered his upcoming final counselling session, and the knot in his gut tightened. As useful as Sam Kerr's investigation into his psyche had been, he dreaded their conversations. "I have to be back by one."

"We can make it."

It had been a while since Dion had last crossed the bridge to Vancouver. The bigger city had once been a hub of fun to him — nightclubs, shopping, music festivals, the PNE. He focused on the present to shrug of the past, and took the Trans-Canada to East Hastings, Hastings to lively Commercial Drive. He managed to find a parking spot not far from the supermarket, and he and Leith completed the last block-and-a-half stretch on foot.

Inside the supermarket, in the vegetable section, they found Tiffany Tan misting broccoli with a hose. She didn't stop spraying when Leith asked her to take a ten-minute break to speak to him in the privacy of the store manager's office. The manager, he told her, had already given the okay.

"Here's good 'nuff," she said.

So Leith explained what he wanted to know. "Just where the money for the van came from. That's all. It's a simple question."

"Gift from my dad. Like I told the Viking."

"The what?"

"Constable Sean Urbanski?" Dion said.

"Sounds right," Tan said.

"If we have to speak to your whole family, and Amelia's, we will," Leith told her. "We'll find out in the end in any case, but not without a lot of trouble for everybody across the board, which I'm hoping to avoid here with your help. I don't think you're telling the truth, and I have to follow up. That's all."

She shrugged and sprayed a tray of carrots, then moved down toward the celery, bok choy, radishes.

Leith turned to Dion. "Could you go wait in the car? I'll just have a word with her."

Back behind the wheel, Dion put on his dark imitation-Porsche sunglasses and watched people passing by. His own line of inquiry, which in retrospect was beginning to feel less likely, held nothing but silence and doubt. Gilmartin had not called him to admit that he knew Ken Poole had assaulted Tony Souza and/or invaded Gilmartin's home and shot him point-blank.

Maybe, even if he was right about Poole, he should assume he wasn't. Drop the investigation. It would be so much easier. But the consequences ... Ken Poole, free to take advantage of other young officers. If Dion was right about all this, it meant Poole was losing his grip. Maybe next time the victim of his abuse would disappear.

He closed his eyes behind his dark glasses, and didn't open them again until Leith returned.

"It seems Foster supplied the cash," Leith said, buckling in as Dion fired the engine and joined traffic. "Tan got the feeling Foster wasn't altogether up front with her. She'd go away for a day, not on a regular schedule, but about once a week, and come back with fun money. She wouldn't tell Tan what the deal was, but it seems the cash was enough for the down payment on the VW — about four hundred a month."

Dion looked at Leith with new respect. "You're not wet. You got all this out of her, and she didn't once spray you?"

"My charm, I guess. There's something else. Even with the money she was bringing in, Foster was depressed, Tan says. She doesn't know why."

"Sounds like she was selling herself."

"Sounds like it," Leith agreed.

They crossed the bridge in silence, but for one observation that wouldn't go into either of their reports: "She's torn up, you know," Leith said. "Tiffany. They were close."

"I know," Dion said. "I got that."

* * *

Today, in their last forty-five-minute session, Dr. Kerr spent much of the time giving Dion space to talk. When he ran out of things he thought she wanted to hear, she told him some things she mistakenly thought he wanted to hear. About isolation, self-awareness, endogenous and reactive depression. Dependencies and addictions, the chemistry of the brain, electrolytes, trigger points.

He fiddled with his key chain, his heart thudding. Eleven minutes left.

She talked about being honest and overcoming the fear of self-expression. Perhaps try a creative outlet, like painting, she suggested. He said he was doing some photography. And in a way, he was. Since his bad shot of JD on the cliffside, he had taken a few street shots, two of which he had saved into a folder on his laptop. One was a small dog yapping at him by the Starbucks, and the other was a man on a bicycle half disappearing out of frame. All were blurry, none fit for an art gallery, and he didn't know why they mattered.

Kerr was interested, but he told her it wasn't anything to speak of. She gripped the edge of her desk as if winded. "Is there anything you want to say, then?" she prompted. "Anything you want to talk about in particular? Sports, cars, anything?"

"No," he said. He made sure to infuse deep satisfaction into his next words. "I feel like we've come a long way. You've taught me a lot. I feel pretty strong. Pretty good. This has been useful. Thanks."

She gave him a leery stare. She extracted a sheet of paper from her file drawer and started circling items from a list of titles, telling him he should read more, find bridges with the rest of the world, perhaps through literature — poetry, fiction, biographies, essays. "The world is full of heroes," she told him, "and the most immediate form of connecting with those people, other than face to face, is through the written word. You should try it sometime."

He took the list from her, folded it into a pocket-sized square, and looked at his watch. Time served. He was done, but for the bottom line. He couldn't resist asking, hoping to get it over with. "Are you going to tell me the verdict now?"

She looked at him in surprise. She had put on reading glasses to examine a form in front of her — probably his progress report with its blanks to be filled — but she laid a palm on the paper now. "There is no verdict, Cal. You're not on trial."

"I totally am on trial," he said. "If you think I'm not fit, guess what the sentence will be."

"We're not there yet."

"I hope you round your figures up, that's all." He stood.

She sat back in her big chair and stared at him. "We've spent a cumulative eight hours together, and it's only in the last sixty seconds you open up to me like this?"

"I've been as open with you as I can be."

Too offended to bother answering, she started writing, and he wondered if, with his one stupid question, he had just blown all his hard work of being good. He was dismissed, verdict pending.

* * *

Late in the afternoon Dion went with Leith to Wings and Things, a hobby store in West Vancouver. Leith told him the place had been recommended by the president of the flying club, Thomas Frey.

Dion was not hugely interested. Murder by RC had become a sideline, to him, a distraction, a red herring, a false lead, and he was here in this hobby store just keeping Leith company.

His suspicions about Poole still oscillated, depending on his mood. Or the time of day. In the middle of the night he tended to believe he was right, while in the light of day the doubts crept in. But if he was right, then Amelia Foster's crash had nothing to do with the hole in Craig Gilmartin's clavicle. Gilmartin and Rory Keefer were two different storylines connected only by a chance encounter on the highway. Dion had Amelia Foster's storyline worked out, too, and it was nothing to do with mini RC fighter jets or drones. She had a mysterious secret life, maybe sex related, as did Rory Keefer. Maybe hide-and-go-seek was the code name for their get-togethers, and Keefer was paying her. Then something went wrong. He had ended up chasing her down the highway and, either by accident or design, he had killed her. Keefer had then been killed in revenge for Amelia's death by somebody else who had been involved.

Highly speculative guesswork, of course, but workable. Foster and Keefer were one package, Gilmartin another, and the fact they got combined was nothing more than a mix-up at the post office.

As for the potshot taken at Gilmartin down by the Quay, Dion decided that it was exactly what everyone had thought at the beginning, a random shot. But it was a random shot that had provided Ken Poole with the smokescreen he needed for a second, fatal shot. Then blame Gilmartin's death on some faceless hit man. Perfect.

Yes, for sure, the plane-as-weapon theory was nothing more than a flight of fancy, and the Squamish detachment had gotten it right that Mrs. Vlug had been frightened by a bird.

Dion looked around the hobby shop with interest as he and Leith waited for the bald man behind the counter to finish dealing with the few browsing customers. He was only along for the ride, but it was a nice enough ride. The place was stacked and stuffed with product and had an oily smell, like an automotive aisle. There was a counter lined with fat, well-thumbed catalogues, paint pots and lacquers and solders on shelves, a balsa wood rack, cabinets filled with miniature gadgets. He looked upward. Bright kites and gliders were strung overhead, and off to one side, solar-powered things wobbled and spun. The door jingled, the other customers were gone, and the bald man was looking their way. "Yes, gentle-men, can I help?"

The man's name was Farzin. Leith told Farzin what he was interested in: clientele. "Do you have a mailing list of any sort to keep track of enthusiasts who, say, want to know about the latest lines in any particular field — like remote-controlled micro fighters?"

"In what?" A cupped ear. "Sorry? What did you say?"

"Remote-controlled —"

"Never heard of such a thing," Farzin said. He waited a beat, then asked, "Maybe you're meaning radio-controlled?"

"Sorry," Leith said insincerely. "I've had a crash course in all this, but that's one thing I must have missed."

"I'm pulling your leg. Call it whatever you want. But *RC* usually means radio-controlled, just so you know."

Leith smiled. "As you can see, I have a lot to learn."

"We all do, sir," Farzin said. He plonked on the counter a heavy binder that he said contained the names and phone numbers of people who put in special orders, along with the parts and purchase order numbers. "Goes back for as many pages as the book will hold. Then I throw away."

Leith thumbed through the loose-leaf binder full of grubby lined paper. At his side, Dion saw handwritten names, numbers, a column of codes.

"Wow," Leith said.

"That, for instance" — Farzin pointed to a five-digit entry dated two years back — "is a ball-shooter assem-bly for a 1981 Solar Fire pinball machine. I have contacts worldwide when it comes to special items like this."

"You also have a great memory, which makes my job a lot easier. But I've got a general question for you first." Leith described Mrs. Vlug's devil-tongued ghost to Farzin, and asked if a plane or a drone could fly about dressed up like that.

"Well, a drone for sure," Farzin said.

"You could dress up a drone like a ghost and make it hover at will, from quite a distance?"

"Of course."

"Could you do the same with, say, a micro RC jet?"

"Much more likely a drone. And you say it made a sound like a swarm of bees? That's definitely a drone."

Leith directed a sigh at Dion, who read his thoughts. Their trickster's MO was getting complicated.

Next Leith asked if Farzin had any RC or drone customers specifically interested in outfitting their machines in disguises. Farzin said none sprang to mind. Did he have a lot of repeat customers? Of course. Did he know any of his RC/drone hobbyists by sight? Of course.

"Don't have a mailing list or anything like that, for ads or newsletters aimed at your RC crowd?" Leith asked.

"No, sir. Do I look like I have time for newsletters?"

"Could you maybe go through the latest entries in this book here and tell me if you can match any of these names with RC airplane buffs? I'm especially interested in a year-round customer."

Farzin pored through names till he came upon one entry that made him smile. "This guy comes in quite frequently. Really friendly, nice guy, could talk your ear off."

Dion took down the particulars anyway.

In the end Farzin gave them nine RC fanatics to check out, mostly first names only. "Is there anybody on this list who strikes you as, well, eccentric?" Leith asked.

"They are all eccentric. It comes with the territory."

"But anyone who stands out in your mind as being just a little more off than the rest, say? We're looking for someone who's maybe using his or her plane to cause serious mischief in the community. I'm afraid that's about all I can tell you."

"Serious mischief." Farzin raised an eyebrow. "You will want to look at Lefty Duggan, for sure."

"I'm not surprised," Leith said, "with a name like that."

"I had forgotten about him. He used to come in here a lot, last summer. Flash big wads of cash, irritate the other customers. Wanted the best of everything for his planes, got mad if something was not to be had."

"Did he ever say anything to alert you that he might be up to something illegal?"

"No, no. Just had *bad* written all over him."

Dion thought Lefty sounded too good to be true.

"Came in here alone, did he?" Leith said.

"As far as I can recall."

"How old, approximately?"

"About seventeen, eighteen."

"Any idea what his real name is?"

"I have no idea, sir. I'm sorry."

"Anything else you can tell us about him?"

"Well, he's left-handed for sure," Farzin said with a wink.

Twenty-Six

SWERVE

December 24

LEFT-HANDED LEFTY DUGGAN was a disappointment, a rude youth whose worst crime was arrogance. The kid came across as rotten enough to be a thrill killer, but Leith discovered he had an alibi for the night in question, namely Europe.

The Duggan lead was ditched, and Leith and the team began pounding the pavement, making calls, checking out the nine names on the list — or the two hundred and forty-eight names, because the nine from Wings and Things were simply pooled in with the rest of the RC community — the many club members and subscribers to RC magazines and web pages.

The list was whittled down first through checks on the computer, bringing those with criminal records to the top. Some leads were followed up, others weeded out after a phone call or two. By the end of the week, eighteen names remained, with a focus on five, all male, between the ages of sixteen and thirty-three. All but one of the five had a record which might reflect an anti-social personality. All had been questioned once, and none had a credible alibi for the night in question. Leith divvied the five names amongst his team for some intensive follow-up and sent them on their way, hoping for results, but by no means holding his breath.

* * *

JD was assigned a couple of names in the Blueridge area, one of them a Perry Javits, nineteen years old. He'd had some scrapes with the law, but minor stuff. The front door of the home opened to JD, and a wheezy little woman with a red face looked out at her. "Perry's on the living room sofa," she said.

In a living room with an enormous fake Christmas tree, Javits was sprawled on the sofa watching a TV show, the loud, violent action-adventure kind of bullshit that was rotting the minds of youth across the nation. Javits looked at JD with incidental interest, but didn't bother to unsprawl or to mute the noise. He was a long-haired brat, big for his age, his face still filled out with baby fat, but dusted with peach fuzz. He wore an earring, T-shirt, nylon workout pants, and nothing on his feet but mismatched socks. He was chewing gum.

"Could we talk?" JD said.

The brat uncoiled, shut off the TV, and answered her questions. He had a thirty-four-inch Delta Ray RC plane, but no longer ran it. "Too much screwing around, so I quit."

"When's the last time you ran it, and where?"

"Deer Lake, Burnaby, last summer."

"Recall what you were doing on December fourteenth and fifteenth of this month?"

"Nope."

"What if you thought about it for a minute, hey?"

Javits thought about it for a minute, chewing his gum, but still couldn't remember.

"Any chance you were travelling around the Sea to Sky Highway in the early morning hours of the fifteenth, out past Horseshoe Bay?"

Javits shook his head. "Why would I be *anywhere* in the early morning hours?"

"Who did you fly it with, Perry?"

"Why?"

For the tedious process of corroboration, JD thought. "Because I'm asking," she said.

"A pal, I guess."

"What pal?"

"Don't you need a warrant for this crap?"

"Not for a few simple questions. What's the name of this pal of yours?"

"We don't hang out no more."

"My condolences. What's his name?"

Javits seemed to think about it. "John Smith."

"Okay, how about the real name?"

Javits shrugged. "Fine. Scott Mills."

"Look, you —"

"That is his real fuckin' name!"

Satisfied by his outrage, JD jotted down the name, along with the last known cell number Javits managed to find for Mills.

"I'm going to talk to your mom alone for a few minutes now," she said. "I may have more questions for you later."

Nervously, Mrs. Javits told JD what she knew about Perry's plane-flying hobby, and what she said jibed with her son's account. He had been avid about the sport for a couple of years. Used to pile into the car with a friend of his — sure, Scott was the name — and head off to go flying.

"Just them two?"

"Well, and Scott's girlfriend," Mrs. Javits said, and for the first time she smiled. "Cute kid. Wish Perry would get a nice girl like that, instead of ... well."

JD pursued the "instead of" for a while, but it seemed Mrs. Javits didn't want to talk about Perry's love life. She did recall the nice girl well, though.

"Dezi. Don't know her last name."

Dezi? JD bottled her dismay. "A local girl?"

Mrs. Javits didn't know that, either.

JD called Leith as she walked down to her car. The case, she told him, had just taken a swerve.

Twenty-Seven

SUGAR AND SPIES

IN LIGHT OF JD'S INFORMATION, Leith called a meeting. The detachment had a wistful, closing-time, Christmas Eve feel, as though nobody was 100 percent present. "I have a feeling this is going to be a long night," he said when JD finished relating what the Javitses had told her. Perry Javits was only peripherally of interest, but there was a new name on the board, Scott Mills, and Mills was only of interest because of the name pinned up next to his: Dezi Novak.

"Look, before we jump the gun," Leith told the group, "all we have right now is a young woman who has been connected to a man who is interested in RCs."

"A girl connected to an RC flyer," Sean Urbanski said, "a girl who magically appears at the scene of a crime — likely to be murder by RC. That's pretty big."

"Yes, but Novak came in of her own accord," Leith said. "She volunteered her statement. We wouldn't have known her name if she hadn't come forward. Thoughts, JD?"

With her lean body, short brown hair, and seeming contempt for cosmetics, jewellery, and frills of any kind, JD sometimes got mistaken for a guy. She didn't seem to care. Only her voice gave her away, at least when she made an effort to sound pleasant. But it seemed to Leith she had spruced herself up lately. Maybe it was new trousers and a sweater, or something. Or a more stylish crewcut? In any case, she now leaned forward in her chair, warily eying the group of men as if waiting for insinuations to start. "Thoughts?" she echoed.

"You seem to get along with Novak. You were saying you even took her to a shooting range a few days ago. Possibly, you've got more insight into who she is than any of us here."

"She seems like a good person," JD said.

"So did Susan Smith, I bet, when she wasn't murdering her kids," Urbanski said.

Leith ignored him. "So the tour of the station and the shooting range — is that the extent of your association, JD? Or is there more?"

"That's about the extent of our association," she told him. She had crossed her arms and was regarding him coldly.

He pressed her for more, a rundown of all conversations she'd had with the girl.

"As you know, she's interested in a career in the force," JD said. "That's about all we've talked about. She asks me about the job. Application advice and whatnot. But not like she's trying to figure out some way to get inside and plant a bomb. She's enthusiastic and she's genuine. Doesn't mean she can't be a criminal as well, but I doubt it. I really do."

"Did she pull off any shots at the range?" Torr asked.

"As my guest. I gave her some instructions, and with permission and oversight, she pulled off one shot. She didn't land a bull's eye, but it made her day anyway."

Leith was thinking that if JD was male, questions about sexual impropriety would be buzzing through his mind now. But this was JD, who was just being a mentor to a hopeful recruit, and what was wrong with that? "Have you made plans to see her again?"

He could tell the question made her uncomfortable. Maybe she had inappropriate feelings for the girl, or maybe she was painfully aware that everyone in the room was likely thinking that very thing. "No, but she's got my phone number," she said. "My thinking was, if she wants to adopt me as her big sister, that's okay by me. I'm not so sure about that now."

Leith nodded. "You'd better keep your distance till we look into this further."

"I'm one step ahead of you there," JD said with a grimace. "My search on her came up empty, by the way. No direct hits, no flagged associations. Also, if she really is, or was, Scott Mills's girlfriend, she failed to tell me about it."

Leith was relieved to change the subject, and addressed the room at large. "Let's turn up whatever we can on Scott Mills, then. Re-interview Perry Javits. Get an address on Mills, but don't get in touch yet. Also give Craig Gilmartin and his family a discreet warning about both these individuals, Mills and Novak."

After the meeting concluded, a meet up at Rainey's was talked about, along with the subject of chipping in to buy Craig Gilmartin a welcome-back-to-the-world gift, as he was being released from the hospital on Boxing

Day. Leith remained seated, distracted by his upcoming task. How would he arrange to investigate a wholesome young woman like Dezi Novak?

JD sat down beside him, and he looked at her.

"If you're thinking there's anything going on between me and Dezi, there's not."

"Okay," he said.

"But I have to tell you something, and I feel really bad about this. I did get closer to her than I should have. She looks up to me, like I'm some kind of superhero. It went to my head. Pride — it's one of the deadly sins."

Leith laughed. "I'd hardly call encouraging a young person —"

"It gets worse," she interrupted. "She knows where I live. When we were driving out to the range, I kind of stupidly pointed out my apartment building to her. Total lapse of judgment. So what do I do if she gets in touch? Or worse, shows up on my doorstep?"

Leith raised a eyebrow. "You think she will?"

"Maybe. Christmas is just around the corner. I wouldn't be totally shocked if she decided to give me a present. We talked quite a bit about personal stuff. I have the feeling she doesn't get a whole lot of affection at home. Her mom is single, and always dating guys who get distracted when Dezi's around."

Leith got it, and nodded. He was thinking about the options and the consequences of using JD's friendship with Dezi to learn more about the girl. "I don't know, JD. If you're willing, it could be useful. Sounds like she's opening her heart to you. Want to carry on, see what comes of it?"

He could see that JD was already steeling herself against the ugly task. "I don't like it," she said. "But I'll do it. As long as you okay it with the boss."

"I'll ask him," Leith said. *Poor JD*, he thought, looking at her profile— chin up, but with disappointment in the lines of her mouth. *The one time she lets down her guard, it turns into a sting.*

Doug Paley joined them at the conference room table. He had done a few computer inquiries into Scott Mills, Dezi's boyfriend. Mills was not on the hobbyists list, but he did have a record, going back three years. Assault.

"Aggravated?" Leith asked.

Paley shook his head. "Plain assault. Got probation and a no-contact order from a chick. Maybe nothing, but I'm definitely interested in this guy."

* * *

JD hauled bags of groceries up to her apartment, one in each arm, like two unwieldy children. On reaching the third floor she was not completely surprised to see Dezi standing in front of her door, 303, just off the head of the stairs. Standing there as if she had been waiting for hours, sagging with boredom, but never giving up. If this had been yesterday, it would have been kind of nice. Now, minutes after a briefing about this very eventuality, it was kind of frightening.

"Dezi, what the hell?"

"Oh my god, I've been standing here for *days*!" Dezi cried. "I got the most perfect Christmas present for you, so I wanted to bring it by. Here, let me help you." The girl seized both hefty bags, freeing up JD to fetch her keys from her pocket.

"Now, c'mon, whatcha doing here, Dezi?" JD said, shoving the door open and retrieving the bags.

"Nothing, except it's almost Christmas, and Mom says we're going out to Abbotsford tomorrow to see her parents for a few days, and I've got to help clean up and stuff, so this is really my last chance to see you for a while."

The suspect had idled her way inside the apartment as she spoke. She stood just inside the open front door, not barging in, not being presumptuous, but lingering hopefully, cute as a button, for an invitation to get past the threshold. JD deposited the groceries onto the counter in the kitchenette, then sat heavily on one of the steel and vinyl kitchen chairs. She beckoned. "Come in, Dezi. Shut the door. There's juice in the fridge, if you're thirsty."

"Just water's fine," Dezi said. She poured herself a glass and sat down, looking around with interest. "What a nice place. I can't wait to get my own apartment."

"I bet. How's your relationship with your mom going lately?"

"I'm keeping it civil," Dezi said. "And she is, too. I think the trick is to stay out of each other's hair."

"And try to put yourself in each other's shoes."

"Yes, I know. That's what I've been doing. I'm not sure she knows how."

JD went to put the kettle on. She would make some tea, the nerve-soothing kind, as her nerves were definitely jumpy. "I've kind of been worrying about what I've been telling you," she said. "I don't want to leave you with the false impression that signing up will be a piece of cake."

"No, you made that clear enough."

"I think I was working so hard to be encouraging I might have glossed over some of the hurdles. That's all."

Dezi's face fell. "That's exactly what I said to Constable Leith — I've heard there are all kinds of hurdles to jump."

"Sure, and like he also told you, I think, honesty will get you over most of them. Unless you've been in real trouble, Dezi."

"What kind of trouble? I told you about my fights with my mom. I've also skipped school a few times. I just couldn't face the other kids some days. But just a few times, and it was nothing serious."

"Been there, done that," JD said. "That's not the kind of trouble I'm talking about, and I think you know it, Dezi."

Dezi nodded, and JD marvelled at how this grim but fantastic opportunity had landed before her. With mentoring as an excuse, she could ask the kid all kinds of personal questions. She was seated at the table again, facing her pupil. "You ever hung around with anybody who's done something wrong? I mean seriously wrong. Even that could be a problem."

"I've never hung around with anybody who's done anything seriously wrong," Dezi said, but the concept seemed to upset her. She had tensed — maybe with anger, maybe anxiety. "Not that I know of. But what if my friends were in trouble, and I didn't know about it? That doesn't count, right?"

"What counts is knowledge. You told me you don't have a boyfriend. Is that true?"

Dezi shook her head, denying any such thing. She sighed, then glanced sideways and her face brightened. "*Nutella*! I *love* Nutella. I could *live* on Nutella." She was ogling a jar peeking out of one of the grocery bags on the counter.

JD looked at the bag, looked at the girl, and like a predator, offered candy to a kiddie. "There's bread in the bin," she said. "Make yourself a sandwich. No, really. Help yourself."

Dezi was already at the bread bin, peeking inside. "You want one?" She had taken off her jacket and was wearing a tight pink tank top over faded blue jeans. She stood at the counter with butter knife in hand.

JD said yes to the sandwich, and as the evening progressed, she put on her comfy off-duty clothes — slack-assed grey joggers and a sweatshirt — and she and Dezi moved to the undersized living room to watch TV, pig out on Nutella, and chat between bites. JD asked again about a boyfriend, and this time a name came out — there was a boy who liked Dezi, who she hung around with sometimes. But it was nothing intense, she said. Just friends. Scott Mills was his name.

"Is Scott a good guy?" JD asked.

Dezi looked doubtful. "He swears a *lot*, and he talks big about stuff, but he's just kidding around."

"What kind of stuff?"

With a squirm and a wince, Dezi seemed about to say, *I don't want to talk about this right now*. But perhaps she recalled the warning about honesty being the best policy. "Stuff like robbing banks and stealing cars," she said, low-voiced. "But he doesn't mean it. Just being a macho jerk. Other than that, he's fun. And he's cute. But if you think I shouldn't hang around with him, I won't. Seriously."

"You'd trade in your friend for a career?"

In what looked like a fit of exasperation, Dezi gave her a piercing stare. "I just want to do it right, JD. Sometimes I don't know what's right and what's wrong."

"Hey, don't worry about it," JD said, hoping she was telling the truth. "You're a good kid, and everything will be all right."

After a moment's reflection, Dezi nodded. "You're right. I overthink stuff. Everything will be all right. And lookit." She placed a tiny gift-wrapped box on the coffee table. "This is for you, JD."

"Aw, thanks, kiddo." JD opened the box. Twinkly little rhinestone earrings, just as she feared. "Now all I need to do is to pay someone to jab steel spikes through my earlobes," she said, with a smile to soften the sting.

Dezi had been sitting close beside her, watching the wrapping come off with hungry, gift-giver antici-pation, and now looked disappointed. "You don't have pierced ears? Seriously? Oh my god. Who doesn't have pierced ears? You'd be so pretty," she said, and edged closer and reached out, touching JD's cheek, skimming her fingers toward JD's earlobe in what sure as hell felt like a lover's caress.

At the first touch JD lurched, but inwardly. She shift-ed position, putting distance between herself and the outstretched hand. She looked away from the longing in Dezi's eyes and down at the earrings in the box, which now seemed to sparkle tragically. She set the gift down and stood, sending the message loud and clear.

Dezi looked stricken. She stood, too, mumbling something about her curfew, and merry Christmas and all that, as she looked about for her jacket.

Making small talk, hoping to reassure the girl that all was still good between them, JD walked Dezi down to the front door of the complex and saw her off. She watched through the glass until the little yellow Sidekick had vanished down the avenue, but remained staring outward. The world was dark and sleety, and across the street, was that a man? With a jolt JD realized she was right. Hooded in black, he stood on the opposite sidewalk, maybe looking this way. She stared at him, and the man turned and walked away, hunched and hurried.

She pushed the door open and stepped onto the concrete landing, following him with her eyes, tempted to shout out, *Hey there, stop! Who are you?* But he was well out of earshot, and had gotten into a vehicle. Her view of him was blocked by a frustrating mess of lampposts, shrubs, and, wouldn't you know it, a fucking cube van. She jogged down to the street in time to see brake lights come on, saw the car zip out and tear away down the avenue in the same direction that Dezi had gone. She couldn't see what make or model the car was, or even its general class, let alone colour or licence plate.

"Damn," she said.

Coincidence, maybe. Maybe nothing to do with her at all, or with Dezi, but it sure felt like some kind of surveillance. And now the girl could be in danger. She turned to rush back inside, and said "damn" again, louder, because the apartment door had long since wheezed shut, and now she stood on the steps in the rain, in T-shirt and joggers and flip-flops, without keys or phone.

She pushed out the building manager's buzz code and waited, swearing.

Twenty-Eight

STAR LIGHT

AFTER A LONGER THAN expected day in the office, Leith was clearing his desk to head home. If anything further happened on the file, somebody else would have to deal with it, because his dance card was punched. Tonight Alison's sister and brother-in-law were coming over for the Christmas Eve dinner of turkey and all the trimmings that Alison was busy preparing now. Tomorrow they would travel in tandem to the Island for a full-tilt family get-together in Parksville. Not his family, which was based in faraway North Battleford, but Alison's. Sheer madness, he'd told her, to ride the ferries on Christmas Day. But the reservations were made, the relatives were thrilled, and it seemed there was no going back.

Dion approached, looking like he had something important to say, but Leith spoke first. "Hey there, season's greetings. Any plans for tonight?"

"Well, yes," Dion said, holding up a piece of paper. "Scott Mills —"

"I mean, it's Christmas Eve," Leith interrupted curtly. He banged his file drawer shut, locked it, pocketed the key. "Tonight, tomorrow? Feasts and festivities? A present under the tree you're just dying to open? C'mon, you must have a life outside these walls."

Apparently not. Having waited till Leith was done, Dion got back to business. "Scott Mills is listed at an address out in Lions Bay, which also pings as the address of Karl Gold-Seton. I don't know what that's all about. Karl's a lawyer. He used to do criminal work, but he's pretty much retired now. I've contacted him, and he'll be at his firm's office in downtown Vancouver tonight. It's a staff party."

"A staff party on Christmas Eve? Kind of unusual."

The RCMP party had been held in the first week of December. Leith had put in an appearance. Dion hadn't.

"Or some kind of party," Dion said. "I know Karl from court, from a few years ago, so he said I could come down and talk to him there, if I want. So that's what I plan to do. I told him it's about Scott Mills, but that's all. I'll tread carefully. As I said, I don't know the connection, whether Mills is a tenant or a relative or what. Far as I remember, Karl doesn't have any kids, but I could be wrong. Either way, hopefully I can get an interesting angle on Mills from his perspective."

Leith was watching him skeptically. There was something inhuman about a man who didn't mope at having to work on Christmas Eve, and there was nothing mopey about Dion's expression. He had no Yuletide plans or aspirations, and apparently didn't regret it. All he wanted for Christmas, it seemed, was permission to follow up a lead.

"Sure, okay." Following up on Scott Mills wasn't Leith's fight tonight, and neither was the problem of Cal Dion. "Have fun."

* * *

The office was on the seventeenth floor of a building near Georgia and Thurlow. There was a bit of a hoopla in progress, not so much a staff party, as it turned out, as a bigwig get-together of some kind. Glitter dust and party favours were everywhere, and Christmas tunes of the Frank Sinatra variety played — *let it snow, let it snow, let it snow*. Rain lashed the windows and blurred the view. The guests all looked like lawyers to Dion, from what he could tell, as Karl Gold-Seton beckoned him down the corridor to a smaller office with an equally spectacular view. The furniture was sharp and spanking clean. The city glimmered in wraparound splendour, traffic flowing like red-and-gold beads below, and a partial view of the Lion's Gate Bridge stretched out into the distance.

Karl Gold-Seton had welcomed him into the office as "Sergeant Dion." Maybe he was misinformed about the rank, but more likely he was joking, judging by his hearty laugh. He had always been a laugher. Now he asked Dion why the fuck he was working tonight, of all nights, and what had his dear boy, Scott, gotten himself into? "Must be pretty damn serious to bring you over here on a special night like this," he said. He had poured two tumblers full of Scotch and dropped into an executive chair, waving Dion into another. The lawyer looked no different than he had a few years back, except his thick thatch of hair was no longer salt and pepper, but stark white. He still had big teeth and big gums, and his rosy complexion looked like good health gone overboard, maybe dangerously so.

"Scott Mills is your son?" Dion asked, puzzled. He recalled Karl bragging about being a childless bachelor, not too many years ago.

"It's a euphemism." Karl waved at the air as if dispersing smoke. "Guess I didn't read the small print when I married Maria last year. He came with the package. You know those emails with attachments, you open them up and bang, you got a virus? Well, that's my Scott."

"So he's your stepson?"

"Afraid so. Suck up that Scotch before it evaporates, Sergeant. It's no mean swill and doesn't deserve to be exposed to air for long."

Dion told Karl he was just putting together some background on a case, and Scott's name had come up. "It's probably nothing, but if you could keep it to yourself, for now, that inquiries are being made?"

Karl's glass went up. "Absolutely. Cheers. And let me say I was sorry to hear about your buddy Ferraro, by the way. And about *you*, for that matter. God, when I heard the news, I thought you'd both bought the farm. Kind of lost track of you after that, so I'm glad to see you're still alive." He laughed as if he couldn't possibly mean it. "Much as I hated you," he added, and laughed harder.

Dion leaned back in the comfortable leather chair. The liquor in his mouth was good. Karl was right — no mean swill at all.

"Not as much as you hated me, of course," Karl said, sobering. "Wow. At the end there, you were taking it all a tad too personally. Thought I'd have to take a restraining order out against you. Holy Cow. It was just a job, man. You try and put 'em away, I try and spring 'em, then we all get drunk and have a laugh. You forgot the drill. Good thing Luciano was there to rein you in."

He was referring to the last trial they'd both participated in, a rough one for Dion on the stand, facing off in court with this unflappable perpetual laughing machine. Though the culprit had been convicted in the end, Dion had still been smarting from a previous trial, one in which the killer had walked, thanks to a legal technicality — or sloppy police prep, depending on who was asked. A different case, different court, different defence lawyer, but Dion had been sore enough after his testimony to lift a fist in the hallway as he and Karl passed each other. A fist drawn back, only symbolically, a snarl, and Looch telling him to chill.

"I was a little pissed off," Dion said. "Sorry," he added, though he wasn't, much. After all this time, he could still feel the heat of the moment. "You tried to make me look like an asshole."

"You were an asshole. One of the best, though. I'm still shocked to my foundations you're not up there in chevrons by now, kicking ass."

They talked shop for another quarter-hour before Dion turned the conversation back to Scott Mills, whether the young man had any hobbies, whether he had a girlfriend. Karl wasn't aware of any of the above, but he didn't have much to do with the kid. "He's actually staying in the guest cabin out back. Which is great.

Out of sight, out of mind, for the most part. He's just turned twenty, and taking some graphics course at Cap U, so if I keep my fingers crossed hard enough, he'll fuck off in a year or two. Spread his wings, fly the coop."

"You must really love the kid."

Karl made a rude noise. "Why was I so foolish as to tie the knot at my age, you ask? You know Raquel Welch? That's what his mom looked like. Still does. And she seemed nice, too. How could I not ask her out for dinner? And when she showed up poured into that sparkling neon pink dress — *oof* — how could I not propose? We laughed, we cried, we splashed through the surf with our trousers rolled to our knees and threw rose petals in our wake. Not quite, but yeah, we got married."

Dion learned little else about Scott. Karl felt Maria spoiled her son rotten, and if the kid wanted a certain toy, he got it. Yes, he had at least one drone. Flew it around the mansion, dodging furniture. Kid was quite a whiz, in fact, but when he knocked over Karl's wineglass one day, that was it. Enough. Out.

"Still pretty sure he did it on purpose," Karl grumbled.

As always, Karl was not only a laugher but a talker, and he seemed in no hurry to end the conversation and get back to his party of lawyers. Neither was Dion in any hurry to finish his Scotch and leave. So he talked and listened — mostly listened — and enjoyed himself more than expected.

Finally Karl saw him out, saying, "But this is sad. Running around asking questions on Christmas Eve. You should be at home with loved ones. Mom, dad, sweetheart — nothing?"

"Not really."

"An orphan, so young? Unfortunate." For the first time he sounded grave. "My father keeled over when I was ten, but my mother is threatening to live forever. Eighty-nine and still going strong, except for the stroke. Knocked her down, but she got back up, and pretty soon she'll be running marathons again. You okay to drive? Hope I didn't ply you with too much Scotch."

"I'm fine. Thanks for taking time out to talk, Karl. I appreciate it."

As he started for home, stray glitter in his hair and clothes, bits of the conversation swirling in his mind, Dion realized he needed to talk to somebody, anybody.

He signalled and pulled over on busy Georgia Street. He stepped out of his car and looked at the night sky for answers. The rain shimmered down, light and cold. He opened his mouth as if coming up for air, as thoughts took shape and then flitted away again, leaving him banging his forehead with a palm. Passing drivers stared. A couple of cars wore antlers, like the hatchback of the RC club president who was afraid of heights. Phone out, he found Leith in his contacts and connected.

"I have some thoughts about Craig Gilmartin," he said, when Leith came on the line. "I have to tell you. Now."

* * *

The houses along Leith's modest North Van cul-de-sac sparkled with Christmas lights, and music spilled out from several homes. Leith's place was a nice little bungalow backed by a tangled greenbelt ravine. By the time Dion arrived, it was later than he had imagined, and the home he walked into was dark and silent. But messy in a cheerful way, as if there had been a lively party going not long ago. Leith wore a Mark's Work Wearhouse–type lounger set, grey T-shirt and plaid flannel pants. The set looked brand new. The lights were down in the living room, no sign of anybody else up and about. The scent of pumpkin pie and blown-out candles lingered in the air.

"We're all kind of in bed." Leith said, but with a generous gesture invited Dion to sit at the dining room table. It was covered in a white tablecloth, not so clean, with a few dishes left on it, along with some wineglasses stained with dregs and an uncorked, unfinished bottle.

Dion didn't sit. He was taking in the scene and regretting his intrusion. "I'm sorry," he said, nearly whispering. "I forgot it's Christmas."

"Christmas Eve."

"We can talk about this tomorrow instead, then."

"I'm in Parksville tomorrow. Don't worry about waking anybody. Frankly, you could run the Holiday Train through here and they wouldn't wake up. No need to whisper. So, you're going to tell me who shot Craig?"

Dion sat down and stared at the artificial Christmas tree in the living room, lit up with gold lights and colourful baubles. He fixed his gaze on the glowing star on top. There was a child in the house, he recalled with a start. That's where Leith's mind would be — on the things that really mattered. His plan to tell Leith about Kenny Poole was already picking up its skirts and fleeing. *Because what if I'm wrong?*

Leith said, "Well?"

"I've thought it over," Dion said, embarrassed. "On my way here. I'm actually not … not a hundred percent sure now."

"Doesn't matter. Tell me anyway."

Dion shook his head, his mind made up. "Sorry. I have to check a few things first."

"All right, then," Leith said, elbow on table, chin resting in palm, any exasperation he was feeling hidden behind splayed fingers. "What about Scott Mills, then? Get anything?"

"No. But I'm starting to think we're off base with the RC plane theory, at least in part. I'll summarize for you, if you want, and go."

"Sure thing."

"Look," Dion said. "Why have we come to this plane theory? A delirious dying girl says something about a screaming bird, Craig hears an engine whine. So Bosko comes up with the plane idea. Then we went and proved it's possible, and finally Dezi Novak has a boyfriend who flies planes for fun. This is how witches get burned, right?"

"Circumstantial, sure," Leith said. "But we're far from burning anybody at the stake."

"Still, what if there are no planes or drones? What's more likely? Sex and intrigue, that's what."

Leith said nothing.

Dion continued. "Rory Keefer and Amelia Foster were both up to something fishy. Maybe they were in a relationship and neither of them wanted their spouse to know. Something went wrong that night — an argument, a breakup. Keefer ran Foster off the road, maybe not deliberately. From there we don't know what happened to Keefer, but there are endless possibilities." He paused, seeing that Leith's face still rested in his palm and his eyelids remained droopy. "It's still guesswork, but it's a lot saner guesswork than planes knocking cars off the road and kids hunting down the witnesses. Isn't it?"

"It's worth considering," Leith agreed without enthusiasm.

"It's just too unlikely."

"Kids setting fire to homeless folk for kicks is unlikely, too," Leith said.

Dion got the point.

"But I take it you've got some reason for stepping the theory back?" Leith asked.

"I'm close to finding out what really happened to Craig Gilmartin. And it's got nothing to do with Amelia Foster's crash. That's the part I wanted to tell you about."

"Which you're not willing to tell me about yet."

"That's right," Dion said. "Also, the potshot was just a potshot, but the man who tried to kill Craig later that night used the potshot as a smokescreen, knowing we'd tie the events together, to make us think there was some kind of hit out on Craig. That's why I think the airplane is a red herring. Gilmartin and Keefer are not a bundle at all."

He was done.

Leith sat back. He looked more interested now, but maybe for the wrong reasons. "You don't look so well, Cal. Are you okay?"

The delicious-looking leftovers on the table before Dion were beginning to distract him. "I'm actually kind of hungry."

"Ha. I can fix that, at least!"

Leith brought out a plate of leftover roast turkey covered in Saran wrap, along with reheated gravy, cranberry sauce, and a clean wineglass for whatever was left in the uncorked bottle.

Dion ate and drank hungrily.

Leith helped himself to a small plate as well. Chewing, he said, "You have backup for any of these ideas of yours?"

"That's what I'm going to be looking into." Dion speared a slice of turkey and stuffed it in his mouth. "But I thought I should let you know before the team wastes too much time on Dezi and flying planes. It's just so much smoke and mirrors." He pushed aside his plate and stood, still chewing, swallowing, feeling better. "Thanks."

"You're welcome," Leith said. "This is not how teamwork works, you realize that?"

"I know. Special circumstances."

"You're not going to risk life and limb again, are you?"

"'Course not."

"And you'll update me soon as you firm up these ideas of yours?"

"I'll let you know. Good night."

At the door Leith warned him again. "Don't get into hot water."

"I won't."

"Merry Christmas, Cal."

"For sure."

Dion left for the other side of town, part two of plan B next on his list.

Twenty-Nine

STAR BRIGHT

MIDNIGHT WAS LONG PAST when Dion pushed the buzzer. A voice rumbled through the metal mesh of the intercom speaker, asking who was there. Dion said he was here to talk, and was buzzed in. On the seventh floor, Ken Poole waited in his doorway, wearing a shabby terry robe over pajamas. "Well, merry Christmas," he said. He didn't look thrilled. "Come in."

The apartment Dion walked into was much as he remembered it from eight or nine years ago: a bachelor pad with signs of an attempt to be classy on a budget, though any contemporary classiness it might once have boasted was now tired retro; the lines of the furniture clunky, the veneer wearing thin. Poole was around fifty, "married once and never again", as he'd said a few times over the years.

In the cramped living room, a crime flick was paused on TV, mid-scream. The only signs of Christmas spirit were a lot of empties and a beer parlour stink. "Well, sit yourself down," Poole said.

Dion took the armchair. Poole dropped into what looked like his habitual place at the end of the sofa, judging by the cushion fatigue, and picked up the stein of beer he'd been working on. He didn't offer a brew to his guest. "What's up?"

"I think I know what happened," Dion said. "I'm going to run it by you, see if you agree."

"Okay."

Poole showed no sign of fear, though his expression was guarded. Ready for it, expecting the worst. Dion got to the point without preamble. "You tried it on with Tony Souza. Maybe you actually got your way. He was so messed up by it that he killed himself. But Gilmartin was his close friend, and he knew what you'd done, and you knew he'd say something sooner or later, probably sooner, so you had to take steps. A window came open, and you shot him. How am I doing so far?"

Poole was thinking it over, his half-empty beer stein dangling between his knees. "How are you doing so far? Hmm, good question, Cal. Not sure what to say. You're already in counselling, so that's been covered. There's a helpline number I can give you, but this is obviously more of a crisis situation here, so best to go straight to emerg. I'm sure they'll give you something for it. I'll drive you over, if you want."

Dion didn't blink. This was a classic Poole manoeuvre, responding to threats with obnoxious wit. "Who did you invite over for your birthday, Ken? Tony, and who else?"

"I didn't make any passes at Tony. You think I'd make that mistake twice? Jesus Christ."

"You invited him to your apartment. That right there screams at me."

"You know," Poole said, the heat rising to his face, "nothing actually happened that night. I shouldn't have said what I said. I was testing the waters, but nothing else. You said no, I said fine, and I didn't touch you. I wouldn't touch you. Then you fell over my coffee table like the stinking drunk you were, misinterpreted a helping hand, and decided I tried to molest you." He snorted.

"Don't rewrite history. Lucky for me I was stronger than you."

"Believe what you want."

"Just like you tested the waters with Tony, once the others had left. Maybe he was a little drunker than I was, or maybe he actually went along with it — I don't know, but whatever happened, he came away traumatized enough to end his life. You're in a position of trust. You knew that if it came out, you'd be finished. You couldn't let that happen."

Poole made a rude noise. "So, in your fantasy, I molested Tony, he killed himself, and then I tried to kill Gilmartin on the off chance that he knew."

"I'm sure you figured out that Gilmartin knew. Maybe not in so many words, but you talked to him, just like I did. You figured it out. He's a shitty liar, and you caught that Tony had confided in him. You thought you had no choice. So that night, after he'd been targeted in the drive-by, you decided it was too perfect an opportunity to pass up. You stopped at your apartment, grabbed the gun, drove him to his place, and left. Except you didn't leave. You walked back up those stairs, shoved the door open, and as he ran, you used the gun on him. He turned, but didn't have time to register who you were."

Dion knew why Gilmartin hadn't recognized Poole as the door was punched open. Poole had changed, like Jekyll to Hyde. He had become unrecognizable in his walk, talk, and aura. That was why. "I'm sure the piece is long gone by now," he added.

"The piece is long gone, you're right. It was a bad idea and I ditched it a month after I scooped it. I thought I told you all this. Hey!"

That last word was an angry shout, and Poole had stood so abruptly his beer sprayed over the carpet. Dion leapt to his feet, too. Poole shook a finger at him and roared, "I get it. This is a sting, isn't it? It's about the fucking gun?"

Dion roared back at him, telling him to stay put, not move, keep his hands out in full view. It wasn't a fist fight with Poole he was worried about, but a firearm stashed close at hand. Being unarmed himself, there was no doubt who'd win the draw.

But already Poole's anger had peaked. He put down the empty beer stein and raised his arms in mock surrender. "So you're taping this, huh? Nice. What a guy. So hey, let's put it all on the record while we're at it, my part *and* yours." His arms had lowered but were held away from his body, proving he would make no unexpected moves. He enunciated the next bit clearly enough that the tape recorder or receiver he thought Dion was wearing could pick up every word. "We were searching a crack shack, and located a nine-mil Glock that was clearly a ghost —"

"A forty-five," Dion said.

"It was nine-mil. I took it, thinking it could come in handy down the road. I recall you congratulating me. What did you call it? A cool score."

Dion decided to run with it. Let Poole think this was a sting, and maybe he'd spill all. "What matters is how you used that gun on Gilmartin," he said. "That was a ballsy move. How did you figure you'd get away with it?"

Poole stood still for a moment, as if listening to Dion's breathing, analyzing the space around him, and finally seeing through the lie. With a cheery wink he collapsed back into his groove on the sofa. "You're a lone gun, aren't you?"

"Doesn't mean it's not a sting."

"Show me the recorder, then."

Dion sat, too, debunked. "No recorder, but doesn't matter. It's over, and you know it. Tell me what happened."

"I'll tell you what happened," Poole said. "Life happened. I'm safely stuck here in my hell. I'll be single till I die. I don't do the bars. I don't look at guys twice these days, unless they're in mags or on the screen. You think I'm stupid? I don't go there. A few of the rookies came over, girls and boys. We had pizza and beer, they wished me happy birthday, I told them some real-life cop stories, and they left. Souza left with them, and I went back to jerking off in the dark. There — you got it, princess."

His shocking words rang true to Dion. But he wasn't ready to give up. Cops made great liars, as he well knew. "You stopped off here on your way to driving Gilmartin home."

"For the gun? I think you mean the camera." Poole smiled angelically.

Dion, who had crossed his arms to show who was boss, began to feel foolish. He jammed his hands in his pockets instead.

"Lil Hart was off to her sister's wedding that night," Poole said. "Her camera had just crapped out, so I told her she could borrow my Canon PowerShot. Great little point-and-shoot. You may want to corroborate that with Lil. But you're such a smart young dick, I'm sure you already thought of that."

Dion was beginning to wonder what his theory had actually been hinged on. The fact he resembled Souza, the fact Souza had killed himself, the fact he had privately kept an eye on Poole all these years, expecting something like this to happen? It was beginning to feel badly *off*.

Poole seemed to have grown tired of smirking. "Anyway, I'm insulted by your lack of faith. If I wanted to kill Gilmartin, he'd be dead, not winged." He got up and went to his fridge in the adjoining kitchenette. He pulled out not one beer but two, and from the freezer a second stein. "Truth is, I'm really sorry about that night."

"You fucking better be."

"Not about that," Poole said. He gave Dion the mug and a beer. "About having to listen to your righteous lectures for the next month and a half. But bygones. Just for my edification, why don't you deconstruct your newest allegations for me."

Dion popped his beer can and poured, feeling miserable. Gilmartin was partly to blame, he decided, for looking like he was harbouring secrets. But Gilmartin had every right to be confused. It was Dion's own fault, for going at the rookie like a rabid evangelist, demanding answers with questions that had not surprisingly been misinterpreted. Look before you leap. He should get the warning tattooed on his hands. For some reason the bright star atop the Christmas tree in Leith's home came to mind, and he wished he could start life over again. Backspace the last two years, to the hour before he'd spotted Stouffer walking along the road in Surrey. Backspace, and drive on by.

But here he was, and of all the places in the world, Poole's stuffy little apartment was the right place to be. Fitting. He and Poole deserved each other on this drizzly night when everybody else was making merry. "Nothing to deconstruct," he said. "I ran it by Gilmartin, and he went pale and started stuttering, so I knew he was hiding something. I guessed what that was, and maybe ..." The corners of his mouth pulled down, the closest he would come to an apology. "Maybe I guessed wrong."

Poole startled him again by slamming a fist on the sofa's armrest. "I know what happened," he said. "Damn!" He went on to explain that Souza had cut his hand that night, trying to unscrew a beer cap that wasn't designed to be unscrewed. He'd then gone rummaging in the bathroom for a Band-Aid, and must have found something he wasn't supposed to.

"My bathtub mag," Poole said. "The one I'd forgotten about under the cabinet. And then he went and told everyone else. *Fuck!*"

It was coming together to Dion, what had happened. Souza had shared the news with Gilmartin, and Gilmartin was too virtuous to pass it on. Maybe Gilmartin had told Souza a thing or two about the perils of rumour-spreading. "I don't think Tony told everybody," he said. "I'd have heard about it, if he had. And whatever Craig knows, he's going to keep it to himself. He didn't tell me, even when I leaned on him. I think you're safe."

"Safe," Poole echoed. He chugged beer as if he couldn't get drunk fast enough.

"Anyway, who cares what you read in your tub after hours?"

"My employer, my relatives, my entire social circle," Poole said. "The guy at the corner store who knows me by name. The old ladies in the park. God. That's who."

"You're really that deep in the closet? I'm the only one who knows?"

"You and Craig fucking Gilmartin." Poole grimaced. "Could be worse. I could have actually shot the little bastard."

They sat and commiserated in silence, until Poole said, "Funny how you got at least some of it right. Just not the important bits."

It was funny enough that Dion gave a disgusted guffaw. Poole asked how counselling was going, and Dion told him. He accepted another beer as he talked, and it turned out to be the most fun he'd had in weeks, describing how Samantha Kerr had tried to get to his soul, and how he'd foiled her. As one bad cop to another, he could say things to Poole he couldn't tell anyone else. It was purgatory. It was dark and depressing, but in a hilarious way. Poole had turned the TV to the music channel, a screenshot of mistletoe with classic Yuletide tunes playing, and this, too, was funny.

In the middle of "Jingle Bells" Poole ran out of beer. But no matter, as he had a direct line to a bootlegger. Within the hour a weedy-looking woman delivered a top-up to his door: a case of foul high-octane with a steep bootlegger markup.

Stocked up, they talked about old times well into the dawn of Christmas Day, two outsiders with nowhere better to go. It was such a blast in the end that Dion had to leave his car on the street and cab it home. The regret didn't seep in right away. Not until he was back in his own apartment, looking in the mirror. His face seemed out of alignment, and he knew purgatory came with its own set of problems. He had shared with Poole the joke of his own existence, but some fears had surfaced as well. His fears were tied to secrets, and with Poole being a cop trained to weed secrets from fears, he had to wonder: what had he given away?

Thirty

THE CONTROLS

December 25

EARLY IN THE MORNING on Christmas Day, Leith was on the ferry, heading to Parksville and trying not to think about work. For the most part he did a good job of it, but when Alison took Isabelle off to the washrooms, he had nothing but the back of another passenger's head to look at — and the ocean, which was much of a muchness in the middle of the Georgia Strait. So he made a call.

The line connected, and a deep, rough-edged voice said, "Dion."

In that one word Leith heard the effects of hangover, and he hoped it was a sign the man had found some festivities to take part in after all. "Last I heard," he said, "you were going off to single-handedly solve the Gilmartin case. So, what have you got?"

"I succeeded in proving myself wrong, that's all," Dion said bitterly. "But no harm done." He didn't sound as if he believed himself. He sounded like a bag of gravel.

Leith was relieved. Dion's investigations could be minefields of trouble, so if he came out with all limbs intact, that was something to celebrate. "At least you tried. I hear you're on shift today."

"A lot of us are," Dion said more cheerfully. "JD contacted Desiree Novak's mother yesterday to let her know we need to set up an interview. JD told the mom it could wait till after the holidays, but Ms. Novak wants to know what's going on, and she insisted on coming in this morning, soon as possible. She's bringing a lawyer, too. I'll be sitting in."

"Holy," Leith said, looking at the flat grey-green water, the strips of clouds not yet touched by dawn. "Well, keep me posted. But only if it gets hot."

"I will."

"Even if it doesn't get hot. Keep me posted."

Dion said goodbye, and added, with surprising conviction, "Merry Christmas!"

* * *

JD had to cancel plans to drive out and visit her sister and her sister's hubby and kid in PoCo this rosy Christmas Day. She wasn't heartbroken. Though she was fond of her niece, she was *not* fond of her brother-in-law, and there was an iceberg between her and her sister from way back when. The gift-giving would have been awkward, as always. Breakfast would be pancakes, coffee would be weak, and the laughter would be false. No, her regrets weren't huge, and an unplanned day at work was her Christmas present.

She wasn't alone. Dion was here in his civvies, busy at his computer. Even busy at his computer, he was clearly a changed man from when they had been friends before, JD thought, looking at the slope of his back. The ding to the head had shut him up, calmed him down. Tamed him.

"Hi," she said. "Dezi's here. Ready?"

"I am."

Dezi looked small and frightened as she accompanied JD and Dion to the interview room, followed by Dezi's mother, Maddie Novak, and the lawyer Maddie had brought along. Maddie was slim and blonde, and didn't look a lot older than her daughter. JD suspected mother and daughter probably got *You two could pass for sisters* often enough. Maddie looked almost as frightened as Dezi. Her lawyer did, too, in a way. It turned out he was a civil litigator who happened to be a friend of Maddie's, just coming along for moral support.

The interview was recorded, and JD did the talking, with Dion sitting in as observer and scribe. There had been some debate as to whether someone less personally involved should interview the girl, but in the end JD had drawn the short straw. "Your name's come up in an investigation, Dezi," she opened. "And it's got to do with the boy you told me about — what was his name again?"

Dezi tilted slightly away from her mother and answered meekly. "Scott."

"Scott Mills," JD said. "Tell me about him."

"I don't want to get him in trouble."

"Why d'you figure he'd get in trouble if you told me about him?"

"Well, that's why I'm here, right? Because of him?"

"You're here for a few reasons."

"Am I in trouble, too?"

The simple question carried extra weight, considering the recent conversation Dezi had had with JD. This was not about stolen chocolate bars or skipping classes, and there was a lot at stake, JD realized. The girl was afraid her dream job was about to disappear, and maybe she was right. JD held her gaze and spoke softly. "All you can do is be upfront with me. However you're involved, if you've done something you shouldn't have, we'll find out. It will be a lot better if it comes from you."

The lawyer asked to speak to Dezi and Maddie alone.

"Of course," JD said.

This wasn't an arrest, and Dezi could chat with whomever she wanted for as long as she wanted. Or exit stage left, for that matter. Off Dezi went with her support team to a private room to talk, and JD waited with Dion, both of them looking at the witness's empty chair as if the answer was about to materialize. "What d'you think?" JD said.

Dion counted off the key points. "Novak and Mills are friends, and Mills flies planes and drones for fun. Somebody might have used an RC plane to drive Amelia Foster off the road, and might then have gone after the witnesses, one of whom was probably Rory Keefer, which we're quite sure of because his wife recognized his voice on the 911 call."

"Even though he tried to disguise it," JD said. "And Dezi just happens to be at that crash that was possibly caused by an RC plane."

"It's still thin."

"But compelling," JD said. "Right? What have we got on Scott Mills?"

"Address, crime sheet, vehicle — he drives a '96 GMC pickup. And if you get anything useful out of Dezi here, an arrest warrant."

"I will," JD told him. "Just watch."

* * *

She did. Dezi opted to talk without her mother and the lawyer present this time, and JD thought maybe Dion should lay off, too, stay in the monitor room and give Dezi at least the illusion of privacy.

Alone, Dezi looked smaller and more frightened than ever, JD thought. She was also ready to talk, and opened up about Scott Mills. She had met him over a year ago, and wasn't truly interested in him, much, but they would hang out at the PNE, at the beach, at the movies. Her mom didn't know about him. Scott was a bit older and a little rough edged, and she was sure her mom would have put a stop to the friendship.

"I thought you said your mom doesn't really care what you do, so long as you stay out of her hair."

Dezi shrugged. "She can be like that sometimes. But she does care about me."

"What did Scott do for fun, besides the PNE, the beach, the movies?"

"Mostly he likes his expensive toys. He's super good at flying, too. We go over to Deer Lake sometimes and he'll fly those things for hours. Kind of cool, but it gets boring."

"Not your thing?"

"No. That quadcopter drone thing he's got is neat, though. He showed me how to use it, but took the controls away after I crashed it into a tree. Those things cost a lot."

"Do you guys hang around with anyone else?"

Dezi seemed to hesitate. "No, not really."

"Nobody at all?"

"Perry, for a while. But I don't think they're friends anymore."

"Why? What happened?"

"Scott's pretty much a loner," Dezi said with a shrug. "Except he likes me."

"He's serious about you, is he?"

"In a way."

JD suspected Dezi was withholding something. "How close are you with Scott? Are you two having sex?"

Dezi looked startled. "Are you even allowed to ask that?"

"Afraid so. Doesn't mean you have to answer. But it's not a crime if you are."

Dezi lowered her voice. "He's never actually tried. I don't think he's interested in that, but he does like showing me off like I'm his girlfriend whenever we're out." She shrugged. "But we're actually just friends without benefits. Literally."

"And you feel he's a good friend? Doesn't try to control you? You're free to come and go, date other guys if you want? He makes you laugh?"

"All of the above. Most of the time he's a really great guy, except when he's being a jerk."

JD decided it was time to let Dezi in on the theory, if only to get a reaction. She asked if Scott ever talked about using his skills with his flying toys to startle drivers, say, on a highway?

Dezi frowned. "Well, he talked about it, but he was kidding."

"You think he was kidding?"

"I know he was kidding. He had to be."

"Did he use his plane to scare that girl into the ditch that night? And don't tell me you don't know anything about it, because you were there, Dezi. You were there."

Dezi stared across the table, maybe waiting for the question to turn into a joke. When it didn't, a look of horror crept over her. "You're saying he really did that, what he said? I don't believe you!"

"What did he say he did?"

"After those kids went off the road in a van, he said he did it. We were in the park and he was playing with his plane, the jet, and he made it dive at me. He said he drove that van off the road just like this. But he lies all the time, just to get a rise out of me. I said, 'That's sick,' and he laughed, and I thought he was just joking. You're saying he really did that? And did it to that girl too, Amelia?"

JD was too focused on Dezi's face to take notes, not wanting to miss a beat. Scott Mills had told Dezi he was responsible for the van accident. It was really all she needed for now, enough to make an arrest. But more was always better. "Did he tell you he'd done anything else?"

"No."

"Ever dress up a drone as a ghost, scare people with that?"

Dezi blinked, and almost smiled. "He did that, yes! But just for fun. He put a little skull on it, and gauze, and made it fly around, chasing after me."

"Not just for fun if you're a driver on the highway and it comes flying at you."

Dezi lost the grin. "He never said anything about that."

"I think you'd better run through that night again, your drive to Squamish and back."

"I told you."

"And I'm not buying it. We think Scott Mills caused that crash. You're his friend. Just a wild coincidence that you happened on the crash that he caused?"

Dezi's eyes were searching the corners of the room, maybe looking for an escape hatch. But there was no way out, and she placed her hands over her eyes and groaned.

"Tell me," JD urged.

The hands came down, but Dezi wouldn't look up. "Grey Man," she said. "That's who did it."

Grey Man? The words brought a memory and a shiver to JD: darkness and rain, and a figure standing across the street cloaked in shadows, only to slither away before she could confront him. But grey had other meanings. "You're saying a senior citizen did it?" she joked.

Dezi stared at her, then gave the briefest smile. "No, Grey Man, that's what I call him, because that's all he wears. I don't know his name. Him and Scott are friends, I think. And he likes me."

"Tell me about it."

"Maybe like three months ago Scott and I were at Deer Lake," Dezi said. "And he pointed and said that guy over there had the hots for me. I saw a man sitting on a bench watching us. I hadn't noticed him before. He had a hat on, and a coat, and I couldn't see his face. And I thought Scott was just being a dick, but then a week later I saw him talking to that same man downtown — I'm pretty sure it was him — and when I came near, the guy kind of turned and walked away, fast. I asked Scott who he was, and he said, 'Just a car salesman,' and laughed. He said the man was going to get him a deal on a sports car to die for."

"Scott had enough money to buy a sports car?"

"Not judging by that old truck he drives. Maybe his mom was going to buy him a new car, I don't know. But he wouldn't tell me about it, so I felt like there was something illegal about the deal. Scott's stepdad is rich, but he doesn't like Scott much. That's what Scott says. His stepdad's a lawyer, and he's got a really big house in Lions Bay, and Scott has his own place there — well, it's a guest cabin, actually — which I've been to once. It's all in a big park, almost."

"Does Scott work?"

"No, he's going to school, at Cap U. So he never has much money to spend, and whatever he gets he blows on his dumb toys. So I don't know why he was talking about buying a sports car. And then what happened next is he asked if I wanted to go for a drive with him and this guy, in the guy's car. "

"And did you?"

"I didn't want to at first, but Scott said it would be fun and we'd get a free meal out of it. So we did, a couple days later. That was in October. It was a nice car, but nothing fancy."

"Make, model?"

"I'm sorry, I don't know. It was a black four-door, and that's about all I can tell you."

"So you saw the man, finally. Describe him for me."

"Again, I can't. Scott drove, and the guy sat in the back seat and didn't say much. I couldn't see his face, and I wasn't about to stare, was I? I didn't really want to talk to him, and he didn't say anything, either. It was weird."

"No conversation at all?"

"Just him and Scott, just a word or two I couldn't hear. And later he told Scott to pull over. We got out, and he gave Scott money so we could go for a nice dinner, and said he hoped we could do this again. And that was all, that time."

"And did you do it again?"

Dezi nodded. Her face pinkened with what JD took to be shame. "Just once, the night I went out to Squamish, the night I stopped at the crash. I didn't tell you the whole truth, JD. I'm sorry."

"Well, you're telling it now," JD assured her. "And that's what matters. Go on."

"We'd gone for a drive again that day, and this time, when it was over, Scott pulled over where we'd left our cars, and I got out, but Scott stayed in the car with him. I should have minded my own business, but I was so curious about what they were up to. It was kind of exciting. Like being a detective. I drove around the block, then parked farther back, where I could watch them. They talked for a long time, then Scott went to his truck and took off, and I followed Grey Man."

She glanced at JD as if expecting anger, saw only patience, and went on. "I wanted to know where he lived. Instead he drove out to Porteau Beach. I drove in, too, and parked. There were two cars in the parking lot — one was Grey Man's — and down by the water I saw him and a girl. They looked like they were arguing, and my heart was just pounding. I didn't know what to do. Then the girl came running up toward me, and she looked scared. She jumped into one of the cars and tore out, practically burning rubber. Grey Man was walking up the beach toward me, and now I was scared, too. I could see he was talking on a phone as he walked. I peeled out of there, hoping he didn't see me. I got back on the highway, and I came upon the crash, and you know the rest."

"You came upon the crash of the girl you'd seen arguing with Grey Man?"

"I didn't even put it together then. I didn't know it was the same girl on the beach. But now it all seems connected, now that you told me about Scott. If that was her, and Scott really does use his plane to make cars go off the road, then I don't know. He lives right close by to where the crash happened. So is he sitting there doing that to people? What's going on, JD? I don't understand."

Dezi was hugging herself, and there was nothing false about her dread. She looked so pale and shaky that the source of her fear might have been sitting in the room with them.

JD took a short break to go over the latest with Dion. There would be more questions for Dezi, but more than likely she would have to be released. Scott Mills, on the other hand, was going to be tracked down and shackled, now that they had Dezi's incriminating statement about the van. Not great, but at the very least, it was fuel for a warrant.

Thirty-One

HEIDI

December 25–26

IN REACTION TO THE WORD *takedown*, Dion's heart was beating fast. He paced the room and made a call to Leith, who was far away on the Island, but wanted to be kept in the loop. "Are you busy?"

"We're all heading out for a walk on the beach," Leith said. "Then the women will prepare dinner, while us guys get to sit around drinking brandy and watching them work. A good old-fashioned Christmas. How's it going at your end?"

"We're putting on Kevlar. Going to arrest Scott Mills. Desiree Novak gave us grounds for a warrant. And this being Christmas is perfect, 'cause we've established that there's a family gathering at the Gold-Seton residence, and Novak says Mills hasn't got much of a social life besides family — he's close to his mother, anyway — so we're pretty sure he'll be there."

"Great. Well, I'll be waiting for the news," Leith said. He sounded a little wistful, Dion thought. As he ended the call, he realized that he wished Leith was here to take part in the arrest — then he wondered why he wished it. But he was interrupted by JD letting him know Bosko had given the go-ahead, and the action was about to get underway. He jumped to it.

* * *

In the end Kevlar wasn't necessary, because Scott Mills wasn't at the Gold-Seton residence, neither in the main house nor in his guest house at the back of the estate. A lot of people were present in the mansion, but at the moment their babble of conversation was blocked out by a heavy door. Dion stood in somebody's study — probably Karl's — looking at Karl's angry wife, Maria. The little white dog at her feet was also angry, backing up its mistress with steady growling and the occasional warning yap. The woman herself was well-dressed in black satin and high heels, a little overweight, polished and shiny, and smelling of perfume and fragrant liquor. Her earrings swung and sparkled as she expressed her anger. She made a stark contrast to the three quiet cops in dark blue, all doing nothing at the moment but listening to her speak.

"Of all the days, you pick this one to swoop in and embarrass the hell out of us," she was saying. "Is that some kind of wicked sense of humour on your part, or just systemic sadism?"

"Time was of the essence, ma'am," JD said. "We understood Scott would be here, and we wanted to speak to him right away. He's not, so we'll make it nice and quick and be out of your hair, as I said, if you'll tell us where he is."

"And as I told you, I do not know where my son is. He's an adult. He doesn't have to report his every move."

"You must have a few ideas of where he could be."

"I'm afraid I don't."

"When did he call to say he wouldn't be at your party?"

"This morning, about ten a.m."

"No discussion as to why, ma'am?"

The *ma'ams* were delivered coldly, JD hitting hard. Dion and Urbanski were playing the steely-eyed backup men, ready to get mean if called upon. Of course they wouldn't get mean. If asked to leave, they would. But it didn't hurt to put on a show.

"No discussion. I suppose he had something more exciting to do than hang around with his mom and step-dad and a bunch of their aging friends."

JD put to Maria the night of Amelia Foster's crash — any idea what Scott was doing then? The woman consulted her phone, presumably looking at her calendar app. "That was a night Karl was out," she said, and put the phone down. "And since Karl and Scott don't get along, Scott took advantage of our eighty-inch 4K television. He watched some godawful wrestling competition. You're going to ask what time. I'm sure he came over when he smelled dinner, hoping to be fed, and stayed until Karl's headlights showed up in the driveway, which would have been around one a.m."

"When did he smell dinner?" JD asked, with no trace of humour.

"Between six and seven."

"Who else was here then?"

"Just myself. We ate, talked a bit, then he went to his TV show, and I went to the den to read."

"I guess the godawful wrestling must have been pretty loud. Didn't that bother you?"

"I was one floor up, and the floors are solid, and he kept the volume down, as I told him to. No, the noise hardly reached me."

"You weren't watching him, then. He might have stepped out at some point?"

"Well, I could see his vehicle from where I was reading, and it didn't move. If he stepped out on foot, it wouldn't have been for long, and he wouldn't have gotten far. I suppose he could have dashed around the grass for a bit. It's a large estate. But more to the point, why? If he wants exercise, he has a pass to the gym. How silly. No, I can assure you, he was here that night, glued to his TV and his snacks."

"Watching sports alone?" JD said doubtfully.

"Yes. What's wrong with that? He's smarter than the average joe," Maria said. She was trying hard to be classy, Dion noticed, but sometimes her working-class roots showed, along with a fierce protectiveness of her son. "Sometimes being smart drives people away. He doesn't have a wide circle of friends."

"Who is in his narrow circle of friends?" JD asked.

"I don't have a clue."

"Any women in his life?"

"They wish."

"You never saw him with a girl?"

"There is a girl in his life, but he's trying to 'shake her loose,' is how he put it to me."

Dion and Urbanski shared a look. *Wow.*

"Yeah?" JD said. "What's the name of this girl he's trying to shake loose?"

"I don't know her name and I've never seen her. I mind my own business, unless he wants to confide. And he doesn't do a lot of that, so there you go."

"So he's kind of smart but anti-social, would you say?"

"Smart and self-contained."

JD ploughed on. "Where was your husband that night?"

"Is he suspected, too?"

"No, ma'am. Just in case I need to confirm your information."

"My *story*, you mean," Maria hissed. But she referred to her calendar again as her little dog rumbled with hatred and stared daggers at JD. She found the entry. "It's not in my calendar, but I recall he visited Heidi in the early afternoon, till about six, likely. He then attended a planning committee meeting downtown. He's involved in a New Year's fundraiser event we'll be attending. If you want the particulars of that, you'll have to ask him."

"Who's Heidi?"

"His mother. She lives just down here at Skyview Manor."

"The assisted living place?"

"That's right."

JD nodded at her steely-eyed backup men. Time to hit the road. As Urbanski had informed Bosko in his initial phone report, the arrest was an epic fail.

"Not only that," Urbanski complained as they drove back to the detachment to take off the riot gear, "We blew Christmas Day harassing high society."

"Awesome way to spend Christmas, seems to me," JD said, from the passenger seat. She looked at Dion, who was driving. "Not a bad way to celebrate the birth of Jesus, right, Cal? Harassing the lawyers?"

Dion heard the question but didn't answer. He was thinking about Karl's mother, and he didn't know why.

JD sighed and addressed Urbanski in the back seat instead. "So Scott wants to shake Dezi loose, hey? That one bowled me over."

"Don't bet on it," he replied. "Could be the classic *she wants to dump me so I'll dump her first* kind of manoeuvre. See it all the time."

"What d'you think?" JD asked Dion. "Who's shaking who?"

"Right," he said absent-mindedly. Whatever it was swirling in his mind was important, he felt. But oh, so elusive.

* * *

Boxing Day, and the malls had sucked nearly all of humanity off the streets and paths of North Vancouver. Dion took advantage of the quiet to cycle along the Spirit Trail, half hoping he would run into Kate again, preferably on her own this time. But even if she was walking with Patrick, he would do a better job of leaving an impression. On both of them. He would boldly suggest a coffee date to Kate, just as friends, while transmitting to

Patrick that it wasn't over till it was over. She would say yes, of course. Patrick would be obliged to show how little he cared, but he would be knocked off balance a bit, and that would make him edgy, maybe even start an argument when they were home alone, and Kate would see her latest boyfriend wasn't such a prize after all.

But he didn't run into Kate or Patrick. He leaned his bike and stood on the path to study the waves. Being near the ocean still opened wounds, but now at least he had figured out why. Memories were bittersweet, and it was the delineation that bothered him — the past so sweet, the future so bitter. The sea's scents and sounds, its wheeling gulls, its wide openness that suggested great power and endless possibilities, all closed to him now. The sea was a kind of background music to what had been the time of his life.

Himself and Kate on the beach, soaking up the rays. Or swimming, the cold splash and gasp with the first plunge. Salt on the tongue and sand underfoot. Grit as he ran his palms down her back. As they dried in the sun, the sand fell away like a shed layer. She felt different in bed after a swim in the sea, her hair tangled and ropey, but clean in a cleaner way. They slept better and fought less. Everything tasted great after a day by the sea.

That's why it hurt to look at the waves.

He looked anyway. The sea tried telling him it was time to give up on Kate, focus on somebody new. He never had trouble meeting women, on one level. The trouble was the second level, which never seemed to happen.

"It's because I don't want it to," he said, trying to figure it out. "I just have to want it more."

A beautiful woman cycled by. They smiled at each other, and he watched her go, half convinced. As she disappeared, another woman filtered through his thoughts. Faceless, and a lot older. Eighty-nine, Karl had said.

Dion couldn't imagine being eighty-nine, the bulk of life behind him. Karl had said his mother could run a marathon, even after a stroke, but Dion didn't believe it. It was probably just a way of saying she would be okay.

But would she? The concept of being eighty-nine, in assisted living, and recovering from a stroke made his own troubles seem petty. But that wasn't why he was thinking about Heidi Gold-Seton, a person he'd never met, never seen, who was nothing to him but a name.

Nothing but a name ...

"Wait a minute!" he shouted at the gulls. "Whoa!"

He picked up his bike and got back on the path, standing on the pedals to go faster. He needed to be at his desk, write it down, be certain about it — then make some calls.

Thirty-Two

IN THE WINGS

December 26

WITH JD BESIDE HIM, Dion drove to Lions Bay and the assisted living facility, Skyview Manor, where Heidi Gold-Seton lived. "It seems like kind of a stretch," JD said, as they joined traffic on the Sea to Sky. She said it again, sounding it out. "Heidi Gold-Seton, hide-and-go-seek. Crazy. Crazy but brilliant." She stared at Dion as he drove until he had no choice but to ask her what was on her mind.

"You're so different," she said. "But you're so the same. I can't figure you out."

"Having your head bashed will do that," he said. "I'm getting over it."

"Going to be your old self pretty soon, you think?"

"Why?" he said, glancing at her. "D'you miss my old self?"

"God, no. You were a royal jerk. I couldn't stand you. Good riddance."

"I'll be a royal jerk again soon. Just watch me."

At Skyview Manor they were asked by staff to wait in the common dining room for their eleven o'clock meeting with Mrs. Gold-Seton. Here, Dion occupied himself getting coffee, while he considered JD's insult and how to retaliate. At the counter he filled two cups, thinking maybe he would just disengage. But that would be like running away. Best to fight fire with fire. Back at the table he said, "You've changed, too. You're … snippier."

"Yeah, because I've lost my few good friends on the force, including you, even if you were a jerk. And Looch. I'm not blaming you, Cal. But nothing's been the same since."

Dion almost said, *But I'm here*, though he knew what the answer would be. *No, you're not.* She had always liked Looch more, anyway. She had found a brother in him. With Looch around, she had been a happy person. Everybody loved Luciano Ferraro, and everybody missed him, and Dion had gone and killed him, and JD was lying when she said she didn't blame him.

There was still no sign of Gold-Seton. The cafeteria was nearly empty but for a small gathering over by the window, laughing it up. A radio played.

At 11:02, JD said, "Let's head over there."

They found her unit, and Heidi Gold-Seton let them into her clean, well-kept apartment. "Sorry," she said shortly. "Was just heading over to get you. Still adjusting to the lower rpm."

Dion had been expecting another Mrs. Vlug, but Mrs. Gold-Seton was on a different spectrum. Square-bodied and erect, in spite of her walker. Her face was squarish, too, and resolute. Her hair was cut short and white as snow, but her eyes were almost black. And steady. Unnervingly steady, as she stared at Dion with a cynical slant to her wide mouth.

"Well?" she said. "What's up?"

"Just a few questions," JD said.

"So you said when you called. Please, sit down. You want coffee or cookies, or something?"

Dion was thinking he would rather have Patricia Vlug as a grandmother any day.

JD declined the refreshments, and they sat at the table. Looking around, Dion saw a large cage over by the window. Mrs. Gold-Seton had a bird, as Mrs. Vlug did, but the bird, too, was on a different spectrum — a lot bigger, and brilliant blue with yellow markings. It was also quiet, motionless, maybe dead. No, it twitched an eye, lifted a foot, set it down again, and shuffled down its perch. A beautiful but grumpy-looking bird.

Mrs. Gold-Seton said, "That's my surviving hyacinth macaw. A talker, usually, but having one of his days. His mate died last year, and he still moons over her." She called out, "Hello, Ralph!"

The bird nodded once.

"His real name is more glamorous," she explained. "But I call him Ralph. That's my deceased husband's name: the Honourable Mr. Justice Ralph Seton. They're much alike. Well, what do you want to ask? I have a hair appointment at eleven forty-five."

"I remember Justice Seton from court," JD said. "I liked him."

Mrs. Gold-Seton studied JD, maybe suspiciously, maybe assessing whether she should warm to her or not. "Thank you," she said coolly. "He was enduringly likable."

JD got back to the point. "We're here about your son Karl's stepson, Scott Mills."

Heidi's brows went up, and Dion expected her to say something nasty, as Karl had done, likening the boy to an email virus. Instead she leaned forward with a worried wince. "Scott? What's happened?"

She was familiar with Scott, then. And in a positive way.

"Nothing's happened," JD assured her. "We need to talk to him, but it seems he's out and about. We thought you might be able to help."

This wasn't true. They didn't expect her to produce the kid. Up to now they hadn't expected her to give two figs for him. All they were here to do was take a look at her, see if her name had anything to do with the case, or was just some kind of phonetic foul-up. Then find out what her connection was, if any, with Amelia Foster, who had worked at the Skyview as a care aide.

"He's not in trouble, is he?" Mrs. Gold-Seton asked.

"No, no," JD said. She paused. "You seem fond of him. Do you get together much?"

The woman scowled. "I haven't been able to get around so well these days" — *no marathons*, Dion thought — "so not as much as I'd like. Can't even drive my car," she said, and gestured toward the window.

Out the window was the facility's organically configured parking area, and before her unit sat a little white Porsche Boxster.

"That's your ride?" Dion said.

She had noted his surprise, and he realized that his surprise could be taken as offensive. "That's my ride," she stated glumly. "Had exactly three spins in it before my stroke. Being the passenger just isn't the same, is it?"

"When will you be back behind the wheel?" asked JD.

Dion feared the question would be a painful reminder to the older woman that she would never slam pedal to the metal again. But Gold-Seton didn't look hurt, and her answer was another shock. "Doc says with rehabilitation, I'm looking at another six months before I'll be driving again. Meantime, I sit and have coffee, I walk to the end of the hall, come back and have more coffee, and try to avoid the nitwits around here. He does visit, though, when he can, which is always pleasant."

"Who?" JD said.

"My step-grandson, Scott — the one you're here about. And I wish you'd explain why."

"When was he last in to see you?"

"Not for a while. When he can manage, he comes by on the weekends. But he's a busy boy. Goes to Capilano University. Digital Arts. He's between semesters, but he's looking for a job to help with tuition, so doesn't have a lot of spare time. I told Karl to help him out, but Karl's a bit of a tightwad, thinks young people should fend for themselves. 'Makes 'em strong,' he likes to say. Let me think. It was about two weeks ago, mid-December, when Scott came by last."

"He didn't visit for Christmas?"

A slight frown. "Odd, yes, but I haven't heard from him. I've asked Karl and Maria about him, and they say he's busy. Too busy to visit, I suppose, but I'm not going to gripe about it. I do like him. He reminds me of my son Evan." She sat in silence for a moment, then gestured to a nearby cabinet. "Last time Scott came by he brought those flowers and that card."

Dion obliged by admiring the roses and lilies in their vase, desiccated but attractive. The card propped before them depicted an English country garden blowsy with sunlight. Behind the card and flowers stood a tri-fold hinged picture frame of ornate pewter holding photographs of yesteryear.

He walked over to pick up the card and take a look at Scott's handwriting, but there wasn't much to see, as Scott had relied on the factory's salutation and simply scrawled his name at the end of it. "Nice," he said. No date.

JD was going into the folder she had brought along for the photograph of Amelia Foster obtained from Tiffany Tan. Foster was very much alive in this particular shot, a plump, shy-eyed, smiling young woman in a soft-blue sweater, her short, glossy hair held back by combs. Until recently she had worked at Skyview, so there was a good chance the two women had met. And if Foster really had been trying to say *Heidi Gold-Seton* as she lay dying, perhaps they knew each other well.

JD presented the photo to Mrs. Gold-Seton. "Do you know this woman at all?"

Mrs. Gold-Seton grumbled something about her reading glasses and went to find them, while Dion studied the photographs in the pewter frame. Gold-Seton returned with her glasses on and took the photograph from JD. "She looks familiar," she said. "Who is she?"

"This picture is a few years out of date," JD told her. "Her hair would be shorter now."

Mrs. Gold-Seton returned the photo. "Nope. Don't know her."

For the third time Dion was surprised, and this time disappointed as well. He had been sure she would break the case wide open for them, say she knew Foster, provide the lead that would reveal what had led to Foster's death. JD tucked away the photo. "Does the name Amelia mean anything to you?"

"Of course. A brilliant young woman who was an advocate for equality, a pilot who flew across the ocean and, on July 2, 1937, disappeared off the radar. You look like her, in fact."

JD, the wannabe pilot, smiled briefly. "The Amelia I'm talking about is actually the woman in this photograph," she said. "She worked here from April to mid-October in housekeeping. Her full name is Amelia Jeannette Foster."

"Good grief," Gold-Seton said. "She's the young woman who died on the highway just two weeks ago."

"That's right."

"Is that why you're here? What's she got to do with Scott?"

"We're still a long way from knowing that ourselves," JD said. "I'm sorry I can't tell you more."

Gold-Seton removed her reading glasses and shook her head. "Maybe she's one of the girls. I'm not a people person. When housekeeping wants to clean my apartment, I vacate, let them work in peace without an old woman glaring at them. Never chat with them, as some do."

"Here's another name for you, then. Desiree Novak, or Dezi?"

"Don't know that name, either."

"Did Scott ever bring a girl with him when he visited, about sixteen or seventeen, blonde, very pretty?"

"He never brought anybody. Now, I'm getting thoroughly tired of your evasions. Was Scott involved in the crash? The papers said it was a single-vehicle accident and that she had lost control."

"We think he may have some knowledge about it."

"He's a potential witness, then? Why don't you just say so?"

JD seemed to be losing steam. She looked to Dion for advice.

"Is this Karl?" he asked, pointing at one of the photos in the hinged frame.

The woman switched her glare from JD to him. "That's Karl on the left," she said. "Went through a few wives, but never had any kids until he married Maria."

Neither *Karl* nor *Maria* was said with love, Dion noticed.

"So at least I finally have a grandson," she said. "Who I swear is more of a blood relation than any of my official kith and kin." She sniffed. "And one who I am hoping is not in some kind of trouble, though I'm starting to think he is, with all your fancy footwork."

JD seemed to realize her PR charm was getting her nowhere, and got to the point. "There have been some accidents along the Sea to Sky here. Drones and other flying objects are attacking cars. Scott likes his flying toys, and he lives right uphill, so of course we'd like to talk to him."

Mrs. Gold-Seton had been staring at JD throughout her disclosure. Now she threw her head back and laughed. When she was done laughing she said, "Scott wouldn't hurt a fly. He's the kindest young man I've met since, well, Evan. You see that boy in that photo?"

Dion picked up the hinged frame and peered at the central photo, an informal shot of a young family of four: husband and wife and two small boys.

"Not that one," Mrs. Gold-Seton snapped. "On the right, the dark-haired boy by the gate. That's Evan. He died two years after that photograph was taken. Scott is so like him, in looks and spirit. I'm not a fanciful woman, but I'll go so far as to say I feel I've connected with my younger son through Scott."

On the other side of the room, the macaw said, "Peek-a-boo."

Mrs. Gold-Seton stared distractedly at her pet. "Where he got that from, I don't know. It's not the kind of nonsense I'd ever teach him."

So Evan was the dreamy-eyed boy leaning on a rustic gate in the photo in the right-hand wing of the frame, Dion was thinking. The photo in the left-hand wing was a studio shot of a proud young man in lawyer's robes. Definitely Karl. He had the same big teeth and challenging eyes as the man who had made Dion's life miserable in court, but with coal black hair. The picture struck him as touching. He glanced at Heidi Gold-Seton and thought of the passage of time, the years of change she had lived through. When she was born, cars still had to be cranked, probably, and the Great Depression and the Second World War were just around the corner. She had gone from that to this — a marathon, indeed.

JD was looking at the photographs over Dion's shoulder. "So that's Ralph Seton as a young man," she marvelled. "Great photograph. Mind if I take a snapshot?"

Mrs. Gold-Seton didn't mind at all, and JD captured it with her phone camera as Dion held out the frame. He placed it back where he had found it, behind the dead roses, and JD sat back down to deal with one last question: confirming Karl's alibi. Mrs. Gold-Seton recalled a recent visit from her son, but couldn't say whether it was the night of the Amelia Foster crash.

"Thanks, you've been very helpful," JD said. "I hope you're back on the road soon."

Mrs. Gold-Seton grumbled acknowledgement, and as they left the macaw called out, "Goodbye."

* * *

"Maybe we misjudged poor Scott," JD said, back at the car. "His step-grandmother, at least, seems to think the world of him."

Dion was still puzzled by the disparity between Karl and Heidi's opinions of Scott Mills. It was like they were speaking about two different people. He said, "If Mills manipulates planes and causes crashes for kicks, he could be a people manipulator, too, sucking up to her. He wasn't born into money, he just lucked into it through his mom. Maybe he wants to make sure he's an heir to Heidi Gold-Seton's estate. Maybe Foster knew he was pulling the wool over her eyes, and was trying to warn us."

JD gave his idea the thumbs down. "Mrs. Gold-Seton vacates the room rather than chat with housekeeping. Foster was probably a nice enough woman, but you get to know people, even if they're dead, and I can tell you, she wasn't any kind of saint. So why would she give a hoot if the grandson to one of the residents here was a worm in disguise, sucking up to granny to get his name on the will? I'd say nice try, but dead wrong. Foster wasn't trying to warn us with her dying gasps to not let Mrs. Gold-Seton get duped. That's just stupid. Sorry, Cal, but you're wrong. She was simply hallucinating about a game of hide-and-seek, like we first thought."

JD was right, and Dion nodded. Behind the wheel, he turned the key. The engine growled alive and cool air punched out of the vents and riffled his hair. JD snapped on her seatbelt. "You keep not showing up at Rainey's. Too bad, 'cause it's lots of fun. You should come along, like I keep telling you. Oh, wait, I forgot, you're gone."

"I'm not gone, I'm right here," Dion snapped, and saw too late it was a trap.

"No," she said with mean satisfaction. "You're *not*."

Dion felt cold, and it had nothing to do with the vent shooting air into his face. He manoeuvred the car out and aimed for the exit.

"Sean is throwing a party New Year's Eve," JD said. "If you're really here, you'll be there."

"Of course I'll be there."

"Sure you will be. Sure, sure."

He frowned as he drove. Ever since hearing of the party, he had harboured a secret intention to find some

last-minute excuse to not go. Parties were sensory overload, stressful, and it was frankly too much work trying
to compete with his old fun-loving self. But JD's attitude
changed everything. He'd show her.

Thirty-Three

GHOST

A CREATURE OF HABIT, Leith brought a packed lunch to work most days, and the type of sandwich never varied, since he felt that ham or salami, cheese, mustard, and crispy iceberg lettuce was about as good as it got. But today he somehow ended up with JD in a small Vietnamese restaurant just off Lonsdale, eating something called spicy lemongrass noodle soup. It was good, but he missed his sandwich.

As they were sitting and talking, mostly gossiping about colleagues, out the window they saw a bear-like man strolling by. Mike Bosko. He didn't see them. "Sit very still," JD said through her teeth. But the warning was unnecessary, for Leith had already gone still as a rabbit under a hawk's shadow.

Together they watched Bosko raise a hand to somebody in greeting. The somebody turned out to be Dezi Novak, dressed in jeans and a hoodie, being pulled along by three small dogs on leashes.

The large man and the slight young woman stopped on the sidewalk and talked, like actors on a stage, but muted by heavy glass.

"They know each other?"

"Met briefly at the detachment," Leith said. "Having quite a friendly little chat there, aren't they?"

Bosko and Dezi seemed to be discussing the three little dogs that were skittering about at the ends of their leashes.

"She walks dogs for people," JD said. "It's a side job."

"Wonder what they're talking about now," Leith said, as the conversation on the sidewalk seemed to grow serious. Bosko was nodding as Dezi spoke, then Dezi nodded while Bosko spoke. Which he did at some length. When he was apparently finished, Dezi said something, looking indignant. Then the two went their own ways. Or at least Dezi did, while Bosko turned to Leith and JD, sitting motionless in their window seat, and gave a little wave.

"Damn," JD said. "He knew we were here all along."

"I swear he's not human," Leith said.

The door swung open, and Bosko entered the restaurant. He took a seat next to Leith. "Well," he said, "that was interesting."

"Do tell," JD said.

"I'm not sure how ethically sound it is," he said. "But it went like this. I've been keeping tabs on the case, but I don't feel I'm a hundred percent on top of it. I did recall her name, though. I greeted her and reintroduced myself. She asked if we had found Scott Mills yet. I said we hadn't, and reminded her that if she heard from him, we should be the first to know, and she should not engage with him in any way. She said of course, but I thought I saw something in her eyes that said otherwise. Now, probably I'm wrong, because I'm not the most perceptive guy, but let's just say I listened to the doubts in my head and leaned on her a bit."

The waitress, who spoke little English, came over and waved a menu inquiringly at Bosko. *Now just watch him speak to her in fluent Vietnamese*, Leith thought. But it didn't happen. Bosko told the woman that he wasn't staying, and she nodded and went away. "I told her that I thought she wasn't being upfront with me," he continued. "I recalled you telling me, JD, that her dream is to join the RCMP, so I leveraged that for what it was worth."

"I've been harping on that theme myself," JD said.

"It's a useful hook. I could see I was hitting a nerve, and maybe I went a little further than I should have, but I told her I think she's got knowledge that's critical to our case. She said that's not true, that she's told us everything. I said I personally don't believe that. She asked me why I don't believe her, when everybody else does. I don't think she was too impressed with my strong-arming, and I'm afraid I didn't win any confessions, either. Sorry, JD. You might have to do some remediation there."

JD was interested. "How exactly did she let you know she wasn't too impressed with you?"

"It was kind of scary, actually. When I said I didn't believe her, her eyes flashed daggers. For a moment there I thought she'd come at me, sink her teeth into my arm."

"Seriously?"

"Not altogether. But she was obviously hurt. 'You don't know anything about me,' she said. 'I'm not a liar.'

When I refused to back down or apologize, her eyes filled with tears. She said you, JD, had her back, and so did everybody else, and I don't know anything."

"That's what she said, 'You don't know anything'?"

"Verbatim."

JD shook her head in wonder. "Try looking at it from her perspective. She knows how critical honesty is. It's high stakes for her, higher than for you or me. You've dashed the hopes of a future cadet, sir."

Leith tried to play the optimist for a change. "I think a little strong-arming was a good idea. She'll mull it over, see she has no choice. We'll be hearing from her soon."

* * *

Dion was at Park Royal, the big mall in West Van that Looch used to call "the pod" because of its expansive space-colony feel. Acres of sterile whiteness with drone shoppers drifting between the food court and retail stores in stoned bliss.

He was in a menswear store, trying on shirts and obsessing over his upcoming attendance at Urbanski's New Year's party. He remembered Sean's parties and could picture himself in the scene. Before the crash he'd been happy and sharp-witted. He'd been a looker, a catch, and, well, full of himself.

These days he coped with work quite well, but the party scene remained a challenge. Standing in corners with nothing to say, a tongue-tied fool pretending to fit in. Maybe the new shirt would give him the boost he needed to prove to JD he was still *here*.

It was a fitted dark-maroon poly-cotton blend, with the faintest vertical stripes to offset the sheen. It snugged nicely to his body, but he wasn't convinced about the cut of the collar. The saleswoman said the look was *luscious*.

"Yeah, maybe," he said, and she buzzed off, leaving him to ponder the problem alone. Just not sure about the collar.

What would Kate think of the shirt? He still bought clothes with her in mind, and sometimes he consulted Looch. He missed Looch more than ever these days — where was that closure he'd heard about? He could hear Looch telling him the collar would look good in a 1970s disco, which made him think about his embarrassing confrontation with Kenny Poole on Christmas Eve. Thoughts of Kenny led to Tony Souza, which led back to himself and the trouble he was in.

Reflected in the mirror, the saleswoman was watching him. He paid for the shirt. Out in the pod's atrium he realized he had lost his bearings and didn't know which exit would take him to his car. But there was something else that had been nagging at him all morning, and he needed more info. Something to do with a ghost. He sat on a bench and called Leith.

"Yo, Cal," Leith answered.

Yo?

"Just a quick question," Dion said. "Do we have a picture of Scott Mills on file?"

"A mug shot, sure."

"I didn't see it. What does he look like?"

"Why?"

"Something Heidi said. I'll explain later."

Leith did his best to describe the mug shot, but the words formed no clear picture in Dion's mind, even with eyes squeezed shut. Leith broke into his thoughts to ask again why Mills's appearance mattered.

"She said he looks like Evan," Dion said. "Her dead son." He watched shoppers float by. They, too, carried crisp designer-brand bags of merchandise.

"I have no idea what you're talking about, but that's fine." Leith said. "Call me when you're ready to explain."

"Sure. I'll go take a look."

He disconnected.

Half an hour later he was in the case room, looking at Scott Mills's mug shot. He snapped a picture with his phone for reference and left the detachment. On the steps of JD's low-rise he pressed the button and was buzzed in. He climbed the stairs and found her standing with arms crossed in the doorway of her apartment, apparently unwilling to let him pass. "How the hell do you know where I live?" she said.

"It's on file now, since Desiree Novak paid you a visit, remember? You've become a person of interest."

She didn't return his grin, but allowed him in. Her apartment was smaller and darker than his. Messy, but nice enough. A lot of books, comfortable sofa, good-sized TV. Some travel souvenirs, but not a lot of knick-knacks or photos on the wall. He wondered if she'd ever had a boyfriend.

"Don't analyze me," she snapped. "Just tell me what you want."

He showed her the shot on his phone of Scott Mills's sullen face, a mug shot taken for the police file a couple years back when he got booked in for assault. Mills wasn't bad looking, but he was pasty, heavy. Muscular, but not well-maintained. His hair was sandy blond and cut short, to the scalp. He had bully written all over him. "It struck me as strange," Dion said. "Mrs. Gold-Seton saying that Scott looks like her dead son, Evan. I didn't know what Scott looked like at that point, but even so, it didn't seem right. And this proves it. They don't look anything alike, do they?"

JD looked at Mills's face on Dion's phone. "I wasn't paying attention to Evan. I was looking at the judge." She pulled out her own phone and scrolled through images till she found the one she had snapped of the tri-fold frame. "No," she said, zooming in on Evan's face. "He and Mills don't look alike at all. But resemblance can be all in the soul."

"What soul?" Dion said. "This guy's not like Evan, inside or out. Evan had dark hair, dark eyes. Look at him." He pointed to the face on JD's phone. "He's soft. And Mrs. Gold-Seton said he was kind, wouldn't hurt a fly."

"Some might say effeminate," JD said.

"Anyway, it doesn't matter what Evan was really like. It's about how he's not at all like Scott Mills, is what I'm saying."

"Maybe it's just her wishful thinking. And don't forget, she needs glasses."

"Only for reading. Not for studying people. You saw how she studied us. And does she look like the kind of person who gives in to wishful thinking?"

"We only met her for fifteen minutes. We don't know her. Think about it. She's trapped in a place she doesn't want to be, misses her dead son, wants to see Evan in Scott, so she does."

Dion shook his head. "No. Something weird is going on."

"An imposter?"

They gazed at the two photographs, then JD whistled low. "How about this," she said. "Heidi Gold-Seton never saw Scott Mills. Someone else brought flowers, someone who did look like Evan. Check out this guy." Again on her phone, she zoomed in on Evan's face to show Dion. "Who does he look like to you?" She waited a beat, and when it failed to click for him, said, "Amelia Foster, that's who."

* * *

By the time Leith arrived in the case room, three portraits had been pinned to the corkboard. The latest person of interest was a man named Evan Gold-Seton, but apparently he was dead. Long gone from this world, in fact. JD described Dion's revelations about Scott Mills and Evan Gold-Seton being such different people, and then her even bigger revelation about Scott Mills possibly being impersonated by Amelia Foster.

The leap seemed at best sketchy, in Leith's mind.

But looking at the enlargements on the board, at Evan's gentle, dark, and humorous eyes, and then at Amelia's, he thought, *Then again ...*

Thirty-Four

RED

December 27

SEAN URBANSKI SLAPPED a print on Leith's desk and declared he had just broken the alibi Scott Mills's mom gave him for the night of the Amelia Foster crash.

Leith looked at a low-res photograph of sushi on a table, and somebody off to the side reaching in with chopsticks. A partially cut-off caption above said, *Yummy sushi extravaganza birthday bash.*

Leith told Urbanski he was too tired and not smart enough to play games right now, and to please explain the significance of the picture.

"It's a screenshot from somebody's Facebook page," Urbanski said. "But to keep it simple for you, that lady with the chopsticks is Maria Gold-Seton." He leaned over and tapped the date of the posting. "Taken on the night this sushi-eating lying bitch told JD she was at home with her son, Scott. Scott was watching TV and she was curled up reading, she says, so Scott couldn't be out causing mischief with his toy planes."

"This is Maria Gold-Seton's Facebook page?"

"No. Her posts are set to private, but she neglected to hide her friends. So I mined their pages instead, and found this. Boom! Bottom line, Maria was out partying, not keeping an eye on Scott like she claims. Get it?"

Leith wished he could be so enthusiastic. The sushi picture remained blurry and indefinite to him. "How do you know that's her? Was she tagged?"

"Nope. This was nothing but an accidental photobomb. In fact, that's one thing I'm going to be asking this friend whose page this is. Did Maria get you to remove any photos or tags from that night? But I'm telling you, I recognize her. That's Maria Gold-Seton."

"Well, what are you waiting for?" Leith said. "Go firm it up."

* * *

Two cars were sent to pull in Maria Gold-Seton and Scott Mills, but both returned empty. Nobody home, and nobody answering their phone, though the old GMC pickup registered to Scott Mills sat in the driveway down by the guest cottage where he lived. Leith and JD were discussing the hassle of applying for a search warrant when Kenny Poole showed up with Constable Raj Sattar at his side. Sattar had been in the party sent out to effect the arrest, and according to Poole, he had something they might want to hear.

Leith and JD listened.

"Just as we were walking away," Sattar said, "this little poodle dog came at the window, barking, just furious, just yapping away at us, you know what I mean? It's one of those bay windows up off the ground about eight feet, triple-glazed, I'm betting, so you couldn't hear it through the glass — but it caught my eye, this white thing hopping up and disappearing again. It was hilarious, right? But everyone, like Corporal Wallace and all, was heading back to the vehicles and yelling at me that it's time to go, and I almost did, but I wanted to see how high it would hop. So funny, its little paws just smacking at the glass. I love animals. Pretty tiny for a guard dog, hardly bigger than a squirrel, but boy, squirrels can bite."

"Get to the point, Sattar," Poole said.

"So I turned to go," Sattar said. "But then I saw it was leaving smudges, this dog's snout and paws. And that struck me as … what's the word? As wrong, not fitting. Such a fancy house, probably plush carpets everywhere, and this dog's running around in mud? I don't like not following orders, but I went a bit closer to check, and it seemed to me the mud was reddish. But what do I know? I'm no mud expert. Probably it got its feet in the food bowl, is all. I hurried back to the cars. I reported what I'd seen to Corporal Wallace, but he didn't seem too bothered by it. It's only when I got back and told Kenny — Constable Poole, I mean — he thought it should be reported right away."

Wow, and good thing he did, Leith thought, thinking of the search warrant to be applied for. In filling it out, he would put a more ominous twist on the constable's observations, leave out any suggestion of food bowls or mud. Getting the go-ahead would be a snap now, thanks to Sattar's love of animals.

* * *

The potentially bloody paw prints got an expedited warrant. In the late afternoon of December 27, the team was on its way to the Gold-Seton estate at Lions Bay, where they would join forces with Squamish members. The day was moody and damp, and the grounds were quiet as Leith drove up the long private drive, following the ERT cavalcade. It was his first time to the park-like estate, and beside him JD was being his guide. That brushy lane to the left — she pointed — would lead to Scott Mills's cottage. They'd check it out after the main house, which was that castle-like structure up ahead.

They arrived at the perimeter and waited at the side of the car while the ERT members scoped the exterior and then gained entrance.

"Not answering phones, bloody paw prints all over the living room window," JD said. "Call me alarmist, but this isn't some giant misunderstanding that's going to end up in sheepish grins and eggnog toasts all round."

She was right. Minutes later came the news of discovery, and it was grim. They listened as the house was cleared of threats. Medics entered and medics left. The ambulance waiting at the wings departed. The coroner entered. The Forensics Identification Unit head stopped to talk to Leith, then went in along with two team members, loaded with equipment. Much of the ERT team left. Members of the press arrived, but were kept behind the lines. Dion and Urbanski had joined Leith and JD by their car to watch the to-ing and fro-ing and to listen to the chatter on the radio. An ERT member left the home in a rush, rummaged in the back of an SUV, then rushed back in, lugging a pet carrier.

Finally the ERT team leader strode down the steps and confirmed that three bodies were inside, a female and two males. Also found was one antsy dog, alive and well, but now sedated. The dog was like a live blotting sponge, just covered in evidence, as Sattar had described, and the house was going to be a nightmare to process, in large part thanks to the dog.

Leith learned that at the other end of the estate, Scott Mills's cottage sat deserted, with his truck sitting cold outside. The cottage's front door was not only unlocked, but swinging open in the breeze, as if the resident had left in a hurry. There were signs of upheaval inside, but no obvious violence.

"We'll check out the cottage next. For now it's our turn here." Leith looked with reluctance at the face of the mansion. Time for the crime-scene bunny suits and more horror stories for that memoir he had no desire to ever write.

Inside the home, an electronic ring tone could be heard jangling from somewhere above, accompanied by its lonely echo. Within the foyer, not far from the front door, the body of a sturdy young man lay sprawled belly up, as if it had been blown backward by a punch. The force of his fall had knocked over furniture in the foyer, smashed a vase and scattered the flowers. His face was damaged beyond recognition, likely by a close-range bullet. Leith suspected this was Scott Mills. JD agreed; those were the clothes and physique of a young man.

Dion had not stopped to speculate, but had moved with some speed across the foyer and through a larger room, following the line of contamination marked out with tape by Forensics, maybe searching for the source of the haunting ring tone. Leith left JD with the body of Scott Mills and followed Dion, finding him stopped halfway up a broad stone staircase. A body lay head downwards, blood gathering in its lower extremities and pinkening the visible quarter of its face.

This dead man was heavier than the corpse by the front door, and older, with a mop of silver hair messily flopped, stained red, and visibly polluted with brain matter. He seemed to be reaching for his phone, what looked like the latest iPhone on the market. It sat on the stair tread below his fingers. It had stopped ringing, but now started up again: a pop version of "Auld Lang Syne."

When the phone fell silent, for good this time, Dion looked around at Leith and said matter-of-factly, "This is Karl Gold-Seton."

Too matter-of-factly. "Stay to the path," Leith warned, because Dion had stepped closer to the body than he should, as if to lend it a hand getting back to its feet. "Let's see the third victim."

They gave the body wide berth and entered a room on the third floor that had been flagged for them by the ERT to check out. It was a lounge or library of sorts with bookshelves and a chandelier, arched windows veiled in gauze and velveteen. One window sash was flung open, and the air was frigid and sea scented. The view was an impressive swatch of Howe Sound, Leith noticed abstractedly. He focused on the furniture. The seating was massive and old school, with rich chocolate-brown leather affixed to oak with brass studs, leafy curlicues carved into the wood. The largest piece of the set, a slightly curved five-seat sofa, had been shoved out of place, rucking the oriental rug into wavelets over the sleek hardwood floor.

The body lay behind it, Leith had been advised, in the narrow space between wall and sofa back. Dion was the first to go over and take a look, then he moved back to give Leith his turn.

Leith got an acute view of the dead woman, from the perspective of her feet, her body little more than a darkened topography of flesh and blood-soaked fabric. The medics would have checked her for signs of life, but only as a formality, leaving her as they found her, an integral and bizarre part of the scene. She lay stretched along the baseboard, as if crushed into place. She looked like a player in a hide-and-seek game gone badly wrong. Her feet were bare, with pearly-pink toenails. Leith shone his flashlight toward her face and saw her nostrils were bloody. He could smell urine. A blood-spattered handbag lay on her chest, open, its contents spilled. The woman's arms were curled up toward her face in an awkward self-hug, pressed into place by the pressure of the sofa back. One hand curled around something shiny — a smartphone.

Not so much a hide-and-seeker as a blizzard victim frozen in the middle of placing her last call, and one of the most surreal crime scenes Leith had ever stared down upon.

JD had slipped into the room, glancing at the open window that was letting in gusts of December air. From behind Leith, she said, "And that's Maria, right?"

As if in response, the phone in the dead woman's hand pinged.

Leith straightened to let JD take a look at the body squeezed into place by the sofa.

"She had time to consider jumping out the window," JD theorized. "But too far to fall. So she hid instead, trying to call for help. The killer took a running shove, pushed the sofa against her, knocked her out. Maybe the impact killed her? Is that possible?"

Leith didn't think getting crushed by the sofa — even one this weighty — would have killed her, or caused all that blood. Knocked her out, maybe, restricted her movements, sure. Cause of death would have to be determined in the morgue, but he was betting that bullets would be found along with the impact injuries.

Leaving JD to maintain continuity, he beckoned to Dion, and they went back to the cold outdoors, to Leith's vehicle.

"Are you all right?" Leith asked, as he and Dion shed their bunny suits.

"Yes." Dion sounded surprised, maybe offended. He tamed the ends of his necktie, which were trying to flap loose in the breeze. "Why?"

"You knew the lawyer, right?"

"Not well. We were on opposite sides of the fence. We weren't friends."

"Still, you knew him. It's a shock, when somebody you know dies. Especially like this."

Leith persisted only because he had the feeling Dion was reining in some heavy emotion. Maybe not grief so much as shock, but whatever it was, sharing was probably a good idea. But Dion wasn't the sharing type. He shrugged off the suggestion, agreed to meet up back at the detachment, and strolled away to his unmarked car.

* * *

It's only hunger, Dion told himself. He felt light-headed and queasy. Breakfast had been light. Too light, apparently. In the dim privacy of his vehicle, he checked his eyes in the rear-view mirror and said aloud, "I'll stop in Horseshoe Bay, grab a bite."

The ferry terminal settlement of Horseshoe Bay was just minutes away. He pulled in and drove through the village, but couldn't find a parking spot, and gave up the plan of stopping for a bite. He wasn't in the mood for food, anyway. Still queasy, and for some reason perspiring. The case spiralling out of control was getting on his nerves. Just needed to ground himself. Driving through the community, he decided not to head straight back to the highway, but to proceed westbound into Whytecliff Park, take a brief break.

Whytecliff was a giant rocky outcrop with beaches fanned out at its base and woods all around. He turned into its shady entrance and rolled forward. The park was nearly empty in the winter chill, with only a few cars at the far end of the generous lot. His plans were vague, and his mind seemed emptier than usual. He would stretch his legs, release some of that crime-scene tension. Maybe stand on the cliffs and take in the sights, breathe in the briny air splashed up from the breakers below, put life back into perspective.

In the end, the idea was hijacked by physiology. Bile rose to his throat, and he steered at a wild angle into the nearest parking space, managed to switch off the engine, fling open the door, topple from the driver's seat, and barely make it to the bushes to throw up his last meal.

He leaned, then, hands on his knees, and spat till the taste had left his mouth.

He rinsed his mouth with coffee from a paper cup in the console, a leftover from an earlier drive, spat again, and felt worlds better. But embarrassed. He straightened and looked down the lot. Nobody had seen. He looked at the sky. It was red.

Thirty-Five

MOVING TARGET

December 29

THE FIRST FORTY-EIGHT had passed since the deadly shots rang out in Lions Bay. A lot of detail had been filled in since, but not the main one, the whopper detail: the killer remained nameless.

Leith studied the chart. A rough time of death had been added. At around 11:00 p.m. on Boxing Day evening, Karl Gold-Seton, his wife, Maria, and his stepson, Scott, had their lives ended in swift consecutive order — at least that was the safe assumption — ending up as figures on a diagram in a police incident room, alongside the crime-scene photographs. Leith looked again over each element of the wall display. He had just finished his lunch — cramming it in, not tasting much — and now was immersed in the gore affixed to the wall like an ill-conceived art show. He crossed his arms and thought about life, death, and ruthless twists of fate — but not for long. He was here to consider the facts, not philosophize.

There were plenty of facts to mull over, each with its myriad sub-facts that the forensics people would have to sort out, the lands and grooves and residues and spatters. The weapon had been a semi-auto pistol. The ammo was .45, the rifling a possible match to the slug that had punctured Craig Gilmartin. The bullet count, all told from all three floors, was twenty-two, so likely more than one reload. Twenty-two shots, but oddly enough, only a few had landed inside the victims. The walls had received most of the killer's wrath — low shots fired seemingly at random.

Aside from the chaotic wall shots, the shooting had been fairly focused. If the order of attacks followed logic, then the young male adult, Scott Mills, had died first. He had caught one bullet in the face, two in the chest.

The lawyer, Karl Gold-Seton, had died next, maybe on his way downstairs to find out what the hell the commotion in the foyer was. Probably he had been on the verge of changing his mind and retreating. One bullet in the gut had toppled him forward. His body had thudded down the smooth marble stairs, dragged by gravity — the blood smear said it all. A bullet to the back of the skull had dispatched him.

His wife had fled upstairs. Her slippers left behind on the second-floor landing were a good indication of where she had been when she turned to run. In the upstairs library she had likely flung open a window, either to cry for help or jump to safety. But there was no one to hear her, and nothing below but a deadly fall. She was trying to dial 911 — a safe guess — when the sofa she had taken refuge behind was pushed into her with force. As she lay pinned and helpless, she was shot in the torso four times from above. Meaning the killer had jumped up onto the sofa and fired down on her, probably using up the last of his ammo.

Forensics assured Leith there would be evidence, saying that with this kind of rampage, there always was. Leith knew better. In his past, he had worked on a few rampages that had never been solved, cold cases that he hoped one day would be closed. He looked at the pins flagging bullet holes. He looked at the photographs of gouges riddling the Gyproc wallboards, mostly in the foyer. More holes in the wall upstairs in the library, where the woman had been killed. Maybe the killer had lost control of his trigger finger. Maybe the gun was faulty. More likely the shooter was firing as he proceeded through the place just to scare his victims. Brazen, cruel, sadistic. This man — Leith assumed it was a man, and a powerful one at that, the way he had rammed the poor woman with that sofa — had a serious grudge against the family. Where had the killer gone after he was done here, and who else had he left mown down in his wake? Wrath like this didn't just stop.

Dion appeared next to him, a cup of coffee in hand. He gestured at one photograph of the bullet-riddled wall. "Shows what kind of sharpshooter he is," he said with contempt. "Not great with moving targets."

Leith looked at him. Was that some kind of dark joke? "What d'you mean?"

"Not even winged," Dion said. He gave Leith a searching gaze. "The dog."

The dog! "Hm, oh," Leith said. He eyed the chaotic line of holes in the Gyproc. "He was trying to shoot the dog. That's a good hypothesis."

Dion frowned at him.

Leith breathed out a sigh of relief. Calling it relief might be overstated, but now that the barrage of low shots had a reasonable explanation, he could worry less about a cruel and vindictive killer on the loose, offing people at random. He turned to the photographs of the cottage where Scott Mills had been living. A mess, but no apparent violence. A wheeled suitcase open and half filled with clothes. What was known about it? Nothing but a series of guesses, which he summed up now. "Mills was packing to leave town. His mother concocted an alibi for him. The two of them, at least, were involved in something. He was running from our inquiries. Somebody didn't want him to leave — or to live. Maybe Maria was a target, too. Maybe the killer wasn't just clearing the house of witnesses, but had a bead on her as well."

Dion indicated the latest person of interest tacked to the board. Somebody with a sense of humour had printed out a blank Facebook avatar for a mug shot. Dezi's Grey Man seemed like a good prime suspect.

JD walked in. "Well hey, guys! Our canvassing efforts have paid off. We've got a witness. A local resident. She didn't see or hear gunshots, or see anybody coming or going from the estate, but a car pulled out in front of her, coming off Bayview. She followed it to the highway, where it turned left, then she lost sight of it. Boxing Day, almost midnight, not a lot of traffic in that neighbourhood — that's the only reason she remembers."

JD tapped the spot on the blown-up map of Lions Bay, and Leith saw that any car leaving the Gold-Seton home would have no choice but take this route. There was no other exit. "Fantastic!" he said. "We've got a description?"

JD shook her head. "About all our witness can say is that it was a car, a darker colour, one occupant, who she only saw from behind, kind of an anonymous bump above the headrest."

"Well, look at me," Leith snapped. "I'm just covered in goosebumps. You call this a tip?"

JD wasn't one to grin, but she did now. It was a suspiciously coy grin, too, and he realized she had been holding back. "I almost forgot," she said. "There was a distinguishing mark on the car."

"Damage?" Dion asked.

"Better than damage. A business name plastered across the rear trunk hatch. She recalls the name clearly because it was 'cute,' she says."

"Cute?" Leith echoed. Some words didn't mesh with murder, *cute* being one of them.

"And it is being followed up as we speak," JD added. "But there's more. The business name she mentioned actually pinged something in my mind." She turned to Dion. "Remember Tom, our pilot who's afraid of heights? Remember that custom-made sling he had for carrying his plane and gear to the lookout?"

Dion stared at her. "I remember a bag, sure."

"It looked professionally made. I didn't think much of it, except that the business name sewn on the shoulder strap was kind of clever, if the proprietor's name happened to be Taylor."

Leith lost patience with JD as he had lost patience with Urbanski and every other riddler on the North Shore — and there seemed to be a lot of them. "Do me a favour and tell me what we're looking at here. This is a murder inquiry, JD, not a guessing game."

She pinned a piece of paper to the board, then slapped it proudly. "I had our witness sketch it for me."

Leith studied a pencil drawing of the rear of a vehicle. Their witness was an even lousier artist than himself — and that was saying a lot — but he felt the first warm ray of hope as he viewed the highlight of the masterpiece. Across the back of the car's trunk, written in block letters, were the words *Taylor-Made Custom Upholstery*. Below *Upholstery* were seven smaller X's.

"What are the X's?" he asked, though he could guess.

"A phone number," JD said. "The witness couldn't remember a single digit. But the team's all high-fiving anyway. I know, what kind of killer would drive a car to the scene with his phone number and logo on display? I know it's bad luck to celebrate too soon, but we're getting so little — hang on," she interrupted herself as her phone buzzed at her hip. "Fingers crossed."

She took the call, listened, and gave a thumbs-up to Leith and Dion. Her smile said it all; the individual who ran the business called Taylor-Made had already been tracked down.

Like the pessimist he was, Leith worried as the team gathered around for a briefing that JD had done just what she'd suggested — celebrated too soon. This lead, linking a car at the Lions Bay murder scene with Thomas Frey, would prove false in the end, and their killer was still on the move. Possibly the distraction would do nothing but allow Grey Man to vanish for good, leaving no clue to his identity except for one scary nickname.

Thirty-Six

UNSTITCHED

AS JD HAD SAID, would the killer be so stupid as to drive a car that could be picked out of a lineup, thanks to the distinctive wording on its trunk? Without that sign it would likely have gone unnoticed in a world that teemed with cars, so many of them much of a muchness. Even makes and models were indistinguishable to most people, at least in passing. Like trying to pick one sardine out from its school.

Leith and JD discussed the question on the drive to Ms. Corinne Taylor's bungalow off the Mount Seymour Parkway. Even before leaving the car, climbing the stairs, and pressing the buzzer, Leith knew a few things about her, thanks to a combination of Google and social media, PRIME-BC, and ICBC records. Taylor was in her fifties, self-employed, had no criminal record, owned a recent model Ford Focus sedan, and was married to Thomas Frey, who happened to be the model airplane flying club president who had assisted Leith with his RC knowledge.

Frey was fifty-two, had no criminal record, had previously worked as an engineer in northern Alberta, but was now employed by Pacific Blue Cross as a group service representative — whatever that was. The only alarm bell going off about Frey right now was the decal on his wife's car. *Just one bell, but a damn loud one*, as Leith had told JD.

Taylor herself answered the door. Tom wasn't home, she explained, but was due back any moment. He had just gone to the store for cigarettes.

She was visibly nervous — who wouldn't be? — as Leith and JD took seats in the living room, which was chaotically colourful, bolts of fabric and textiles everywhere. Leith explained that this was a murder investigation, and he needed to know where she had been and what she had been doing on Boxing Day.

"Murder?" she said.

"We have to follow up every lead," Leith said, reassuringly, letting her know this was probably nothing, nothing at all. Which really, it was anything but. She balked at first, but accepted his smile at face value. "I was at home," she told him, with a blank-eyed stare. "I wouldn't go out there if you paid me. It was Boxing Day."

Leith nodded. North Van traffic was bad enough without Boxing Day madness, the sales and gift exchanges, the traffic snarls and fist-shaking, goodwill and peace on earth blown to heck as Christmas shifted gears. "Didn't go out at all?"

"Other than a neighbourhood walk early in the morning, no."

"What about Tom?"

"Tom was home all day, too."

"All day, all night?"

"Yes, of course."

At the mention of her husband, the woman had become slightly defensive. Leith wondered why. And why the *of course*? It was like a pianist striking a wrong key, discordant but interesting. He put it aside for the moment, and asked her about the lead-grey sedan he had passed in the driveway. "That's your car, the Ford Focus?"

"It is," she said.

"Taylor-Made," he said. "Your business, I take it?"

"Yes. As you can see" — she waved a hand at the fabric bolts, pattern charts, sewing machines around the room — "I do custom upholstery for people. I have a workshop, but when things get busy, it kind of spills out here."

"Great business name, anyway."

"Thank you." She smiled through her nervousness. "Eye-catching, d'you think?"

"It caught my eye," he assured her.

Taylor did her best to return his smile. "Good thing I kept my maiden name," she said. "Frey would hardly do for a seamstress, would it?" Leith's reassuring smile broadened. "Though I would have been going back to Taylor anyway, by the looks of it," she added, and her mouth flatlined again. "Anyway, my marriage is not your problem, and I talk too much."

She mime-zipped her mouth.

Leith liked people who talked too much. It made his job easier. "That's all right, really. Does Tom help in the business at all?"

"Not a bit. He's got his own work. We're like two separate planets, lately. I don't know him anymore. Oh god, there I go again. I'll say nothing. You ask your questions and I'll try and help."

"I'm pretty much done with my questions. We're really here to see Tom. So ... what's the strangest custom upholstery job you ever got?"

His clumsy attempt at casual, ice-breaking conversation failed, and her response was terse. "My business is strictly by the books. I pay my taxes. I fall below the GST amount, so I don't have a registration number."

"You're really not in trouble over your business," he assured her. "I just noticed the decal on your car, and JD and I were saying it's pretty clever."

"Yes, well." She relaxed slightly. "Work's been slow lately, so a friend suggested I start advertising. So far I've gotten all my business through word of mouth, but it's true — it's time to get more professional. That, plus I was trying to show Tom that I've got brains, too. He thinks he's the only one who can think for himself. So I went out to the stationery store and stuck *Taylor-Made* on the back there. The phone number's quite small, though, isn't it, under the word *Upholstery*? Maybe kind of hard to read?"

"No, it stands out nicely, I think."

She nodded, but her happiness seemed tarnished by some private thought. "It's already drumming up business," she said, as if in defiance of her own doubts. "I got my first call just this morning. The lady said she saw my sign, took down the number, gave me a call."

Leith was interested, not so much in Taylor's business acumen as in the timing of her decaling job, along with her mysterious ambivalence about it. The sign was a recent thing, and something about it bothered her. He wondered if it had to do with the killer's fatal oversight.

"A waterproof, colour-coordinated barbecue cover," Taylor said, as if to herself. She was knitting and unknitting her fingers and staring at the floor. "To match the patio decor. Should be easy enough."

"Sounds like the sign was a smart move," Leith said. "So you stuck the decals on just recently?"

In an odd response, her face clouded over. "Hmph," she said. "Yes."

Leith waited, but she didn't explain the *hmph*. "Was there a problem?"

"Well, it may be just a symptom of our deteriorating marriage, but instead of being impressed, he was pissed off. Tom, I mean."

Leith nodded sympathetically, hoping she wouldn't zip her mouth again.

"I applied it on Christmas Day," she went on, "and it's not as easy as it looks. You have to space the letters evenly, keep them straight. But I hurried through it, when he was out. I was going to surprise him with it, you know, thinking he'd be pleased. Though nothing pleases him lately. I don't know where we went wrong."

"Marriage can be a tough road," Leith said.

The lame platitude seemed to comfort her. "You can say that again."

"So what happened with the decaling?" he pressed.

"What happened is I forgot all about it until two days later, when he comes bursting into the house in a big tizzy asking what the hell I've done."

"So that's the twenty-seventh?"

Immediately Leith regretted the pointedness of his question, as she turned wary eyes on him once more. "Why? Does it matter? What on earth has he done? It's serious, isn't it?"

He nodded. "I'm sorry."

She nodded in return, but instead of clamming up, she continued with something like satisfaction. "Yes, that was the twenty-seventh. He was not happy when he saw the sign. I don't know what the big deal was, but obviously it's got something to do with your serious case, am I right?" She went on as if she didn't expect an answer. "He used to be so easygoing about everything. A bit of a neatnik, a bit *anal* when it comes to houseplants or socks, but otherwise not terribly fussy. So apparently it's not the decal itself, but how it's messed up his plans, whatever those are. I'm guessing he borrowed my car, and I'm guessing he didn't realize he was driving around with an advertisement all over its backside."

"Does he often drive your Focus?"

"No, never. He's got his own vehicle."

She gazed toward the window, maybe looking for a sign of her husband's return. By now Leith couldn't tell whether she was gloating or grieving. "What's taking him so long?" she murmured.

JD, silent till now, asked, "Corinne, are you sure Tom was home all night on Boxing Day, day and evening?"

"I was sure, until you two showed up."

"Do you share a bedroom?"

Taylor laughed. "Not anymore, we don't. He's got his

space and I've got mine. Now he can look at his girlie pictures all he wants."

"Internet porn?" Leith asked.

"I don't know. Go take a look, if you want."

"Could he have gone out that night, and you didn't notice?" JD said.

Taylor seemed to weigh the possibility. "I was asleep by ten, as usual. He has access to my car keys. So yes, he could have."

They continued to wait for Frey's return. Leith considered taking up Corinne's offer to check out her husband's computer, but decided he didn't want to jump the gun, not without discussing it with the team. Taylor asked if she could get some work done, and Leith said it was no problem. She seized a piece of upholstery, sat down again with a small instrument in hand, and began to viciously rip at stitches. "This seam is all wrong," she said to herself. "What was I thinking? What a mess."

* * *

Tom Frey wasn't coming home. His wife had provided a list of possible locations he might have gone to, but the list wasn't promising. Safeway, some gas stations, the liquor store. Cars had gone out to prowl the areas in question, but Frey had not surfaced.

When too much time had gone by, Leith looked at his watch. "Corinne, where is he? You must have some idea."

She repeated that she didn't have a clue. She was watching a sitcom on TV now, not laughing at the jokes but was dabbing at her eyes with a Kleenex. Leith fully believed that whatever Tom had done, she wasn't a part of it.

At 6:15, JD arranged for a shift of cars to watch the house, and she and Leith departed, with nothing to do now but wait.

Thirty-Seven

SPOOKED

December 30

BY MORNING, THOMAS FREY was officially a missing man, the contents of his computer had been searched, and it was found that one folder contained over a hundred shots of Dezi Novak. They were surveillance-type shots only, no close-ups, no *together* shots, which told Leith the girl was unaware she was being stalked.

Yes indeed, Grey Man had surfaced.

Leith stood admiring the diagram on the case room's whiteboard. JD had drawn it out in her neat and precise dry-erase calligraphy. The diagram sported five names in boxes, and the boxes were connected by lines into a circle, with other lines radiating out to other connections and complications. The five names were *Novak, Foster, Mills, Frey,* and *Grey Man.* JD had creatively drawn an infinity symbol around two of the names, *Frey* and *Grey Man,* to show that they had merged. The connecting lines showed that Dezi knew Scott Mills, and Mills had — quite probably — been killed by Frey. Did Dezi know Tom Frey, and did she realize he was Grey Man? She would need to be brought in once more for questioning, and this time she would be leaned on until she told what really happened.

But where was Thomas Frey? He and his white hatchback, reindeer antlers no doubt discarded, had vanished into the blue.

* * *

The skies were turquoise, the air sharp and clean, and Ken Poole was working up a sweat. He had driven to Ambleside Park for his usual jog. He ran not out of zest for living, but out of fear. Heart trouble and all its consequences had wreaked havoc in his family tree on both sides for as far back as the branches could be traced. Paralysis, incontinence, brain damage, early death. He had seen the effects and dreaded them, and so he jogged every day, early morning or late at night, whenever his schedule permitted. Usually it was around his neighbourhood, thudding up and down the avenues like a tired horse with blinders on.

But this was his day off, and so he had driven across town to the popular park in West Van, with its long walkways abreast sandy beaches and its holiday atmosphere. Lovers in winter jackets strolled arm in arm, dogs romped off leash in their designated romp zones, and some, like Poole, went forth in solitude.

He jogged and puffed, ignoring the other joggers and walkers. When his Fitbit told him he had done enough, he slowed to an easy lope, and finally stopped to rest on a bench.

He looked at the sea, at the Squamish Nation Welcome Figure standing at the end of the spit, its arms out to the brilliant blue sky. The winter air cooled the sweat on his temples, and he shivered.

The call he had to make had been weighing on him for the past few days, ever since that off-the-wall Christmas visit — Dion barging in with his wacky accusations, followed by his obvious embarrassment, then a night of talking. That rambling, coded conversation loosened by liquor. Even laughing, Dion was afraid, and what was that all about? There was something he wanted to confess that night, but in the end, instead of unburdening, he had come to his senses and called a cab.

Poole dialed and waited.

Dion came on the line, sounding guarded. Poole's number wouldn't be in his contacts list; it would show up as *unknown*, and he would be expecting a telemarketer. Some kind of machine thrummed in the background, a rhythmic *whup-whup-whup*. Possibly he was in a laundry room. "I've got something important to tell you," Poole said. "What are you up to? Have a few minutes to meet?"

As expected, there was hesitation. Then, "What for?"

"I'm not going to get into it over the phone. Cap Mall, the Starbucks, half an hour. Up to you, man. But you might as well jump in your car, or it'll drive you crazy, wondering what I have to say. Right?"

Dion was smart enough to agree.

* * *

Capilano Mall was down-to-earth and on the small side, with big-box stores all around — nothing like the Pod, where Dion had bought his shirt. The Starbucks had quasi-alfresco seating set up outside its front doors, except the fresh air was mall air. Half an hour after the call from Poole, Dion was sitting across from the man at one of these tables. Each had a coffee in front of him. Other than *hi* there had been no chit-chat about weather or work. Now Poole beelined to the point of the meeting. "I know you're in shit. I just don't know how deep. What's going on?"

So that was it. As feared, Dion had said too much on that Christmas visit, lulled by strong beer, and Poole had sussed him out. He shrugged. "Not deep."

"What is it?" Poole said. "You wanted to tell me, so tell me. I'm here to help. You know it."

Dion shook his head. He hadn't confessed while drunk, and he sure as hell wouldn't now, sober.

Poole shrugged. "Fine, then. But I thought you should know, whatever it is you're up to your neck in, you're being watched. Within the force. By your own people."

Dion's heart began to thud. He stilled his body — no raised brow to give himself away, no twist of the mouth — and waited in silence for whatever Poole was going to tell him next.

"Back in the summer," Poole said, "I was in the detachment, in the underground parking. I was sitting in my car, but I wasn't going anywhere. No reason. Just one of those moments when I needed a minute to decompress."

"Sure."

Poole hunched forward and lowered his voice, not enough to look fishy to the other Starbucks patrons, but enough that nobody could overhear. "Car pulls in," he said. "Right? Dave Leith and JD get out. They walk to the exit, disappear. Door clangs shut. Couple seconds later, Leith comes back, goes to his car. Gets something out of the glovebox. Heads for the stairs again, but stops by your car, seems to check his pockets for something, looking around."

Along with his thudding heart, a knot now tightened in Dion's stomach.

Poole had paused to chortle from the side of his mouth. "Not a natural-born spook, this Leith guy."

"No," Dion agreed.

"So I see him hunker down, and he removes something from the wheel well of your car. Or attaches something — I dunno. Removes or attaches, one or the other. Take a wild guess what that thing was."

"Why are you telling me now? Why not then?"

"Because for one thing, I didn't know it was your car at the time. I've seen you driving it since. For another, I didn't know till you came over the other night that you're in trouble. For a third, from where I was sitting, I couldn't see exactly what Leith was doing over there. It meant nothing to me then. But adding up all the parts, I think it's safe to say you're being tracked. Or you were in the summer. Who knows if he still is, but I wanted to warn you — no strings attached. That's all."

"I appreciate it. But why do you feel you have to warn me? Why don't you just stay out of it like you should?"

"Because," Poole said. He looked irritated. "Just because, is why."

Dion stood, feeling sick, afraid he'd throw up all over the table, which would really blow his cover. He had hardly touched his coffee. "Thanks for telling me," he said. "Don't worry about it, though. It's nothing. See you later."

"Hope so," Poole said. But he didn't sound hopeful at all.

Thirty-Eight

THE DEVIL IN THE DETAILS

DEZI HAD JUST LOST her friend Scott Mills in the most horrible way, so it was no wonder her face was puffy and her eyes were red and swollen. She sat across from JD in the interview room and talked about her confusion, her grief, and her self-doubt in a voice so hoarse she might have been shouting for hours. All of it looked and sounded like the real McCoy of shock.

By now JD knew for sure that Dezi wasn't the shooter. Her alibi was solid. She hadn't been anywhere near Lions Bay at the time of the murders, was in fact visiting her grandparents in Abbotsford with her mother, Maddie.

But maybe she knew who was responsible, in one guise or another.

It was guises they were talking about this morning.

No, Dezi didn't know the name Thomas Frey. Neither did she recognize his picture. JD saw the lack of recognition in Dezi's eyes as she looked at the photograph obtained from Corinne. She asked Dezi to describe Grey Man again for her.

"I only saw him those few times," Dezi said. "At the park, and then when we went for a ride, and then at Porteau Beach. I mean, I could guess, if that's all right."

"Guess away."

"I think he was older, like fifty or something. Average size, average weight, I'd say. He wore that long grey coat, and a hat. It was shaped like an outback hat, I think. And he kept his collar up and wouldn't look at me straight. I saw his eyes, though, once. He had nice eyes."

JD asked her to describe his eyes, beyond *nice*, but Dezi couldn't. He seemed to work hard to avoid even that kind of contact. "I'm thinking he was burned or something, and that's why he didn't want to show his face. But that's just totally speculating."

JD remembered Thomas Frey's face being pitted with acne scars along one cheekbone; otherwise he was unremarkable. Remarkably nondescript, if anything. "Did you ask him why he was so shy?"

Again Dezi shook her head. "I didn't want to be snoopy."

"And he didn't volunteer anything about it?"

"No. Like I said, we barely talked. Mostly he just said one or two words to Scott."

JD asked Dezi if she had ever noticed Grey Man, or anyone for that matter, following her, watching her, maybe aiming a camera at her.

"There was one time," Dezi said. "Maybe early December, a guy way down the block had this big camera, and he might have been aiming it at me."

Big camera probably meant a DSLR with a telephoto lens. Like the Canon Rebel JD knew Frey owned. "Could that have been Grey Man?"

Dezi shook her head. She didn't know, hadn't been worried about it at the time. "I'm careful. My mom's been warning me about strangers ever since I was little. I would have noticed if I was being stalked."

"A guy with a big camera aimed your way didn't alarm you?"

"I couldn't even say if he was aiming it at me. He could have been aiming it at anything. A tourist, you know." Dezi didn't look convinced by her own assurances. She looked miserable and guilt-ridden. "I should have been more observant. I'd have made a lousy cop anyway, I guess."

"Now, come on," JD said. "Nobody's blaming you for any of this."

"I know. But I feel like shit."

It was the first time JD had heard the girl swear. It jarred the ears. She asked Dezi to cast her mind back to the night of the Amelia Foster crash. Had there been another vehicle in the area where the accident happened, perhaps pulled over?

Dezi didn't think there was, but maybe. Yes, quite possibly, in fact, there were a couple of vehicles in the pullout as she drove past. Or maybe just one. But again, she couldn't be sure. She gave JD a gloomy stare. "You're thinking Grey Man killed Scott? Why? Something to do with that girl in the crash? Or was it because of me?"

"All I can say right now is that you'll be watched around the clock," JD said, "you and your mom and your home, till we know better. But you be extra careful, right? Eyes open."

Dezi nodded.

"Did Scott ever seem to be afraid of Grey Man?" JD asked.

"Not that I could see. Scott always dissed everybody except him, so I guess he liked him."

"They seemed close?"

"Not like friends. I actually thought it was just about cars. But was that just a lie? Scott said Grey Man liked me, that first time, but it never occurred to me that was the whole point of us hanging around with him, going for drives with him. But is that what it was?"

Probably, JD thought. "It's possible," she said.

Dezi pulled a worried face, as if assembling in her mind the clues she had missed. "Taking pictures? That's really creepy. I hope you catch him soon. I won't be able to sleep till you do."

The girl had worked out the stalker-kills-boyfriend theory neatly enough, JD thought. But so she should. After all, she was going to be a detective one day, if everything went right.

Though her faith in that day actually arriving had faded. Even if Dezi was only peripherally involved in this maelstrom of violent crime, it could impact her chances.

But just how peripheral was Dezi? That was the question.

* * *

In the lunchroom they sat at a table, JD with her cup of strong coffee, Dion with his decaf.

"How did I do?" JD asked.

"You did great."

"I don't think Dezi has a clue who Grey Man is."

Dion had come to the same conclusion while monitoring the interview.

"She's telling the truth about that part," JD said. "The other part bugs me, though. I was wondering if you got the same vibe. Toward the end."

"The part where she's creeped out to learn the guy is stalking her," Dion said. "It all sank in too fast, and the follow-through was all wrong. Right?"

"The sinking in and follow-through are where people always screw up," JD said.

"Let's go play it again."

As they walked upstairs to view the video recording of Dezi's interview, JD said, "So, have you thought of a good excuse yet?"

From her snide tone, Dion knew what she was referring to. Urbanski's New Year's party. "I'm going," he said. "Wild horses couldn't keep me away."

Thirty-Nine

WINGOVER

December 31

NEW YEAR'S EVE.

Dion was so sure that he wouldn't be going to Sean Urbanski's party this evening — especially since learning of Leith's espionage — that when he found himself driving across town in his best clothes, including the new maroon shirt with the collar tips he had come to actually like, he was surprised. It was like he had blacked out between noon and now, and had gotten spiffed up on autopilot.

He parked down the road from Sean's place. The streets around the area were narrow and parking was awkward. He trudged up the hill, wine bottle under his arm, climbed the steep steps, rang the bell, and was welcomed by Sean's partner, Kyla, into their comfortable home full of lively music, laughter, sparkling conversation.

After the first whump of depression following Poole's warning about Leith, Dion had begun to feel oddly light and reckless. Almost footloose, almost happy. Maybe he was looking forward to resolution more than he even knew.

Kyla was saying, "I haven't seen you in ages, Cal! How are you?"

Her arms being open, he gave her a hug, and said she looked great. She went about pointing out who was here, as if he was a stranger. Aside from friends of hers, there was the usual platoon of cops. JD Temple was a shock to the eyes in a slinky outfit instead of her usual drab slacks and sweater. Lil Hart and her husband, Wayne, were talking to Tara from general duties. Some civilian staff he couldn't name. There was David Leith and his wife Alison. Dion had never met Alison face to face, and he eyed her with interest. Of course, Doug Paley and Louise were here — Dion waved at Louise — and the guest of honour was young Craig Gilmartin with his arm around a girl in round glasses. "So who's protecting our city if you're all here?" Kyla asked him cheerfully. "Right?"

He didn't stay long on the main floor. After joining in conversation with Sean, Doug, and Lil for a few minutes, he glared at Leith's back, smirked at JD — *see, I did come* — then used the excuse of needing a cigarette to go outside.

So much for giving up smoking. Immediately after his grim meeting with Poole at the Capilano Mall, learning he was on the radar, he had bought a pack and smoked one on his way home, saying aloud as he drove, "I'm dead anyway."

He had the pack with him now. He didn't go out the front door, but upstairs to the snug covered deck he remembered from Urbanski's parties in the past.

Here, with the light switched off and the blasts of music from downstairs muted, he found chilly peace. He stood at the railing and took in the great view down the hillside to the North Shore, the Lion's Gate Bridge, Vancouver's gleaming downtown across the Inlet, the island ranges hulking, barely visible, in the dark distance. Soon there would be fireworks shooting and spiralling through the heavens, and maybe other partiers would join him then, but for now the cold kept everyone away. He looked at the cigarette in his hand — his alibi — unlit.

Quitting had been surprisingly easy, and getting hooked again was surprisingly hard. He stuck the cig back in its carton, put the carton back in his pocket, and sat down on the rattan bench to gaze at the night sky, blanking out, thinking of nothing.

The glass patio door slid open, and somebody was sharing the night air with him. At first all he could see of her was a long dark coat and the sheen of gold hair, but he knew right away what was happening. Either Kate had just joined him, or he was home in bed, dreaming. He sat straighter. She sat beside him, her face now visible in the ambient light.

"Well, hi," she said.

"Hi," he said.

"So, what happened is Patrick wanted to go to this other house party in Kits with old friends. Except his old friends are also his ex's old friends, so she'll be there, so I don't really want to be. She glares at me, Cal. And I think she knows witchcraft. So when Doug called, inviting me over, I thought, perfect, I'll see my old friends instead.

Then I got here, and everybody pointed upstairs, so I came to say hi. Hope you don't mind."

"No," he said. "No, I don't mind."

She was laughing, maybe at the look on his face. He smiled, too. Then they shared the view in silence.

His nerves were in knots again, his stomach doing flip-flops. He was no longer blanked out and thinking nothing, but desperately trying to decide what his next move should be. Anything he thought of doing or saying seemed wrong, so he said and did nothing.

He wished she wasn't here, but when she stood to leave, he felt sick with dread that she was about to disappear, this time for good. He was fumbling for his cigarettes when she pointed indoors with her thumb. "Champagne time. The year's about to turn. Are you coming?"

* * *

As the countdown began, he was outside with the other partiers, Kate at his side. Everyone had put on coats. Some, like himself and Kate, remained on the porch, while others meandered to the lawn and street, armed with pots and wooden spoons, or sparklers, or in the case of Sean Urbanski, an arsenal of firecrackers bought in Chinatown, ready to ignite the moment the calendar flipped to the first moment of the first day of January. Dion had done well. He had managed to say a few smart-sounding things to Kate, asking how she was doing, how the art show had gone, apologizing that he hadn't attended. He had talked to her, probably artlessly, about Patrick and the chance that Patrick might go back to his ex. She doubted it. But even so, he felt good. If nothing else, he felt he had made some amends for how he had treated her after the crash.

Midnight struck. Kate linked her arm in his, huddling against him in the chill. He cheered loudly with the rest of the neighbourhood, and gave Kate's cheek a traditional New Year's kiss, maybe not as platonically as he should have. The flashes and bangs and showers of sparks continued up and down the street. Past Kate at his side, Dion noticed JD on the steps, not cheering but answering her phone. She wore over-the-knee boots and a fluffy coat over her snug velveteen dress. She looked great, and he waited for her to put her phone away, so he could hand-signal an approving "okay" her way. But she didn't.

The spin of happy thoughts began to slow, then go in reverse. He let go of Kate to watch JD on her phone, trying to read her lips. She looked serious, and his curiosity pinged.

He saw JD climb the stairs to go into the house, beckoning Leith to join her. "Excuse me," Dion told Kate. "Back in a minute. Don't leave."

"I won't if you won't."

He followed their voices to the quiet backwaters of the kitchen, where JD was saying to Leith, "No, I'm not kidding. Our boss is missing."

* * *

It was hardly a crisis, but it was definitely strange. Under the bright, unromantic detachment lights, Leith listened to Jim Torr's somewhat jokey explanation of why he had put out the alert of one missing boss. JD and Dion listened at Leith's side.

Torr described receiving two reports, neither alarming in itself, but when put together, they added up to at least a *what the fuck*. "First report this evening was a suspicious-looking character in a car," Torr said, and cited the address of the person who had called in the report, a quiet street below Keith Road. "She says this character sat in his car, in the dark, for about an hour, kind of hunched down. I asked her to get me a licence plate, but she was too afraid to go outside. She starts telling me how useless us cops are, and tells me to send a patrol to check this weirdo out for her. By the time we got there, the weirdo was gone. What else could we do? Got a statement from the lady and filed it. Now for part two of the mystery. Hour later, I get a call from Sarah Bosko. Husband's not answering his phone for the last hour. She asks if he's here at the office. I say no. I ask her where she believes he is, and she doesn't know, but thinks he might be out socializing." Torr paused. "Some cozy relationship. If I didn't know where Tina was on New Year's Eve, I'd say it was time to start dialing D for divorce."

"So where's Tina tonight, Jim?" JD said.

"At home in bed, alone, with champagne and a negligee, waiting for me," Torr said, and Leith interrupted again, telling them to stick to the point. He was thinking of Alison back at a party full of strangers, alone. Like himself, she wasn't a mingler. It was how they had met — two wallflowers at somebody else's wedding, held in a school gymnasium. They'd met, said hello and not much else, danced in the dark under a disco ball that flung out electric stars, and in the end, found comfort in each other's clumsiness. Tonight he had offered to take her home or call a cab before heading to the detachment, but she had chosen to stay. For his sake, he thought, but she'd gotten it wrong; the knowledge of her waiting was keeping him on edge. In a fit of exasperation he exclaimed to Torr, "Mike Bosko doesn't answer his phone for an hour on New Year's Eve, and he's a missing person?"

"Hang tight," Torr said. "There's more. Know where Bosko lives? Right across the street from our chickenshit caller who could have gotten a licence plate for us. Plus the weirdo's vehicle sounds a lot like Thomas Frey's, a white hatchback station wagon. Plus Sarah Bosko says Mike always answers his phone. Always. I tried Bosko's numbers myself, both of 'em. Both went to voicemail."

Leith was starting to see Torr's point. He was feeling as chagrined as Dion was looking right now, Dion who had been standing starry-eyed next to a lovely woman as the fireworks went off. His plans were trashed, too, apparently. Seemed there would be no more partying for either of them tonight.

Forty

BLUE MURDER

January 1

DION FOUND IT STRANGE to be out at this time of night, driving around town with JD, both of them looking like a million dollars in their New Year's Eve best. JD had wanted to change, but Dion had convinced her not to. They were out on a wild goose chase, sparked by a series of misunderstandings, and the night was going to end up as a big joke, he said. They might as well do it in style. She had agreed they might as well look picturesque as they chased geese, so now, in her soft purple-black jacket and tall boots with fancy buckles, she steered her ratty Subaru station wagon through the streets of the city, heading toward Bosko's home.

Dion sat in the passenger seat, scanning cars and pedestrians. He was looking for either Bosko's silver Toyota Corolla, or for his familiar bear-like figure on foot. What would happen if Bosko turned up dead, he wondered. That could be the end to his troubles, that's what.

He scowled and switched off the thought. JD was pulling over without hesitation, as if she knew where she was going. She shut off the engine, stepped out of the car, and headed toward a plain little house.

Dion followed. "You've been here before?" he asked as she rapped her knuckles on the front door.

"Bosko threw a garden party in the summer," she told him. "I went. A lot of us went. You weren't around. You were in one of your *I'm quitting* snits."

The bungalow was small and rundown, not the kind of place Dion expected a man like Bosko to live. Maybe it was a rental situation. Maybe Bosko wasn't putting down roots, was planning on transferring out. Again, that could be an end to his troubles, and a far better one all around.

A slight woman in her forties opened the door, and JD greeted her as Sarah. Sarah invited them in to talk. In the living room, which felt to Dion like a safe-house set-up — practical and efficient, but uninspired — Sarah could offer no clues to her husband's whereabouts other than those she had already provided. Mike might have intended to drop in on his parents in West Point Grey, she said, but it was a loose arrangement. She had already called his parents. She had learned that he had phoned them around noon, as was typical, to wish them the best, but he had not planned on an actual visit till tomorrow.

Yes, she was a little worried.

"There's probably a good explanation," JD said. "The problem with cellphones is everyone expects immediate connection, and if it doesn't happen, it's scary. Right?"

"Yes, I know," Sarah said. "And the problem with Mike is he's not the type to forget his phone is on silent mode or low on juice. We have a tacit understanding not to call each other when we're out at events unless it's important, so it's not unusual that he didn't call me. What's unusual is he didn't answer. Or call back."

"There wasn't a plan to call each other during the big countdown?" JD asked.

"No. Maybe it's strange to you, that Mike and I aren't doing New Year's together. It's just we have different friends, different interests. We live together, but sometimes our phones are our only way of holding hands."

Not just a safe house, but a sham wife, Dion thought.

"I get that," JD said. "And I'm sure Mike's okay, but we are taking this seriously." She warned Sarah about the unknown lurker spotted in a car out front earlier that night. "I don't mean to upset you, but do keep an eye out. And don't hesitate to give us a call, for any reason. Do you have a friend you can go stay with?"

"Well, now I'm really worried," Sarah said. "Go." She ushered them to the door. "I'll take care of myself. Just go find him, please."

* * *

It was nearly 2:00 a.m. by now, and with no better lead, Dion agreed with JD that visiting Bosko's parents on the other side of the bridge would be as good a starting point as any. The first day of the year remained cloaked in darkness, and patrol cars cruised the near-empty streets like sleepy sharks.

It wasn't until they were crossing the Lion's Gate Bridge that Dion realized he had known all along how Bosko had spent at least part of this day. It had been niggling at him from the start. "Dim sum!" he cried.

JD stared at him. "What?"

"That's where he was tonight, JD. Dim sum. With a friend."

* * *

When, though — who knew? And the identity of the friend was another question mark. Dion told JD about overhearing Bosko telling Sean Urbanski of his New Year's plans. "And the friend he was talking about, I think it's the same one who loaned Bosko the plane. An old friend and colleague, is what he called him. I just can't remember the name. Head for downtown, and I'll see if I can track this down."

"Arlo?" JD said. "At the pub he was talking about his friend Arlo."

Dion reached the E Division headquarters in Surrey, where Bosko had worked before North Van, and after some runaround and explanations, he was rerouted to the cell number of an officer who had worked with Bosko. The woman he spoke to said, "Mike's not answering his phone? Yeah, that's Code 3, for sure."

Dion asked if she knew a friend of Bosko's named Arlo. Did she have any idea who that might be, and how that person could be reached?

The woman told him that would be Arlo Kirk, now retired from the force. She said she shouldn't be giving out Kirk's number, but she would. "Got a pen?"

A minute later Dion had not only the phone number, but also the address of Arlo Kirk jotted down. It was on 6th Avenue, near Rupert and Broadway. He stuck the note on JD's sun visor, and she headed for the Georgia Viaduct. Dion tried Kirk's number, meanwhile. It, too, went to voicemail.

* * *

"This should be it," Dion said, looking at house addresses — never easy in the dark. The home he was looking at was one of the smaller, older models, dwarfed by monster houses on either side. Dwarfed but not intimidated, its archway, shrubs, and every inch of fence blazing with Christmas lights.

"Bosko said Arlo's a little obsessed," JD said. "He wasn't kidding."

Dion stared at what was probably the living room window, shrouded by drapes. Lamplight shone within, and there was evidence of a flame-like flickering. "They've got a fire going, so they must be home."

JD had pulled in behind a silver sedan on the quiet avenue, and she was looking at the vehicle's rear. "That's Mike's car," she said, having double-checked her notes for the plate number. "So, yup, he's here. Drank too much and crashed at his buddy's place. He didn't answer his phone because the music was too loud or his pal had convinced him to turn it off. It was New Year's Eve, the one time of year he decided somebody else could deal with trouble. Let's get lost before they spot us lurking and we have to explain how stupid we are."

Dion shook his head. "You heard what his wife said. He'd be ready to answer, if only in case she called. She called, and he didn't answer, and something's wrong."

JD sighed. "So now we're going to go knock on their damn door, wake them up, and have a lot of explaining to do. Fine. Serves him right."

Nobody answered the door when she rang the bell. Nor when she knocked, nor when Dion knocked louder. Nobody peeked out the windows of the monster houses on either side. Music emanated from the house across the street, another New Year's party still going strong, but again, nobody looked out to see what the fuss was.

JD clipped down the steps in her fancy boots. She found a crooked concrete path leading around the side of the house to the shadowy backyard, and vanished. Dion followed. In the rear of the house was a carport, and in the carport was an older white Chev Impala that he guessed belonged to Arlo Kirk.

"I'll try the back door," he said. He climbed wooden stairs onto a landing of sorts, opened a screen door, and pounded on the wooden inner door with the side of his fist. He looked down at JD and past her at the front of the Impala. Even from here the car looked dewy and cold. He thought about Bosko's silver Corolla lodged against the curb out front as if it had been there for days.

He checked his watch: 2:20 a.m. Ordinarily, most people would be asleep by now, but this was the early morning hours following New Year's Eve, and if two buddies were bothering to get together to celebrate the event, wouldn't they stay up till at least midnight, probably more like 1:00 a.m.? Bosko struck Dion as long-winded and tireless. Around one or one-thirty the friends might have started to think about sleep, but even so there would be a sense of life lingering now, a light still on, somebody in a bathroom brushing their teeth. And even if they had both retired to sleep, somebody would have rolled out of bed by now to respond to the hammering on the door.

No. This place felt deserted. As he'd told JD, something was wrong. He tried the door handle and found it locked. Next to the door was a sliding window accessible from the small landing he stood on. He tried pushing the window and it slid open an inch. He pushed it further and found it didn't jam up against a safety catch. From down in the dark yard, JD called up quietly. "Hey. What are you doing?"

"Look at this," Dion said. "The window's open!"

"So what? You're not going in there."

"Kirk's a cop. He wouldn't go out and leave his window unlocked."

JD said she had heard of stranger things.

Dion pushed the window open wide and tested the old wooden sash for strength. It seemed solid. JD had come up the stairs meanwhile. She grabbed the back of his jacket and tugged. "No way we're going in there. I'll make a call."

"That'll take forever," he said. He was still thinking about Bosko's car on the street, Kirk's car in the driveway, the silent house, unsecured window, and two unanswered phones. He called into the house and got no answer. "I'll go in, scout around. Only be a second."

The window was placed high and barely man sized, but if he climbed on the deck's bannister he could weasel his way in. He clambered up, thrust in one leg, gripped the upper window frame, got the other leg in. He slung his body inside, and found himself bridging awkwardly over a double kitchen sink full of cold and sudsy dishwater. Trying not to break anything, he twisted around to climb down to the linoleum. He paused mid-climb to call out again. "Hello? Police! Arlo Kirk? I'm from the North Shore RCMP. Anybody here?"

No answer. He continued to work his way off the sink counter. Piled dishes slid with a clatter, and a wineglass fell to the floor in pieces.

Dion stared at the broken glass, then at JD, who was hissing at him through the open window, "I'm not going to let you get shot alone. Let me in."

He opened the door, and now they were both in the kitchen. It was messy, but lemony clean, and it smelled pleasantly of fresh-baked muffins.

"You broke their fucking dishes," JD said.

"I'll pay for it." Dion said. He called out once more, "Sergeant Bosko? It's Cal Dion. Arlo Kirk, are you there? Anybody?"

Silence.

JD spoke through her teeth. "The neighbours are calling 911 by now. ERT is on its way. We're going to get tasered."

"Don't worry about it."

She scraped the soles of her boots on the doormat. "Right, what's to worry about? We're just tracking a killer, unarmed and without a warrant. Best case scenario, we're facing two dishonourable discharges for B and E-ing a cop's house."

Dion was already moving down the carpeted hallway. JD followed, looking more like a lost movie starlet than a cop. The first room they passed was the living room with its street-facing window. A lamp was on low, casting the muted glow Dion had seen from the car. The room was overcrowded with an enormous sofa and two extra-large easy chairs. In the hearth a fire danced —they paused to marvel that it wasn't real, but a silk flame underlit and teased to life by blown air. "Cool," JD said. "Everything you could want from a real crackling fire except heat."

They moved along. There was a bathroom, fairly messy, nobody hiding in the tub enclosure. The master bedroom was empty. It sported a king-sized bed, nobody hiding underneath. Nobody in the closet, either. Judging from the clothes in the closet, JD said, a big man and a big woman lived here. Or a big cross-dresser.

Further along they discovered a messy craft room of sorts, with a clutter of photo albums spread over the floor. Then there was a games room with dartboard and pool table and nowhere to hide, and beyond the games room were more doorways still. In the hallway Dion glanced at JD, exasperated. The little one-storey house was bigger than it looked from the outside, a labyrinth — and still the basement to explore.

The last door on the main floor opened into another bedroom. With the light flicked on, Dion took in a room painted blue, smaller and considerably neater than the master bedroom. A guest room. On the chest of drawers sat somebody's car keys, and under the bed, when he crouched to check, was a breathing pool of darkness wearing eyeglasses. He saw the gleam of a gun barrel, gave a warning shout to JD. He tried to spring back as the being under the bed gathered itself and swarmed out at him faster than he could hope to escape, and in the moment of chaos there was a flurry of motion, a blast, gunpowder in the air, and he was on the floor, his back thudding against the wall as a second shot rang out. Somebody was shouting. Two voices competing. He'd been hit, too stunned to feel the pain. He squeezed his eyes shut, wondering where the bullet got him, whether he was going to die.

At least JD wasn't dead. He now recognized that it was her doing most of the shouting, and she sounded damn healthy. He still felt no pain. He opened his eyes and saw her kneeling in front of him. Close, within arm's reach, busy wrangling with the man from under the bed, the man slammed face first on the floor, JD on all fours on top of him. Or not quite on all fours, but pressing him down with one knee. She had hold of his uppermost ear in one fist and his short salt-and-pepper hair in the other, and was mashing her free boot heel to one side as though stomping on ants. Not ants, Dion realized, but the man's gun hand, which was by degrees splaying its fingers and releasing its grip.

The man was shouting insults and protests, thrashing but stuck, trapped by both cop and bed frame. Both of Dion's arms worked, he found, and a quick self pat-down found no gaping holes, no spilled guts. JD kicked the gun out of the man's reach with a warrior cry of triumph. Dion did a home-run slide to grab the weapon, and once he had it in his fist he scrambled back against the wall, levelling its muzzle at Thomas Frey's noisy face with a shout: "Shut up, lie still, don't move!"

Frey rolled a one-eyed glare his way, but lay still and stopped screaming blue murder. He was done.

Still sitting with his back against the wall, gun in hand, Dion drew in a deep breath and pieced together the mad series of events. Frey had come crawling out gun first, JD had bounded past Dion and up onto the bed, and from there dropped onto the shooter with her full weight. The gun went off, but the bullet missed its target, Dion, probably by inches. A second shot flew wide.

"I could use some help here," JD snapped. She told him to grab a nearby extension cord. He did, and helped her use it to bind Frey's wrists behind his back.

With her prisoner frisked and disabled, a folding knife seized from his jeans pocket, JD stood at Dion's side, wobbling a bit, to catch her breath.

But only for a moment, before digging into her fluffy coat pocket for her phone and making the call. She asked for police — and ambulance, too. "Just one," she said. Ambulance, Dion supposed. No, she explained, the injured man was breathing fine. She might have broken the fine bones in his fucking gun-wielding wrist, that's all.

She finished the call, and she and Dion stood looking down at their prisoner. "If you're okay here," Dion said, "I'll go check the basement."

"She didn't do anything," Frey rasped, his face down on the nubby carpet. "I did it all. She had nothing to do with it. You broke my hand. It hurts. I can't breathe."

"Don't talk till you've consulted a lawyer," JD told him. She made a brutal kicking motion at the back of his head, a kick he didn't see or feel, since it didn't connect. There was jubilance in her dark eyes when she turned to look at Dion. He saw relief, too. "I thought you were hit," she said.

He started to say, "So did I," but stopped. Something in Frey's last words startled him.

I did it all.

All what? It had been in response to Dion saying he was going to check the basement. "You did all what?" he said sharply.

But Frey didn't seem to hear, too busy moaning about his crushed hand.

Dion left the room at a jog. JD shouted after him to stay put, backup was here. Sirens wailed to a stop outside. He found the basement stairs and flicked on what turned out to be a low-watt bulb, and made his way down. At the bottom he tried to locate the main switch for better lighting, but couldn't. He swore, as he had no flashlight, and his smartphone beam didn't cut through the tungsten gloom much. He used it anyway. The unfinished basement was sprawling, a maze of shadows complicated by support beams. Junk everywhere. A hoarder's paradise.

Movement caught his eye — a slow, drifting glitter between obstructions, down on the floor at the far corner of the basement. Blood escaped a pile of clutter and made its way toward a floor drain. He stumbled toward the clutter, and saw behind a heap of boxes a body — the bottom half, heavy legs in blood-soaked trousers. He brought his arm to his face in defence against the stench of death that he expected, that he knew so well. Upstairs, he could hear the heavy footfall of men, and voices ringing out loudly: male voices and the shrill tones of a woman, not JD.

With his arm still up he walked toward the bloody legs, knowing with a sick heart what he would find attached.

Forty-One

FLYING

SIRENS, POLICE, AMBULANCE, the homeowners, and Mike Bosko — they all seemed to arrive within moments of each other. JD had opened the front door as the first VPD officers had arrived, knowing what she must look like in her slinky red dress, her short hair tousled, her kohl-lined eyes — first and last time in her life she'd use that muck — smudged and streaked. Dion had just disappeared downstairs and wasn't there to back up her story, so she shouted at the cops that she was North Shore RCMP responding to a report of a break-in.

Not exactly, but it sounded more credible than the truth, and hopefully they'd think twice before tackling her to the ground.

They didn't tackle her, in the end. She was leading them to the guest bedroom to introduce them to Thomas Frey when two civilians who must be the Kirks showed up, demanding to know what was going on.

There was a lot of talk, and JD shouted over the noise, asking the Kirks if Mike Bosko was with them, where was he? Getting no satisfactory answer, she headed along the hall toward the front of the house, and there he stood, alive and well, showing his ID to the constable at the door.

"JD," he said, staring at her in surprise.

"Lookit," she said, too exhausted for deference. "Cal's downstairs looking for your remains. You better go tell him you're alive."

"What? I'm afraid —"

"I think he probably saved your life, by the way," she said, but before she could elaborate, she was called away by one of the uniforms on the scene to finish explaining what the hell was going on here.

* * *

Dion pulled away the boxes. He was shaking inside. Why did he care so much? He had seen death before, up close and hands-on. He had lost friends and brother officers and had accepted their loss without falling apart like this. And Bosko wasn't a friend. Not even close. In the final analysis, he was an enemy. So what was the matter? Why did his death seem like the end of the world?

Bad got worse — it was not just murder, but mutilation. As the boxes fell aside he saw that the upper half of the body was missing. Gone completely. It had been cut at the midriff. Quite neatly, too. Dion stepped back in horror, tripped on clutter and landed hard on the concrete, rump and elbows splashing in the warm river of blood, the blood wetting his hands and clothing as he struggled back to his feet shouting out in fear and disgust.

A bright light shone and a bulky figure was coming his way, calling out. Dion tried to run backwards, or sideways, not sure what he was running from, but his legs got tangled and he began to fall again, corkscrew fashion. The bulky figure dashed forward and grabbed his arm, steadied him, saying, "Hey, hey, take it easy."

He stared at the man who steadied him. The flashlight had been set down and was no longer blinding him, but illuminating the truth.

He stared at Bosko, then down at his own wet palms. Water.

He stared down at the bloody corpse and saw only two fat, badly stuffed Santa legs, life-size, black-booted, and clad in red velveteen. He looked at Bosko, and his anger welled up, fuelled by humiliation, until it blew out of him in a gust of anger. "We've been trying to contact you!" he bellowed, for the first time in his life shouting full throttle at a superior. "You didn't answer your phone! Why the *fuck* didn't you answer your phone?"

"I'm so sorry," Bosko said. His hands were up, *don't shoot*. "You can blame Arlo for that. But listen."

Dion listened. Already his anger had cooled, giving way to regret. Not only had he shouted at Bosko, but used the F-word at him, and in his dazed state of mind the transgression inflated into a crime.

But it was a crime Bosko chose to overlook. "I haven't had time to sort out what's happening here," he said. "But I'm starting to jump to conclusions. And JD says you saved my life. What's that all about?"

"Thomas Frey is what it's all about. He was hiding under the bed in the guest room. He had a handgun, and he fired at me. JD ..." Dion paused, catching sight of the grotesque Santa legs, and his anger flared again. "What *is* that?"

"Let's go," Bosko said. "It's Arlo's idea of fun," he explained, as he led the way upstairs. "You didn't think that was *me*, did you?"

Dion glared at the slow leak escaping from the hot water tank — apparently it needed service — and stomped up the stairs after his superior.

* * *

Much of the rest of the night was a blur for Dion. Leith arrived, still nicely dressed. Torr and Paley were here, too, and a woman in a sparkly cocktail dress who might have been a VPD VIP, amidst uniformed officers. It was like a house party colliding with a roadside disaster colliding with an official debrief, with nobody in charge and everybody asking questions. Within Dion's periphery, people came and people went, and the clips of conversation he took in made no sense. JD was trying to describe the events of the last hour, but it was a patchy story.

JD: "... kept trying to call you, and then Cal ..."

Sylvia Kirk: "Well, it's because he's always on his phone, so ..."

Arlo Kirk: "... the one night his phone malfunctions ..."

Mike Bosko: "It didn't ..."

David Leith: "But how did you know ..."

JD: "Kind of cool, actually."

Sylvia: "No, Dave, full disclosure, Arlo switched it off when Mike was ..."

Bosko: "I was wondering why it was so …"

Leith: "… okay, but why didn't you just …"

Arlo: "If you just did like me and turned the damn thing off once in a while …"

Somebody: "Ma'am …"

Somebody else: "Look, can somebody here give us his lowdown? He needs medical …"

Leith: "Jim, you'd better accompany …"

JD: "… Frey, I told you. Thomas Frey. It's a broken finger, at worst. Jesus."

Somebody: "Excuse me, when will you be …"

Somebody else: "…the crime scene …"

JD: "… soon, okay? I think we're …"

One of the somebodies: "Looks like you're all going to have to clear out."

And finally, somebody new, an older man with a bullhorn voice: "*Now!*"

* * *

There was a major exodus from the Kirk home to the Burnaby RCMP detachment, where they could debrief in the calmer setting of a spare case room. Here Dion did most of the explaining, since JD said she was losing her voice. She had scrubbed off her makeup and was looking more herself. Dion had scrubbed his face, too, and with adrenalin levels back to normal, he felt good. He and JD had saved the day, after all.

As had Arlo, by sabotaging Bosko's cellphone. If Bosko had answered his phone, the alarm wouldn't have been raised, and he would have ended up walking into the trap. Likely he would be dead. Possibly Arlo and Sylvia would have joined him at the morgue.

Tomorrow Leith would be dealing with Thomas Frey, but for tonight, everyone was going home to get some rest. As Sylvia said, there would be a lot of prayers of gratitude uttered tonight.

When all the other cars had left the detachment's parking lot, Dion and JD returned to JD's ratty Subaru. She drove back toward the bridge, and in the passenger seat Dion thought back over the night's events, and the way it had ended. Via text, he had lined up a coffee date with Kate, and he had at least a day pass to Bosko's respect.

Bosko had thanked him for a job well done, in front of everybody. He hadn't mentioned the farcical Santa-legs confusion, nor Dion's bellows of fear. He had even clapped Dion on the back at one point, which felt like friendship. It felt like more than that, like inclusion into a safer world. It wasn't — it couldn't be — but it felt that way.

His eyes closed as JD carried them over the bridge. She was singing to herself, another first, but he couldn't catch the words. Maybe he was dreaming, but he seemed to be gaining altitude, looking down on his troubles, watching them dwindle to specks. He was airborne, that's what it was, and he held on to the feeling as best he could, just for a while.

Forty-Two

FALLING

January 2

WERE FREY AND GREY MAN one and the same? Had this two-faced creature driven a blade into Rory Keefer and put a hole through Craig Gilmartin? Or had he worked in concert with Scott Mills, who was no longer around to give his side of the story? Or was he in cahoots with Dezi? JD had told Leith of her doubts about the girl — completely unsubstantiated, but bothersome. Dion agreed with her. There was something off about Dezi, and it couldn't be ignored.

But for now they focused on Frey. Leith spent an hour with JD, preparing for the upcoming interrogation. They were wondering what had gone wrong in the man's life, because from all indications, he was an upstanding individual who'd had no past brushes with the law. Not the kind to tear through a house shooting everything that moved, nor to lie in ambush with a loaded gun.

Reports from the medics and jailers said he was behaving well, even now that the painkillers had worn off.

So when, and how, had this schism started?

"We all start out good, then ego comes along," JD said.

"But this?" Leith indicated the file stuffed with gory photos.

"Mid-life crisis, emotional breakdown, infatuation. No question he's Grey Man, and he's got a hard drive full of Dezi pics."

In any case, Leith pointed out, Frey's inexperience was advantageous to the interrogation. He was so new at being bad that he'd be a crappy liar, right? JD told him not to count on it. She advised him that if Frey proved uncooperative, Leith could always try using Dezi as a pitchfork.

Leith said he would do that, and arranged to have his prisoner brought in.

* * *

"Well," Frey began. "I won't say I regret any of it. That wouldn't be honest."

First sentence out of his mouth and already he's headed for the psych ward, Leith thought.

But he gave a nod of understanding. He and Frey were alone in the softer of the interview rooms, because intimidation wouldn't do spit with a man like Frey. It was *easy does it* with this type of madness.

"I never really lived, till I saw Dezi," the prisoner went on. "I wouldn't have met her if not for Scott. Scott and I had become friends, in a way. He looked up to me, middle-aged man willing to talk to him, not bully him. You know, a kind of a father figure."

"I hear you're popular with the kids in the flying club," Leith said.

"I understand kids. You don't push them, and they won't push back."

"I see."

"I didn't meet Scott in the flying club, actually. I saw him in the field, flying his plane, and he was amazing. What a talent. We talked a bit. Later I saw him again, same park, but now with a young girl, trying to teach her how to fly. I remember it so vividly. The trees, the sun sparkling through the leaves. I think I fell in love with her on the spot, and nothing has been the same since. I was going to go over and talk to them, but changed my mind. I didn't want to disturb them. I just wanted to … watch. I sat on a bench. I couldn't take my eyes off her. Next week, the same. I didn't want to break the spell, spoil everything by being introduced."

"How would that spoil everything?"

Frey looked at Leith as if he was mad. "Look at me. Would you fall for me?"

Definitely not, Leith thought.

"No," Frey said. "You'd dismiss me, as would she. And after that, I would no longer be able to watch, either, as she'd know who I was. So I refrained. As soon as I could get Scott alone, I asked about her. Was she his girlfriend? He said she was, but I didn't believe him. He didn't give off the signals of wanting her, if you know what I mean. Later, he let it slip that he didn't have feelings for women. Can you imagine?"

"Who did he have feelings for?"

"Nobody. I think he and Dezi were about as platonic as could be. Just friends, at least from her end. As for him, he was probably using her as a prop, so other men would think he was some kind of player."

Frey inhaled deeply and sat back with eyes closed.

Leith didn't know where Frey had gone, but he didn't mind the recess. He glanced at the Mirropane. He couldn't see JD, but she could see him. "So you fell in love with Dezi. Did you try to talk to her?"

"I didn't have the nerve."

"But you followed her, took pictures of her."

"Oh. You found those, did you?"

"Yeah, we did."

"Tell Corinne I regret all that," Frey said. He didn't look sorry, in Leith's eyes. "But it was never real, with her. There was no spark. She'll understand."

"Sure. I think you went further than stalking Dezi, though. I think you met her. Took off your mask, so to speak."

"I never took off my mask, so to speak," Frey said. "I always remained in the shadows. She didn't know anything about me. Didn't even know my name. I think in a way she felt my admiration, and enjoyed the mystique, but it never went further than that."

Leith gave it another push. "You actually had a relationship with her. You had sex, didn't you?"

Frey seemed to be only half listening. He gave a shudder as he came back to earth. "No, that's an absolute falsehood."

Leith could see Frey was struggling to slip back into

his incognito wonderland, following pretty girls in his mind, taking them home with him, in the form of photographs, to study at his leisure. Worried that Frey would disappear down that rabbit hole for good, Leith decided he needed to consult with JD. "How about lunch?" he said, cheerfully.

* * *

Leith's lunch consisted of a sandwich and a speed-read of every statement Dezi had made, followed by a review of the case with JD. They went over the span of events from the van-load of kids plunging into the sea to Frey popping out from under Bosko's bed with a loaded .45. Was Dezi really standing on the sidelines, or did she have blood on her hands as well?

"The way she snapped at Bosko when he pushed her," JD said, explaining how her suspicion had shifted to the girl who had once been her friend. "I'm thinking that was her mistake. He pushed her, she snapped at him, and next thing you know, there's an attempt on his life. And the way she tried to seduce me. She's a manipulator."

"And a damn good one," Leith said.

JD leaned forward. "You know what you're going to have to do with this guy?" She mouthed the answer, for his eyes only: *lie*.

Leith was thinking the same thing. He went back to pick up with Frey where they had left off, and it only got wilder.

* * *

"What you're saying isn't lining up with what Dezi's told us," Leith lied. "So what aren't you telling me, Tom? How did you end up in Lions Bay blasting holes in people?"

"You've talked to Dezi?" Frey's brows went up, and for a moment Leith thought he wasn't going to fall for the old ruse, *we already know everything, so might as well spill.* But the brows went down again, and the shoulders sagged, which either meant Frey had taken the bait after all, or he was changing tactics.

"I'll tell you what led up to Lions Bay," Frey said. "But it's got nothing to do with Dezi, so I'm not sure what she might have told you. Anyway, to begin with, it was all about a car."

"What car?" Leith asked, though he thought he knew: the sports car Dezi had said Scott was intent on buying from Grey Man.

"Scott's grandma had a stroke," Frey said. "And since she could no longer drive her little hot rod, Scott decided she should bequeath it to him, and it was just a matter of convincing her. The problem was, she wasn't his real grandma. Scott's mom married a guy named Karl, so Gran was actually a step-gran, and from what Scott heard, she was a cranky old bitch. He figured, probably rightly so, that if he went kowtowing to her, she'd just throw him out on his ear."

Leith compared what he was hearing with what he knew. Some of it wasn't matching up. "It wasn't a car deal you and Scott were making?"

"I had nothing to do with it, except Scott asked for my advice on how to win Grandma over, and I told him the obvious. Be nice. He said his mother gave him the same useless advice, plus something about washing his mouth out with soap. I have to say, she had a point there. He said he wouldn't know how to begin being nice, and he too had a point. I also told him to stop dressing like a thug, so he put on a nice sports jacket and plaid shirt and went over to see Grandma. But her place was being cleaned and she wasn't in. This is all stuff he told me later. Then he got talking to the housekeeper who was cleaning the apartment, about cars and birds, and the two of them hatched an idea. It's a strange one, so hold on to your hat."

Leith nodded to show his hat was held.

"I never meant to hurt anybody," Frey said. "It just went so wrong. Scott claims it was the housekeeper's idea, because there was something she wanted from the old lady, too. This housekeeper —"

Leith interrupted, "You know her name and you know what happened to her, right?"

"Amelia Foster," Frey admitted, with no sign of regret. "I had nothing to do with her death. And again, I only know about it because Scott told me. As Scott put it, this Amelia person had kind of a boyish look, and she thought herself a bit of a con artist, too. What got her thinking about it all was her resemblance to Grandma's dead son, which she knew about because there was an old photograph in the lady's apartment, and she knew a bit of Grandma's history from other employees. Amelia decided that she could schmooze her way into Grandma's heart by pretending to be Scott, while more or less channelling the dead son. Do you follow so far?"

Leith said he was following.

"Know how the son died, by the way?" Frey asked.

"No. How did he die?"

"A car crash. How ironic is that?"

"What did Amelia get out of the con?"

"A bird," Frey exclaimed. "A big blue bird that talked. She had become attached to it and wanted it, was afraid it would go to a bad home after Grandma died. So she wanted the bird, and Scott wanted the car. Two items that a dying woman might easily hand over to somebody who cared about them as much as she did."

Leith sat back to marvel. The story seemed too strange to be true, yet too strange not to be. So this was all about a car? And a *bird*? "The plan seemed to be working out?" he asked.

"Better than Scott hoped," Frey said. He directed a hoot of laughter at the ceiling. "Too good. Grandma adored the imposter, and I guess where it went wrong is the imposter came to adore Grandma. The two of them got along great. They talked about travel, birds, nature, fast cars. One day Amelia broke the news to Scott. First the good news. Bird and car would be gifted to Scott upon Grandma's death. The old lady had sent a note to her family attorney to avoid any squabbles over it after her demise, stipulating that Scott should get the car. The bird was a more informal gifting. Of course Scott could have the creature, as he clearly loved it."

Leith waited with interest for the bad news that must have followed the good.

"The bad news," Frey said, "was twofold. A, Grandma's prognosis was actually not bad, and she was expected to be driving her Boxter again by autumn, and B, Amelia was done with the gig. She was quitting." Frey smiled broadly. "I remember the day Scott told me. Early December, over at Deer Lake. He was bombing his plane around to blow off steam. I said, 'Well, at least the car will be yours, somewhere down the road. But he was afraid. If Amelia went to the authorities, he could end up in jail."

Frey sat for a moment in thought, and for the first time became serious. "Things just got away from me. Scott had set up a meeting with Amelia out at Porteau Beach, where he would try to convince her to carry on with the scheme and not rat him out. But he was too angry to deal with her. He wanted me to do it. I took the request at face value. I had no inkling of what he had in mind, lying in wait with his plane to frighten her off the road."

"So is that what happened?" Leith asked.

"Believe it or not, I do believe that's what happened. I met Amelia at Porteau, and tried to reason with her. She told me to go to hell, and she left. Scott intercepted her, and she crashed her car. At least that's what I take from what he told me on the phone soon afterwards."

"Why would you do all this for Scott? What did you get out of it?"

"Ah," Frey said. "Scott and I had struck up a deal. I loved Dezi, and I had come to see that Scott was no good for her. He was going to drag her down with him. I said I would do this favour for him if he cut off his friendship with her."

"So you played the negotiator with Amelia in order to save Dezi from Scott's influence, is that your story?"

"That's right. Turns out Scott was not only foul-mouthed and corrupt, but a liar and murderer, and he had no intention of cutting off Dezi as promised."

Leith had a map of the Sea to Sky on the table, and he placed a finger on Porteau Beach, north of Lions Bay and north of the spot where Amelia had crashed. "You went there alone, did you?"

"I did."

"Dezi was there, too, though, wasn't she?"

Frey ogled him. He cleared his throat, and his eyes darted around the room. When he was done looking for an alternate story, he heaved a sigh and nodded. "It was a night of surprises. I didn't expect Dezi to follow me. I also didn't expect Amelia to be so nasty about it all when I showed up instead of Scott. She told me she wouldn't let us defraud Grandma, and she started to march back to her car. I phoned Scott to let him know I had failed. He said something about heading her off at the pass, and then he hung up on me. I didn't know what he meant."

"Why did Dezi follow you?"

"I don't know. She's Scott's friend. Maybe she worried that he was getting in too deep. Which he certainly was."

"And what happened after Amelia fled?"

"Dezi left, and I left. We came upon the crash, and this was moments after it happened, I assume. I had seen lights veering in the distance, followed by a bunch of flashing. We both pulled over. Dezi jumped out of her car. Neither of us knew that was Amelia down there. You couldn't see the crash from the road. I stayed in my car, but she ran to help. As I was sitting there, Scott phoned and told me what he had done, that he had successfully driven Amelia off the road. He asked me what was happening. I told him people had stopped, were down there helping Amelia. I said Dezi had gone down, too, trying to help out. As we were on the phone, I saw a man climb out of the ditch and get into his car. I advised Scott, and he said I should follow the man, find out if Amelia had said anything to him. And I did. I followed him all the way to Horseshoe Bay."

"Why obey an order like that?" Leith asked, working to keep the anger out of his voice, anger at the image he couldn't get out of his mind: Rory Keefer tied to a tree, covered in blood.

"Because for the first time in my life, I was enjoying myself." Frey said it with a flare of vicious delight that made Leith want to hit him. "Because I wanted to show the world what I was capable of. Because I didn't want Dezi to suffer for Scott's crimes, and I knew one way or another he would pull her in. All kinds of reasons. That's why. This was the turning point in my life. This was *real*."

"And Dezi was going to thank you after you were done? Was that the idea?"

Frey ignored the question, perhaps because he had no answer, and went on with his confession. "I followed the man to Horseshoe Bay, and found him talking on a pay phone. It was a dark, secluded place, middle of the night. Nobody could see. When he turned around, I hit him with the Maglite I keep in my car. Scott arrived in his truck, and we loaded the man into the back. I left my car in the ferry parkade and then drove the man's vehicle and dumped it behind the Superstore. From there I walked home. The next day Scott picked me up. The man was in the back of his truck, still kicking. We went to the Maplewood forest, and we took him into the woods, and we killed him."

Just like that, Leith thought. "And why?" he asked again.

Frey lifted his face. "For Dezi. Everything I did, I did it for Dezi."

"You killed Scott. How does that help Dezi?"

Frey snorted. "Isn't it obvious? He was murdering people. He was trouble. He was leading her down the path to hell and he wasn't keeping his end of the deal. She'd end up in jail, if she kept hanging around that guy. I had to get him out of the picture."

"And Scott's parents?"

"I killed them, too, because they got in the way. I killed all of them. Just couldn't get that fucking little dog."

* * *

In the long meeting that followed, everyone agreed that woven through Frey's story was a stinking trail of bullshit. But to Leith, a truth came through the narrative as well. What wasn't being said spoke louder than words, like a negative space, like a void pattern in blood spatter. Like an object that had been present through the violence but since removed. In spite of the tangled story and Frey's clumsy attempts at obfuscation, the truth was plain to see. It was a thrill kill team, and young Dezi Novak was at the controls.

Forty-Three

FALLEN

January 3

DION WORE BOOTS, jeans, sweater, parka, and a toque to protect his ears. He had just reached his destination: high above the world, the snowy plateau overlooking the Burrard Inlet that Looch had brought him to in the past. He hadn't approached via Fellridge today, but from Lions Bay below, in his role as guide to the Forensics members who were searching and photographing Scott Mills's ledge. Dion had driven with them up from Lions Bay as far as the rough spur would take them, as Mills would have done. They had then climbed on foot from its dead end to the killing ledge. A different trail, same destination, and a far easier and faster route than from above.

He had left Forensics out of sight below and climbed the rest of the way, for the sake of the view. He wanted to take another look, now that he was still feeling the lift of Kate's renewed friendship and Bosko's gratitude. He wondered if he would get a rejuvenated thrill in this new state of being.

When he'd recovered from the exertion of the climb, he looked out to sea. An uneasiness crept over him. The happiness and sense of reawakening wasn't flooding into him, as he'd expected. Far below, the ferries continued to carve their routes between terminals as if nothing had changed. The glob of pale sun overhead was only a halo in the clouds, and he felt no redemption. Not even a flutter.

He thought about Souza's jump. A mystery, everyone said. So young, so healthy, so good-looking. His whole life ahead of him. Why couldn't he just speak up, reach out for help?

Dion wasn't as mystified by Tony's decision as others seemed to be. When depression hits, the only mystery is how to carry on. Depression may come out of nowhere. It might have nothing to do with what's in the mirror, or the bank account, or the love life. Depression is an undertow, and unless a person has waded into it, they can't know the pull.

Someone called out a hello, and Dion turned to see Leith clambering down the difficult path toward him, also bundled like an arctic explorer hitting the icefields.

"Hey," Leith greeted him, breath gusting out white. "How's it going?" He passed Dion to check out the awesome view.

Dion thought how almost supernaturally lucky Leith's presence was. A confrontation between them was overdue, and could there be a more perfect time or place?

There being no possible friendly segue that he could think of, he said, "You've been tracking me. Why?"

Leith turned from the view and blinked at him. "What? No, I'm doing the rounds of all the —"

"Not now," Dion said. "This summer. You put a tracker on my car. What's up? Mind explaining?"

* * *

The drop-off beside Leith was not sheer, but it was decidedly unfriendly. Where he stood now, he realized, one good shove would send him to his death. "You want to go back to my car?" he asked, and used the question as an excuse to walk away from the edge and back toward the safety of the ascending trail.

"Let's just talk here," Dion said, not budging.

Leith stopped and jammed his hands into his jacket pockets. He had been about to say a bunch of nice things, like happy new year, congratulations for a job well done, etc. But that wasn't going to work now. Nothing worked with Dion, and Leith was coming to see how moonlighting as a spy for Bosko was poisoning both their lives.

The tension was getting to him. Alison thought it was the stress of the new posting that was keeping him awake nights. She didn't know what he was up to, playing detective in the cheesiest way, latching that low-tech tracker to Dion's car. Foiled, as it turned out. With nothing to go on now, except rumour and Mike Bosko's vague instructions, Leith had justified to himself that giving up was in order. Until something new came up.

And now something new had, according to Bosko, and the tension would soon be over. But not until Leith had closed this chapter of deceit and betrayal. And since Dion wanted answers and was being blunt about it, maybe this was their chance to do just that.

"I tracked your car, yes. Because you're a suspect. The investigation hasn't made the books yet, but it's going to."

Dion nodded. "I figured. Bosko, right?"

"Bosko is running it pretty much on his own. He's got his reasons. He's had little to go on, so far."

Dion nodded again. Along the cliffs behind him grew hardy little evergreens, and with every gust of wind the dry snow flailed off their branches, momentary ghosts that danced and scattered. He didn't seem to feel the cold, his attention riveted on Leith.

"But there's new evidence," Leith said. "It's over, Cal. It's time to talk."

"What kind of new evidence?"

"A witness. She's made contact, agreed to talk to Bosko."

The words had less impact than Leith was expecting. No gulp, no *holy cow, I'm cooked*. Dion continued to watch him like a lip-reader waiting for a punchline. But he must be wanting closure as much as Leith did. They both knew that a witness coming forward almost certainly meant there was something to come forward about, and it wasn't to discuss the weather.

Leith had found himself in the role of hostage negotiator a few times in the course of his small-town RCMP career. He knew about the power of empathy. "You're tired of running," he said. "I can feel it. You want to get this off your chest. So talk to me. Better me than a stranger, because I get where you're coming from, and I care about you. What d'you say?"

Dion looked out to sea as if to consider the offer — but when he turned back to the conversation, he was clearly not bathed in the clean light of absolution. "There's nothing to tell. I've had the feeling Bosko was after me for something, I don't know what. Something to do with the crash, I'm guessing. Does he think I crashed my car on purpose, got my best buddy killed for some reason? Somehow fixed it that we'd get hit on the passenger side by a speeding car in the middle of nowhere? Kind of bizarre."

The last thing Leith had expected was a cranky but down-to-earth comeback. There were times when he felt Dion was ready to break, but this was not one of those days. There was also the tempting sliver of a chance that he was telling the truth.

Whatever the truth was, his refusal to spill made Leith's job easier. Let somebody else twist his arm. And pull the switch, if that's what it came to. "It's not what happened in the crash, and you know it," he said, letting Dion know he was done. "It's what happened before. But here's the deal. I've given it a shot, and it's not my case. If you want to keep on keeping on till you're arrested, best of luck, okay? It's out of my hands."

Now they were both looking out to sea in silence. Finally Leith said, "Most people go out of their way to stay out of trouble. Some people stumble into it. But some, like this Scott Mills guy, don't seem happy unless they're reinventing it."

They were back to business, and Dion looked almost grateful, maybe getting the allusion to his own stumble. He listened attentively as Leith related his gut feeling that Dezi and Scott were in the plane game together, that she knew everything about the Gold-Seton plot, that it was her idea to go after Amelia Foster when she defected, her idea to go after Keefer to silence him, and ditto with Gilmartin. Even serial killers seemed to prefer having some kind of goal when they went looking for victims. It upped the ante for them, Leith supposed.

"Are you anywhere close to charging her?" Dion asked.

Leith shook his head. "We have nothing on her. Frey's keeping her out of the story. So far he's happy to be the boogeyman, and she's just a naive girl who hangs around bad men. We can't prove otherwise. We need something solid on her, something with teeth. Better get back to finding that thing. Coming? I'll give you a ride back down."

* * *

Dion followed Leith, thinking that the problem with flying was the falling. Leith's words had caught him at a bad time, when he was feeling hope. Now he was sinking once more. He was back in the darkness of a gravel pit, shovelling dirt. He paused for breath and turned to see his co-conspirator's face oddly illuminated. The question continued to nag him. Was Looch talking on his phone? And looking up, there was the girl straddling her dirt bike. To this day anyone with pink hair gave him a jolt.

He had shouted at Looch, watched those tail lights flicker on, a puff of dust as she fled, and he had leapt to life, too, diving for the wheel of his car, Looch falling into the passenger seat that would get him killed moments later. They took up pursuit via the road, didn't have the advantage of the hills, trying to cut her off.

He should have let her go and faced the consequences. How had he hoped to catch her, and what would he have done if he had?

He hadn't stopped to think about it. Hadn't stopped to think, period.

The gravel pit road intercepted an empty byway. Middle of the night, deserted. Trying to predict her path, stepping on the gas. Sudden glare of headlights merging at speed with his own.

The end.

He had woken after a number of weeks, and ever since, he had been waiting for the pink-haired girl to come forward. She never had, apparently. Till now.

Forty-Four

DASHED

BOSKO'S WITNESS STOOD outside the North Vancouver RCMP detachment, chomping gum. The woman was not a teenager, and she had never had pink hair, nor operated a dirt bike. She was a widow, an ex-kinesiologist, and she was here to tell her story. Not today, but tomorrow. This afternoon was a practice run, nailing down the route, because the devil was in the details, and public transit was a plethora of details indeed.

Her name was Brooke. She knew her way around the North Shore well enough, having lived here in the past. She didn't know the bus routes, though, especially from Burnaby, where she now lived. When Sergeant Bosko had asked where she'd like to meet, she should have chosen somewhere closer to home, but her brain was fragile these days. Slippy and slidey. "Doesn't matter," she had said, so he had gone ahead and set up the time and place: a coffee shop not far from the detachment.

Bosko sounded nice on the phone. He had wanted to meet right then and there, but accepted her request for a day or two later. He said he was grateful for her coming forward like this. He sounded like he cared about her well-being, too. He would make everything all right again.

She stood and looked at the building, a sight as painful as every other reminder of what she had lost. Moving east hadn't helped, and neither had returning west. Nothing helped. What had finally prompted her to make the call, when she was ready to just let it all go? Christmas, that's what. This was her second Christmas alone, and damned if she would go through another without bringing Cal Dion to justice. Her life could only move on if his was stopped in its tracks.

It occurred to her as she stood staring at the building where Dion continued to work that she might in fact bump into him. Christ! She was turning to rush back to Lonsdale to avoid the unthinkable when somebody called her name. A female voice. She turned to see one of the gang walking along the sidewalk toward her. JD Temple.

She heard herself respond brightly. "JD, hey, how are you?"

Such a natural, commonplace greeting. JD was an enemy, too, if only by association with Dion. JD was now studying her in the casual but observant way of cops. She would be noticing the changes, the lost weight, the Sally Ann clothes, the tangled hair. "I'm good, Brooke. How are you?"

"Surviving." Brooke forced a grin.

JD had always been sharper than any of the men she worked with. "Were you coming into the detachment? Somebody in particular you wanted to see?"

"Happened to be in the neighbourhood. Just wondering how you're all doing. How's Doug?"

Doug Paley had been one of Looch's best friends on the force. Brooke had seen Doug at the funeral, JD at the funeral, everybody except Dion at the funeral. Doug had seemed grief-stricken, but what did he know about grief? Within days he would have moved on. More like hours, in the fast-paced world of law enforcement. He wouldn't be stuck in a loop like Brooke was, handicapped by missing parts. Because that's what Looch was to her: vital missing parts.

JD walked backwards for a few steps, beckoning. "C'mon, then. I'm heading down to Rainey's. Doug's already there. Come and say hi."

"God, no. I don't want to see Cal."

JD appeared to understand the aversion. Again, she was a sharp one. "No chance of that. He's not in today."

So Brooke ended up in the pub where the crew used to gather when Looch was alive, where she'd join him from time to time. The music was as loud as ever, but now it made her want to cringe instead of get up and dance. She said hello to Doug Paley and Jim Torr, who said hello back to her. It was like nothing had changed. How outrageous! Nothing, except Looch was gone and she was thinner. She asked for a glass of water to keep her hands busy, and tried to calm the whirligigs of panic in the pit of her stomach.

Must stay sober. Chat a while and go. She sipped water, smiling as the men and JD fell into conversation.

They were trying to include her, but maybe she had a force field around her that wouldn't let her out or them in. She knew she made them feel guilty. She knew they wished her gone. They began to ignore her and talk shop, and she began to plan her departure.

As she inched toward the edge of her seat, two more arrived, a heavy-set man and a blonde woman, both in civvies. Brooke almost could name the man, but couldn't quite. Kevin or Ken. He maybe recognized her, too. Doug was asking her if she still taught or practiced kinesiology. She said she had given up the discipline, too busy working at adjusting to life without Looch. "I can't seem to get it together," she said. She raked back her hair and tried to smooth it down. Her hair felt awful, like tangled nylon against her palm.

"We all miss him," Doug said. He sat too close and gave her arm a squeeze. "Can I get you something stronger than — what's that watery stuff you're drinking?"

"Water," she said, and almost giggled. Doug had always made her laugh. But not like Looch could make her laugh. Where had all the laughter gone?

Doug bought her a highball, and the liquid swirled in her mouth with a heavenly burn. Around her, the conversation became loud and lively. Leaving wasn't so easy, especially when she found a second drink in front of her. All would be okay if she didn't mention Looch again, or her plans for tomorrow. She bore through the cops talking about the cop life. The blonde lady cop was already standing, swallowing her beer and heading out. The heavy-set guy also seemed ready to call it a night, wrapping his scarf around his neck, zipping his jacket. It was JD who leaned across the table and asked Brooke again what brought her to North Van, if she was living in Burnaby.

Something about the question rubbed Brooke the wrong way. *Mind your own fucking business*, Looch's voice boomed in her head. She said instead in a thin, clear voice, "I've come to put away the man who killed Looch, that's what."

The table went quiet, and all eyes latched onto her. Now that it was out she felt good. She wasn't just telling one man in a suit, but the world at large. Double the pleasure, double the damage.

"What d'you mean, Brooke?" JD said.

Brooke sat straighter. "Looch would still be alive if not for *him*." The name she could barely think, let alone say. "It's his fault. He killed Looch."

"It was an accident," Doug said, still close, still being a shoulder to cry on.

She didn't want his damn shoulder. She laughed at his choice of words. "Accident? Killing people in the middle of the night is no accident. It's murder. Does nobody get it?"

Caution now in all their faces, and doubt. They were listening to her but wondering if she was mad. She poked the air, saying, "He was always bad news, and you know it. How many times have you covered for him? I told Looch, I said, 'He's going to get you in deep shit one day. Stay clear of him.' But he didn't, and I was right. Look what happened."

"We loved Looch," JD said, "and we miss him, but come on, Brooke. Looch and Cal were both yahoos. If they got in trouble, they got in it together."

Brooke couldn't believe her ears. "Looch was a good man," she cried.

But they were banding together now, blocking her. That's what cops did when one of their own was threatened: create a line and plug their ears, *Maintiens le lie*. Jimmy Torr and Kevin or Ken were talking now, ignoring her. She raised her voice. "The night Looch died, he phoned me. He was frightened. He wanted to know what to do. You want to know what he said that he and Cal had just done? You want to know what that first-degree, lying piece of garbage got my Looch into?"

JD was watching her with cool interest. Doug Paley asked Brooke if he could call her a cab. Brooke heard herself becoming shrill. She slapped the table and told them, "He didn't just kill that man. He killed Looch. He killed Looch's beautiful, happy family. He killed me. He killed the kids we never had. And he's just carrying on as if nothing happened. It's not right!"

JD told her not so kindly to get a grip. Instead, Brooke lost her bearings. She looked at Doug, but he didn't look back. She stood and told the group, "It's not going away. I've made enough calls from pay phones, trying to stay out of it, and nothing happened. So I'm here, in person. Look at me. Tomorrow I'm going to see Sergeant Bosko, and I won't leave till he does something about this. Get it?"

Their attention came and went, and she could tell they were tuning her out. Just like in her nightmares, she was shouting the truth at people who refused to listen. Ken or Kevin was on his feet, saying good night to Torr. He nodded at Brooke and left. Doug Paley asked the waitress for another beer, but didn't offer a top-up to Brooke. JD asked Brooke if she could give her a ride home, maybe she wanted to talk?

"No," Brooke said. "No way." With tears streaming down her face, she made her way toward the exit. With a backward glance she saw the group of three at their table, pretending to be lost in conversation but in fact watching her go. Like a pack of wolves tracking a deer and calculating the rate of return.

* * *

At 10:30 that night Leith got a call that hustled him out of his pajamas, back into his street clothes, and over to the detachment. JD and Dion had also interrupted whatever they were doing to come in for the breaking news. They preceded him to the evidence section to show him what they had. Thomas Frey's white hatchback had been located.

"So where did they find it?" Leith asked.

"Parked a few blocks away from the Kirk residence," Dion said.

"But it's what we found inside that's going to make your day," JD said.

Leith studied the upshot of what was found within the vehicle, and JD was right — it made his day. He gave the thumbs-up and sent her and Dion to arrest Dezi. When they were gone, he arranged another chat with Thomas Frey. This time he would find out what really happened the night of Amelia Foster's crash.

* * *

A change had come over Frey. Leith could only describe him as mellower than mellow, and he saw it as madness descending.

With the new evidence before him, Frey ditched the fairy tale and answered questions openly and honestly. He didn't seem conflicted about ratting on the love of his life, and Leith understood why: it wasn't Dezi the human being that Frey cherished, any more than a trophy hunter cherished the gazelle he'd just shot and had stuffed. Dezi was nothing but a hard-on concept to play with in Frey's mind's eye. In an abstract way, he had had his way with her and was done. She was a moment in time, smashed like that little red Mazda, unfixable, gone. Frey realized that even if Dezi somehow deigned to visit him in jail sometime down the road, which she wouldn't, his mask was off, the mystique was gone, and he was exactly what he looked like: a middle-aged nobody.

"You're right," Frey said. "She pushed it along. In fact, it was more her idea than Scott's to go after Amelia, and I'm pretty sure she had murder in her mind all along."

"So let's try this again," Leith said. "Describe the meeting at Porteau Beach for me."

"Sure. If I can have another 7-Up, please."

With a fresh pop in hand, Frey seemed almost buoyant. "Dezi and Scott set up the meeting with Amelia, and Dezi drove out to the beach in her Sidekick. She told me to follow. As protection, I think. Or just for someone to show off to, maybe. I did follow, but only thinking I would keep her from doing something she'd regret. I stood back some distance while she walked up to the girl down by the surf. It was dark out, hard to see. And cold. Amelia was expecting to meet Scott, and I could see she was confused. I don't think she and Dezi had ever actually met before. The two of them talked for a while, and I couldn't hear the words, but I could see that Amelia was becoming alarmed. She tried to walk back to her car, but Dezi stood in front of her, being the little bully she is."

Frey chuckled at his memories. "But Dezi's quite small," he went on. "And Amelia isn't, so Amelia pushed past her and marched toward the parking lot. Dezi dogged after her, throwing stones — literally — and laughing. Taunting her about Grandma, saying she'd put rat poison in the old lady's meds and she was going to die a horrible death."

Leith sat straighter, but Frey assured him, "There was no rat poison. But by the look on Amelia's face that night, she believed it, and she couldn't get to her car fast enough. Dezi's a scary little girl, you know. She's got the knack. She'll hook you in and leave you demolished. Just look at me. Look at Scott. I know toward the end there, she scared the shit out of him, too. He was packing his bags to disappear when I showed up and, well, dealt with him."

Scott Mills's fear was news to Leith. Casually crossing his arms, he said, "But he didn't move fast enough."

"No, he didn't."

"He realized you were Dezi's loaded gun."

"Oh, she kept me loaded, all right," Frey said. "I'd given her a phone so she could call me any time of day or night, talk dirty as long as she wanted." He reflected a moment. "She never did talk dirty for long. And I know she was just using me. I see that now. You're thinking it's time for me to repent? Sorry, but no. And the judge will order that I go through a violent offender program, and I'll do it, but I'm not going to regret any of it. No, sir, hearing her tickling little voice in my ear was all it took to make me dance." He gave Leith a ghastly grin. "'Scott's going weird on me. He's got to go.' That's what she said. So I got him. Poor Scott. He didn't go down easy, and I didn't mean to harm his parents. Really, I didn't. But you know how it is. After the first, the rest is easy."

Leith said nothing, thinking of Amelia Foster racing to Lions Bay to stop a poisoning that wasn't real. He steeled himself for the next area of discussion, the killing of Rory Keefer. But the discussion was shorter than he thought. "I didn't take part in that," Frey said. "I draw a line at that kind of violence. I stayed in my vehicle."

"But you didn't draw a line at shooting Craig Gilmartin."

"I had nothing to do with that, either."

"You didn't drive along and shoot at him from a van?"

"No, that would be Scott and Dezi. But I did arrange wheels for them. I know a guy who rents out vehicles, always gives me a deal. He also loaned me the flashy car to drive Dezi around, impress her. A Mercedes. Of course she wasn't impressed. She's seventeen. I should have pushed for a Camaro."

"Tell me about those drives. Was Scott always behind the wheel?"

Frey blinked at him. "Just for the first drive, when I wanted to see her up close. Smell her. I gave them a few bucks to get something to eat after that. The next time, though ..." Frey actually licked his chops. "The next time I saw her walking along, I worked up the courage to glide up alongside her, as if I'd come upon her by chance, and I invited her to hop in. She was *so* beautiful in the passenger seat beside me. Allowed me to park in dark places, touch her leg. I'm no fool. I know a carrot on a stick when I see one." Creepily, Frey cooed in a little girl's voice, "*Don't, mister. Not yet.* Oh, she had me wrapped tight."

Leith inched his chair back a bit and wondered how long it would take to wash off this interview when he got home in the early morning hours. "So who shot Craig Gilmartin in his home?"

"Scott found a couple of guns in the man's car. Rory Keefer's. Scott must have given them to Dezi, before he knew better. Dezi slipped me the .45 later to take care of him with. She said she hoped I was a better shot than Scott, who had only winged the cop, it turned out. I told her I was actually quite a sharpshooter. And I am. Except when it comes to little white poodles, it seems."

"She asked you to eliminate Scott," Leith said, "and you did, just went and shot a young guy in the face, did you? I thought you were his father figure. I thought you were friends."

Frey play-acted shock. "Put yourself in my shoes. If Dezi had asked you for help the way she asked me, her hand on your crotch, you'd have done the same."

After a pause, Leith decided not to stand up and throw a chair at the man. Instead he asked, "What about Mike Bosko? What was that all about?"

For the first time Frey looked uncomfortable, but maybe only because he was recalling his mashed fingers, bruised but not broken, as it had turned out. "Dezi's got this idea she's going to be a police officer. You probably think that's funny, but it's true. She's dead serious. She thought the head honcho was trying to ruin her career. I told her she was being paranoid, but she insisted. And I obeyed."

Leith had to smirk, thinking of Dezi's desire to be a cop. *Good luck with that.* But then he thought further, and realized there was a chance she could be acquitted. She could then emigrate, find a place where cops were in short supply, a place where background checks were lax. It could happen.

"Yeah, that's not going to happen," he said, more to comfort himself than to inform Frey. He was tiring, ready to end the interview, resume in the morning.

"If it's not asking too much, I have a request," Frey said.

"What's that?" Leith was on his feet, itching to leave.

"Those photos you found on my computer, they're clean, aren't they?"

"They're not what I'd call clean."

"But you'll let me have a couple, won't you? For my cell?"

Leith walked out and let the door slam behind him.

He got a call from JD as he sat at his desk, catching up on his notes. She sounded half pumped, half furious. "So just as Dezi's mom was letting us in the front," she said, "we saw Dezi slipping out the back. We had to chase her all over North Vancouver, but we got her."

"Great news," Leith said. "Everyone's okay?"

"We're fine. Cal fell in a creek and twisted his ankle, and I'm waiting for the ambulance guys to check him over. But I'd say he's going to live."

"Good to know."

Leith returned to the evidence room to re-watch the video taken off the microchip found in the dash cam of Thomas Frey's abandoned hatchback. Several hours of useless footage had been downloaded, and one priceless set of frames — silent, low-res images that would have been automatically overwritten if Frey had put in another day of driving. Leith thanked his lucky stars that hadn't happened.

It was likely that Frey had overlooked the dash cam unobtrusively suction-cupped to the windshield and motion activated, a precautionary measure taken by many forward-thinking drivers in case they ever had to dispute a fender bender.

The device was a department store cheapie, not great at capturing night scenes, but good enough for Leith, thanks to the extra-tall lamp standards set up on the section of highway where the clip in question had been recorded.

Yes, a lot of good stuff here. The rear licence plate of the little yellow Sidekick could be read as the vehicle pulled into the broad cone of light, and the young female driver of that car was clearly visible once she had hopped out. And the footage came time-stamped, and the time could be checked against the camera's current settings for accuracy, and it so happened that the time and date assigned to the clip matched that of Amelia Foster's crash, and all that was going to look fabulous in court.

Leith slouched forward, and with the mouse, scrubbed back and forth through the dark and grainy footage: out on the Killer Highway, tail lights in the distance veer to the left and vanish. The Sidekick driving ahead swerves to a stop in the pullout, and the driver gets out, looking ahead, then turning back toward the dash-cam vehicle as it too pulls to a stop. Making eye contact with whoever is at its wheel, she laughs and points toward the catastrophe she's helped orchestrate.

Subtle evidence, for sure, Leith was thinking. *But with that beaming face, try and tell a jury you weren't in it for the thrill. Just fucking try.*

He freeze-framed on her grin and pressed Print.

* * *

"I'm sorry, JD," the detainee said. "It kills me that you hate me."

JD ignored her. She was in the driver's seat, with her prisoner in the back, safely behind bars. The cruiser was parked near the spot where the takedown had happened, and JD was watching as Dion was checked over by a couple of female paramedics. He had a blanket around his shoulders, and his hair was still beguilingly wet. He was demonstrating his limp and wincing a lot. The paramedics seemed to be taking their sweet time assessing the injury. *Big baby*, JD thought.

There was a tightness in her chest, and she knew its source. Sorrow. *Did I really like her?* she wondered. *Yes, I did. I loved that sadistic, manipulative, heartless monster I've ended up putting in handcuffs. How is that possible?*

Silence from the back seat. Finally, JD looked in the rear-view mirror and saw Dezi was turned away, gazing out at the dark, wet street. Despite her last words, spoken with a whimper, she looked blank now. Like her emotions had gone into hibernation.

"Dezi," JD said.

The girl's eyes met her own in the mirror.

"I would have liked teaching you the ropes."

"Yeah," Dezi said, something flashing across her face. Innocence. "That would have been so cool."

Then she was looking out the window again, back in some darker place where JD would never belong.

Forty-Five

INTO THE BREACH

January 4

KEN POOLE HAD SEEN the day break. He sat in the driver's seat of the sedan he had borrowed, looking down the rainy avenue in Burnaby, waiting. It was a neighbourhood of low-rises; they had pushed out the single-family dwellings that had once lined these streets, nice houses with grassy yards and picket fences. Now these squat apartment buildings from the '70s and '80s were themselves under threat. In the distance, high-rise condos were going up above the morning mist, each topped by a crane adding yet another storey.

Poole's happiest days had been spent in a nice house with a picket fence, not far from here. Days of popsicles and innocence. Look at where the world was going, the groping race to the top, the squeeze for elbow room, the crush for jobs, young people in sleeping bags under bridges, everybody angry about something, his own anger adding to the buzz inside his head.

Screw the buzz. He slouched and went back to his paperback. It was a western, and the good guy was galloping like mad across the plains to save the day. The cowboy would go through hell, but by the end he would have won back the girl, and probably the ranch, too. It was just a matter of turning the pages.

He flipped another page. He had no idea when the woman he was waiting for would emerge, so to be safe he had returned before daybreak. By a process of extrapolation, having a good idea of Bosko's schedule, he knew the meeting would have to be set for this morning.

He was right. The glass door he was surveilling swung open, and out she came, fussing with her handbag. She had cleaned herself up since yesterday. Her hair had always been her pride, he recalled — long and glossy and chestnut brown. Going a bit grey now, but neatly combed. Makeup applied, she was dressed for success, looking fit and pretty and determined.

He stepped out of his car as she reached the sidewalk. He called out to her. She looked his way in surprise and headed toward him, couldn't seem to recall his name. He introduced himself, and explained that he had been tasked with escorting her to the meeting. She seemed flustered, but went around and sat in the passenger seat. Only when they were on the road, driving along Hastings toward the Second Narrows Bridge, did she voice her doubts. "But Sergeant Bosko doesn't know where I live. He doesn't even know my name."

"He's a cop," Poole told her, with a wink. "He's got ways. Don't worry about it." He glanced at the clock on the dashboard of the car he had borrowed for this purpose, the old but respectable gold-brown Taurus his mom kept in her underground parkade but never used these days. The plates were borrowed from another car in another parkade that could never be connected to him. He'd thought of everything. "You want breakfast?" he asked. "Mike says he might be a bit late, so I'm to take you for a bite, if you'd like. Up to you."

"Coffee would be nice."

"Sure thing. I know just the place."

Instead of turning right toward the bridge, he hooked a left toward Highway 1. Brooke was startled. "Where are you going? The bridge is that way."

"Can't meet in North Van," Poole told her, watching the road. "You can see why, right? This is an IHIT case. They've set up a safe house in Surrey."

He could feel her eyes on him. He could feel her fear.

He told her not to worry, and they both fell silent as the road peeled away under them.

On the freeway he picked up speed, heading out to the Fraser Valley, where the land spread out flat, much of it farmland, but great swaths of it wild and undeveloped. A place of beauty — and endless possibilities.

ACKNOWLEDGEMENTS

I think it's commonly accepted that crime fiction writing is a strange pursuit, and the writers who do it are often full of self-doubt, facing the near-daily question, *Why?* So when you find a writing buddy who gets it, and can give you near-daily reassurance that there's some point to it all, although she's not sure what that point is, either, that person is a valuable find. So I'd really like to thank Judy, a.k.a. JG Toews, for being my go-to writing buddy, sounding board, and ballast. And the great thing is, I know she feels the same about me, which makes it all more or less debt free.

JG also was my first reader of the first draft. I'd like to say it needed no repair, but I can't, and it did. She made sure to let me know where I'd gone astray.

My substantive editor Allister Thompson took over from there. He's been with me from the start, helping me shape the arc of the series, which is as difficult as painting clouds. He's also rapped my knuckles on occasion, for which I'm thankful — once the sting wears off.

Copy editor Catharine Chen truly cared about this book — I can tell — and zoned in on specific problems that led to much fine-tuning. Finally, Jenny McWha, my editor at Dundurn, has amiably shepherded all of this along, which I much appreciate.

So a lot of minds went into giving *Flights and Falls* wings, and I'm grateful for every pointer, criticism, and encouragement.

Yet sometimes nothing seems to make sense, and when that happens there's one guy whose solid voice of reason always buoys me. He won't read this, as he doesn't read crime fiction much — even mine — but I'll thank him here anyway — love you dearly, son.

NOTE: I have taken liberties with some of the geography and businesses of the Lower Mainland, though hopefully its essence remains intact.

BOOK CREDITS

Project Editor: Jenny McWha
Developmental Editor: Allister Thompson
Copy Editor: Catharine Chen
Proofreader: Megan Beadle

Designer: Laura Boyle

Publicists: Michelle Melski and Tabassum Sidiqui

DUNDURN

Publisher: J. Kirk Howard
Vice-President: Carl A. Brand
Editorial Director: Kathryn Lane
Artistic Director: Laura Boyle
Production Manager: Rudi Garcia
Publicity Manager: Michelle Melski
Manager, Accounting and Technical Services: Livio Copetti

Editorial: Allison Hirst, Dominic Farrell, Jenny McWha, Rachel Spence, Elena Radic, Melissa Kawaguchi

Marketing and Publicity: Kendra Martin, Elham Ali, Tabassum Sidiqui, Heather McLeod

Design and Production: Sophie Paas-Lang